M

WITHDRAWN

gone with a
handsomer man

gone with a handsomer man

MICHAEL LEE WEST

Minotaur Books
New York

This is a work of fiction. All of the characters, organizations, and events portrayed
in this novel are either products of the author's imagination or are used fictitiously.

www.minotaurbooks.com

ISBN 978-0-312-57122-1

First Edition: April 2011

10 9 8 7 6 5 4 3 2 1

To Tyler West
who kept watch

But one thing's settled with me: To appreciate Heaven well,
'Tis good for a man to have some fifteen minutes of hell!

—WILL CARLETON,

"GONE WITH A HANDSOMER MAN"

one

All I ever wanted in life was true love, a set of copper cookware, and the perfect recipe for red velvet cake. The last thing I wanted was to end up on Charleston's six o'clock news, accused of murder and a slew of other crimes.

It started Monday, the first week in June, when I thought I'd gotten the dates wrong for my cake baking class. Numbers don't usually stick in my mind. This one did because it was my twenty-ninth birthday, and my fiancé, Bing Jackson, surprised me with the darlingest gifts—pastry bags, a fifty-three-piece Wilton Supreme Cake Decorating Set, and eight prepaid classes at the Vivienne Beaumont School of Cake Design.

Before we left Bing's house in Mount Pleasant, he opened a bottle of Moët and we toasted our upcoming wedding. Then we drove across the river into downtown Charleston and turned down East Bay Street. He pointed to a redbrick building with a giant neon cupcake sitting on the roof.

"Teeny, this is where you'll be every Thursday from 7:00 to 10:00 p.m.," he said. "Classes start June fourth—that's only three days from now."

A lot of women might have gotten suspicious over the exact details, but not me. Bing was all about timing. Thanks to the giant clock inside his head, he'd never been late to a real estate closing or open house. His Rolex was just for show.

"Teenykins, I signed you up for this class because I want you to make our wedding cake," he said. "But I don't want something traditional. How about an eighteen-hole golf course? You can do sand traps and little spun-sugar balls."

"You bet." I threw my arms around his neck. We were getting married in August—only ten weeks to go—and my thoughts were already skipping ahead to the wedding. Maybe I could make the groom's cake, too, something unusual like a giant tee or a Big Bertha driver.

On Thursday night, I put down the top on my beat-up turquoise Oldsmobile and drove from Bing's house across the Cooper River. The school's parking lot was empty and I began to fret. Was I Miss Vivienne's only student, or had I arrived a tad early?

I leaned toward the rearview mirror and combed my windblown hair—it's long and blond, prone to tangles. Normally I didn't drive with the convertible top down, but my air conditioner was broken. I grabbed my cake decorating kit, along with the enrollment packet, and walked to the door. It was locked, and a memo was taped to the glass. Due to circumstances beyond Miss Vivienne's control, classes had been rescheduled and would commence *next* Thursday.

I walked back to my Olds and drove back to Mount Pleasant. When I passed a grocery on Ben Sawyer Boulevard, I did a U-turn and angled into the parking lot. I came out with an apple walnut salad with raspberry vinaigrette, a wedge of brie, and a cheesecake sampler. Nothing beats fresh, simple food on a sticky hot summer night in Charleston.

It was almost eight o'clock when I turned down Rifle Range Road. The sky curved above me like an oyster shell, ribbed and grainy. Even though it was still daylight, the moon was on the rise, moving through the clouds like a dropped pearl. Long before Mama left for good, she used to say a full moon cleared troublesome matters of the heart, wiped the slate clean, and resolved unfinished business.

My heart wasn't burdened in the least as I sped down the highway. I turned into Jackson Estates, a new subdivision the economy had flattened. Bing owned all thirteen acres, and his green stucco house sat in the rear, surrounded by peach trees and empty lots. A real peaceful setting. But the minute I pulled into the driveway, I knew something was wrong. First, my bulldog, Sir, didn't shoot out of the doggie door to greet me. Second, a white BMW convertible was parked under the mimosa. The license plate read SOSEX-E. Not a good sign. Not at all.

From the backyard I heard laughter, the high, twittery girlish kind. I stayed in my car, trying to get a deep breath, but the air was thick and moist. The last thing I needed was an asthma attack. I grabbed my inhaler and took a puff; then I got out of the car.

Weeds brushed against my legs as I walked around the house. Our badminton net stood in the middle of the backyard. A boom box sat on the patio table, and Muse was singing "Ruled by Secrecy," which isn't about cheating but ought to be. I started to holler for Bing when a naked brunette ran across the grass and swung her badminton racket at the birdie. I ducked behind a peach tree and saw Bing and a tall redhead race toward the net. They were naked, too.

I sucked in air, and it whistled through the thin gap between my front teeth. For weeks now, Bing had been pressuring me to do something kinky, but I had no idea he'd wanted a trifecta. Tears stung my eyes as I looked at the women. They had perky chi-chis, no tan lines, and no cellulite.

Me, I'm a little too short and curvy, with brown eyes and the aforementioned blond hair. When I was a little girl, Mama would get drunk and call me Possum Head. Sometimes she'd get on a roll and point out my major failings: my elbows were too far down, my teeth resembled a picket fence, I was too sweet and gullible, and my hair looked like something that grew in the Okefenokee Swamp. After she'd sober up, she'd hug me and say, "Teeny, nobody's perfect. Besides, you've got a good heart." Now that heart dropped to my navel and tapped a code: run, Teeny. *Run.*

The redhead grabbed the birdie. She was all legs and hair. Instead of hitting the birdie with her racquet, she giggled and threw it over the net. It was a prissy throw, but the brunette sacked the hell out of it. Bing took off running, his dangly parts swinging.

I'd stood in line at Target to buy that badminton set. Bing had fussed when I'd called the white thing a birdie. He'd told me to call it by its proper name, a shuttlecock. Speaking of which, his privates jiggled violently as his racquet smashed into the birdie. It shot over the brunette's head and thumped into my herb garden.

"You get it," the brunette told the redhead, then she struck a pose— hand on her hip bone, one leg bent at the knee, like she was a contestant in the Miss Tall Gal Pageant. The redhead squatted beside the rosemary bush and glanced around for the birdie. She wasn't a knockout like her friend, but she was graceful.

Bing slipped under the net, his straight blond hair falling into his eyes, and placed the edge of the racquet under Miss Tall's chin. Her head tilted back, and Bing kissed her pouty, bee-stung lips like he'd never kissed me.

I flattened my palms against the warm grass. A tear hit the back of my hand. St. Andrews Episcopal was reserved for our August fifteenth wedding. It wasn't too late to cancel, right? I'd found true love once. I didn't expect to find it again. But I didn't have to settle for this. I could still opt for those copper pans and a good cake.

My bulldog sniffed Miss Tall's leg. She kicked him and Sir yelped. That did it. I wouldn't let this skank abuse an innocent dog. I swallowed back tears. Things weren't perfect between me and Bing, but I had no idea he was a man-whore. There's no canary in the coal mine for cheating men.

The redhead held up the birdie and looked past Bing, straight into my eyes. "Hey, there's a girl watching us," she yelled.

I ducked low as Bing and Miss Tall broke apart. I'm mostly a calm person, but I wanted justice. I could break off a switch and beat their bony asses. But girls like that worked in a team. I'd end up in a body cast.

"This is private property," Bing cried. "Leave now, and I won't call the police."

"You can call Jesus, for all I care," I said.

Sir's head twisted when he heard my voice. I gazed up into the dark branches, each one loaded with unripe fruit. I grabbed a low branch and shimmied up the trunk—not so easy in shorts. My legs would be a scratchy mess.

"Who is she?" asked the redhead. She walked toward the net.

"My fiancée," Bing said.

"I thought it was a dwarf," said Miss Tall.

I couldn't argue with her. I'm barely five foot two. When I was a kid, I was short in a noticeable way. It's how I got my name.

Bing tipped back his head. "Teeny, why are you in a tree?" he hollered up.

"Why are you naked?" I called down.

Sir ran to the tree and barked. I pulled off my engagement ring and threw it at Bing. He jumped back, like I'd hurled a watermelon. That gave me an idea. I grabbed a peach. In a month it would be ripe, but now it was hard and heavy. I reared back and tossed it at Miss Tall. She ducked and it hit Bing's shoulder. "Hey!" he cried. "Cut that out."

"Screw you," I yelled and lobbed another fruit. It smacked against Miss Tall's hip. She screamed and threw her racquet at the tree. I grabbed another peach and aimed it at her mouth, but she ducked again. The fruit hit the boom box; it fell over and the music stopped.

I tossed another and another. One peach smashed the redhead's nose. Her chin snapped back, and blood trickled out of her nostrils, streaming over her lip. Bing stepped in front of her and spread his arms, shielding her.

I fired down two more peaches. One whizzed over Bing's head, but the other slammed into his nether region. He screeched and doubled over. The redhead hung back, crying over her busted nose, but Miss Tall looked ready to fight. I threw peaches as fast as I could. It was like the old days when the pickers' kids and I had fruit fights.

"Dammit, Teeny. Get the hell out of that tree," Bing cried. Though he was still bent into a C, he herded the women to the patio, into the house. Even the dog went. I stayed in the tree until Bing came back. He dared me to move as he put on his clothes.

The police arrived a few minutes later. I started to climb down, but my hair caught on a branch. Bing's entourage came out of the house. The women had gotten dressed. The redhead pressed a bag of frozen brussels sprouts to her nose.

"You're going to jail," she yelled.

"I'm not the criminal," I said.

"This is prespousal abuse," Bing cried. "Nobody hits me."

I didn't get scared until two policemen advanced toward my tree. One was tall with pointy ears and the other had a caterpillar crawling on his lip. Then I saw it was a moustache. The pointy-eared cop ordered me to climb down. While I tried to explain about the naked women and my snagged hair, Bing yelled, "I'll get my chain saw."

He walked toward the garage. "Bing, no," I cried. In my mind, peach trees meant love, shelter, and comfort. I'd grown up on a peach farm in Bonaventure, Georgia. Bing knew how I felt. The engagement was broken, but the tree should stay in one piece.

The mustached cop looked up at me. "Lady, it's against the law to hit people with peaches."

"Too bad I didn't yank them baldheaded," I said.

"This ain't funny," the caterpillared cop yelled.

Bing returned with the chain saw. I was in trouble now. Even though this was Mount Pleasant, I totally expected to get slapped with the death penalty. A mighty buzz filled the air as Bing leaned toward the tree.

Bark churned in the air as the blade cut a wide kerf. The trunk cracked and leaned sideways. The cops lowered it to the ground and hand-cuffed me.

Needless to say, the wedding was off.

two

I'd crossed the Ravenel Bridge a hundred times but never in a police car. The officer booked me at the Charleston County Detention Center. After I was photographed and fingerprinted, I called the only person I knew in this town—Bing's stepmother, Miss Dora.

It was a natural choice. Back in April, she'd hosted our lavish engagement party, but Bing hadn't even thanked her. Despite his antagonism, Miss Dora and I had become friends.

I was bussed to night court with two other women. One had hired a hit man to knock off her boyfriend's wife, and the other had shot ten people with a paint gun at Terri Sue's Klip 'n Kurl after an altercation over hair braiding. My crimes were small in comparison. Surely my case would be dismissed.

The bus turned into the courthouse parking lot. I took a deep breath and gave thanks that I hadn't let Bing talk me into selling the farm. Bonaventure, Georgia, was a three-hour drive from Charleston. In just a little while, I'd be home.

Miss Dora hired Mr. Alvin Bell to represent me. He looked a hundred years old and smelled like gin rickeys. The air between us filled with alcoholic vapors as he explained that I was being charged with assault and vandalism.

"But I didn't vandalize anything," I said.

"You broke a boom box," Mr. Bell said.

"I didn't personally smash it," I said. "I threw something at it."

"Just the same, you destroyed Mr. Jackson's property." Mr. Bell leaned closer. "Are you telling me everything?"

"I might be an accidental vandal, Mr. Bell, but I'm not a liar." This wasn't completely true. In my whole life, I'd managed to keep every commandment except number nine—unless cohabitation with Bing counted as a sin. I'd always been mindful of my lies and kept track of them on a yearly basis, starting with January first. So far, I'd only told a dozen. One more violation and I'd be up to the unluckiest number of all: thirteen.

"How can I be in this much trouble?" I asked Mr. Bell.

"You can throw peaches at a fence, but if you aim them at people or animals, it's criminal assault. I know a case where a girl got jail time for throwing a cat at her boyfriend."

"I had no idea it was this easy to break the law, Mr. Bell," I said.

"That's what keeps me solvent, my dear." He patted my hand. "You can't call people liars. That's defamation. But it's perfectly legal to call them assholes."

"What's going to happen to me?" I whispered.

"Remember, you're innocent until proven guilty. If the complainant doesn't show up, the judge will dismiss the charges."

"Teeny!" cried a voice behind me.

I glanced over my shoulder and waved at Miss Dora. She sat on a bench all by herself in a raspberry linen suit. Her swimmy blue eyes glanced around the courtroom, then she fingered her short, poofy white-blond hair. No one, not even Bing, knew how old she was. She looked to be anywhere from fifty to seventy.

I smiled, then turned around and glanced up at the bench. The judge's black robe had long, crinkled fold lines down the front and a mustard stain on the bib. As the night wore on, his edicts got harsher and harsher. The woman who'd paint-balled the beauticians was slapped with six months unsupervised probation and was ordered to stay away from the shop. The woman who'd tried to kill her boyfriend's wife was carted off to the state hospital for psychiatric evaluation—thirty days involuntary commitment.

Bing and the girls showed up with an attorney, not his own personal lawyer but one who worked for the city. When my case was called, the judge listened to the arresting cops. Then he listened to Bing and the women, who all but said I was a rabid polecat. Finally, Mr. Bell asked me to take the stand so I could tell my side of the story.

My legs shook as I walked to the witness stand, but my voice was strong as I swore to tell the truth. I explained about the canceled cake class, the naked badminton game, and my ninja attack. Then I went back to my seat.

The attorneys argued back and forth, but even to my own ears, I sounded guilty. Apparently Bing had gotten an emergency restraining order. The other attorney claimed I was a flight risk because I'd lived in Charleston County for only a few months.

Mr. Bell called Miss Dora to the stand. She took up for me, but the judge didn't seem impressed. He got a weary look in his eyes and sentenced me to forty-eight hours of community service and six months unsupervised probation. I had to pay a fine and couldn't leave South Carolina until probation ended—exactly six months from today.

"And Miss Templeton," the judge said, "stay away from Mr. Jackson."

The judge called for a recess. The bailiff said, "All rise."

Everyone stood except Miss Dora. She started talking real loud about kangaroo courts and plea bargaining. Her brassy voice always made me think of Ethel Merman songs, motorcycle gangs, pure grain alcohol, and home hair coloring gone wrong. She was an interior designer here in Charleston, but her personality put off a lot of people. Apparently she'd been named after a hurricane that hit the Georgia coast in 1964, and she'd been stirring up trouble ever since.

The judge flashed her a hard stare. Mr. Bell's face turned red. "Dora, you better rise or he'll hold you in contempt."

"Honey, my cup runneth over with contempt," Miss Dora whispered. "I've seen that man naked."

The three of us walked into the hall, where a janitor pushed a wet mop over the floor. Bing hurried out and never looked in my direction.

"Don't you be thinking about going near that boy," Mr. Bell said.

"No, sir," I said. I feared jail more than I feared bees and snakes.

"Alvin, you're frightening the poor girl," Miss Dora said. "Teeny, don't listen. One of my drapery hangers got slapped with unsupervised probation and he didn't even have a parole officer."

"Teeny won't have an officer." Mr. Bell patted my arm. "Just be smart. Don't leave the state. Don't drive over the speed limit. Don't jaywalk. Be a model citizen and those six months will fly by. It's summer now, but it'll be December fourth before you can say Jack Robinson."

three

Miss Dora and I walked out of the courthouse into the muggy night air. We climbed into her Bentley, and she dumped her purse between us—a large Hermès bag, which she affectionately called The Black Hole, thanks to its tendency to suck objects into a vortex. Tonight the purse bulged with fabric swatches, marble chips, and a fan deck from Sherwin-Williams.

From the depths of the bag, her cell phone rang. She reached inside, pulled out a gilt drapery finial, and located the phone. She answered with a breathless hello. A tinny, hysterical voice rose up, but Miss Dora cut it off.

"I'm so sorry you're troubled," she said. "But it'll have to wait till the morning. I've got a family crisis. Toodle-loo."

She rang off and turned onto Azalea Street. "A client is having a hissy fit," she said. "Apparently the wrong furniture was delivered—a hideous brown leather sofa instead of a silk settee. The poor woman is hysterical. Mark my words, she'll call back."

Halfway to I-26, the phone trilled again. This time, Miss Dora didn't bother to say hello. "Look, darlin', there's two ways of doing things," she told the client. "Your way and my way. Let's do it my way from now on."

"Humphrey Bogart said that in *The Caine Mutiny*," I whispered.

She winked at me and resumed her conversation. "You're talking way too fast," she told the client. "Start at the beginning."

I settled against the window and remembered the engagement party Miss Dora had thrown for me and Bing. It had been a warm April night, and her guests had spilled out of the Queen Street house into the courtyard.

During the party, Miss Dora had pulled me aside and pointed out prominent Low Country citizens, adding salient points about their personalities, marriages, and household decor. She waved to a sharp-nosed woman in a blue dress. "Look at those diamonds, Teeny." Miss Dora whispered the woman's name. "She's one of the richest women in South Carolina. But she's miserable. Just like Vita in *Mildred Pierce*."

"You mean she eats her young like an alligator?" I said.

Miss Dora smiled. "You're familiar with that movie?"

"Yes, ma'am."

"Teeny, you're a keeper. You put me in mind of my baby sister. Gloria and I were rabid film buffs. She was an ash-blonde, just like you. Same big old brown eyes. Same cute little gap between her front teeth. Big boobs and curvy hips. She was made for childbearing. And she had a turquoise convertible, just like you—a Chevy, not an Olds."

"Had?" I asked.

Miss Dora's eyes teared up as she told me how Gloria's convertible rear-ended a truck filled with giant pumpkins. "It's like Gloria has come back to me," she'd said, squeezing my hand. "I know you aren't her, but it just makes me feel good to be around you."

Remembering the party made me sad. That same night, Bing and I had spent a little time in Miss Dora's azalea pink guest room.

Now, from the other side of the Bentley, I heard a loud shriek, and images of Miss Dora's guest room evaporated.

"What the poop!" she cried. "I think she's been drinking. Every other word is gibberish."

She dumped the phone into her purse. "You know what, Teeny? Bing's an asshole for letting a jewel like you get away."

She steered the Bentley into traffic. In the distance, I saw lights from the Ravenel Bridge.

"Now tell me about the peach fight," Miss Dora said. "And don't leave out a thing."

"You heard what I told the judge," I said. "Have you really seen him undressed?"

"Bunches of times. The judge and I had a little fling when I first moved to Charleston. But he had the littlest penis I ever saw in my life—in fact, I called him Pencil Pecker. I quit him and married Rodney Jackson."

As she headed toward the historic district, I wondered if the memory of the judge's private parts had distracted her.

"Aren't you taking me to my car?" I asked.

"I like a man who's well endowed in *every* way," she added, ignoring my question. "Which is something the Jackson men aren't. But they're gargantuan compared to Pencil. And yes, I know you want your car. I'm sure you're worried sick about that bulldog of yours. But do you really think it's wise to go near Bing Laden after he took out that restraining order?"

She drove through the intersection of Queen and Meeting. I'd thought for sure we were going to her house on Johnson's Row. I looked back at the Mills House Hotel, then I glanced at Miss Dora. She was just being Dora-esque—scatterbrained, late for appointments, a notorious no-show.

The traffic thinned after we drove past St. Michael's Episcopal. Miss Dora pointed out houses she'd decorated, adding assessments of her clients. "Stingy," she said, gesturing at a redbrick. "Social climbers," she said about a white clapboard. When she spotted a blue stucco she hadn't decorated, she flipped her hand and said, "Fugly."

She swung onto Tradd Street, nosing the Bentley around parked cars, then she drove past Church and Bedon's Alley. When she hung a left onto East Bay, I expected more of the deco-tour but she made a U-turn and angled the Bentley in front of a three-story pink house with gray shutters. A sign next to the door read SPENCER-JACKSON HOUSE, CIRCA 1785.

I'd never been inside this house, but I knew its history. It had been in the Jackson family forever; it was high maintenance and needed a full-time custodian. Bing's uncle Elmer had lived here rent-free, but he'd died three weeks ago. After the funeral, Bing and I had driven by the house and I'd asked if he was going to sell it. "Never," he'd said. "The Spencer-Jackson House proves my family is Old Charleston."

"Miss Dora, why're we stopping here?" I blinked at the iron gate, into a breezeway that was lit up with gas lanterns. At the end of the corridor, faint lights twinkled in a private garden.

She ignored me and dug through her purse, muttering to herself. Two men in sweats jogged by the Spencer-Jackson and moved toward a blue house with black shutters. On this side of East Bay, the houses were fitted together like marzipan confections—cotton candy pink, blueberry, lime, saffron, watermelon ice. Across the street, the homes were cream, white, or beige, as if their more colorful neighbors had sucked the life right out of them.

The joggers cut across the street, past a white Winnebago plastered with cat-related bumper stickers, and headed toward the Battery. Behind them, I saw a wedge of Charleston Harbor. It spread up and out, all streaked with lights.

I fidgeted with my Ventolin inhaler—all I'd brought with me from Bing's house. The matron at the detention center had let me keep it after I'd explained about my asthma. My chest tightened when Miss Dora pulled a hot pink tasseled key chain from her purse. I fit the inhaler between my lips and took a short puff.

"Here are the keys," she said.

"To what?" I asked.

"To the Spencer-Jackson House," she said. "Your new home sweet home."

four

I glanced up at the pink monstrosity and took another hit of Ventolin. "I can't stay here," I cried. "Bing will pitch a fit."

"No, he won't," she said. "He hates this old house. He prefers McMansions."

"That's not true," I said. "He hates the traffic in the historic district, but he loves this house. It's a feather in his social cap. If I move in, he'll call a SWAT team." I totally believed this.

"Are you kidding me?" Miss Dora cried. "Why, just the other day he called the Spencer-Jackson a firetrap. He said taxes were eating him alive."

"The problem isn't Bing's feelings about this house," I said. "It's his feelings towards me."

"Darlin', I hate to be crude, but Bing Laden is sniffing after poontang. He's not thinking about you." Miss Dora combed the tassel with her fingernails. "But there's a reason I want you here—a selfish reason. I decorated this house myself. I used some of my finest antiques, and I haven't had time to move them. What if a burglar stripped the place? Or a fire could break out and everything would be lost."

"So buy smoke detectors."

"The Spencer-Jackson has a state-of-the-art alarm system. But when a place sits by itself, it falls into ruin. I'd just feel better if I had a house sitter. You're stuck in Charleston till December. You might as well stay at the Spencer-Jackson."

"Can't I spend the night with you?" I crossed my arms and gave the house a spiteful look. "I won't make a peep."

"You know how much I love having you around. But my house is in turmoil. I'm redecorating and painters have taken the beds apart. There's no place for you to sleep."

"The floor's fine," I said.

"Just stay here tonight. First thing tomorrow, I'll have Estaurado bring your car."

"Who?"

"My new manservant. I hired him a few weeks ago. He's an illegal, but don't tell." She pointed toward the intersection of East Bay and Adgers. "The house comes with off-street parking. There's a lot just around the corner."

She sounded like a high-pressure saleswoman, forcing me to take a giant pink dress on approval, only this dress wasn't my style. And it was way out of my price range.

"I don't know," I said. "Maybe I should go to a hotel. I'll find an apartment in the morning."

"Well, that's an option." She twirled the key. "But how will you afford it? You'll get stuck with umpteen deposits. Phone, utilities, cable TV. And you're unemployed, aren't you?"

I nodded. After Bing and I had gotten engaged, I quit my job at the Food Lion bakery. He didn't want me cooking for other people.

"The Charleston job market isn't booming, darlin'," she said. "And remember, you're in trouble with the law. You'll have to check that little box on your job application, the one that asks about criminal history. If you check 'no,' it's a felony. Anyway, I doubt you'll get a job. Don't get me wrong—you're a talented cook. Nobody can beat you making key lime pie. But you don't have formal training. Charleston used to have a chef school, you know. The town is filled with degreed chefs."

"I've got a savings account," I said. But I only had a few thousand dollars; I'd been putting back money for a Jamaica honeymoon, hoping to surprise Bing, but tra la la, he'd surprised me.

"Look, you're tired," Miss Dora said. "Let's call it a night. Bing's nursing his wounds. He won't know you're here. Just go inside and fix yourself a cup of tea. Elmer's only been dead a few weeks. The kitchen is stocked with basics—you might have to buy milk and eggs. But other than that, you're set."

A cup of tea did sound nice. But everything else felt wrong. She reached around me and opened my door. "If Bing lets you stay—and I'll talk to him—you won't have to dip into your savings. If the roof leaks, just call a repairman and send the bill to Quentin Underhill. He's a lawyer, but he takes care of the Spencer-Jackson."

She pushed the pink tassel into my hand. "The alarm code is Bing's birth date."

"What if I break something?" I looked up at the house. It was so pink, it made my head hurt. It was real pain, like when ice cold strawberry sorbet hits the roof of your mouth.

"Teeny, the only thing you're breaking is my heart," Miss Dora said. "Listen, if you need me, I'm only a few blocks away. The house looks imposing, but it's down-to-earth. Really. Think of it as a beautiful lady who's had a difficult life. Once, she was a gorgeous debutante. But she fell into ruin, maybe prostitution, and people deserted her. Now, look—she's Botoxed, lifted, tucked, and filled with collagen. Why, she's a symbol for us all. Isn't she?"

I couldn't argue with that. As I climbed out of the car, a ship's horn blew and I stumbled backward. Miss Dora leaned across the seat. "Think of it as an opportunity. Why, people would give their eyeteeth to live south of Broad. Now, dry your tears, darlin'. Go forth and carpe diem a little."

five

The stench of gasoline and brackish water blew around me as I watched Miss Dora's taillights move toward the Battery. I hated to see her go. If I'd had cash or credit cards, I would have walked to a hotel. But I couldn't loiter on the sidewalk because those joggers were coming back, and a police car was right behind them.

I unlocked the iron gate and stepped into the narrow brick corridor. Three gas lanterns flickered against the wall, shadows pooling between them. The wind shifted, carrying delicate fragrances: lemon balm, camellias, sweet almond, and fresh cut grass. The joggers ran by the gate, and I flattened myself against the wall. The police car inched down the street. Then it passed.

My footsteps clapped over the bricks as I passed by long shuttered windows and potted ferns. Most houses on Rainbow Row had two front doors—one at the street, which was meant to keep out the riffraff, and one inside the breezeway. A gray door was on my left, framed by two concrete cherubs. I unlocked it and went inside.

Shrill beeps rose up. If I didn't locate the alarm box and punch in the code, the police would come back. I groped for the light switch, found a panel of them, and hit each one. Light blazed from a three-tiered crystal chandelier and filled the hall with a cozy glow. But the alarm kept beeping. I saw a box next to the door. I punched in the numbers and the noise stopped.

My footsteps echoed as I walked to an oval staircase. Paintings of angry-looking women stared down, silently warning me not to touch anything. I'd never seen this much finery, not even at Miss Dora's home, and it scared me.

I stopped in front of a table and dropped the tasseled key chain into a crystal bowl. A piece of glass chipped off and skittered to the floor. I leaned over to examine the bowl. Waterford. I'd been in the house three minutes, and I'd already damaged a priceless artifact.

A sick feeling came over me. I squatted beside the staircase, fit my inhaler into my lips, and sucked in the bitter Ventolin. I was dying for a cup of tea but when I get tired, I get clumsy. Even if I drank water from the tap, I'd break the faucet. If I stayed longer than a night, I'd want to cook barbecued ribs and fry a batch of coconut shrimp, but a house like this cried out for cheese soufflé and cold watermelon soup.

I couldn't see myself cooking here. I'd inherited the untidy gene— all the Templeton women had it. We cooked from scratch, creating feather-light biscuits. But we also made epic messes. I wasn't built for high-class living. I let the dishes pile up in the sink; I didn't always eat at the table. Home was a place where I could eat Oreo Cakesters in bed. Only I couldn't get home. And I was stuck in a museum.

After a while, I got to my feet and grabbed the banister. It shifted to the right, like it was ready to fall down. The stairs gave indignant squeaks as I climbed to the second floor—a sign that the Spencer-Jackson House and I weren't going to get along.

"Oh, shut up," I told the staircase. When I reached the landing, I turned on the light. A gallery ran the length of the house, and the walls were lined with more pissed-off women. An arched window was open a crack, stirring the raspberry silk curtains. I caught the scent of sweet almond and thought of Mama. If she were here, she'd say, "Teeny, this house needs a little dirt. Go make mudpies."

The smell followed me down the hall, into a room with pink toile wallpaper and bedding. I unlocked the window and it glided right up—no broken glass or scuffed paint.

I kicked off my shoes, pulled back the covers, and sank into the feather mattress. As I snuggled under the quilt, I thought about Bing. Was he hurt? Were those girls still with him?

Last New Year's Day, when my beloved Aunt Bluette lay on her deathbed, she'd made me promise I wouldn't turn away from love. She'd practically raised me and knew how I was. "Teeny, don't be afraid to let people see your frightened heart," she'd said.

I'd nodded and crossed my fingers behind my back. On that day, January first, I'd started an annual lie tally, and I'd just told fib number one. But I wanted her to leave this world with an easy mind and not worry about me in the hereafter.

"I don't want to look down from heaven and see you waiting tables at Hooters," Aunt Bluette said, even though I'd quit that job two years earlier. I'd given it up because the tips were shitty and my boss had gotten too fresh. Aunt Bluette had put her foot down and said I needed a more peaceable job, so I'd started working in the Food Lion bakery. At first, I wasn't trusted to decorate the cakes, so I worked the counter and doled out free cookies to kids. The bakery ladies warmed up to me, and before long I was making special-order cakes.

Bing Jackson showed up at Aunt Bluette's funeral and came back to her house with the mourners. I tried to place him as he walked around the dining table, piling food onto a plate. Spiral ham, bacon-deviled eggs, chicken and rice, seven-layer salad, and lemon chess pie. He gave me his card, Rodney Bingham Jackson III, and said to call him Bing. He'd been in Savannah when he'd read Aunt Bluette's obituary. He was sorry for my loss, and if he could help in any way, such as listing the peach farm with his real estate company, just let him know.

Bonaventure was an hour's drive from Savannah. I sized Bing up right fast. An ambulance chaser. Out for himself. If he thought I'd hire him to sell this farm, he could think again. I was all set to show him to the door when he claimed he'd bought peaches from Aunt Bluette last year. He'd also bought one of her upside-down cakes with an out-of-this-world crumbly topping. He'd never tasted anything that good, even at Poogan's Porch in Charleston.

"Your aunt was a culinary genius," Bing said.

It was true. The secret topping called for crushed pralines and pecans, with dark brown sugar, unsalted butter, and a dollop of molasses. The peaches were steeped in vanilla brandy for a solid month.

He smiled. I smiled back. If you want to get to me, just talk about food.

After the funeral, he kept coming around, driving all the way from Charleston. I talked to him through the screen door and wouldn't even invite him in for coffee. Part of me didn't trust him and the other part was grieving for my aunt. I tried to pack up her clothes, but they smelled just like her—vanilla extract and lemon furniture polish.

The more I packed, the harder I cried. I felt woozy, as if I had twirled in a circle and fallen into a hole. There were gaps all over our orchard where trees had died. Aunt Bluette's handyman, Mr. Tom, would yank them out with the tractor, leaving pits. I had a hole inside me just like that. Somewhere in the dirt-dark black, the truth was hidden, the truth of me, who I was and who I would become. But I was too grieved to think about the future.

One afternoon I heard a car pull up the gravel drive. Bing got out of his Mercedes, and the sun hit his blond hair. I dried my tears and he took me to O'Charley's for a steak dinner and said, "You and I, we're alike. You lost your aunt, and I lost my daddy. We *get* each other, you know?"

We drank two bottles of wine and went to his motel room. "Teeny, I love your brown eyes," he said. "I love your name. Teeny. It suits you to a T."

The lovemaking was nice but unremarkable. No fireworks, just a little *pffft*, like the burp of a Tupperware container. If he'd been a pot of chicken soup, I would have tasted the broth and thought, *It needs something else.* I would have added salt, Tabasco, a grind of pepper.

Prior to our date, I'd been in love twice. My first love, Cooper O'Malley, left me with a broken heart. My second, Aaron Fisher, up and died. What did I know about sex? Maybe it was just like getting used to expensive French wines when I had a taste for spritzers.

"Was it good for you, too?" Bing asked.

"Oh, yes," I said. Lie number two.

The next morning, Bing and I ate breakfast at Waffle House. While we lingered over a second cup of coffee, a rainstorm hit and we waited for it to clear. When we finally got back to Aunt Bluette's, a hackberry tree had fallen on the roof. I'd never had to face a household emergency by myself.

"Relax," Bing said, "I'll tend to this."

He went into the attic to check for leaks. Then he started making phone calls. Tree surgeons and a gutter man descended. I liked Bing's efficiency, and he was a good kisser. So, why wasn't I bowled over? He was a man-angel who'd swooped down to rescue me. Besides, I couldn't run an orchard by myself. If I stayed in Aunt Bluette's house, I'd have to let things go. My job at Food Lion wouldn't cover the propane bill, much less the upkeep on a hundred-year-old home.

Bing's eyes said, *Trust me. I'm the one.* Though I couldn't have said why, he reminded me of Aunt Bluette's antique settee—the one with cream brocade, goose-down cushions, and carved rosewood feet. The perfect blend of beauty, comfort, and function.

My Baptist guilt had prevented me from living with a man who wasn't my lawfully wedded husband, but it didn't stop me from driving back and forth to his house in Mount Pleasant. Bing thought a two-carat diamond would fix things right up. I bargained with Jesus and asked Him to cut me some slack. After all, the modern world made Sodom and Gomorrah look tame.

I closed up the farmhouse, packed my turquoise Oldsmobile, and moved to Mount Pleasant. I planted an herb garden, organized the closets, and baked red velvet cupcakes. Bing worked long hours, but I didn't want to complain. Then, an advertisement in the *Post and Courier* caught my attention. A Charleston neurosurgeon was selling a bulldog puppy. I drove to a white mansion on South Battery, and the doctor brought out a brown and white puppy. It ran in circles; then it stopped and tilted his head as if he'd just noticed me. A broad white stripe ran down the center of the pup's flat, mashed-in head. The undershot jaw widened into a grin. Honest to god. The doctor sold him cheap, claiming he couldn't stand the drooling and snorting.

I was a little nervous as I drove back over the bridge to Mount Pleasant. I wasn't sure how Bing would react, but it was love at first sight for him, too. "Look at these teeth," he said. "A dog like this commands respect. Let's call him Sir."

The name took. I house-trained Sir in a week, using little bits of cheese as a reward. Bing hired a carpenter to install doggie doors in the people doors. We taught Sir to fetch a stuffed squirrel—not so easy with that atrocious underbite. Every night we helped him onto our high cannonball bed. Sir would circle and circle before flopping down between us, his stubby legs stretched out behind him.

Those days were so sweet, and they stayed in my mind the way lemon meringue pie lingers on the tongue. Now they were gone. We'd only been together almost six months. That came to 4,320 hours. I'd read in the *National Enquirer* about short-lived celebrity marriages. Rudolph Valentino left his bride six hours after the wedding. Britney Spears's first marriage ended after fifty-five hours. Ethel Merman and Ernest Borgnine, 768 hours. Nic Cage and Lisa Marie Presley, 2,160 hours.

Now I was all alone, sleepless in Charleston.

A car rumbled down East Bay Street, and lights ran over the walls. When I rolled over, the mattress shifted like it might crash to the floor. I held real still and thought about food. When I got nervous, I had my own ways of calming down; I made up unusual recipes that weren't necessarily edible but suited my mood.

What I needed was my family's private cookbook, but it was locked up at Bing's house. No matter what had happened between me and Bing, I couldn't lose that book. Long before I was born, my aunt and her sisters began a Templeton tradition. They started with a spiral-bound Baptist cookbook, covered it with blue plaid, and painted *Templeton Family Receipts & Whatnot* across the front. Whenever one of the sisters got peeved, she wrote a recipe—not a normal one, mind you, but one that helped her relax. Some people have punching bags, time-out rooms, or Prozac. The Templetons had a cookbook. Our recipes were fanciful, listing umpteen lethal ingredients. Not that we'd ever tried them on anyone. It was just our way of venting.

I pictured Bing's peach tree. Too bad I'd used the fruit as ammunition or I could make You'll Get Yours Peach Icing. It calls for 1 cup heavy whipping cream, 1/3 cup sugar, and 1/2 cup pureed peaches. Reserve the pits and beat the cream until it stiffens, about five minutes. Add sugar. Fold in peach puree. Set aside. Smash the pits with a hammer. Retrieve seeds. Place in a mortar and use pestle to pulverize the seeds until they resemble your heart. Cry a little. Smile when you remember that peach seeds contain cyanide. Shrug because they aren't fatal unless consumed in humongous amounts. They have been known to cause explosions in the digestive tract.

Quick note to self: Mix seeds into peach puree. Spread icing onto a layer cake and serve it to the skanks who stole your husband-to-be. Refrigerate to prevent spoilage.

six

I was dreaming of monster cheesecake, the kind that's drizzled with dark chocolate, when I heard gunfire. I sat up and listened to the rhythmic pops. Was a robber downstairs shooting Miss Dora's antiques? I looked around for a place to hide, but the noise seemed to be coming from the street.

I got dressed, hurried downstairs, and grabbed the tasseled key chain. My pulse thrummed as I went out the gray door, into the corridor, and peeked through the iron grille. I half-expected to see a sniper or furniture thief; the sidewalk was empty except for a long-legged brunette. She was busily hammering an ornate sign into the strip of grass between the sidewalk and street.

It was the naked badminton player, the pretty one Bing had kissed and kissed, only today she wasn't naked. She wore a blue silk dress, high heels, and an ankle bracelet.

"You!" I cried and unlocked the iron door.

"Stay away from me!" She lifted the hammer.

"Put that damn thing down," I said. "You're liable to hurt someone."

"*Me?*" She stepped back.

"Does Bing know I'm at the Spencer-Jackson House?" I asked. Stupid question. Of course he knew. And he'd sent this woman to do what?

Attack me with a hammer? I repressed an urge to snatch off her ankle bracelet. If throwing fruit was criminal battery, stealing jewelry would slap me in the state penitentiary.

"I'm not telling what he knows." The woman lowered the hammer. "But I'll tell you what he said. He told me your folks were pygmies."

"They were not," I cried. "For your information, Miss Tall Gal, five foot two isn't tiny." Actually, I was more like five foot one and three quarters. I wanted to defend my genetics but I couldn't. I'd never known my dad. He could have been a pituitary dwarf.

"Bitch," I said.

"My name isn't Bitch. It's Natalie Lockhart. And I refuse to be verbally abused by a garden gnome." She shoved her hand into a straw handbag. "I'm calling Bingo. I'm calling him right now."

"Bingo?" I laughed. I couldn't help it.

"Shut up. What do you know about lovers and their nicknames?"

"Not much," I admitted. "What do you know about decency?"

"I'd love to chat, but I'm late for the day spa."

She would go to a place like that. I glanced at my unpainted toenails. A day spa wasn't long enough for me. I needed a year-long immersion in Pond's cold cream.

A horse-drawn carriage filled with tourists clomped down the street. A lady in a straw hat stood up and clicked a digital camera in my direction. Natalie flashed an irritated glance at the carriage. She ran to her BMW, climbed inside, and drove toward the Battery.

I walked back to the sign. It was black, surrounded by an ornate wrought-iron border:

For Sale
Jackson Realty
by Appointment Only
Natalie Lockhart, Broker

I went inside and called Bing's office. His secretary said he'd taken the day off, that he'd been attacked by a crazy girl. The judge had forbidden contact, but he hadn't been specific. I dialed Bing's cell phone. He didn't answer, so I called his house. When he didn't pick up, I wondered if he'd disconnected his answering machine, the one we'd taped together in happier times. I started to hang up when Bing answered with a curt hello.

"It's me," I said.

"When did they release *you* into the wild?" he asked.

"Last night."

"Big mistake," he said. "I just hope your debt to society is a big one."

"Big enough," I said.

"I just got home from the hospital," he said. "They did a CAT scan on my head. I'm waiting for the doctor to call, so make it fast. What the hell do you want?"

A good question. I wanted a lot of things. I wanted to know if he was hurt or putting on, I wanted to know why he needed other women. I had questions for myself, too. Did I want Bing or a life by myself making cakes?

"Your secretary said you weren't feeling good."

"It's feeling *well*," he said. "Not *good*."

I hadn't called to discuss my swamp grammar. A few months ago, Bing took a business English course. He was self-conscious about his Southern accent and wanted to show off to all the Yankees who came down to the Carolinas to buy beach houses. He wanted me to talk better, too, but when I got excited, I just had to speak what was in my heart.

"If you called to apologize, forget it," Bing said.

I sighed. What I'd wished he'd said was *I love you, Teens. I've always loved you.* And I'd say, *Prove it. Buy Natalie a ticket for the Space Shuttle.* I gathered up my courage and said, "I am sorry you got hurt. But the reason I'm calling is, I just talked to your girlfriend Natalie."

He was silent for a moment. "Where'd you see her?"

"I'm at your uncle Elmer's house."

"You're where?" he cried.

"Miss Dora gave me the key."

"Damn her. I should've known she'd pull something like this."

"She's redecorating, or I'd stay with her."

"Well, the Spencer-Jackson House isn't hers," he said. "You can't stay there."

"I know. Natalie told me."

"How'd she know you were there?"

"Didn't you send her?" I asked.

"No. Absolutely not."

"She put up a 'For Sale' sign."

"She *what*?" he cried.

I waited to see if he'd continue. When he didn't, I said, "Bing, I know you're mad. But is there any way I can stay for a few days? Miss Dora said you need a house sitter. You won't kick me to the street, will you?"

"You hit me in the head. You've got twenty-four hours to get the hell off my property."

"But Miss Dora said—"

"Don't mention that bitch's name to me. She shanghaied my poor daddy and then fed him nothing but fried foods. He'd still be alive if he hadn't tangled with Dora."

I pictured Bing sitting at the pine kitchen table, rubbing his hands together. He always did that when he talked about Dora. I was pretty sure our bulldog lay stretched out on the floor, his lips vibrating with each exhale.

"Teeny?" Bing said. "You still there?"

"Just tell me why you cheated," I said.

"I didn't get to. I didn't even know they were coming over. They showed up with a cooler of lemon margaritas. Next thing I knew, they were naked."

"You didn't have to join them, did you?" My hand was trembling so bad the phone knocked into my jaw. I was having trouble understanding how two women just happened to show up on the very night of my first cake class. If it hadn't been canceled, I wouldn't have known the truth about Bing.

"At the time it seemed like fun," he said.

I was tempted to call him an asshole, which was perfectly legal, but I held back. Women stayed with bastards all the time. I'd heard on *Oprah* that relationships can be sticky. Some kind of hormone gets secreted, and it traps you to the other person. You're afraid to peel yourself away because you might leave behind a piece of yourself. When insects land on flypaper, they might break loose, only to leave behind a leg. They buzz off, thinking, *Wow, what a clean break.* And their foot is still wiggling on the paper.

"Bing, I know you're upset," I said. "But I'm flat broke. I can't rent an apartment till I find a job."

"Go back to your farm."

"Can't. I'm on probation here for six months."

"Well, that's too fucking bad. And don't start in about your childhood. I don't want to hear that shit about your mama and them. I don't feel one drop of pity for you."

I wrapped the phone cord around my wrist, hating myself for having told him about Mama. It had been a huge step for me, a catharsis, and I'd put everything behind me. Now Bing was using the past against me. Fine, I didn't need this house. I'd just call Mr. Bell and ask him to talk to the judge. I didn't know doodly-squat about the law, but maybe I could get special permission to live in Georgia. No way could I afford to stay in Charleston until December fourth.

"I can't go anywhere without my clothes," I said. "They're at your house."

"No problem. They'll be waiting for you in my driveway. Anything else?"

"My dog." I swallowed. "I want Sir."

"No, ma'am. You're a little jailbird. You're unfit to raise a dog. Don't even think about sneaking over here with a T-bone steak and dognapping him. That's grand theft. And you'll be violating the restraining order."

All this time, I'd tried to speak softly and carry a big stick just like President Roosevelt said to do, but I couldn't hold back another second. "You're worse than evil," I said. "You sent me to cake school so you could womanize in the backyard, and *I'm* the bad guy?"

"You're not a guy. You're just a bitch in trouble—and you're a violent bitch, too." His voice screaked up at the edges. "Never in my life has a woman hit me."

"I didn't mean to. But when I saw what I saw, I went crazy."

"A normal woman would cry and pack a suitcase, not climb a tree."

"Is that what you wanted? For me to catch you?"

"Teeny, I swear. Have you been sniffing oven cleaner? Hell, no, I didn't want to be caught. You know how I hate confrontations."

My knees wobbled and I dropped to the floor. I wished he and those women were dead and gone, killed in a twenty-car pileup on the Savannah Highway. A tear ran down my cheek into the corner of my mouth. It tasted salty. Tears from crying jags aren't like the tears you get when you chop onions. I read that somewhere. Bing didn't care about trivia; he cared about grammar. He'd even bought me a word-a-day calendar. But sometimes he dropped his guard and dropped his *g*s like a natural-born Charlestonian. "*Darlin', don't wait up for me,*" he'd say. "*I'm workin' late this evenin'.*"

I was like those *g*s. He'd dropped me, too. And it wasn't 100 percent Natalie's fault. I bet she'd never write him a love note with incorrect grammar. Just the other day I'd left one that said, *Your the best.* And Bing had written back:

Dear Crackerbilly,
It's <u>you're</u> the best, although <u>you</u> <u>are</u> will work, too.
Love you anyway,
Bing

"Answer me one thing," I said. "Why did you ask me to marry you?"

"Don't ask stupid questions. You're cute. And I loved you, I guess." He exhaled. "Can we discuss this later? I could be bleeding internally for all I know. And my head is killing me."

"I need to settle my housing situation."

"Oh, all right. Meet me at McTavish's Pub at five o'clock tonight and we'll talk. You remember McTavish's?"

"No," I said, biting down on the word. Clearly he'd taken another woman to that pub. Who was he mixing me up with?

"The pub is a few blocks from Uncle Elmer's," he said. "And Teeny?"

"Yes?"

"I'm not a cold-hearted bastard. It just looks that way. I might let you stay at Uncle Elmer's for a while. Who knows? After we leave the pub, maybe I'll take you out for dessert."

His lighthearted tone sounded like the old Bing, but I didn't trust him. I hung up without saying good-bye. He liked to tell people we'd gotten engaged because I wouldn't give him the recipe to my peach cobbler. That's sort of true. I'd sworn to Aunt Bluette I'd keep it a secret. I may be tasteless, I may be short, but when Teeny Templeton makes a promise, she keeps it.

seven

Here in Charleston, you can't swing a squirrel without hitting a professional chef, but I was determined to find a cooking job. While I sipped coffee, I studied the phone book and made a list of restaurants and cafés. Then I locked up the Spencer-Jackson House and stepped into the brick corridor. A bulky pink envelope lay just inside the entry gate. I tore open the envelope and found my car key and a note from Miss Dora.

> *Dear Teeny,*
>
> *Estaurado parked your car on Adgers and filled it up with gas. I'm cleaning one of the guest rooms today, but it's a sight! It won't be ready for a while. Hang in there.*
>
> *Love, Dora*

I pushed down my disappointment and headed down the sidewalk. The noon sun burned my shoulders as I walked down East Bay. Even before I got to the corner, I spotted my turquoise Olds in a lot off Adgers. My car key wouldn't fit on Miss Dora's tasseled chain, so I'd have to be extra careful not to lose it. I put down the convertible top, drove out of the parking lot, and turned onto the cobbled street where the old cotton warehouses used to be. I headed toward Folly Beach and stopped at one of Bing's favorite restaurants, The Sailmaker.

"Our pastry chef is from Le Cordon Bleu," the manager said. "We're not even hiring dishwashers."

I thanked him and drove to the next restaurant on my list. A café on West Hudson offered me a waitressing position, but I was still pumped with optimism and turned it down. By the time I'd worked my way across Charleston, I'd been rejected by eighteen restaurants. I drove to Sunset Smorgasbord on Washington Street. It was Bing's favorite place in the world. We had eaten there every Friday night.

I glanced at my watch. Three o'clock. Perfect. I'd arrived during the lull between lunch and supper. I gathered up my courage and went inside. The restaurant was empty except for two middle-aged women in the corner booth. I asked a waitress if the owner was available. She told me to wait by the nautical ropes. Smells drifted from the kitchen— garlic fried shrimp and Parmigiano-Reggiano. The food at Sunset Smorgasbord was fresh and memorable, but the décor was corny: red booths, mounted sailfish, nets filled with shells and plastic crabs.

Mr. Fortino came out of the kitchen and smiled, as if he recognized me. He led me past the salad bar, which resembled a boat, to a booth in the back. He squeezed into the seat across from me, and the table pressed into the front of his Hawaiian shirt. This was a man who appreciated good food. I started in about how I was a self-taught country cook and really needed a job.

Mr. Fortino held up his hand to shush me. "Miss, I thought you was engaged to that real estate tycoon who eats here. What's his name, Bing something?"

"Jackson," I said. "We broke up. And I really need a job."

"Wish I could help, sweetie. But I don't have no openings. I got a kitchen full of illegals. If a waitress spot comes open, I'll keep you in mind."

"Thanks." I started to scoot out of the booth, but he caught my arm.

"Don't worry. Cute as you are, you'll find a job." He pointed at me. "Be thankful you're away from that man-whore."

I blinked. He hadn't said a bad word, but it still hurt my ears.

Mr. Fortino lowered his head, looking at me from under his eyebrows. He was mostly bald except for long black strands that he combed straight back. "I seen you and him coming to eat here week after week. You sitting prim and proper in your cotton dress, ordering manicotti, and him going to the men's room to rub naughty parts with my wife's baby sister. Didn't you notice something was funny? The way he ran back and forth to the bathroom?"

I'd never heard a man speak in such graphic terms, but Mr. Fortino wasn't trying to shock me, he was telling the truth. I averted my gaze and said, "Bing told me he had a sick stomach."

"Right. 'Sick stomach' is man-whorese for 'Don't follow me, let me hump in peace.' The man has no taste. If he ate out a wildebeest, I wouldn't be surprised. He cheated on his first wife—I forget her name. But she wasn't sweet like you. I couldn't believe it when he was engaged to you and tapping that brunette chick."

I blinked and blinked. Finally I said, "Natalie Lockhart?"

"No dick in Charleston is safe with her around," he said. "Bing wasn't the only one she snookered."

I rubbed my forehead. So this had been going on awhile.

Mr. Fortino spread his stubby hands on the table. "I'm telling you this cause you're a nice lady," he said. "You tipped my waitresses extra when Bing threw down a few dollar bills. Do me a favor. If he asks you to take him back, do a 'fuck you' dance all over his face."

I thanked him and drove toward Rainbow Row. On impulse, I swung into the Harris Teeter on East Bay Street for baking supplies. I hit the half-price-candy rack in case I had a sugar attack. Bing thought I was a little too curvy. I am. There is no way to be skinny if you cook like me. Plus, I hate to exercise. Why risk an asthma attack? Me, I use housework to keep from getting too stubby, but mostly I don't worry and I don't count calories. My philosophy of dieting can be summed up in five words: when I'm hungry, I eat.

Down the street, I stopped in a funky consignment shop and bought a red blouse, striped pants, and a purse shaped like a giant lemon, all for less than ten dollars.

When I got home, I put my car key in my change purse, then I carried the groceries to the kitchen and set them on the counter. The island was black granite, and it caught my reflection as I moved around the large, square room. I opened a white cabinet and twirled the built-in spice rack. I removed an empty peppercorn tin and replaced it with a jar of Hungarian paprika.

Next, I found tea bags in one drawer, a copper pan in another. I filled the pan with water and set it on a burner. The gas whooshed up, then tamped down into a quivering blue circle, casting light on the brick backsplash.

While I waited for the water to "smile," as the French say, I checked out the appliances. The double convection ovens needed cleaning; the warming drawer was filled with fine bread crumbs. I flipped the switch to the garbage disposal. It sputtered and emitted a sharp whine. I shut it off.

I wasn't going to get along with this room. Wherever I'd lived, I'd developed a relationship with the kitchen. I'd fallen in love with Bing's state-of-the-art appliances, and I'd had great rapport with Aunt Bluette's antique stove and temperamental ice box; but I'd had a tumultuous union with Food Lion's kitchen. I had battle wounds to prove it. Once, a springform pan had exploded and dumped blistering-hot graham cracker crumbs and cheesecake onto my wrist. I still carried a dark brown, half-moon scar.

I found a stool in the pantry and pushed it against the counter. As I shoved cornmeal and sugar bags in the tall cabinets, I wondered if my shortness had made Bing take up with a giantess. He was six foot two. Me, I wore high heels that deformed my poor feet, and still people had stared at us, as if trying to figure out how a tall man and a short woman could fit together.

On my way down the stool, I paused to rearrange the tall spices that wouldn't fit into the lazy Susan. Too bad Bing hadn't picked someone his own size. I'd had no clue he was a player. I'd just assumed he had a low sex drive—not terribly low, mind you, just not what you'd expect from a thirty-year-old man. I'd been clueless. I'd baked layer cakes, played with my dog, and weeded the herb garden. Meanwhile, Bing had disrespected me on a daily basis.

I put away the stool, walked into the garden, and picked lavender, piling it into my shirttail. Then I went back inside and made a vanilla peach pecan coffee cake and drizzled it with royal icing. I sprinkled lavender on top. When Aunt Bluette fixed this cake, she'd added a few pulverized peach seeds—not enough to be poison—because it added a hint of almond.

Just thinking of her made me feel sad to my bones. I wandered into the pink living room and curled up on the settee. Worry begets worry. Quiet begets quiet. Peace begets peace. Mama used to say I attracted trouble. She blamed it on the year I was born, 1980, when John Lennon got shot. But all of the Templetons were nervous people. Only two aunts were still alive. Goldie was a professional clown and lived somewhere in Tennessee with her psychic daughter, Tallulah Belle. Aunt Pinky lived off the coast of Georgia, tending to wild donkeys, while her son Ira made talking Jesus dolls. I loved my family, even though some of them were flat-out weird, but Aunt Bluette and the farm were my heart.

When I was little, I'd sit on her lap and grip the steering wheel while she drove through the orchard, checking the trees for blight. She'd shift gears, and the engine would sputter. She was the eldest Templeton sister. Mama was the baby. They didn't always agree about my upbringing, but Aunt Bluette never argued with Mama, she just went about things in her quiet way.

On Wednesday nights, Aunt Bluette and I went to the Pack-a-Pew party at First Baptist. We'd leave Mama sitting at the kitchen table, her head bent over a spiral notebook, cookbooks piled around her. It looked like she was planning a menu, but she was matching rock-and-roll songs to recipes and Bible verses, the way a foodie would pair wines with the entrée, adding complementary music.

When Aunt Bluette and I got home, Mama would tear out pages from the notebook and set them in front of me, just as proud of her imaginary recipes as if she'd cooked a steaming hot bowl of actual soup. Aunt Bluette said Mama was feeding me the only way she could.

Mama was right fond of ZZ Top's "Poke Chop Sandwhich" paired with Isaiah 65:4, along with a tried-and-true recipe for pan-fried pork cutlets—so moist and butter-like you could cut them with a spoon.

Mama was totally fixated on dead musicians: John Lennon, Jimi Hendrix, Jim Morrison, and Elvis—especially Elvis. She had a life-sized *Viva Las Vegas* poster on her bedroom wall. She even paid a man to build me a Graceland dollhouse. When she had one of her spells, she'd get to thinking that Elvis might not be dead after all, and she'd stop writing recipes and keep a log of the King's sightings.

When she got like this, Aunt Bluette did her best to set things right. She'd take Mama to the garden and make her weed. If it was raining, they'd sit in the kitchen and string beans. I'd stretch out under the table as the kitchen filled with noises—beans ringing against the side of the metal pan, water streaming off the roof, the rise and fall of Mama's chatter. She knew she was talkative and poked fun at herself. "I'm the Mouth of the South," she'd say. But once she got going, she couldn't stop no matter if it was motor-mouthing or acting wild.

If Mama acted up during peach season, Aunt Bluette would steer her to the kitchen and put her to work. "Come on, Ruby," my aunt would say. "Let's make jam."

One time Mama set a pot to boiling, then she leaned across the counter, moving her hands like she was treading water. "Teeny, did I ever tell you how I got pregnant with you? I went on a church trip to Daytona Beach. That's where I met your father. Well, one of them."

"Ruby, hush," Aunt Bluette said. "The child is listening."

"No, she isn't."

"God is listening," Aunt Bluette said. "God has ears."

"How do you know? Have you seen Him?"

Aunt Bluette muttered something about blasphemy. Mama wandered over to the stove and dipped a peach into boiling water. The skin slid off in one piece. She held it up. "Just like a debutante stepping out of a ball gown," she said, then frowned. "What was I saying? See? That's what happens when you interrupt me, Bluette."

"You should see a doctor," Aunt Bluette said. "It ain't natural to talk this much."

"But I have things to say. Teeny has a right to know who her daddy is." I tugged at her skirt. "Who is he, Mama?"

She squatted beside me, her eyes shining. "Well, I'm not sure. He's either a green-eyed proctologist or a hashish dealer with a fuzzy red ponytail. Cute as buttons, both of them. I'm waiting to see who you take after, so I can sue his ass."

"Don't hold your breath," Aunt Bluette said, pointing at me. "Teeny's like us, brown-eyed and blond."

"That explains it." Mama giggled. "I'm the mama and you're the daddy."

Aunt Bluette ignored her and ladled preserves into a Ball jar. "Get me more peaches," she said.

"You can't order me around. I won't be trapped on this farm," Mama said. "One of these days, I'll fly away, and you won't stop me."

I stared up at her. I didn't think she'd go; she was just talking big. But I couldn't be sure. I grabbed the hem of her dress. "Take me," I said, tugging hard. "Don't you go without me."

She didn't leave that day. But she was like a bird fluttering around a cage. If you leave the door open for a second, it will escape, darting from room to room, smacking against windows, searching for a way through the glass, beating its wings harder and harder, wanting nothing more than to fly up into the blue.

eight

Late that afternoon, I set out for McTavish's Pub. I paused by Natalie's sign, then I yanked it up and slid it under the hedge. Pronged shadows fell across the sidewalk as I started up East Bay Street. Most of the time the light in Charleston was clear and polished as if filtered through a fine net. This afternoon, it was thick and woolly as if it had been wrung out of a bright yellow washcloth.

The pub wasn't far, so I left my Oldsmobile at Adgers and turned onto Exchange Street. I saw a blond man, but he turned out to be older than Bing. He held open the door to Carolina's Restaurant while an elderly woman with a walker shuffled inside.

I breathed in the smells of fried pork bellies, bacon butter, and fried flounder. Carolina's made the best peach jam in the south, even better than Aunt Bluette's.

Bing had loved my preserves. Aside from his career in real estate, I knew basic details: He was a native Charlestonian. He'd grown up in the Queen Street house with his tycoon daddy, Rodney Jackson, and his debutante mother, Genevieve, who'd died of a brain aneurysm when Bing was a junior at Clemson. His LSAT scores were shockingly low. Rather than suffer through the exam a second time, he got his broker's license and went to work for his daddy.

Bing hated wasps, bad grammar, sunburn, headaches, ice cold water, jalapeño peppers, weird night noises, and black-and-white movies. He liked chocolate, 70-degree weather, matching socks, and Ping golf clubs. His idol was the late golfer Payne Stewart, who'd traipsed around in kilts and had won two US Opens and one PGA championship but had died young. Bing was a Virgo to my Gemini, and when I'd read his daily horoscope out loud, he'd listen patiently, like I was a crazy aunt who'd just gotten released from the local asylum.

So I knew factoids but nothing juicy. The trouble was, he'd buried his sore spots. Not that I wished him to have any, but he was bound to have at least one. I'd shown him my embarrassing stories and cracked pieces.

Just the idea of seeing him tonight made me reach inside my pocket to make sure I'd brought my inhaler. My hand shook a little when I opened McTavish's tall oak door. I stepped into the pub and waited for my eyes to adjust. Smoke curled along the low beamed ceiling. The smell of fish 'n' chips wafted from the kitchen and mixed with the faintly bitter scent of Guinness. Antique golf clubs and pictures of St. Andrews lined the green-and-red plaid walls. Now I understood why Bing had chosen this place.

I headed toward a long mahogany bar and passed a pool table, where two elderly men rubbed blue chalk on their cue sticks. On the wall behind them, a dartboard with Prince Charles's face was filled with holes. A lady in purple shorts smiled at me from the jukebox. She pushed in a quarter, and a minute later Elvis began singing "Softly, As I Leave You." Mama used to pair that song with Psalm 65:10 and soft shell crabs.

I didn't see Bing anywhere. I slid onto a leather stool. The bartender swaggered over and spread his hands on the counter. His sleeves scooted up, showing Celtic cross tattoos on both wrists.

"Peach martini, please," I said, and the bartender reached for the schnapps. Behind me, the billiard balls cracked, and laughter rose up into the smoky air.

The bartender returned in a flash with two peach martinis. "It's happy hour," he said. "Enjoy."

I took a sip and kicked off my flip-flops. The stool beside me creaked. I glanced up as a dark-haired man sat down and ordered a Guinness. He wore ragged jeans and a faded blue t-shirt with LAWYER OR LIAR—YOU MAKE THE CALL printed across the front. As he leaned his elbows on the counter, a curl fell down over familiar gray eyes.

Please god, not him.

Not Cooper O'Malley.

I'd imagined this moment a thousand times, and here I was, wearing flip-flops and wrinkled shorts. The last time I'd talked to O'Malley was eleven years ago. He'd stood in my aunt's parlor and told me he couldn't see me anymore, then I'd promptly had an asthma attack. I'd done my best to forget him, not an easy trick in a small town. I'd stopped reading the newspaper so I didn't have to keep tabs on his heart-stomping ass.

Maybe I should ignore him now. I reached for my second martini, took a sip, and glanced sideways. He smiled. Damn, men that gorgeous should be outlawed. The bartender brought Coop's beer. It had a stamped clover in the foam.

"Another drink, cutie?" the bartender asked me.

"Please," I said, thinking about crazy girls with hammers. I fished a peach slice from my glass and bit into the tangy flesh. It tasted like a fallen fruit. They're stronger and slightly alcoholic, with a flavor like schnapps or brandy. My mouth filled with the memory of Aunt Bluette working in her roadside stand, weighing bags of fruit and chatting with customers while honeybees hummed over the bins.

The door opened, and warm night air pushed into the bar. I glanced at my watch. Five forty-five and no Bing. Cooper lifted his glass mug. His t-shirt was stretched over his shoulders, each deltoid muscle round as an Elberta peach. I'd never wanted to touch a man's arm this bad—

well, except for *this* particular man's arm. I wanted to push my hand under his sleeve and feel his peach of a muscle, the way I had when we were younger. If Bing strolled in, he'd think I was flirting. Well, so what? He had it coming. Tit for freaking tat. Except our "talk" would go out the window, and I'd end up totally homeless.

The bartender brought my drinks and cleared the empty glasses. I reached for my martini, and the voice inside my head made a tsking sound. I needed gas money, not alcohol. Too damn bad. I tossed down the drink. It felt cold against the back of my throat. Now I understood why Mama did what she did. Her mind was crawling with snakes. No place to be still, no peace, only the slick edge of pain. Alcohol was a cheap way to step out of her own skin.

"You come here a lot?" Coop grinned and dimples cut into his cheeks.

"My first time."

"You don't recognize me, do you?" he asked.

"I'd know you anywhere, O'Malley," I said. Even if he did look a little different. And more handsome, if that was possible. In high school, he'd been thinner, and his long dark bangs had fallen into his eyes.

His smile widened and I saw the tiny scar on his chin. When he was six years old, he'd tumbled off a merry-go-round at Lakeside Elementary, and I'd held my mitten against the wound until his daddy, Dr. O'Malley, had arrived.

"Whatever happened to you?" I asked. I was referring to why he'd dumped me all those years ago.

"After Carolina, I went to Yale law. Then I lived in England." He shrugged. "What about you? How'd you end up in Charleston?"

"Long story." Well, what was I supposed to say? I could tell him about Bing and my criminal record. Or I could describe the Food Lion bakery and how I'd distributed pecan sandies to members of the Free Cookie Club.

You're drunk, I thought, mentally adding an apostrophe between "you" and "re." I stared into my glass. No more peachtinis for me, at least not tonight. If I understood anything at all, it was the chemistry of food. Bread won't rise without yeast. When vinegar hits baking soda the gasses whoosh up and unstop your sink. Hot water makes sugar crystallize, and the result is rock hard candy. You can even turn a lemon into a battery. A martini was a chemical. And it was changing me, changing my brain. Oh, I would regret this in the morning.

"I heard about your aunt's passing," Coop said. "I'm so sorry. She was a nice lady. "

"I miss her."

"Death is tough. I lost Uncle Ralph a year ago. I thought I'd see you at the funeral home."

"Aunt Bluette was getting radiation therapy," I said.

"Bonaventure won't be the same without her," he said.

"Or without your uncle," I said. Ralph had taught biology at the high school. Twice he'd been chosen Teacher of the Year for inspiring bored, hormonally driven teenagers to care about cell division.

"Damn, I didn't mean to get maudlin." Coop finished his beer and leaned into the space between us. "You smell like vanilla cake from the bakery."

"A bakery?" I laughed.

"I really do smell vanilla," he said.

I touched my nose to my shoulder. It did smell faintly sweet. Vanilla is supposed to increase blood flow to the nether regions. I wondered if it was affecting his.

"I made a coffee cake today," I said.

"Homemade?"

"Is there any other kind?" I smiled. He wasn't flirting. But I was.

He eased off his stool, walked over to the jukebox, and dropped a quarter into the slot. On his way back "Don't Be Cruel" began to play.

He leaned across the bar, and his hand knocked into the glass I was holding.

"Damn, I'm sorry," he said.

"That's okay." I blotted up the spill with a napkin. "It's happy hour. I've got a spare drink."

"But I ruined your blouse." He waved one hand. "Just take it off. Take it off right now. There's a one-hour dry cleaners on East Bay."

Seriously? Wait, he was kidding.

He leaned closer and sniffed. "Peach schnapps?"

"90 proof," I said.

"Potent stuff," he said. "I could pass out on Broad. A horse-drawn carriage might roll over me."

"Or snag you," I said. "You could be dragged for blocks."

He laughed. "Just give me the blouse and nobody'll get hurt."

Normally I wouldn't joke about accidents, but I couldn't help it. The old chemistry was still there, and it wasn't all from my side. Then I remembered why I was here. Coop's job was to defend jailbirds, not flirt with them.

"I can't resist vanilla," he said.

"How can you smell anything in here?" I waved my hand. Cigarette smoke hung in thick strands under the billiard lights. Aunt Bluette always said breathing secondhand smoke was dangerous. Besides, it was time for me to go. I slid my toes into my flip-flops and smiled up at Coop. I wasn't sure what to say—See you around? Nice talking to you? I hadn't seen him in eleven years and probably wouldn't see him for eleven more.

"Nice seeing you again, Coop." I tossed down my drink.

"Don't let me chase you off."

"I'm chasing myself. I have to get up early."

"Let me walk you to your car." He touched my hand and a jolt of pleasure traveled up my arm.

"I didn't drive," I said. "I walked."

"From where?"

"I just live a few blocks away."

"I'll drive you. This neighborhood can be scary after dark."

"I'm not scared. Tourists are all over. And policemen."

"Policemen won't help. See, I'm a lawyer. I know what really goes on. Things that don't make the news."

"And it's your duty to defend me, right?"

"I'd just feel better if you got home safe."

"Maybe I don't want you to know where I live."

"You can blindfold me."

"Then you can't protect me."

"Just let me walk you halfway."

"Half? What good is half?"

He threw a wad of cash on the counter. "How about if you walk me to my truck?"

"You just don't give up, do you?" I smiled.

"You should see me in a courtroom."

We squeezed through the crowd, onto the sidewalk. A breeze stirred the hanging flower baskets. I smelled fried banana fritters, espresso, and cigars. Way off in the distance I heard a blues band playing on a rooftop bar. Coop stopped beside an old red truck. A gigantic hairy beast stood in the back.

"What's *that*?" I said.

"My dog. Don't worry. He's a gentle giant."

I took a breath, remembering dogs could sense fear. The animal was the size of a miniature donkey, with gangly legs and a long tail. As I moved forward, the dog's ears swiveled through the rippled, taffy-colored hair, tracking my movements. The gigantic mouth opened, and a pink tongue slid between curved incisors.

"This is T-Bone," Coop said. At the sound of his name, the dog spun in tight circles, making the truck sway, then he stood on his hind legs and waved his paws.

"T-Bone loves to ride," Coop said. "Don't you, boy? I hate leaving him at home."

"How old is he?"

"Don't know. I found him two years ago. He was half dead. Starved. A broken leg. He's fine now. He weighs nearly 140 pounds, but he could stand to gain a few." Coop patted the dog's head, and the pink tongue shot out, the size of a brisket, narrowly missing Coop's cheek.

"Cut that out, T-Bone." Coop laughed.

The dog woofed and spun again.

"He's got chutzpah," I said.

"That's for sure." Coop grinned. "Come on, let me drive you home."

Why not? I thought. I wasn't taking a ride from a stranger, just an old boyfriend. I glanced at his profile. His nose was just as I remembered, long and straight, as if drawn with a ruler. "Okay," I said.

"Where do you live, sweetheart?"

"East Bay." I looked away so he couldn't see me smile. The way he'd said "sweetheart" put me in mind of Humphrey Bogart in *The Maltese Falcon*.

We climbed into the truck. The light from the dashboard reflected into his face as he cranked the engine. Music started playing. Radiohead was singing "All I Need."

I turned around and looked out the rear window at T-Bone. "Does that tail ever stop wagging?" I asked.

"Never." He adjusted the mirror and I saw T-Bone's reflection.

Coop turned onto East Bay Street. A group of tourists in shorts and sandals strolled toward the waterfront. A little farther down, a carriage moved toward the Battery. Coop tapped the brake. The truck slowed just as the music started to build in a rush of piano, xylophone, drum beats and cymbals.

At the end of the street, a dark car pulled away from the curb. I jumped a little—Bing drove a black Mercedes—but when the car passed under the streetlight, it was navy blue.

Not Bing. What a relief. A Winnebago pulled into the slot, and a plume of dark smoke drifted from its tailpipe.

"I live right there." I pointed to the pink house. If I invited him in for coffee cake, would he think I was offering more than dessert? Even in the old days, we'd never crossed the line.

Coop squinted out the window. "You're selling it?"

"What?"

"There's a sign out front."

I turned. The ornate sign was back. It jutted up from a narrow patch of grass, lashed to the palm tree by a thick metal chain.

"You can stop here." I cracked open the door. "Thanks for the ride."

"May I call you sometime?" he asked. "For dinner or drinks or something? Or you call me. My number's real easy to remember: SUE-THEM. The answering service picks up 24-7."

"Sure." I started to climb out of the truck, and he touched my arm. I turned. From the radio, the music reached a crescendo. We reached for each other at the same time, our movements building like music, the different elements converging—lips, tongues, hands.

The song ended abruptly, and I came back to my senses. I pulled away, my hands knotted against his shirt. I'd kissed someone I used to love. But he hadn't loved me. Why would it be different now?

"I'm sorry. I can't do this." I wrenched away and climbed out of the truck. I ran toward the sidewalk, past the sign. A note was taped to the wrought iron door. *Check Out Time—24 Hours, Bing.*

I flattened the note with the heel of my hand. His handwriting looked odd: the *g* in Bing wasn't curled up like a watch spring. Had he written the note or dictated it to Natalie? He'd sworn up and down he hadn't known about the sign, and I'd believed him.

I ripped up the note. As I threw the pieces at the sign, I remembered an old Gullah recipe called Bye-Bye Bitch. It calls for pepper, gunpowder, and spit from your victim. If throwing fruit is a crime, how in the world would you collect saliva without ending up in the pokey? Why, you'd have to be a dentist—or quick on the draw with a turkey baster.

nine

I went straight to bed but I couldn't sleep. Seeing Coop again had brought back feelings that I'd worked hard to repress. He'd been a year ahead of me at Bonaventure High, but he'd always teased me in a brotherly way. His daddy, Dr. O'Malley, had taken care of the town's ills, including my asthma, and his mama beautified local homes with a gift shop on the town square.

Since the O'Malleys attended First Baptist, I got to see Coop every Sunday, and at the Pack-a-Pew parties. Aunt Bluette said Coop was an Irish Baptist—Dr. O'Malley had been Catholic until he'd met Coop's mama, a Baptist preacher's daughter. I was grateful they'd picked my church because that meant I got to see Coop every day except Saturday. Because I was short and puny, he'd sneak up behind me and set me on his shoulders.

"Put me down, O'Malley," I'd say, full of mock indignation.

Every afternoon, I saw him at football practice. I was in the band, the worst clarinet player in Bonaventure High, and I was evermore marching out of step. Coop would hang around to watch the head majorette, Barb Browning, but I couldn't take my eyes off him.

Not that it did me any good, because Coop and Barb had gone steady since junior high. They were voted "Cutest Couple" their senior year. Everyone assumed they'd get married, but the day after gradua-tion, Coop and Barb broke up.

A week later, he walked up to me after church and said, "Hey, you ready for summer?"

I glanced over my shoulder, thinking he was speaking to someone else. He laughed and breezed on by. I was so discombobulated, I had to go home and put an ice pack on my head. Aunt Bluette kept asking what was wrong. I couldn't tell her the truth, that I'd been infatuated with Cooper O'Malley for years, and when he'd finally acknowledged my existence, I'd acted awful, what Mama used to call Teenified.

Aunt Bluette bought me a tennis racquet at a garage sale and dropped me off at the community center. "But I don't know how to play," I told her.

"Watch," she said. "And learn." Then she drove off and left my ass.

I walked down to the tennis court and sat on a bench. Coop was playing on the first court with a tall, thin girl—not Barb. He cut a strik-ing figure in his white shirt and shorts. After the game, he walked over to my bench.

"What you doing here, Templeton?" he said.

"It's a free country, O'Malley," I said.

"No really." He laughed. "Are you waiting for a court?"

"Aunt Bluette said I needed to get out of the house. She dropped me off."

He glanced at the parking lot. "Where is she?"

"Gone."

"Need a ride home?" He zipped the cover over his racquet.

"The farm's out of your way," I said.

"It'll give us time to talk."

About what? I managed to control my breathing as we walked toward his car. The whole time, he tapped his racquet against mine. Finally he said, "Hey, Templeton, you doing anything next Saturday?"

I shook my head. I never did anything.

"The youth class is having a cookout at Lake Bonaventure," he said. "Would you go?"

I stumbled, and he caught my arm. "Go with the class, you mean," I said.

"Yeah." He shrugged. "With me, too."

Aunt Bluette went to a garage sale and bought me a red polka dot swimsuit, just this side of a bikini, and a matching cover-up. I put the clothes into a paper sack that smelled faintly of peaches. He picked me up in a pastel gray '69 Mustang, an old car that had belonged to his daddy.

During the drive to the lake, Coop tried to draw me into conversation, but my voice was shaky and I gave tight-lipped answers. Besides, a green bug was crawling on his shoulder, and I was distracted. I was afraid to pick it off. What if he thought I was being forward?

When we got to the lake, the whole youth group was there. I headed to the women's restroom to change clothes. I pulled on the suit, then I jumped up and down, trying to glimpse myself in the high mirrors. The suit was skimpy. The bottom fit, but my breasts swelled out the top. I was ready as I'd ever be. I draped my cover-up over my arm and stepped out of the restroom into bright sunlight.

Coop was waiting beside a pine tree, holding a patchwork quilt. He wore a t-shirt and cutoffs. When I walked up, two dimples cut into his cheeks. It was the first time a boy had looked at me that way. I liked it.

Coop sat on the quilt while I picked daisies. Behind us, ski boats sliced across the green water. He wanted to know what I did on the peach farm. I wanted to know about Barb, but I bit down the question and watched a bass boat stir up waves, pushing swimmers into the shallows. The kids whooped and swam back, waiting for the next boat.

Smoke rose from the pavilion. It smelled of lighter fluid and hickory wood. One of the church elders came out and yelled at a girl who'd shown up in a string bikini. I slipped on my cover-up as one of the mothers led the girl to the restroom.

"Come on, Teeny," Coop said. "Tell me about the farm. Y'all grow the sweetest peaches in Georgia. What's your secret?"

It was the first time he'd said my name. A warm flush spread through my chest. I twirled a daisy and told him about pruning and trimming, hot days in the roadside stand, and my quest for the perfect peach turnover.

I held out the daisy. Coop started to tuck it into his pocket, when a strangled cry pierced the air. Way out in the water, a girl was thrashing. Just beyond her, two boats moved into the shallows, their motors drowning her garbled cries.

I sat up and looked toward the chaperones. They were crowded in the pavilion, hidden by a wavy veil of charcoal fumes. I glanced back at the lake. Waves lapped over the girl's head. A white arm came up, her fingers clutching air.

The daisy fell from Coop's hands. He scrambled to his feet and ran to the shore. Just before he dove in, the girl went under. The boats were headed straight toward her. Coop didn't notice. He swam toward the flailing girl. Just before he reached her, she went down. He took a mighty breath and dove.

One boat cut in at an angle and sped toward the place where Coop had been. I ran down the bank and waved my arms, yelling at the boat. The church people ran out of the pavilion and began screaming, too. The boat sped up. Why didn't the driver see or hear a shitload of Baptists waving and hollering?

Coop burst out of the water with the girl. The driver jerked the wheel. The boat veered away, sending up huge green waves. Coop and the girl floated up the edge of the swell, then slid down. He gripped her in a neck lock, keeping her face above the water.

The choir director waded in, but Coop was already kicking to shore. They laid the girl on the bank. Water rushed over her hair, pulling and fanning the damp brown strands over the pebbles.

She sat up and coughed while the choir director pounded her back. She burst into tears, hiccupping every other breath. Several of the church elders hollered out a few hallelujahs, then they went back into the pavilion.

Coop took my hand and led me back to the quilt. We flopped down. Water was beaded in his lashes. "What are you doing tomorrow night?" he asked. "And the night after that?"

We dated that whole summer. He ate supper with us every night, wolfing down second helpings of chicken-fried steak, mashed potatoes, red rice, and peach pie, though he later confessed that his favorite food in the world was egg salad sandwiches made with Duke's Mayonnaise and lettuce, with a grind of pepper.

I wore garage-sale sundresses and dime-store panties that stayed on my body, despite long, intense necking sessions that steamed up the Mustang's windows. Every night, on the oldies station, Elvis sang "That's When Your Heartaches Begin."

I thought mine were ending. Night after night, Coop's hands squeezed my breasts, but never once slipped under my clothing. Then we'd come up for air and he'd draw his fingers across the fogged window. I ♥ Teeny.

Coop's birthday, August ninth, fell on a Sunday. I asked Aunt Bluette if we could fix Coop a special supper. I didn't want to be forward, so I waited for him to call. I didn't expect to wait long, as he'd been calling every night. I baked a chocolate layer cake from scratch and decorated it with yellow icing sunflowers. I couldn't decide if HAPPY BIRTHDAY COOP was proper or too ordinary, so I decided to just write COOP.

Aunt Bluette drove me to Walgreens, and I squatted by the cologne counter. I dithered between Brut Revolution, Hugo Boss, and Drakkar Noir. Finally I settled on Euphoria. I came home, set the gift-wrapped box on the counter, and waited.

Coop didn't call. That Sunday I looked for him everywhere at church. I saw Dr. and Mrs. O'Malley sitting in the fifth row with Mrs. O'Malley's parents. Aaron Fisher sat in front of me and tried to flirt, but

I brushed him off. After the service, Aunt Bluette saw me staring holes at the O'Malleys. She offered to sneakily ask about Coop.

"Lord, no!" I whispered.

"Better to know than to wonder," she said and started toward the O'Malleys.

I grabbed her arm and dragged her to the door. "I'd rather stick pins in my eyes," I said.

The next morning, I was helping Aunt Bluette make squash pickles, when I glanced out the kitchen window. Coop's Mustang drove down our long driveway, stirring up gravel dust. I yanked off my apron and ran to the bathroom, ignoring Aunt Bluette's questions. I brushed my teeth and ran a comb through my hair. It was too late to change—I was wearing one of Mama's old t-shirts that featured Elvis on the front and back.

I heard a knock and ran into the hall. Aunt Bluette beat me to it. She held open the door and smiled at Coop. "Come on in," she said. "Just come on in. Teeny'll be here directly."

The minute I saw the pinched look on his face, I knew this wasn't a social call. Still, I shut my eyes and made a quick bargain with Jesus. If He'd let everything be all right between me and Coop, I wouldn't miss another choir practice.

I led Coop into the parlor and moved a heap of old newspapers. "Have a seat," I said. "Would you like some iced tea?"

"Teeny, we need to talk." He stood by the sofa but didn't sit down. "I don't know how to explain, but I can't see you anymore."

"Why not?" I sat down and tried to catch my breath. I could feel an attack coming on and couldn't remember where I'd put my inhaler.

"Me and Barb got back together." He shrugged. "I'm sorry."

I nodded. Then I started wheezing.

"Teeny, you okay?" Coop asked.

I shook my head. No, I wasn't okay. I'd never be okay. How could I have let myself care so much when he'd cared so little? I stretched out on the sofa, trying not to gasp. Aunt Bluette came running with my inhaler. She stuck it between my lips. "Breathe, Teeny," she said and pushed the button.

I still couldn't get air. She made me take another puff, then she turned back to Coop.

"Would you help me get her to the car?" she said to him.

I ended up spending the night at Bonaventure General Hospital, hooked to oxygen and an IV. While I slept, she made phone calls to get the dirt on Coop and Barb. My aunt's best friend, Miss Wilma, had talked to Dr. O'Malley's nurse, Miss Jane, who reported the lovebirds had been spotted at the Skyline Drive-In, the Dairy Queen, and the balcony at First Methodist, holding hands under the hymn book.

I just knew they were sleeping together. In my girlish mind, I wondered if sex was a binding agent, no different from an egg wash that seals the edges of puff pastry. A word about Barb. She'd tormented me in elementary school, but during my sophomore year, she'd picked me to be her new best friend. Her parents taught at the university in Augusta, and the walls in their house were lined with plaques and diplomas. Their house was smaller than Aunt Bluette's but it was well tended and drop-dead gorgeous, filled with watercolor paintings, French antiques, bone china, and Persian rugs.

"I like warm colors," Lucinda Browning said when she saw me staring at an orange-and-brown afghan.

"I do, too," I said.

"I just made chocolate-dipped strawberries," Lucinda said. "Let me get you one."

She was a true foodie, always in her kitchen making puff pastry from scratch. "The secret is temperature," she told me. "The dough must be chilled and put into a 400-degree oven."

While Barb sat at the kitchen counter and painted her nails, Lucinda showed me how to make Italian granitas in an ice cube tray and how to add bacon bits and chives to corn muffin batter. I could have spent hours looking at her KitchenAid attachments and her full set of Le Creuset bakeware, but Barb wanted to fix me up with guys. When that backfired, she spurned me. Then worms turned up in my home ec cake, and I got an F. A dead crab was also found in my aunt's truck.

Though Barb was a witch, I could see why a guy would pick her over me. She had educated, talented parents. A beautiful home. Gourmet food. But I still thought Coop might show up to the hospital, just to make sure I hadn't gone into a coma or something, but the only O'Malley to darken my door was Coop's father.

Summer ran by like spilled sorghum. I moped on the sticky hot screened porch, taking bronchodilators and reading cookbooks. The radio kept playing "I Do (Cherish You)" by 98 Degrees. Aunt Bluette sat down beside me. "Teeny, you got the pip?"

"No, ma'am." The "pip" was a chicken disease. Once it took hold, it could wipe out a whole poultry farm. If I looked that bad, I wasn't long for this world.

"I'm okay," I said.

"Does this have something to do with Cooper?"

"No, ma'am."

"You're too young to be this heartbroke," she said.

"How do you know what I feel?"

"Everything shows on your face, Teeny. You can't hide nothing. All the Templetons are that way." She was silent. "He didn't get under your skirt, did he?"

"No, ma'am. But I wish he had." I looked up, trying to see if I'd shocked her. Nobody in Bonaventure was more Baptist than my aunt, and no one was kinder. She laid her rough palm against my cheek.

"I just hate seeing you all tore up," she said. "He was your first love, wasn't he?"

I blinked and tears spilled down my cheeks.

"Oh, honey. Don't cry. A lot of folks glorify their first loves. But that's all it is."

No way, I thought. This was hard-core love.

She must have seen something in my face because she began stroking my hair. "Everybody goes through this. Cooper will always be the one you can't forget. But your heart will come back to you. It'll come back when you love again."

The last days of August were hazy, thanks to a rainy spell. A damp, yellow hotness squatted over Georgia. I heard that Coop had gone to college in Chapel Hill, North Carolina, leaving both me and his longtime love.

Right before school started, Aunt Bluette bought me a '88 Olds convertible and paid a man to paint it turquoise. To help pay for gas, I got a carhop job at Sonic. When classes began, my seatmate in biology was Aaron Fisher, the cutest guy in school, the same guy I'd blown off at First Baptist. He passed me a note, *You're totally rad. Go out with me.*

The darlingest guy in school wanted to go out with me? I was totally rad? I was flattered but couldn't respond. My heart felt all crinkly, like a green pepper that's been left too long on the countertop.

Aaron kept passing notes. After six weeks, I wrote back, *OK.* We became the new "it" couple. The popular girls had never talked to me, but now they all wanted to be my best friend. In a polite way, they wanted to know how a girl who wore un-hot clothes could snag the hottest boy. I found their interest disturbing and kept my distance.

I stuck close to my real best friend, Rayette, who lived on a rice farm, and told her I wasn't going to repeat the mistake I'd made with Coop. She called me a fool but gave me a pack of Trojans, just the same.

One night, when Aaron and I went parking at the lake, he put his hand up my dress, and I didn't stop him. I couldn't see into the future, of course. I couldn't know that a year later, Aaron would go to Clemson and die of alcohol poisoning at a frat party, or that once again I'd be moping on Aunt Bluette's porch, listening to sad love songs. The night I gave myself to Aaron, he was the furthest thing from my mind. I opened my arms to a young, gray-eyed man in a gray Mustang while Celine Dion sang "My Heart Will Go On."

Cheesy, I know. It was the right song, wrong man. My heart didn't go a damn place. I put it in a jar, added vinegar and dill, and totally pickled it.

ten

I dreamed that Bing was a giant cockroach, and he mistook the Spencer-Jackson House for a petit four. I awoke at dawn, clawing air, thinking I was trapped on a layer of raspberry jelly.

Then I realized the pinkness was coming from the toile wallpaper. The design showed a girl feeding chickens while a man in a wig sat on a horse watching from afar. The pattern repeated over and over, hundreds of girls, horses, pullets, and wigged gentlemen. I made up stories for them. One man had come to buy eggs and another was a stalker. Another had come home from war and the chicken girl was the daughter he didn't know he had.

What a pity life didn't offer multiple-choice solutions. If it did, I wouldn't have gone to that pub. I would have stayed home and eaten coffee cake, leaving crumbs for the roaches. I wouldn't have kissed Coop O'Malley—not that I hadn't enjoyed it. I had. But lawyers didn't take up with criminals unless they were getting paid by the hour.

Since I couldn't go back to sleep, I prowled around the house. I found an old Electrolux in the hall closet and dragged it down the stairs. Aunt Bluette used to say it was impossible to cry and clean house at the same time. I'm sorry to report she was wrong. I was weepy-eyed when I started vacuuming the dining room. By the time I reached the kitchen, I was bawling.

I cried because I didn't know the law and because I'd thrown dangerous objects. I cried because Bing was a dog-stealing, womanizing asshole. I cried because I'd be homeless in just a few hours and because I was spit polishing a house that wasn't mine. I cried harder because the living room was pink and filled with breakable knickknacks. Then I laughed because I wouldn't have to dust.

I was acting just like Mama. When I was eight, she finally escaped the peach farm by marrying Donnie Phelps, a school bus driver by day, beer guzzler at night. Mama and I went to the dollar store and filled our cart with doodads for Donnie's trailer. It was a triple-wide, beige with white shutters and a front porch. Mama fixed it up right nice, adding wicker from Pier 1 and a straw rug she found at a garage sale. We'd sit up at night and watch the traffic on Savannah Highway. Aunt Bluette lived just beyond the curve, but Mama said we were taking a break from family.

When Donnie wasn't driving innocent children to Musgrove Elementary, he restored antique cars for rich people. He took out a loan to buy a '55 Ford Country Squire wagon. Mama said it was just like the one Jimmy Stewart drove in *Vertigo*. Me and her were major Hitchcock fans. She kind of looked like a brown-eyed Grace Kelly in *Rear Window,* with her thick blond hair and her graceful ways. You'd never know she was country-born, with an eighth-grade education.

Now that we had our own kitchen, Mama started cooking for real, pairing lip-smacking recipes with music and Bible verses, the way she had before.

"Why Bible verses?" Donnie asked her.

"So you can say grace in style," she told him.

Mama was right big on style. She went to the organic farmer's market and paid a fortune for fresh sage leaves.

"Always wash the leaves real good, Teeny," she'd say.

"'Cause they're dirty?" I asked.

"Kinda. But you don't want to accidentally fry a bug."

"Have you ever done that?"

"A time or two," she said. "But I sure hated it."

One night, Mama picked yellow squash from the vine, then brought it into the kitchen to fry. As she was laying the golden crisps onto a plate, she saw a deep-fried baby grasshopper. Her eyes filled. She hadn't meant to kill an innocent little grasshopper—she'd always had a great fondness for living creatures—but there it was, resting on a fried squash round. Before she could remove it, Donnie passed by, stuck out his hand, and gobbled up the insect.

Every Monday she filled his kitchen with homemade bread, the pans all lined up on the counter, the dough pushing up against red tea towels. She saved the stale loaves for me, and I'd crumble them in the yard to feed Donnie's chickens. Then I'd twirl in circles until I collapsed in the grass. Sometimes Mama would stop cooking and twirl with me. We'd clasp our hands and close our eyes and spin through great drifts of smell: bread, zucchini soup, and stew, the sauce fragrant with Chianti. Then we'd fall down together and I'd clap my hands.

"I love you more than beans and rice," I'd say.

"I love you more than anything," she'd say back.

When she got agitated, I tried to pull her into the kitchen and make her cook like Aunt Bluette had done, but my efforts were less successful. She had to be in the mood to bake. Sometimes I'd inadvertently make the situation worse by showing Mama food pictures in cooking catalogs. She'd reach for the phone and order exotic ingredients like saffron, curry, and truffle oil. Donnie got sick of hauling off the empty shipping cartons, which were filled with Styrofoam peanuts. He told her to buy local.

One day he came home and found a three-foot-tall plastic orchid sitting on the coffee table. I cringed, waiting for the explosion. Mama had bought that flower at Mrs. O'Malley's swanky shop for twenty-five dollars, but it was a good buy because it had been marked down from $99.99.

"You bitches been out spending my money?" he cried.

"I got it on sale for practically nothing," Mama said.

Donnie pulled me up by my arm. "How much did it cost, Teeny?"

"A dollar," I said, adding another lie to my tally.

Then one evening, it all fell apart, and it had nothing to do with Mama's buying habits—it was due to Donnie's temper and my clumsiness. Mama and I sat on the porch, sipping milkshakes from the Dairy Queen, watching him clean the engine. "You can eat off this carburetor," he said.

"Like I'd want to." Mama laughed.

Donnie threw down his rag and started toward her. I leaped out of the way, but he grabbed my arm. "Don't you shy away from me, you little bastard." I pulled back and my paper cup went flying. The milkshake hit the engine and exploded.

He blacked Mama's eyes and stomped her in the kidneys. I crouched behind the car, trying not to have an asthma attack. This was my fault, every bit of it. After the flying fur settled, he told her to get inside and fix him something cool to drink. I found her in the bathroom, washing blood off her face. Then she raked through the medicine cabinet and grabbed a plastic bottle.

"What you fixing to do, Mama?" I asked.

"Teach him a lesson. Come on, help me pinch open these capsules." She lifted me onto the counter. I watched her put the medicine in a tall glass. She added a little sugar and salt, then opened an ice cold Budweiser. Donnie stepped into the kitchen and she handed him the glass.

"That's more like it," he said and took a swig. Mama walked to the bedroom and started filing her nails. Her right eye was almost swollen shut. Donnie stumbled into the room and flopped spread-eagle onto the bed.

"Man, I'm dizzy," he said.

"Take you a little rest," Mama said.

He shut his eyes and got real still. Then he began to snore. Mama ripped off the edges of the bottom sheet. "Teeny?" she whispered, "Fetch me the stapler, duct tape, and a Coke."

When I returned, she'd already folded the bottom sheet around Donnie. She grabbed the stapler and went to work. I squatted beside the bed, twitching each time the gun snapped. She fastened the edges of the sheet until Donnie resembled a mummy. He didn't wake up until she wrapped tape around his ankles. "Ruby?" he croaked.

She ignored him and kept wrapping him in tape. Once she started a project, she didn't like to stop. Donnie's arms twitched, but they were fastened tight. He watched her with a puzzled expression and tried to raise up. She pushed him down. Then she reached for the Coke bottle and took a dainty sip.

"What you looking at?" she asked him.

"Goddamn you, Ruby. Undo me. If you don't, I'll kill you."

While he talked, she poured the cola into his mouth. It spilled down his face, onto the mattress. A gargling sound rose up. He spit, and Coke spewed into Mama's face. She turned the bottle upside down and shook out the last few drops. Then she grasped the bottle by its neck and beat the hell out of him. He screamed, his hips bucking up and down.

"Hurts, don't it?" Mama cracked the bottle on his nose. "Teach you to hit me again."

He screeched. I felt bad for him, but he had it coming. I opened my mouth, trying to move air in and out of my lungs. Each breath sounded like an iron door with a rusty hinge.

"Teeny, we don't have time for an asthma attack," she said. "Pack your things."

My medicines were lined up in the kitchen window. I put them in a sack with a few clothes. We ran out to his station wagon. The engine backfired, then it caught. Mama turned onto the highway. I tried not to wheeze. Catching my breath was like climbing a mountain and getting slapped down by the wind. Every now and then, I'd reach the top, only to see another hill.

I hollered when she sped by Aunt Bluette's farm. "Teeny, we can't live in this town anymore." She sucked the back of her hand. "Donnie'll hunt me down. He'll kill me and you both. I'm sorry, baby, but you're only eight years old. I can't let you die. And we can't go home."

I wiped my eyes. Home wasn't Donnie's triple-wide. It was my pink bedroom at the farm. It was Aunt Bluette's hand on my cheek. Home was the place where all my scattered pieces came to rest.

Mama pushed her foot against the accelerator, and we flew into the night, farther and farther from Donnie and Aunt Bluette.

Miss Dora and her man servant, Estaurado, showed up before lunch. He resembled a Spanish version of the Blues Brothers—sunglasses, hat, and a black polyester suit. He was tall and emaciated, with a pointy beard, and cast a spiky shadow along the floor.

Miss Dora bustled around in a pink bouclé suit, her pocketbook swinging back and forth. Her hands and face were a violent shade of red. "Have you been in the sun?" I asked.

"I'm a sight!" Her hand flew to her face. "You would not *believe* what I've been through. I stopped for lunch at Chez Cassie. I'm highly allergic to sucralose. That's what makes things like Splenda so sweet. I don't know how it got into my dessert—or maybe it was that latte I drank—but it did."

"Can people be allergic to that?" I asked.

"Apparently so. The first time it happened, I thought I had a rash. And it didn't hit me right away, so I never associated it with sucralose. After that, whenever I ate something with artificial sweetening, my symptoms got worse and worse. This time, I turned blood red and started itching. Even my ears swelled."

"You poor thing." I studied her face. Her ears did look big.

"Not everybody with sucralose allergies does this." She reached into her purse, pulled out a gold compact, and studied her face. "The emergency room doctor blamed it on my quirky body chemistry. Well, I *am* allergic to just about everything. He pumped me full of steroids and told me to avoid artificial sweeteners like the plague."

"I wish I'd known," I said. "I could have made your supper."

"You're too sweet." She snapped the compact shut, her bracelets clattering. "Estaurado, run and get Teeny's clothes."

He twisted his head, as if trying to understand.

She repeated her command with exaggerated slowness and Estaurado stepped into the corridor. "I have to be so careful with him, Teeny. He misunderstands every word I say. Just yesterday, he told me he was getting sick and threw out a foreign word, *constipación*. Well, I dosed him up with Ex-Lax. Little did I know *constipación* was the common cold."

"Get a Spanish dictionary," I said.

"Oh, I've got several. The man is just too literal—though I'm sure he'd say it's the other way around." She rolled her eyes. "Never mind him. I got into a huge fight with Bing Laden. But I got your clothes."

Estaurado returned with four bulging Hefty bags. "*Su ropa, senorita.*"

"See what I mean?" Miss Dora rolled her eyes. "Now he's mixing up ropes and clothing. Darlin', I'm sure your pretty outfits are wrinkled to high heaven. When I got to Bing's, everything you owned was laying in his front yard."

While she talked, she bustled around the entry hall, straightening pictures and rearranging knickknacks. "This place needs fluffing in the worst way," she said. "It's not formal enough."

I glanced around. If it had been mine, I'd have packed up the silver and the porcelain figurines and popped a fig cake into the oven. This house took itself too seriously. It needed the opposite of formal.

Miss Dora pushed a fat white envelope into my hand and said, "Don't spend wisely—squander it."

I pushed it back, but she grabbed my hand. "Keep it, darlin'. Only god knows what you've had to tolerate the last few months, engaged to that pussymonger. Speaking of men, I was supposed to meet a client twenty minutes ago."

Estaurado shuffled toward me and held out a box. "For you, senorita," he said.

He waved one hand, indicating that I should open the box. I pulled off the lid and saw six tiny figurines laying on a cotton strip.

"What are they?"

"Worry dolls, senorita."

"Why, thank you," I said, touched by the gesture.

His face dissolved into wrinkles as he smiled, and crooked front teeth pressed against his bottom lip.

Miss Dora peeked over my shoulder. "You're supposed to tell them your problems and stick them under your pillow. Speaking of troubles, I'll be in a fine mess if I don't leave this second. Tell you what, I'll try to stop by later. Maybe I'll treat you to an early supper."

"I'd enjoy that."

"See you then." She lifted one hand and wiggled her fingers. "Come, Estaurado."

Miss Dora blew me a kiss and breezed out the door, into the corridor, with Estaurado bobbing in her wake.

I squatted beside the trash bags. Inside the first one, I found a shoe box with a silvery key. It was my spare to Bing's house. I started to throw it away, then I remembered Bing's upcoming trip to Pinehurst. He went every summer to play golf. I'd planned to go too, and I'd lined up a dog sitter to feed and walk Sir twice a day. Maybe I could sneak over to Bing's house and visit my dog. I could also get *Templeton Family Receipts*.

I fit the key onto Miss Dora's chain and dropped the pink tassel into the bowl. Then I pushed the Hefty bags next to the staircase. No need to unpack. I was leaving in the morning, what with Bing's deadline. I hadn't found an apartment, so I'd have to stay at a cheap motel until I found a job.

As I started out of the foyer, my heel snagged on one of the bags, and a black sheath dress spilled out. Bing had bought it specially for our engagement party. It had a high neckline, fit for Sunday school or a funeral.

"Shouldn't I wear a peppy color?" I'd asked him.

"Black is the new white," he'd said. "And don't let Dora say otherwise. That woman looks like a Mary Kay cosmetics trophy. The bitch suffers from pinkitis."

It was true. Miss Dora's house was raspberry stucco, but the interior was pink as a cat's mouth. The night of the party, Bing took me on a tour, pointing out paint colors. "This room is Baboon's Ass Pink," he said, waving at the guest room. He guided me down the hall, pointing at other rooms. "Vaginal Blush," he said. "Nipple Nougat."

We made love in the pinkest bedroom. Then we crept down the stairs, into the real world of Charleston and Miss Dora's friends. Bing introduced me as Christine and said I was a gourmet cook. People were just as sweet as could be, asking about my china and silver patterns, which, thanks to Miss Dora, I'd picked out at Belk.

I couldn't have said why, but after the party, everything changed between me and Bing. We were just too different. I was bashful; he was outgoing. I would take food to a funeral and not tape my name to the bottom of the bowl. Bing craved recognition. Every time I drove by a billboard with his picture on it, or saw a Jackson Realty ad on television, I'd have to get a sugar fix.

A few days after the party, I was watching the local news and one of Bing's ads came on. I grabbed my purse and headed to the door. "I'm going to Piggly Wiggly to buy me some Easter Peeps," I told him. "You want anything?"

"God, what are you, the Swamp Queen?" Bing said. "It's not '*buy me some Easter Peeps.*' Just say, I'm going to 'buy Easter Peeps.' You don't need 'me.'"

Now, barely two months later, the engagement was off. I pushed the black dress into the bag and walked to the kitchen. As I crammed chocolate cherries into my mouth, I tried not to think about Bing or his leggy girlfriends, but I couldn't help it.

I imagined shooting the women with a paint gun. No, that wasn't mean enough. I wouldn't feel satisfied until I'd force-fed them Good Riddance Blueberry Pie. It calls for sugar, Scotch whiskey, and 1½ cups of heavy whipping cream. Add 2½ cups of berries, along with 3 tablespoons of melted blueberry jelly and a dollop of Havoc—a blue, granular rat poison with a rodent-alluring flavor. The berries will mix right in with the fatal aqua-blueness of the pellets. Sprinkle more Havoc into the buttery homemade pie dough, adding a handful of chopped hazelnuts and dried berries. Flatten with a rolling pin, pressing it over the dough this way and that. Make a wish. Pray for an unwrinkled love life. Or maybe that's the problem, maybe I'd stretched it too thin. But never mind all that. A pie like this calls for two crusts, top and bottom, symbolic of the missionary position—which, like pie, is easy to overindulge in.

In real life, I would never make this pie. But I imagined how tart and sweet it would taste, and how it would ooze over the bone china plate. *Come on, girls,* I'd say, *one bite won't kill you.* I'd sit back, watch them eat. Each forkful would deliver sweet explosions of flavor, texture, and death. I could see all the way to their funerals. They'd be laid out in mahogany coffins with leopard-spotted linings. Their dead selves would be dressed in formfitting black Dolce & Gabbana suits, also with a silk leopard lining. Instead of clutching little Bibles, they would hold Neiman Marcus shopping bags and iPhones.

I would never kill a rat. What had a rat ever done to me? I'd use those live traps and call it a day. So I sure as hell wouldn't poison those women. It's flat impossible to poison skanks who never eat carbohydrates.

eleven

Late that afternoon, I walked through the house, admiring how the arched windows reflected on the heart pine floors. I passed through the dining room, and my feet hit a wet spot. I skidded sideways into a mahogany lowboy. A candlestick knocked over and rolled into a puddle of water. I looked up. A stream of water trickled through the chandelier. It hit the long table and streamed over the edge, pattering to the floor.

I ran upstairs to see if I'd left a faucet running. I hadn't. When I opened the closet above the dining room, I saw the problem. The air conditioning unit had frozen and the tray had overflowed, leaking water through the dining room ceiling. I put a punch bowl on the table to catch the drips.

Before I could call a repairman, Miss Dora arrived with a bottle of predinner wine. When she saw the leak, she opened her cell phone and said, "I'll take care of this."

Twenty minutes later, her HVAC men showed up. While they tramped up the stairs to investigate the leak, I opened the wine and we stepped into the garden. A breeze stirred the confederate roses, and golden light fell in long stripes across the lawn. In the back, the garden was hemmed in by an old brick wall, and in the center of it was a gate that seemingly led nowhere, except to other people's backyards. Miss Dora said the gate was original to the house, and it had once led to a kitchen. In modern times, it had allowed Uncle Elmer to trim weeds on the other side of the wall.

"How many more hours until the deadline?" Miss Dora asked.

"Seventeen," I said. "I don't guess he'll change his mind."

"No, he's pretty steamed," she said. "You *did* beat him up pretty bad."

"Seriously?"

"He had a black eye and a huge punk knot on his forehead, maybe the size of a jumbo egg." She lifted her glass. "I *never* knew a peach could do all that. It's a versatile fruit."

"I'll say."

"I remember when Bing told me he'd met you. It sounded like he'd said, 'I met a possum,' but he'd really said, 'I've met an awesome woman.'" She waved her hand, shooing a fly. "Honey, did you have a clue he was seeing two women?"

"Not at all. I knew something was wrong. I never guessed what."

"Because he's good at cheating. I watched his slow work on his first wife."

"Bing won't talk about her. What happened?"

"Gwendolyn was a stockbroker. Worked all the time. They were married three years. She didn't catch him cheating until the end, so don't you feel bad. You can't outsmart a professional liar." She waved at a fly. "The Jackson men need to be cheating on somebody or it just isn't fun."

I hadn't thought of it in those bald terms, but it made sense. He'd needed me for homemade cakes and Sunday pot roast, not entertainment.

Miss Dora clapped her hands, then opened them, revealing a dead fly. "Little bastard," she muttered.

The repairman stuck his head out the back door. "The unit's fixed," he said. "Call if you have any problems. And I'm real sorry about the parking situation."

"What situation?" Miss Dora asked.

"Your housekeeper yelled at me for parking out front," he said. "But I won't do it again."

"What housekeeper?" Miss Dora cried.

"I probably got it wrong." The repairman shrugged. "Maybe it was a neighbor?"

"What did she look like?" I asked.

"Just a lady in sunglasses and a hat." He scratched the side of his jaw. "Anyway, your unit is fixed. But you got a lot of damage to the dining room ceiling. If you need a good drywall man, just let me know."

"Absolutely," Miss Dora said. "And thanks for coming on such short notice."

After he left, she poured another glass of wine. "Wonder who yelled at him? Have you seen any neighbors who fit that description?"

"No, ma'am." I hadn't seen any neighbors, period.

"Well, let's don't worry about it," she said. "Let's think about where we want to eat tonight. Carolina's is just up the street. Or we could go to Magnolia's."

"Whatever you want is fine by me."

"You're such an agreeable girl. How could Bing treat you this way?" She took a sip of wine. "It's a wonder how two sweet things like ourselves got taken in by conniving men."

"Bing can be charming," I said, but that wasn't the half of it. He was handsome and suave, from a fine Charleston family. When he'd showed interest in me, I'd felt like it was Aunt Bluette's guiding hand. But it was just Bing acting Bingy.

"Plus, he's shallow," Miss Dora said. "He probably loved you for a minute or two until infatuation wore off. And when it faded, he was stuck with a pint-size ball of fire."

"Is that how you see me?" I laughed.

"Well, let's just say you have the makings of a fireball." She tilted her head. "If Bing asked you to come back, would you?"

I pursed my lips. He and I were wrong for each other—that much was clear—but that didn't mean we couldn't become friends. Eventually.

"Well?" Miss Dora's eyebrow went up. "Surely you don't still love him?"

"No, ma'am. I'm not carrying a torch or anything. But when I care for a person, it just won't quit. It might be watered down, but it's there." I folded my arms and looked up at the sky. "Just like a part of me still loves Aaron."

"Who?"

"My boyfriend who died—the one from my hometown. He drank too much alcohol at a fraternity party and stopped breathing."

"I had no idea." Miss Dora reached across the table and patted my arm. "You need a vacation from troubles. I'm leaving for Savannah in the morning to look at an antique bed. Come with me. We'll have fun."

I didn't want to hurt her feelings, but I couldn't stand looking at old furniture. Once I'd gone with Miss Dora to a mall where she'd taken hours to examine an eighteenth-century plantation desk. She'd pulled out every drawer, searching for chips and cracks.

"I'm not supposed to leave the state," I said.

"That's right. I keep forgetting." She stood and weaved to the side. "Well, you can at least eat well while you're on probation. Speaking of which, I had my heart set on crab cakes. Are you ready to eat supper?"

"I'll drive." I led her into the house and reached into the crystal bowl for the tasseled key chain. It was empty. I picked up the bowl. Nothing. I bent down and looked under the table.

"What the poop is wrong?" Miss Dora asked.

"The house keys are missing."

"I'm sure they're around here somewhere, darlin'. Have you checked the kitchen?"

"But I remember putting them right here."

"Keys just don't walk off." She walked to the table, opened a drawer, and peeked inside. "Nope, not in here. But they'll turn up. Unless you think the HVAC men took them?"

"They wouldn't do that," I said.

"Well, they're good boys, but even the good ones have drug habits."

"Should I call a locksmith?"

"Teeny baby, you aren't thinking. This time tomorrow, you won't be in this house."

"But I can't lock up tonight." I waved at the doors—each one had a double cylinder lock.

She opened her pocketbook, dragged her hand through tile samples, and pulled up a brass key. "Here's my spare. Guard it with your life. If you lose it, I'll have to get a copy from Bing, and I don't want to do that."

We abandoned our supper plans, and she left. I searched the house for my old key but couldn't find it. I locked the doors with Miss Dora's spare, then I set the burglar alarm, grabbed an Oreo Cakester from the kitchen, and ran upstairs to the toile bedroom. Just to be safe, I dragged a dresser in front of the door. I couldn't imagine anything worse than living in a froufrou place that other people wanted to rob—unless it was living in a car or refrigerator box.

I scarfed down the cakester. If the repairman had stolen the keys, maybe he didn't want antiques. Maybe he was a perv. I dove under the covers. I just had to get through the night. Tomorrow I had to find a cheap rooming house and a job.

I lay there a long time, trying to sleep, but all I could think about was true love. I wasn't going to find it. How many chances did a person get? I'd spent my youth pining for Coop. I hated that Barb had gotten him. I'd never slept with Coop—a major missed opportunity. Aaron and I hadn't made love in a bed, just in the back of his daddy's Eldorado, but he'd been less a lover and more of a friend. In recent years, I'd had a few dates but let's be really real—I compared every man I met to Coop O'Malley. That was plain silly, like longing for lottery money I'd never won.

Even if my own true love had shown up at the peach farm, I wouldn't have known it. The business of running an orchard kept me too busy to notice much of anything. Well, that's not exactly true; I noticed a lot. When the peach blossoms opened, the air turned pink and hummed with bees. I worked in our roadside stand, a weathered building with a rusty tin roof, and weighed fruit for strangers. During the hot noon hours, I'd close the stand and ride shotgun in Aunt Bluette's truck, checking the trees. Every season brought dangers: drought, ice, hurricanes, lightning, briars, fungus, birds. A cold snap could send us to the poorhouse. Winter was particularly hard. When the temperature dipped below freezing, Aunt Bluette and I set out smudge pots, and we sprayed the trees with water, hoping the ice would sheath the blossoms. In the summer, we watched the weather report, hoping for rain, but not too much.

My friend Rayette used to beg me to put on a dress and go nightclubbing in Savannah. But I was happy to stay with Aunt Bluette and watch Food Network. I checked out food DVDs at Hollywood Video, and we watched Nigella Lawson. My aunt and I loved Nigella's unapologetic attitude toward her curves. Aunt Bluette also loved *Iron Chef* and Emeril Lagasse. Each time Emeril said "Bam!" my aunt would make a fist and punch the air.

I was happy we'd had those nights together. I pictured our long gravel drive, the peach trees spread on both sides. Our house had a long front porch with wooden gliders at each end. Inside, our wooden floors were crooked, and if you dropped a marble, it would roll for hours.

My favorite room was the kitchen. A long walnut table with spindly legs sat in the middle of the room. At one end, Aunt Bluette would roll out pie crust, and at the other I would spread out my homework. Our stove had to be lit with a match and gave off the stink of propane. That house was more than a house. It was family, a place where my mother's smell lingered in crevices and empty drawers.

But it was in Bonaventure and I was here. Soon I'd have to find shelter—a cheap apartment or a furnished room. I could do without cable TV; but I'd have to pay utilities and car insurance, and more important, taxes on the farm. If I couldn't find a job, I'd have no choice but to sell the Templeton homestead.

If Aunt Bluette were still here, she'd say, "Teeny, do what you have to, baby. And don't beat yourself up." But when it came to forgiving myself, I always resisted. I wanted to wallow in postmortems and if-onlys. Oh, how lovely it would be if self-forgiveness was one of man's basic needs, something we did automatically. Like breathing.

twelve

The next morning a honking car woke me up. I threw back the covers and walked to the window. A horse-drawn carriage moved down East Bay Street. The view was so beguiling, I decided to have coffee up there. Then I remembered Bing's deadline.

First, I packed my car. Then I looked up Alvin Bell's number in the phone book. His answering service picked up, and I left a message. I didn't have a single regret as I locked up the Spencer-Jackson House and walked around the corner to Adgers. My cell phone gave two short trills. I dug it out of my lemon purse and blinked at the text message.

I STILL LOVE U
COME HOME NOW

It was from Bing. But it wasn't like him to abbreviate "you," even with texting. I called right back and got his voice mail.

"It's me," I said. "What does your message mean? Call me back."

Next, I called the house. No answer. I thought about texting him but was afraid I'd spell something wrong. I looked down at my outfit. If only I'd worn something ladylike, not baggy cutoff jeans and a Wide-spread Panic t-shirt.

I turned the car around and drove up East Bay. Did he really want me back or was this another trick? I hated to waste the gas on a wild-goose chase, so before I got to the bridge, I called his office. His secretary said she hadn't heard from Bing.

I called his house as I turned toward the Ravenel Bridge. I hoped the judge wouldn't find out, because I wasn't turning back. I didn't want to reconcile; I needed to apologize to Bing for hitting him. And I wanted to work out an arrangement to visit Sir.

I passed under the green signs for Isle of Palms and Coleman Blvd/Sullivan's Island and veered right, toward Mount Pleasant. I dialed Bing's house again. Now I was starting to worry. Was he playing with me? While I didn't think he had a bottle of Moët chilling in the fridge, he was up to something. I felt like Bette Davis in *Of Human Bondage*, when she kept wiping off her lover's kisses. Despite everything, I liked Bing tremendously, but all the champagne and gin joints in the world couldn't make me take him back. Seeing Coop O'Malley had reminded me what true love felt like.

Gulls flew over Shem Creek as I drove down Coleman Boulevard. I kept dialing Bing's house until I turned left onto Rifle Range Road. When I drove into the subdivision, I saw the green stucco house peeking between the trees. I half expected to see the white convertible, but the driveway was empty except for Bing's Mercedes, which sat in its usual spot beside the garage.

I grabbed my lemon purse and walked toward the house. The breeze smelled faintly of the ocean. I took a breath and pressed the doorbell. We had one of those bells that could play any song in the world, and since we'd gotten engaged, we'd set it to play the marriage song. It soothed me to hear the familiar ding-dongs.

He didn't open the door, so I pushed the bell again. I heard a skittering sound as Sir ran into the foyer. He shot out the doggie door. I dropped to my knees; he trotted into my outstretched arms and knocked me sideways. He licked my face and hair. I scratched his ears, and his lips drew back.

"Where's Bing?" I asked.

Sir barked and squirmed away from my grasp. I stood up. My shorts and knees were splotched with red paw prints. I rubbed one of the prints, and it smeared.

"You're hurt!" I grabbed Sir and checked his feet. He looked up at me and snorted. He didn't seem to be cut anywhere, so I stood up and rang the bell again.

"Bing?" I rapped hard on the door. "Bing, open up!"

I walked around the side of the house and stepped onto the patio. A silver key stuck out of the lock and the door stood ajar. Typical Bing. Organized, yet messy. Always in a hurry. He had a habit of leaving his key in the door, which just invited burglars. I pulled out the key and stepped into the den, a true man cave, with knotty-pine walls, bookcases, leather recliner, and flat-screen television.

"Bing? It's me," I called. When he didn't answer, I wondered if I'd been wrong about the blood. Maybe Sir had gotten into the trash and had tracked spaghetti sauce through the house.

"It's okay, baby," I told Sir as he jumped around my knees, his jowls swinging back and forth. He wanted me to pick him up, which required both of my hands. I dropped Bing's key in my lemon purse and lifted Sir into my arms. I followed paw prints into the kitchen. It was tidier than I'd left it but smelled odd, like fireworks.

When I got near the door to the breakfast room, Sir began to squirm. I set him on the floor and looked around. The tile counter was bare and glossy except for a bowl of green apples. Bing wasn't one to decorate with fruit. Either Natalie or the redhead had been playing house.

I walked toward the breakfast room. Bing's chair was pulled back at an angle. Then I saw him. He was sprawled on the floor, facedown. A dark puddle spread from his chest and met a smaller puddle near his head. I ran to him and pressed two fingers against his neck. It was warm and still. No pulse. And he wasn't breathing.

I withdrew my hand. My fingers were tipped with red. One word rang out in my mind: murder. I had to call the police. I reached inside my purse for my cell phone when someone grabbed me from behind. Before I could look over my shoulder, pain shot through my neck. My head wouldn't move. A current ran through my body, over and over, until all my muscles went rigid. I was falling, falling into a black hole. My last coherent thought was, *Teen, you been tased.*

thirteen

I was dimly aware of a sniffing sound. The wet petal softness of a tongue hit my face. I cracked open one eye and saw a spotted muzzle.

"Sir?" I croaked. "That you?"

He answered with a snort. I lay there too dizzy to move. If Sir was here, then where was I? The dog licked and licked. His tongue slid over my eyes and curled into my nostril. When I tried to push him away, my hand felt limp and boneless. After a minute, I was able to move my head. I saw Bing. He was dead—violently dead.

My arms tingled and I couldn't think straight. I waited until I could control my muscles enough to sit up. I patted my neck, searching for a bump or wound, but I didn't feel a thing. I clearly remembered feeling a burst of pain, then my whole body going into a knot. What would do that? Had I slipped in blood or had someone hit me from behind? A taser wouldn't knock me out. At least it didn't knock out people on *Law & Order.*

If I had been attacked from behind, whoever did it might still be in the house. My cell phone was lying on top of my purse. I punched in 9-1-1. When the operator answered, I said, "I'd like to report a dead body. Someone hurt my . . . my . . ."

I paused. How to word this? My ex-fiancé? Friend? Maybe I shouldn't be specific.

"He's bleeding," I said. "I think . . . I think he's dead. Please, send help."

"Slow down, ma'am," the operator said, but the smell of copper pennies rushed up my nose and I couldn't breathe. I gave the address and clicked off. I was having trouble remembering what had happened before I'd found Bing's body. Everything was in pieces. The text message. Sir's bloody paw prints. Green apples. And a dead Bing.

I heard a car screech up the driveway. I walked into the hall and unlocked the front door. A big-shouldered, dark-haired officer looked past me into the foyer. "Did you report a murder?" he asked.

Murder? Had I said that? Behind him, the blue lights on top of his car swirled over the trees. "Ma'am?" asked the officer, blinking at my bloody clothes. "Are you hurt anywhere?"

"No."

"You've got blood all over you."

"It's from my dog. He shot out the doggie door." I pointed, and Sir barked. I motioned for the policeman to follow. When I reached the kitchen, I gestured at the breakfast room. "He's in there," I said and pressed a trembly finger to my lips. "I'm pretty sure he's dead."

The officer stepped through the arched doors and froze. His head angled toward his shoulder microphone and he called for backup. Then he blinked. "Ma'am, have you moved anything or touched the victim?"

"I . . . I took his pulse."

He hunkered down and pushed his finger into Bing's neck. I couldn't get my breath. I rubbed my hand over my throat. I needed my inhaler. But it was in my purse, and I didn't want to walk through the blood to get it. My spit tasted like I'd been sucking pennies, and I thought I might be sick.

The officer stood and turned. "What's your name, miss?"

"Teeny Templeton."

"Do you know the victim?"

"He was my fiancé," I said with emphasis on *was*.

He looked at my bare fingers. "And you came home and found him?"

"Yes," I said, then thought of my annual lie tally. Had I just told number thirteen? Technically, yes. This *had* been my home until recently. Misleading a policeman would definitely qualify as a commandment breaker. I shut my eyes and did a quick recount of every lie I'd told so far.

Number one, Aunt Bluette—New Year's Day.
Numbers two through twelve, Bing—January through June.

I stared up at the chandelier, into the tear-shaped prisms. What should I do? I could look the cop in the eye and say, Actually, this isn't my home. But if I told the truth he might get the wrong idea about me. Better to raise the lie count than get slapped into the pokey, right?

In the distance I heard sirens. A man in a dark green suit came into the house and talked to the responding officer. Uniformed policemen streamed around them, followed by men in overalls. I heard the responding officer say my name. The guy in the suit turned. His eyes were the color of his suit, hazel, and protruded from deep sockets. His hair was curly and windblown, jutting up like a Chia Pet. He walked over and introduced himself as Detective Purvis.

"Did you witness the homicide?" he asked.

I shook my head. Bile spurted into my throat, and I bolted to the powder room. Sir scratched at the door while I was sick. I turned back to the sink, switched on the faucet, and ran my hands under the cold water. The door flung open. Detective Purvis reached past me and turned off the tap.

"Ma'am, don't wash your hands," he said.

But it was too late; I already had.

He grabbed my elbows, steered me into the dining room, and pulled out a chair. Sir trotted under the table and growled. I sat down and put my hand on my chest. In the background I heard the officers say that Bing had been shot. I imagined him lying on the floor, and I drew in a wheezy breath.

The detective's eyes narrowed. "What's the matter with you?" he asked.

"I've got asthma," I said. "I hate to bother you, but I need my inhaler. It's in my purse and my purse is in there." I pointed toward the breakfast room.

He left the room and I dropped my head into my hands, forcing myself to take measured breaths. Purvis returned with my handbag. I grabbed my Ventolin inhaler, shook it, and took a puff.

Detective Purvis sat down. "Miss Templeton, tell me again what happened."

"I knocked and rang the bell. Bing wouldn't come to the door."

"Where were you prior to coming home?"

"Charleston."

"Where exactly?" Purvis asked.

"Rainbow Row."

"Why were you there?"

I almost said "visiting" but that would have definitely been a lie. "I've spent the past few nights at a house on Rainbow Row," I told him.

"Which house?"

"The Spencer-Jackson."

"Why were you there if you live here?" Purvis glanced up at the brass chandelier.

"See, Bing and I broke up."

"When?"

"Couple of days ago."

"Why?"

I paused. Surely to goodness they didn't think I had something to do with this. Better to tell the truth and lay it on thick. "I caught him playing badminton with two women," I said. "They were naked."

A muscle twitched in Purvis's jaw. "Okay, Miss Templeton. What time did you leave East Bay?"

"9:00 a.m."

"Can anyone corroborate that?"

"No, sir. I don't think so."

"How did you enter the house?" he asked.

"The back door was open." And it had been—this wasn't a lie. I started to mention the key I'd put in my purse, but he cut me off.

"If you and the victim were broke up, why were you here?" he asked.

"He texted me. So I came over. And found him. Somebody hit me from behind. Maybe they tased me. When I was able to move, I called 911."

"Tased?" He gave me the once over. "Where?"

I showed him my neck. He leaned forward. "Can you show me your cell phone?"

I reached into my purse, grabbed my phone, and scrolled through the menu. The text was gone. "That's impossible," I said. "It was here. I texted him back. And I called, too."

"What did his text say?" the detective asked.

"I love you. Come home now." I took a breath. "I didn't erase it."

"We'll check his phone records. Yours, too." He pointed to my shorts. "How'd you get blood stains?"

"I already told you—the dog jumped on me."

One of the men in overalls came into the dining room. He wore plastic gloves. The detective pointed at my phone. "Would you give that to Mr. Lawson, please?"

Mr. Lawson slid my phone into a paper bag. The detective rose. "Miss Templeton, come with me."

He led me to the kitchen. Men in overalls were putting bags over Bing's hands. A cop with a video camera moved through the kitchen into the breakfast room. A technician put plastic baggies over my hands and slipped rubber bands over my wrists, holding the bags in place.

"What's this for?" I asked.

"Cross-contamination," Purvis said.

"Of what?" I asked.

He ignored me. "You need to come to the station, Miss Templeton."

"Why?"

"There's a lot going on here." He gestured to the men. "You might contaminate the crime scene."

"I just need to get my dog," I said, looking around for Sir. I clapped my hands, and the bags made a muffled whomp. When my dog didn't come, I walked toward the hall. Purvis put his hand on my elbow.

"The dog has to be examined," he said.

"Examined for what?"

He shifted his eyes but kept holding my arm. "You can fetch him later."

"From where?"

"The pound."

"No!" My eyes filled with tears as a bearded officer walked by holding my dog. I turned back to the detective. "Can you take his squeak toy?"

"He'll be fine," Purvis said.

He led me to a white car and put me in the back. I blinked at the metal grid that divided the front and back seats. Before he shut the door, I said, "Wait, are you arresting me?"

"No, ma'am. I just have some questions."

"May I make a phone call?"

"Sure." His jaw tightened. "At the station."

fourteen

The Mount Pleasant Police Department was tiny compared to the large facility in North Charleston. A white-haired volunteer was fingerprinting a woman with frizzy red hair. A man in a Hawaiian shirt had his feet propped on a table. He was watching *Days of Our Lives* on a small television.

An official-looking man waited by the water fountain. His name tag identified him as Louis Qualls, a crime scene technician for the Charleston Police Department.

"She washed her hands," Purvis said, removing the bags from my hands.

"I'll need her clothes," the technician said, then leaned over to swab my hands.

"What's this for?" I asked.

"GPR," the technician said. "Gunpowder residue."

"You won't find any," I said.

The technician ignored me and opened a compartment in his field kit.

A female volunteer took me to the restroom and waited outside the stall while I undressed. I handed my clothes over the door. There was a rustling sound, and a striped jumpsuit fell into my stall.

I got dressed and followed the volunteer out of the restroom. Purvis and the technician were waiting in the hall.

"People think it's easy to get rid of GPR," Purvis said, looking at my hair. "It saturates everything."

I wanted to say it couldn't saturate an innocent person, but I was too scared. They'd find out soon enough that I hadn't fired a gun. I followed Purvis to an ice-cold room with dark paneled walls. Off to one side was a metal table and plastic chairs. A Coke machine stood on the far wall, next to a coffee urn and metal racks filled with chips and candy bars. It looked more like a bus station café than an interrogation room.

I sat down and watched a bald, sunburned man set up a video camera. He introduced himself as Bill Noonan. He and Purvis took turns asking questions. Simple things, like my name, age, address. Then they started rehashing the murder.

"Did you find the body?" asked Noonan.

I sighed. They'd asked this five times already, but I said, "Yeah."

"And you called 911?" asked Purvis.

"Yes, sir. But before I did that, somebody knocked me out."

The men exchanged glances. Detective Purvis did an eye roll.

"Did you get a description?" asked Noonan.

"No. It happened too fast."

"Are you sure someone hit you?" asked Noonan.

"What else could have happened?"

Purvis rested his elbow on the table and drummed his fingers. "You tell me."

"Wait, you don't think *I* hurt Bing?" I cried.

"Could you have hurt him and forgotten?" Noonan asked.

"No!" I made a face.

"We're just trying to determine the facts is all," Purvis said. "Tell me about the altercation between you and Mr. Jackson."

He had asked this before, too, but for some reason my answers weren't pleasing. Now, with the camera rolling, if I explained about Bing and the women, the detectives might learn about my prior arrest and the restraining order—if they didn't already know. And I didn't want to talk until my head cleared. Bits and pieces of the morning were fading in and out.

"Why did you wash your hands, Miss Templeton?" asked Purvis.

"I don't remember." It was the truth. I crossed my arms. "It's too cold in here. I can't think straight with all this cold."

"Do you own a gun, Miss Templeton?" asked Purvis.

"No."

"Do you know anyone who'd want to shoot Mr. Jackson?"

"Is that what happened? Was he shot?"

"Why don't you tell me?" Purvis rolled a pencil on the table.

" 'Cause there's nothing to tell." I burst into tears. A while later, they brought me a phone. I couldn't for the life of me remember Alvin Bell's number, so I dialed SUE-THEM.

The detectives leaned against the wall, pretending not to listen. I turned my back to them. If Coop was in court, I'd just have to leave a message. A woman answered on the third ring. I gave her my name. My chest tightened when she put me on hold. I laced my fingers through the telephone cord. I heard a click, then Coop answered.

"This is Teeny Templeton," I said. "I'm sorry to call, but I'm in a world of trouble."

I explained the predicament, giving him a speeded-up version. "I'll be right there," he said. "And don't say another word to them."

Purvis sat down and crossed his arms while Noonan fiddled with the video camera. "So," Purvis said and leaned forward. "When did you last see Mr. Jackson?"

"I'm not talking till my lawyer gets here." I pressed my lips together.

"We can still interrogate you," Purvis said. "We used to not, but the Supreme Court ruled on it."

"I'm a little nauseated," I said.

Noonan dragged a metal trash can over to my chair and sat down beside me. I laid my cheek against the table, hoping the coldness would settle my stomach. I could hear the detectives shift in their chairs. After a long time, I heard voices in the hallway. The door swung open and Coop walked in, trailed by two officers. The detectives got to their feet and shook Coop's hand.

"Hey, O'Malley," Noonan said. "Didn't know you was practicing criminal law. Thought you gave that up for easy shit. Divorces and disability cases."

"I'd like to speak to my client, please," Coop said.

After they left the room, he sat down beside me and took out a yellow pad. "What's going on?"

I started with the text message and ended with the 911 call. He made some notes, then examined my neck.

"There's two red marks. A stun gun can do that. That's why you're experiencing mental confusion. We'll take some pictures."

The detectives returned. Coop rose from his chair, smoothing his tie. "If you don't need Miss Templeton for anything else, then we'll be going."

"Go with god," Purvis said, spreading his hands.

I followed Coop into the hall. We walked past a coffee machine into a larger hall with glass doors at either end. Off to the side was a square room with desks. The back wall was covered with policeman of the year plaques and pictures of South Carolina's most wanted.

We stopped by a long counter where a fax machine was spitting out pages. Noonan gave me a chilly stare, like I was getting away with something bad.

"Take it easy, O'Malley," Noonan called.

Coop and I stepped out of the building. Heat rippled over the pavement, rising into a cloudless sky. He stopped beside his truck and helped me into the passenger seat.

"Hungry?" he asked.

"No, but I'd like to change clothes."

"No problem."

"Well, there might be. They're in my car. And my car is at Bing's house." I couldn't bear to call it a crime scene.

"Not anymore. Your car has been impounded."

"Seriously?"

"You're a person of interest."

"But my clothes aren't, right?"

"Detective Noonan said it looked like you were leaving town."

"Bing threw my stuff out of his house. Miss Dora put everything into bags and brought them to me." A lie of omission was still a lie, and I'd just told number fourteen.

"Miss Dora?" Coop asked.

"Bing's stepmother."

"You get along with her?"

"She's my friend."

Coop walked around the truck, got in, and started the engine.

"How did Bing die?" I asked.

"The detectives say he was shot. Did Noonan test you for gunpowder residue?"

"A technician from Charleston did. He took my clothes, too. Noonan was upset because I'd washed my face and hands."

"I'll get a copy of the test. The residue can be washed off sometimes. But they'll check your clothes."

"There was nothing to wash off. I don't even own a gun."

"They're just following procedure. You were Bing's girlfriend. The police always start with the significant other. They'll eliminate you soon enough and move to the next person of interest."

He drove to Towne Centre and we walked to the stores. My jump-suit drew stares as we stepped into Banana Republic. I went straight to the sale rack. Coop's phone rang. He walked to the front of the store and put his hand on top of his head. Then he glanced back at me.

Something was up. I grabbed beige slacks and a white blouse and started toward the cash register. I hadn't withdrawn any money from the bank, but I still had the envelope with Miss Dora's money. Even on sale, Banana Republic clothes were sky high. I hated to squander cash when I didn't have a place to live, and even though I was still queasy, I would eventually need to eat.

I paid for the outfit and asked the saleslady if I could change in her dressing room. Her eyes lingered on my jumpsuit, and she pointed to the changing area.

"I'll just be a second," I told Coop and hurried to the dressing room. When I stepped out, he snapped his phone shut.

"You've been holding back," he said. "We need to talk."

fifteen

We walked in silence to the red truck. Coop started the engine and turned on the air conditioner. "Teeny, what in the Sam Hill's going on? You didn't tell me about your previous arrest."

"I was going to," I said.

"When? The police have issued an APB. Now they've got a reason to hold you."

"Hold? You mean arrest?"

He nodded.

"For what? Not murder. 'Cause I didn't do it."

"Relax, they're booking you for trespassing. And violating a restraining order. Apparently you were already on unsupervised probation." He gave me a stern look. "This is bad, Teeny. The DA will argue that you're a flight risk. If the judge sets bail, it's liable to be steep. So, either you tell me everything, and truthfully, or get yourself another lawyer."

"It's a long story." I pushed back my hair. "If I start talking, you'll run out of gas."

"Teeny, this isn't funny. The police think you had several motives. Your fiancé cheated, but he held the financial cards, and you were going to end up homeless. I need to know more about your previous arrest. You were booked for criminal assault and resisting arrest, correct?"

"I didn't know about the resisting arrest part," I said.

I told him everything, starting with Aunt Bluette's funeral. When I finished, he shifted gears and steered the truck onto the highway, toward the Ravenel Bridge. "You taking me to the detention center?"

"I have to."

"Will they keep me long?"

"They can hold you till the bond hearing. Then you can bail out— unless the judge is really pissed. He could deny bail. But I'll try to meet with him in chambers later this afternoon and get this sorted out."

I didn't have enough money for bail. But I knew who did. "Could I borrow your phone, please?"

I punched in Miss Dora's cell number. At the sound of her chipper hello, I burst into tears.

"Teeny!" she cried. "What's the matter?"

"Bing's dead. The police think somebody killed him."

"My god, dear god," she said. "How'd he die?"

"Someone shot him." I filled her in.

"My Lord." She exhaled. "Why'd you go over there in the first place?"

"He texted me—at least, I thought it was him. When I got to the house, Bing was dead."

"You poor thing. But listen, you've got to be strong. We'll need to arrange the funeral."

"Funeral?" I shuddered.

"We just better hope Eileen doesn't show up," Miss Dora said.

"Who?"

"Bing's sister. She got kicked out of the Jackson family. I wouldn't put it past her to kill Bing."

This was the first I'd heard of a sister. But now that I thought about it, my lack of information summed up our whole relationship.

"The Mount Pleasant police issued a warrant for my arrest," I said. "I might need your help with bail."

"Arrest?" she cried. "For what?"

"Because I went to his house and violated probation. They're claiming I trespassed."

"Those bastards! Don't you worry one little bit. I'll be happy to help you. The only thing is, I'm still in Savannah. But I'm leaving right this second. I'll call when I get home."

"The police took my cell phone. Let me give you Coop's number."

"Who?"

"Cooper O'Malley. My lawyer."

"Why didn't you call Alvin Bell?"

"Couldn't remember his number. I'll explain later."

After I hung up, I set the phone on the console. "She'll post bail," I said.

"If there's bail." He chewed the inside of his lip.

We drove in silence over the Ravenel Bridge into North Charleston. I was going to the Big House, where they took bank robbers and child touchers. When Coop pulled into the detention center parking lot, I turned away from the ugly brick building and looked up. The South Carolina flag snapped in the breeze atop the metal pole.

Coop's hand slid across the console, and he touched my arm. "Teeny, the police will interrogate you again. They have the right to do that, but if I'm not present, don't say a word. I don't care what they say or promise, wait till I get there."

I nodded.

"One more thing," he said. "The booking process is demeaning. Being in jail is worse. But I'll do my best to get you out. You've got to trust me."

"Okay." I reached for my lemon purse and pushed it into his hands. "Can you keep this? I've got money and stuff in there. I only need my inhaler."

"Sure. The medical staff will keep your inhaler." He tucked my purse into the backseat.

I climbed out. The heat from the pavement pushed through my shoes. We stepped into the building, cleared the checkpoint, and passed through electronic doors. A lady cop escorted me to the restroom and patted me down. I changed into a striped jumpsuit, then the woman led me to the same processing room where I'd been booked the night of the naked badminton game. For a second time, I was photographed and fingerprinted. The cop who took my picture said, "You back here already?"

"Didn't like the first mug shot," I said. "Thought I'd try again."

When he asked my name and address, I hesitated. Then I gave the Bonaventure address. He led me to an interrogation room. Coop stood next to a wall with a huge grid map of Charleston. The Mount Pleasant detectives sat at one end of the table, and a new cop sat at the other.

"I'd like to speak with my client alone," Coop said.

The woman cop shuffled out, with the detectives following. The door slammed.

"Teeny, there's a problem," Coop said, helping me to a chair. "A woman is claiming you sent her a threatening text message around the time of the murder."

"What woman?"

"Natalie Lockhart."

"She's Bing's girlfriend," I said. "I didn't text her. I don't even know her number."

"A text message was sent from your phone to Miss Lockhart's at 9:42 a.m." He slid a photograph across the table. It was a picture of a cell phone. The display read, *You're next.*

"I can prove I didn't send it. The English is too perfect." I tapped the photograph. "If I'd done this, I would've texted *Ur Next.* Check Bing's phone. See if he kept any of my messages. He used to go wild over my bad grammar."

"I'll mention it to Detective Purvis."

"After I was knocked out, maybe the murderer texted Natalie from my phone."

"They'll check for prints. But Teeny, this doesn't look good." He glanced at my throat. "I'll get photos of your neck and show them at the arraignment."

"Let me take a lie detector test."

"A polygraph isn't admissible in court." He wrote something on the legal pad, then looked up. "I got your bail hearing moved up to tomorrow. But you'll have to spend the night in jail."

I leaned back in the chair and crossed my arms. "Are they charging me with murder?"

"No. Criminal trespass and violation of a restraining order."

"Trespass? But he texted me."

"That's the law, Teeny."

"I've never had a speeding ticket. The first time I saw a real courtroom was the night I got arrested for throwing peaches."

"That will help our case. Right now, all the police have is motive and opportunity. Even their circumstantial evidence—like the text message—is pretty shaky. They'll need physical evidence to convince a jury, like gunpowder residue or an eyewitness. Without a murder weapon or forensic evidence, it won't happen. The DA can't prove beyond a reasonable doubt that you killed Bing."

"Because I didn't."

There was a knock at the door. The Charleston detective cracked it open. "Y'all about finished?"

Coop waved them inside. The Mount Pleasant guys sat down, but the Charleston detective stood against the wall with his arms crossed. Detective Noonan started quizzing me about the text message but Coop cut him off.

"My client denies sending that message. When she arrived at the murder scene, she was attacked from behind. I want photographs taken of the marks on her neck."

The Charleston detective left the room. Noonan leaned closer. "Did you have an altercation with Natalie Lockhart at the Spencer-Jackson House on Rainbow Row?"

I nodded. "She put a 'For Sale' sign in front of the house. It wasn't that big of a fuss."

"Is it true your fiancé gave you twenty-four hours to vacate the Spencer-Jackson House?"

"My client has no comment," Coop said.

"Were you in a relationship with the late Aaron Fisher?" Noonan asked.

Coop looked at me and gave a short nod.

I looked at Noonan. "Yes," I said. "A decade ago."

"Mr. Fisher was a student at Clemson?" Noonan asked.

I nodded.

"He died there?" Noonan asked.

"Yes."

"Were you with him when he died?"

"No."

"Where were you?" Noonan blinked.

"At home with my aunt. In Bonaventure, Georgia. But—"

"What's your aunt's name and phone number."

"Bluette Templeton," I said. "She passed away."

"Can anyone corroborate your whereabouts when Mr. Fisher died?"

"No—"

Coop cut me off with a terse "My client has no further comment."

The Charleston detective returned with a camera and took pictures of my neck. When he finished, Noonan said, "I guess we're done. Bail hearing is at 11:00 a.m. tomorrow."

"Coop, would you call Miss Dora?" I asked.

"I will," he said.

I wrote down her number and he tucked it into his folder. The Charleston detective opened the door, and a policewoman stepped into the room. "Lydia, show the arrestee to her new home."

sixteen

My jail cell was the size of a walk-in pantry. The other inmates watched as the door slammed behind me. The air reeked of pine disinfectant. The inmate in the next cell sat on her cot and scratched her head.

"Hey, Barbie doll," she said. "What you in here for?"

I ignored her and put the sheet on my bed. I lay down, trying to calm myself with recipes, but the thought of food made me nauseated. I barely made it to the toilet. The stench of disinfectant made me sicker.

"You ain't got nothing catching, do you?" the inmate asked.

I ignored her and shuffled to my cot. I drew my knees to my chest and listened to the inmates' chatter. I'd just have to get used to it, because if the judge denied bail, I'd be stuck here awhile. A tear slid down the side of my face and hit my knee. All my life, I'd followed the law. I'd always stopped at yellow traffic lights; even if a U-turn was legal, I wouldn't do it.

My moral compass had formed when I was eight years old, the night Mama beat the crap out of Donnie and stole his station wagon. While we drove to the Georgia coast, Mama sang Elvis songs. She was bruised up, but she didn't complain.

We stopped at Cracker Barrel and she put a little pancake makeup on her face to hide the bruises. We took a seat next to the window and ordered catfish platters. She tipped the waitress extra and bought me a sack of hard candy, counting bills from Donnie's billfold.

When we got near Savannah, she started talking and couldn't stop. "I'm ready for a true blue romance," she said. "A man with a college degree and a sweet temper. He's out there, Teeny. I'm getting close to finding him, I just know it."

She sighed. Her breath smelled like peppermint. She always kept a Life Saver in her mouth because you never knew when you'd meet the love of your life, and you sure didn't want to have sour breath.

We drove to Tybee Island and Mama found a boarding house. She wouldn't tell me how much it cost a day. "Stop worrying about money," she said. "Look, our room faces the marsh. Isn't it pretty?"

"No," I said and burst into tears. All I'd known was the farm. I missed the sound of peaches tumbling on the conveyer belt, the smell of browned piecrust wafting from the kitchen, the mournful sound of whip-poor-wills calling out in the woods.

"Can't we just call Aunt Bluette and tell her we're okay?" I begged.

"I'll do it tomorrow," she said, twisting her fingers together. "Promise."

Mama spread the *Savannah Morning News* on the floor and read our horoscopes. I sat next to the window, fretting over the stolen car and Aunt Bluette. I'd told so many lies since Mama had gotten married, I couldn't stand myself. Late at night, I dug out my falsehoods like they were fish bones, each one transparent and sharp. There were so many of them, I knew I'd never get to heaven.

The next morning, Mama went job hunting. She didn't want to squander Donnie's money on gas, so she walked to town. I spent the day luring ants with crushed vanilla wafers. I had farms on the brain, and I was trying to build one with ants.

Mama came home with blisters on her heels. She stood in the yard, running the water hose over her feet. A woman in a purple tent dress walked by with her Chihuahua. She gave Mama a side-eye look. "Y'all in some kind of trouble?"

"Heavens no." Mama laughed. "We like to keep to ourselves. And we really don't like dogs, so just keep moving."

"Why don't you apply for food stamps? There's a whole slew of government handouts you can get."

Mama ignored her and said, "Get in the house, Teeny."

"Your little girl is cute. You really shouldn't leave her alone all day. Don't worry, I won't report you. But somebody will."

After she left, Mama stared down at her feet. They'd sunk into the ground, water lapping around her ankles. We waited till dark, then we packed the car and drove up to Myrtle Beach, using a big chunk of Donnie's money. We passed the seedy part of the strip and turned into the Wayfarer Motel. It looked deserted. We didn't have money for a room, but it was 102 degrees, and we couldn't stay in the car. We walked on the beach until it got dark. I found loose change on the sidewalk, and Mama bought us two candy bars.

"Eat up. It's good for you," she said. "There's a ton of protein in nuts."

We headed back to the station wagon. "I'll take the front seat," she said. "You get the back."

"We're not sleeping in the car?" I cried.

"You got a better idea?" Her face scrunched up like she was trying not to cry. "Look, it'll be fine. You stay in your half of the car; I'll stay in mine."

That night, the motel came to life. Skinny women in short skirts came out of their rooms and leaned over the rail, flicking cigarette ashes into the oleanders and watching the cars cruise down Ocean Boulevard.

We lived in the station wagon for the next week, washing ourselves in the Burger King restroom. Mama made friends with a busboy from a steak house, and he brought us bags filled with food that people had sent back to the kitchen. He even brought leftover wine. Mama drank while I stuffed myself on onion rings and T-bones that were too rare or too done. The wine made her cheerful and she started singing "Milkcow Blues Boogie." Then she quoted Proverbs 30:30 and gave me a recipe for a strawberry-peach shake.

Her motormouthing hurt my ears, so I held out an onion ring. "Here, I saved you one," I said.

"Eat it yourself, Possum Head. God, it stinks in here." Mama cracked the window to let the smell of food blow out.

"Mama? Are we going to live in this car forever?"

"How the hell do *I* know?"

"It's just hard to see in the dark."

"I'll buy you a damn flashlight, okay?"

"Don't say that, Mama."

"What are you, a little preacher?" she cried. "Lay off me. I'm doing the best I can."

The skinny women knocked on our windshield. They found Mama a job and moved us out of the car, into a room on the second floor. Mama put clean clothes and my inhaler into a bag and steered me to a room on the bottom floor, where an old woman with frizzled white hair sat in a metal chair.

"Teeny, this is Mrs. Phelps. She's babysitting you tonight." Mama thrust the bag into the woman's hands. "If my baby gets winded, she's got medicine. I'll pick her up in the morning."

Night after night, Mama teased her hair and brushed on three coats of mascara. If Mrs. Phelps couldn't keep me, Mama would go to the motel next door and barge up to families. "Can you keep my little girl?" she'd say.

One morning when she picked me up, the station wagon was packed with our things. I didn't ask questions. I was glad we were leaving the Wayfarer. She drove down Highway 17 until it split.

We stayed in Charleston for a day and moved down to Beaufort, parking at Memorial Hospital. We'd go into the hospital cafeteria and fill Styrofoam cups with hot water, then we'd make soup by adding catsup.

On the way back to the station wagon, she pushed hair out of her eyes. "You're a good girl, Teeny. But you shouldn't be around me. Something bad's gonna happen. I just know it."

"Let's just go home," I said. "Aunt Bluette can hide us on the farm."

After a security guard chased us out of the lot, Mama stopped at Wal-Mart and went inside. She came back with someone's pocketbook. We used the money to buy gas and french fries, and we headed to Georgia.

I perked up when signs for Bonaventure flashed by. "Are we going to see Aunt Bluette?" I asked.

"Mmm-hmm," she said and pulled into the Dairy Queen.

"What if Donnie spots your car?"

"He won't." She handed me five dollars. "Run on in and get us two cones."

I cracked open the door, and she grabbed my arm. Mascara ran down her cheeks.

"Mama, you're crying," I said.

"No, I'm not." She wiped her face and smiled. "It's just that I love you so much."

I went inside and ordered the cones. I tried to keep an eye on her, but the windows were pasted up with giant posters of banana splits and Blizzards. The lady handed me the cones, and I told her to keep the change. I ran out. Mama's car was gone. I walked around the building, holding the cones straight out so they wouldn't drip on me. But I didn't see her car anywhere.

I squatted beside the front door and watched customers go in and out. By the time I finished my cone, she still hadn't come back. Her ice cream lost its shape and ran down my arm, spattering against the pavement. The manager came out and squatted beside me.

"Honey, is somebody picking you up?"

I nodded and looked away, struggling not to cry. Mama's cone felt soft and spongy. Flies gathered around the puddles, twitching their legs.

"You from around here?" he asked.

"Used to be."

"You got people here?"

"My aunt." I wiped my eyes.

"What's her name?"

"Bluette Templeton."

"She own that peach farm?"

I nodded.

"I should've known," he said. "You look like a Templeton. Give me the cone, honey, and we'll go inside and call her."

"I can't. It's for Mama," I said. She was coming back. She wouldn't drop me off without my medicine. The manager went back inside. A while later, a policeman showed up and drove me to Aunt Bluette's. She stepped onto the porch, and I dove at her soft legs. Her hand slid down the back of my head.

"Where's Ruby?" She squinted at the driveway.

"Gone."

"You got a suitcase?" Two lines cut across her forehead. "Your medicines?"

I shook my head.

"She'll come back," Aunt Bluette said. "Just as soon as she thinks this through, she'll be back."

"No, she won't." It was the end of August, and she'd dumped me off just in time for school.

"Let's call Dr. O'Malley and get your prescriptions," Aunt Bluette said. "Then you and me'll get her room ready. Run and find the feather duster. It's in the pantry, same as always. I'll be right behind you with the vacuum. Ruby'll be delighted, won't she?"

I rested on the curve of her voice. I'd forgotten how she broke that word into three parts, de-*LIGHT*-ed, with her voice screaking up in the middle. Mama had run off more times than I cared to remember. She'd always come back, but this time felt different.

While me and Aunt Bluette scrubbed baseboards and changed the sheets, we hummed "Bye Bye Blackbird." Just like in the song, we packed up our woes. We made Mama's bed and lit the porch light, but she didn't show up. We never saw her again. She was gone for good.

seventeen

I awoke on the jail cot and listened to a metal cart squeak down the corridor. Breakfast was being served. I was starving, yet queasy. In a few hours, I would go before the judge. Coop had said this was a bail hearing. If the judge set it too high, or denied it, I'd come right back to this cell.

My eyes teared up a little and I wiped them on the sheet. Now wasn't the time for a boo-hoo party. I sat up and pushed my hair out of my face. I didn't have a comb but I didn't want to go to court looking like a hedgehog.

I raked my fingers through the tangles and thought about Bing. I was guilty of mean thoughts, but I wasn't capable of murder. I'd been set up. He hadn't sent me a text message; the murderer had done it. Considering what had transpired between me and Bing, not to mention the restraining order, I could have easily ignored that message and found a cheap boarding house. Or I could've gone straight to Bonaventure. If I'd broken probation, at least I would've had an alibi—gas receipts stamped with the date and time. Eyewitnesses could have placed me in Georgia. And the real murderer couldn't have gotten hold of my phone and sent a phony message to Natalie. Nobody would think I'd murdered Bing if I'd been miles and miles away, right? Instead, I'd turned up at a murder scene.

The cart stopped in front of my cell door. A matronly woman slid a tray under the metal gap. Breakfast smells rose up and my stomach rumbled. I crept over to the tray. I was surprised that prison food was so good. A pat of butter skated over fluffy white grits. Sausage patties were arranged around a mound of scrambled eggs. I lifted the biscuit—it was the fluffiest, lightest biscuit I ever saw—and took a greedy bite. Then, I set it down and reached for the plastic spoon. I was so caught up in tasting the sweet yet savory flavor of grits that I barely noticed when a bony hand inched through the bar toward my biscuit.

"Hey!" I cried. My spoon clattered against the tray. The hand grabbed my biscuit. Before it slipped back through the bars, I seized the woman's wrist.

"That's my biscuit," I said.

"Like you need it, you big-leg girl."

"Drop it," I said.

"Make me." She tried to squirm away, but I sank my teeth into her hand. I wasn't just biting her, I was biting for world hunger, fall guys, injustice. I was biting on behalf of every child whose mama had left them at a Dairy Queen.

The inmate screeched and the biscuit hit my tray. She stepped back, sucking her hand. I felt so ashamed. I'd been in jail overnight and had already had a food fight. No telling what I'd do if I got a prison sentence. I lifted the biscuit, pushed it through the bars, and dropped it onto her tray.

The woman snatched the biscuit, then she scooted her tray away from the bars.

I thought she'd report me for attacking her, but she didn't say a word when a lady officer brought me an outfit: a brown, pilgrimish dress with a white collar.

"Your lawyer brung it," she said.

After I got dressed, the officer handcuffed me with a plastic twist tie. I shuffled into the corridor, toward a side door where other prisoners were lined up waiting for a bus.

When we reached the courthouse, I sat on the bench next to a woman who told me she'd been wrongfully accused of killing a rooster. She'd cooked her boyfriend's prizewinning Rhode Island Red cock and was being charged with animal cruelty.

She grinned, showing a dark front tooth. "You and me's a pair, ain't we?"

While I waited for my name to be called, I rehearsed my speech to the judge.

"Quit muttering!" said the rooster killer. "You ain't having your say. Neither am I. Our shitty lawyers is cutting deals, just like they'd slice a pie."

"She's right," said the woman sitting on my other side. She had a half-moon scar under her left eye. "It's a done deal. All you need to know is, stand when the sorry-assed judge comes in and stand when he leaves. When he asks you a question, say, 'Yes, Your Honor' or 'No, Your Honor.' The Honor part is real important. Judges eat it up. If you don't say it, you'll get slapped with contempt. That's more jail time."

"Thanks," I said.

"Don't mention it."

"Templeton!" called a man in a uniform.

The twist-tie handcuffs stayed put as he led me into the courtroom. The seats were full and people stood along the back wall like they'd come to a free magic show. In a way, it was. Guilty people walked in, and if the stars were aligned, they vanished from society. But the innocent could disappear, too. Now you see me, now you freaking don't.

A new judge sat behind the high wooden desk. He had a crew cut,

John Lennon glasses, and sunburned cheeks. Sunlight fell through the tall windows and hit the empty jury box.

The officer led me down the aisle. Miss Dora sat in the third row. When she saw me, her eyes teared up. She lifted her handbag and mouthed what looked like *Bail*.

I followed the officer into the squared-off area behind a rail. Coop sat at a counsel table, writing on a yellow pad. An accordion folder stood open and papers jutted out. He greeted me with a nod.

Before I could speak, the bailiff cried, "CR-05-409. The State of South Carolina versus Templeton."

I frowned. That sounded awful harsh—the whole state was against me?

The judge glanced at a paper, and his glasses slid down his nose. "We're addressing bail?"

"Yes, Your Honor," Coop said.

"Miss Templeton is being held in the detention center, correct?"

"Yes, Your Honor," Coop said.

"Miss Templeton, you're charged with trespassing and violating a restraining order. Do you understand these charges?"

"Yes, Your Honor," I said in my most reverent, scared-of-burning-in-hell voice.

Coop talked about the South Carolina Constitution and how all people are entitled to bail except murderers. He asked the court to continue my unsupervised probation and to release me on my own recognizance.

At the other table, a man with short sandy hair stood up—I was pretty sure he was the DA. He said I was a flight risk, adding that on the day of my arrest, my car had been found packed with clothes. Coop argued that I was moving to another apartment, not another state. The judge told me to rise. "Miss Templeton, you will post $25,000 bond. You will surrender your passport to your attorney. I'm continuing unsupervised probation, but if you leave the state, you'll lose bail and be put in jail. Do you understand?"

"Yes, Your Honor," I said, even though I didn't have a passport. I was worried about bail. $25,000 was a lot of money, and Miss Dora had brought a small pocketbook.

After the hearing, I followed Coop into the hall. A detention center deputy started to lead me away. "Wait, Coop?" I called over my shoulder. "They're not taking me back to jail, right?"

"Just until the bail is posted and the paperwork goes through," Coop said.

Miss Dora walked up and glared at the deputy. "Is the trial over? Is she cleared?"

The deputy shook his head. "No, ma'am. This was just the bail hearing, not a trial. That's later."

"Teeny is innocent," Miss Dora said. "Y'all should look for the real criminal."

She drew me into a hug, and I breathed in her rose-petal perfume. She pulled back and smiled at Coop. "I'm Dora Jackson. And you must be Mr. O'Malley?"

"Yes, ma'am."

"What was Teeny charged with?" she asked.

"Trespassing and violating an order of protection."

"Why'd they put her in jail over a little thing like that?"

"Because she was on probation when she was arrested. The judge could have come down a lot harder."

"Thank goodness he didn't." She lifted her pocketbook. "Where do I post bail?"

"You need to see the bail bondsman," said the deputy.

Miss Dora turned to Coop. "You *are* awfully handsome. But I'm wondering if you're the right lawyer for Teeny. I don't understand why she had a bond hearing in the first place."

"She was arrested on a warrant," Coop said. "She had to go before the judge."

"All that is just over my head." Miss Dora patted my arm. "I'll be gone all day—back-to-back appointments. If you need me, call."

The officer started to lead me away, but Coop stopped him. "I'll try to expedite the paperwork. Just go with the deputy. I'll be right behind you, okay?"

"You better be, O'Malley," I said.

eighteen

When I got back to the detention center, a female officer took me to a holding area. She removed my handcuffs and escorted me to a hall, where Coop was waiting.

"That was fast." I smiled, then I frowned. "How can I do nothing and be in this much trouble?"

"Happens all the time."

Police were milling about. Coop touched my elbow, and we stepped down a long corridor, through metal doors, into the parking lot. "Your car hasn't been released," he said. "Do you have a place to stay?"

"I have a key to the Spencer-Jackson House."

"You don't own the property, do you?"

"No. But Miss Dora said I could stay."

"Has she given her written permission?" Coop asked.

"No, but I'm sure she'd be happy to."

"Does she own the house?"

"It's part of the Jackson estate."

"I don't like gray areas, Teeny. I'd just feel better if I had a signed document."

"She won't be home until later." I leaned across the seat. "I couldn't talk you into taking me to Bonaventure, could I?"

"You'd violate the terms of your parole. The police would go into a feeding frenzy, and the bondsman would send a bounty hunter after you."

"I'm just kidding."

"Well, I'm not kidding about the Spencer-Jackson House. You shouldn't stay there without written permission."

"Then drop me off at a safe, cheap hotel."

"Could be a problem without reservations. You know how it is this time of year."

"Right." Tourist season was a bad time to be homeless in Charleston. On the other hand, he seemed to be making excuses. That excited me.

"I just live up the road a piece," he said. "We'll make some calls. See if we can't find you a room."

"Up the road a piece" turned out to be a gray clapboard house on Isle of Palms. It resembled a modern schoolhouse with tiny square windows, peaked dormers, and a wraparound deck. Built on pilings, the house seemed to float above the sea oats.

Coop steered onto the narrow, curved driveway. Through the dunes, I saw slashes of the Atlantic.

"Can you handle a stick shift?" He pointed at a gray '69 Mustang in the carport. It was the same car he'd driven in high school.

I nodded.

"You're welcome to drive it."

I glanced back at the Mustang. Coop held on to people and things. Me, I couldn't keep either.

I heard barking from inside the house. Coop unlocked the door and stepped inside. T-Bone let out a woof and pushed his nose against Coop's hand. I froze.

"Relax, Teeny. Just let him smell you."

I held still while T-Bone's enormous nose sniffed me up and down. I was trying not to freak, but the top of the dog's head was level with my boobs. He sat down and extended his paw.

"Can I shake it?" I asked Coop.

"Hell, yes."

I touched the paw. The nails were clipped short, but the paw itself was epic, filling up my palm. Coop opened the door wide. T-Bone scrambled to his feet and shot out. The deck shook as he ran down the steps.

"Will he be all right?" I asked, glancing anxiously at the road. I thought of Sir, locked up at the pound.

"He won't go far," Coop said and dropped his keys into an abalone shell.

"Nice foyer," I said. Light streamed through two skylights, hitting the Ansel Adams prints on the wall. White, cube-like bookcases stood in each end of the foyer. Each cubbyhole held black-and-white pottery vases.

"I can't take credit for it." He smiled. "My mother drove up from Bonaventure and fixed it up—she cleaned out her gift shop."

I glanced at the sleek black bench under the artwork and gave a silent prayer that his mother was responsible for the décor and not his girlfriend. I followed him through the hall, into a beige room with a cathedral ceiling. A black leather sofa sat in front of glass doors that looked out onto the ocean.

Coop picked up shirts, ties, and crumpled McDonald's bags and carried them to the kitchen. He came back, stopped by a bookcase, and switched on the stereo. Music started up, Elvis singing "Suspicious Minds."

"It's a bit early, but you look like you need a drink," he said. "Will gin and tonic do?"

"Only if you're having one."

He turned into a small dining room with black walls. The table had a huge driftwood base with a thick slab of glass on top. White, heavily carved chairs were lined up on either side.

I turned in a slow circle. Turkish-looking pillows were piled on one end of the sofa. Another set of bookcases framed the fireplace with more black pottery. I walked over to one of the French doors. Two white Adirondack chairs were angled toward the water. Each chair had a cushion and footstool. Two of everything, like on Noah's Ark.

Miss Dora had taught me to study people's homes. She said you could learn everything you needed to know about people by their colors, art, and accessories. I'd half expected Coop's shelves to overflow with law books, but there were no books at all. That worried me. In the left case was the TV and video equipment. The right case had three glass shelves with shells on Plexiglas stands. There was a fireplace but no mantle, and no logs in the fireplace, just an empty grate. Nothing on the coffee table either, except for a smear of mustard.

Coop rounded the corner, holding a tall glass in each hand. He handed me one and gave me an appraising stare. It was the same look he'd given me on our first date, a look I associated with desire and treachery, a look that had lied when it said I ♥ you.

I fixed him with my blandest expression—not cold, because I didn't want to send coldness. I wanted to send blankness. I ( ) you.

"Cheers," he said and clinked his glass against mine.

I took a sip and gazed through the French door. The beach stretched out beneath a blue haze. A man and a woman walked hand-in-hand along the shoreline, pausing now and then to kiss. I took a long swallow of my drink and turned away. I couldn't shake the feeling that I'd wandered into an old movie about lovers reconnecting after many years but with poor results. I didn't want to end up like Natalie Wood in *Splendor in the Grass*.

"I've got a phone book in the kitchen," Coop said. "But you're more than welcome to stay here. I've got four bedrooms."

"You're sweet to offer."

"I heard a but in there." He smiled.

I sat down on the black sofa, hoping that was all he'd heard. I wasn't ready to face him. Not yet, anyway. Plus, it was plain sleazy to crash at my lawyer's house—weren't there rules against that? Or was I being old-fashioned? I finished my drink, and images of Bing skittered up into the haze. Maybe Miss Dora had been right. I needed to carpe diem a little more.

Coop sat down beside me. "Maybe I asked this before, but how long were you and Bing engaged?"

"Just a few months." Coop pretty much knew what I'd been up to for the past eleven years, but I didn't know anything about him. He wasn't wearing a ring. And, other than the decorative objects his mother had set out, I hadn't noticed any feminine touches in his house.

"How long have you lived here?" I asked.

"Eleven months."

I wondered where he'd lived before that but didn't want to pry. I lifted my glass, and the ice clinked like loose gravel. "Gosh, I'm woozy," I said. Translation: My fiancé is dead. The police think I killed him in a jealous rage. They took my dog, my phone, and my car. Other than that, nothing's wrong. I'm just peachy.

"You okay?" he asked.

"It's just hitting me, you know? Bing, jail, court. Would you mind if I lied down?" I cringed—had I said that wrong? Was it lie or lay?

Coop showed me to a room with indigo walls and tiny white-framed windows. Beyond the panes, the sky and water met in a dark line. I flopped onto a bed with a carved shell headboard. When I reached down to pull off my shoes, my hand stopped on my knees. I was too exhausted to move. I didn't fall asleep so much as drift. I was a girl in a leaky boat, desperately trying to row myself into a dream. Then I let go and sank down into the salty blue.

nineteen

Way off in the distance, a dog barked and barked. I opened my eyes. Sunlight dappled along the walls like minnows caught in a tide pool. I pulled back the covers. I was wearing the pilgrim dress and brown shoes. But where the blazes was I? A blue room with white windows that looked out into more blue.

Coop's house.

I bathed and put on my brown dress; then I walked into the hall. Doors were lined up on both sides. I opened one and saw a room filled with plants: maidenhair ferns, baby's tears, spider plants, orchids, African violets. A humidifier purred in the corner. Grow lights cast a blue tint over metal shelves, a watering can, and clay pots. Mama used to say, "If you ever find a man with a green thumb, keep him."

Good advice. But what if that man doesn't want you?

I turned back into the hall and let my nose guide me to the kitchen. Coop was forking up bacon and laying it on a paper towel. T-Bone stretched on the floor. Both of them glanced up when I walked into the room.

"Hey, you're awake." Coop grinned.

"What time is it?" I pulled back my hair, wishing I had a rubber band.

"7:00 a.m."

"I slept that long?"

"You needed to. You want toast and coffee, sweetheart?"

There was that word again. I smiled. "Love some," I said.

We ate breakfast on the deck, watching gulls wheel in and out of bright sun. The tide was falling. I set my empty mug on the rail and turned away from the beach. I could see our reflections in the glass doors. We looked so normal, like two people on a date, not a criminal and her lawyer.

"A couple of things you need to know about probation," he said. "You can't carry a firearm. The police can search your home without probable cause. And you can't consort with other criminals."

"I'll bear that in mind." The wind caught my dress and I smoothed it. "What's going to happen to me?"

"Right now, the police are doing forensics. They'll test your clothes for gunpowder residue and for blood. I'm confident the tests will show a contact transfer versus blood splatter."

"What's that?"

"You got blood on your clothing from your dog. If you'd shot Bing, chances are you'd have gotten sprayed with blood droplets. It would depend on the range, of course."

"What about the gunpowder? I should be in the clear on that one. The test won't show a false positive, right?"

"In your case, I don't think it'll show a damn thing. Unfortunately, it won't clear you. We'll know the results in about ten days. Longer if the lab is backed up. I wouldn't fret over it. GPR is corroborative evidence, but it doesn't give the whole picture." He paused. "More coffee?"

"Sure," I said, but I was still mulling over "corroborative." I remembered hearing that word on *CSI: Miami*.

He reached around for my mug, and our eyes met. He stared so long I began to worry.

"Anything wrong?" I asked.

"I'm sorry. I don't meant to gawk. But I'd forgotten how pretty you are."

I smiled. A nice girl would have averted her gaze in a flattered but saintly way and go powder her nose, but not me. He put his hands on my face and kissed me. He tasted sweet and salty, and I sucked his lower lip into my mouth. His cotton shirt felt warm and rough as I slid my hands over his shoulders. My mind was like the surface of a pond, reflecting chaos instead of sky. Making love to Coop would be like throwing a rock into the water, the ripples breaking up the turmoil for just a few moments. Then the water would settle and life would go back to the way it was.

His lips brushed over mine. I pulled back. I couldn't let this go further until I knew how the last eleven years had changed him, and especially why he'd dumped me for Barb.

"Remember the summer we dated?" I asked.

"Every bit of it. I still have that daisy you picked."

That startled me, but I pressed on. "I bought you a birthday present. It's probably still sitting in Aunt Bluette's closet." I paused. "Remember that day you broke up with me?"

"You had an asthma attack," he said. "Scared me to death."

"I really, really cared for you."

"You did?"

I nodded.

"I had feelings for you, too. But I couldn't tell you what happened."

"Tell me now."

"Well, it's like this. One night Barb's car broke down on Broad River Road. She couldn't find anyone to help. Her parents were in Savannah. She called me, and I went. It caught me off guard when she started hitting on me. I tried to resist. I cared about you, Teeny. I really did. Barb must have sensed I wasn't interested in her anymore, so she took off her clothes. My hormones collided with hers in the backseat of her mama's Chrysler."

"I got thrown over for nookie?"

"She blackmailed me. She said if I kept seeing you, she'd tell you what we'd done. But if I dropped you, I could have more of the same. I was blindsided by the sex. And I didn't know how to tell you. I couldn't look you in the eye. I was young and stupid." He ran his fingers through his hair. "I didn't want to hurt you. I just wanted to get laid. My penis took control of my brain."

He looked up at the sky. I looked, too. Clouds gathered over the water, all bunched up like sheep.

"Barb and I became a cliché," he said. "Boy goes to college. Girl stays home. Boy goes wild with a whole campus full of girls. The girl back home gets mad. Truth is, Barb and I were apart more than we were together. It's a long way from Bonaventure to Chapel Hill. And she was crazy-jealous, so I stopped seeing her."

I knew the rest of the story. He'd broken Barb's heart, and she'd up and married Lester Philpot, a local sports legend who blew out his shoulder and became a pharmacist. Then Barb's mom passed away. Because I'd admired Mrs. Browning, I went to the funeral home. Barb stood next to the casket with her new husband. She wore a loose-fitting black dress, and when people came up to pay their respects, the first thing she said was, "I'm pregnant, not fat!"

"I didn't really let you know me back then," Coop said, bringing me back to the present. "But now I want you to know everything."

My formerly favorite subject was offering himself, all of his warts and accolades. I picked up his hand. I liked the way the dark hair lay on his wrists and how blue veins branched across his knuckles.

"So, tell me all about yourself, Cooper O'Malley." I spread my arms.

"I like oysters on the half shell and old trucks." He grinned. "Big dogs. Kindness. Truth. Babies. St. Patrick's Day. Sleeping late. Guinness. Forgiveness. Orchids. Justice. Empathy. Reliability. A woman who really listens. Brown-eyed girls who bake peach cobblers and carry inhalers."

I laughed. He leaned forward like he was going to kiss me again, but I leaned back. He was into truth and justice. And I kept track of my lies.

"What makes you sad?" I asked.

"Cruelty." He tipped back his head. "Law breakers. Funerals. Lies."

Just my luck. He ran his thumb over the rim of his mug.

"What about you?" he asked. "What makes you happy?"

This caught me off guard. Other than Aunt Bluette, no one had ever asked me what I thought about anything, much less what thrilled me. The wind caught my hair and it streamed across my face. I started to ask if Coop had a rubber band when he tucked a lock behind my ear.

"I'm a sucker for dogs with smashed-in faces," I said. "I love laughter. Courage. The color blue. Don't get me started about old movies, peaches, or cast-iron skillets. Or the smell of sweet almond because it reminds me of Mama. And I can't drive by McDonald's without getting a McFlurry."

"What about bêtes noires? Your pet hates?"

I smiled. "Men who use foreign words."

He bowed. "*Touché, ma petite.*"

"I don't like limbo," I said. "Or breaking things that don't belong to me. It kills me to eat the last cookie in the jar. I don't like people who hold back the truth because they think they're sparing my feelings. I don't like unfinished business, either."

"Maybe we should finish what we started." He cupped the back of my head as if I were a boneless infant. His irises were gray, and the soft, neutral color pulled me in. My pulse tapped out a rhythm, *Don't You Dare. Make Him Wait.* There was still enough Baptist inside me to know it wasn't proper to think what I was thinking. But I wasn't a fool. I'd been waiting too damn long for this moment.

We walked into the house. After being in the hot sun, the cool air conditioning felt good on my face. He caught my hand and led me down a short hall. We stopped to kiss under the skylights, where sun fell in broad stripes, then we turned into a white bedroom. T-Bone ran after us, but Coop shut the door.

"Sorry, old buddy," he told the dog through the door. I had the feeling T-Bone knew the routine. Coop put his hands on my waist. His head dropped to my neck, and he pushed his face against my dress. Each time he exhaled, little bursts of air moved through the fabric, warming my skin and leaving damp circles on the fabric. I kept touching his hair, feeling the strands glide between my fingers.

This wasn't a dream. It was real. We were going to make love for the first time.

"I want you so much, Teeny," he said, his voice muffled by my dress. He lifted his head and reached around to unzip me. I moved into the warm space between us and unbuttoned his shirt slowly, letting my palms linger on the crisp linen. His shirt fluttered off; then he pressed against me. I could feel him through my clothes, hard as alder wood.

"I want you, too," I said. I lowered my hand, grabbed his belt, and tugged him closer. He reached down to help. The buckle jangled, and his trousers slid over his hips and hit the floor. Then my dress came off just as fast.

"Can I push Bing from your mind?" He kissed me again. "Can I make you forget him?"

Never in my life had I wanted a man the way I wanted him, but I was scared to put my feelings into words. I turned back the covers and stretched out on the bed. The sheets rustled as he slipped in beside me. I kissed him, tasting sugar and coffee. A thousand times I had imagined him in my arms, and I wanted to remember every detail. The back of my hand traced the dark hairs that ran down the center of his belly, into his boxer shorts. Then I reversed the direction, barely grazing his skin, drawing hearts, *I ♥ you, Coop O'Malley. I'll always ♥ you.*

"It's going to be so good, Teeny," he said.

His hand slipped between my thighs, a place he'd never felt before. My fingers moved through the gap in his shorts and brushed against the damp bead on his tip.

He inched down his shorts, then he cupped my hand between his legs; the flesh was smooth and textured like corduroy. My panties were off in a flash, but he took his time, tracing his thumb over my collarbones, curving down between my breasts. The sheets rustled as he slid down and moved his tongue over my nipples.

"I can't wait any longer," he said. His hand dropped between my legs, moving them apart. I lifted my hips and his hands slipped behind me. He bit his lower lip and pushed his hips forward.

I gasped.

He pressed deeper and deeper.

We moved the way wind shapes dunes, shifting and gathering, ripples molding into peaks, faster and faster, each grain separate yet together.

twenty

I slid my hand over the sheet, feeling the cool wrinkled linen. Outside, I heard gulls crying. I sat up, wincing at the soreness between my legs. Across the room, the bedroom door stood open and my brown dress spilled across a white chair. Coop's shirt lay beside a black dresser.

I sighed. My moral debauchery was complete. Bing was dead and I'd just slept with my lawyer. Worse, I was glad.

T-Bone trotted into the room and flashed me a look, as if to say, Don't even think about getting rid of me.

"I can share," I told him.

His head swiveled when Coop stepped into the room carrying a paper bag.

"I went to the store while you were sleeping." He tossed the bag onto the bed. "You can't visit Isle of Palms unless you own a swimsuit. It's a law."

"Thanks, O'Malley." I smiled.

He started to kiss me, but T-Bone began spinning in circles, growling at his tail. "T-Bone, slow down, buddy. You better get used to Teeny."

A thrill shot through me. The dog must have sensed it, because he showed his teeth and growled under his breath. Coop clapped his hands.

The dog loped to the French doors that led to the deck. Then he stood on his hind legs and pressed his front paws against the glass.

"Aw, buddy," Coop said.

The dog lifted one paw and tapped the glass.

"He's relentless." Coop patted my leg. "Let's hit the beach."

The dog let out a deep bark, then dropped to all fours and trotted out of the bedroom door. "See you outside," Coop told me.

I opened the bag and pulled out a white two-piece. It was a size smaller than I normally wore, but it slipped right on. When I stepped onto the deck, his eyes swept up and down, and he grinned. We walked down to the beach, with T-Bone racing ahead. Gulls wheeled above us as we crossed over a wooden walkway, then trudged through warm, ankle-deep sand. Coop found a flat place above the surf line. He hooked a leash to T-Bone's collar.

"Leash law," he said. "Dogs can only run free before 8:00 a.m."

We spread a quilt on the sand. The beach was deserted on both sides, except for a cluster of umbrellas toward the pier. The wind was flecked with salt, sweeping the surf line into curves and valleys like a woman's cleavage.

Cooper was stretched out on the quilt and propped up on his elbows, reading *Advanced Indoor Gardening*. T-Bone lolled beside him, his paws stretched out like tree limbs.

"Tide's falling." Coop pointed. "See that dark streak in the water? No waves are breaking. That's a rip current."

I nodded, thinking that sea currents weren't the only things to watch out for. I sat next to Coop and watched a man in a red swimsuit jog by. The man did a double take at T-Bone and picked up his pace.

"I can't stop touching you." Coop leaned forward and tucked a curl behind my ear. "I remember our first date. You wore a red polka-dot bikini. The wind was blowing, and your hair fluttered around your shoulders.

I thought I might pass out. I'd never seen anyone that beautiful. You're even more beautiful now, if that's possible."

Then he drew his finger along my chin and moved up, tracing my lips. He slipped his finger into my mouth and grazed my teeth.

"What if somebody sees us?" I asked.

"Sees what?" He smiled. "An innocent kiss?"

"Define innocent, counsel." I put my arms around his neck.

"I submit exhibit A." He took off his sunglasses. We kissed so long, we fell sideways and landed on the quilt. My hair fell all around him, throwing his face into shadow. "And exhibit B," he said. He kissed the edges of my mouth while his hand slid inside my bathing suit.

A shadow passed over the blanket, and T-Bone barked.

"Yodelayheehoo, Boss," said a gritty, masculine voice. "Hey, you gonna represent this girl or suck face? 'Cause you can't do both."

Coop and I broke apart. I looked up at a stumpy man in tiny round sunglasses with green lenses. He grinned, and his brown moustache stretched into a flat line over small teeth. His hair was chin length, brassy blond, with violently dark roots that screamed home dye job. He swept a lock off his forehead, then ran his hand down his frayed shorts. They stopped just below his knees, revealing broad, hairy calves. He gave me a hard stare and brushed a thick finger over his moustache.

"Don't let me interrupt the lovefest," he said and shuffled his feet. He wore tennis shoes with the tips cut off, showing splayed hairy toes.

"You're early," Coop said.

"Yeah? Seems I got here in the nick of time." He scratched his chest, and his nails scraped into his cotton t-shirt with COLDPLAY printed across the front. T-Bone nuzzled his hand, and the man absently patted the dog's head.

"Hey, you old monster," he said, then glanced at me.

"Teeny, this is Red Butler Hill. He's a private detective."

"Pleasedtomeetya," the man said, looking anything but pleased.

"Nice to meet you, too, Red." I extended my hand but he ignored it.

"It's Red Butler to you, girlie." He rubbed his nose. It looked boneless, without a smidgen of cartilage, as if it had been broken multiple times.

"What's with the *Beach Blanket Bingo* shit?" He pointed to the quilt. The sun glinted off a diamond cluster ring.

"We're just sitting here," Coop said.

"Right. And I'm Jesus come down from heaven. Can we go inside?"

Coop got to his feet. Mustering as much dignity as I could, I grabbed a towel, draped it around my shoulders, and stood. T-Bone stepped back as Red Butler Hill picked up the quilt. Sand flew all over everybody, but he didn't seem to notice. He tossed the quilt over his shoulder.

The wind picked up as he strode ahead, past the dunes, toward the raised wooden walkway. All around us, the sea oats clucked their disapproval. Red Butler reached the end of the walkway and jumped off. T-Bone's tail wagged as he waited for Coop and me to catch up. When we got near the end of the walkway, Coop took my arm.

"Come on, Boss. No PDA." Red Butler winked at me. "That's public display of affection, girlie."

Coop laughed. "You're a detective, not my mother."

"The dunes have eyes, man."

We slogged through the deep sand and walked single-file up the stairs to the deck. Red Butler dropped the quilt on an Adirondack chair. His tennis shoes clapped over the wooden planks. He reached down for a paper sack and pulled out a six-pack of Coors Light.

"Refreshments," he said and opened the door with his free hand. The dog shot into the house. The men hung back, doing their "ladies first" thing. I went inside. Red Butler headed to the kitchen.

"Be right back," I told Coop.

"He's okay, Teeny." He caught my hand and squeezed it. "He's always grumpy."

I was tempted to keep holding his hand, but I broke away and walked to the bedroom. I peeled off the bikini, changed into the brown dress, then went back to the living room. It was empty except for

T-Bone, who lay in a patch of sunlight. His ears perked forward, and a moment later Red Butler walked through the dining room holding a beer. He pushed his sunglasses on top of his head. His eyes were a clear, sharp topaz rimmed with stubby gold lashes. The upper lids were flat and straight, as if drawn with a ruler, making him seem alert.

"Where's the boss?" he asked.

"Don't know." I sat at the far end of the sofa.

Red Butler burped. He lifted the bottle and took a long swig. I couldn't believe this rough man was a detective. He seemed like he'd be more at home at a racetrack, placing bets on my guilt or innocence. *Ten dollars says the filly killed her boyfriend.*

T-Bone's ears slanted, and he let out a muffled woof. When Coop emerged from the hall, he was tucking a pale green shirt into cutoff khakis.

"Beer's in the icebox." Red Butler lifted his bottle. "Get you one?"

"Maybe later."

"Suit yourself." Red Butler shrugged. "After I tell you all the shit I found out, you'll need the whole six-pack."

"What'd you turn up?" Coop sat down beside me.

A smile flitted across Red Butler's rumpled mouth. He swaggered to a leather chair and sat down so hard the cushion squeaked, then took a long pull from the bottle. "It's been a wild morning. The coroner ruled Mr. Jackson's death a homicide."

The room began to spin. I leaned back, trying to remember where I'd put my handbag. I opened my mouth and gulped air. Coop put his hand on my leg. "You okay?"

"I need my inhaler."

He patted my leg and got up. He disappeared into the bedroom. Red Butler tilted his head. "Why you need an inhaler?"

"Asthma."

"A cousin of mine has that," Red Butler said. "She's a nervous Nellie, too."

"Whatever," I said, but he'd hit a nerve. When I'd lived on the farm, I'd stashed inhalers everywhere, the way drug addicts hide pills.

"Sure, it's physical." He laughed.

Coop returned with my manila envelope. I dug out the Ventolin, shook it, and depressed it. I held my breath, grimacing as my throat filled with bitter vapors.

"Don't get all wheezy on us," Red Butler said. "I saw the preliminary autopsy report. Mr. Jackson died from a gunshot wound to the chest. Official cause of death is exsanguination. You know what that means, girlie?"

I gave silent thanks to *Law & Order* and nodded, but I couldn't say the words: *bled to death.* "You sure he wasn't shot in the head?" I asked. "It was bleeding."

"A postmortem wound." Red Butler took another swig. "That means the dude was dead before he hit the ground. A scalp wound would gush like a motherfucker, but only if the motherfucker was alive." He shrugged. "Dead, not so much."

Coop lowered his eyebrows. "Anything else?"

"I'm just getting started." Red Butler took a sip of beer. "The deceased had a woman in every zip code. Over in Edisto, a shrimper's twenty-year-old daughter says Bing Jackson is her baby's daddy. So your girlie isn't the only one with motive."

"Bing fathered a child?" I cried. "Is there a woman in South Carolina who hasn't slept with him?"

"Prolly not," Red Butler said.

"Where is my dog?" I asked, not caring if I sounded heartless.

"It's at the humane shelter," Red Butler said.

"Oh, Lord." I drew in a breath. "They aren't going to put him to sleep, are they?"

"Hell, no." Red Butler cracked his knuckles. "Not unless you don't claim him."

"Coop, I need to go."

"Sure, I'll drive you," he said.

"Not today, you won't." Red Butler glared. "The shelter is closed. You can fetch the pooch tomorrow."

"Don't worry, Teeny." Coop touched my hair. "He'll be fine."

"I don't know about you peeps, but I ain't fine," Red Butler said. "I need something stronger than beer. Where you keep the hard stuff, Boss?"

twenty-one

While we drank gin and tonics, Coop and Red Butler discussed my housing situation. They agreed that I shouldn't stay at the Spencer-Jackson House, but when Coop insisted that I stay with him, Red Butler shook his head.

"You're just asking for trouble, Boss," he cried.

"Look," I told them. "Miss Dora gave me a key. The house is loaded with antiques. I was house-sitting for her."

"She can hire someone else," Coop said.

"If you won't let me stay there, I'll have to find an apartment."

"So get one," Red Butler said.

"It's not that simple." I felt the heat rise to my face. "I've got to watch my pennies."

"What's Miss Dora's connection to the Spencer-Jackson?" Coop asked.

"She decorated it."

"That's a non sequitur, Teeny." Coop grinned.

"And she was married to Bing's daddy. She's a Jackson."

"Now that Bing's dead, will his property go to her?"

"I don't know. Apparently Bing's got a sister." I paused. "Look, I don't like the Spencer-Jackson House, but it won't hurt if I stay a day or two.

I can't go back to Bonaventure. I'm trapped in Charleston. I don't have a job. I'm looking, but it's scary."

Coop gave me the key to his Mustang. He and T-Bone followed in the truck, with Red Butler lagging behind in a white van. I turned down Palm Boulevard, then veered right onto the Isle of Palms Connector. As I sped through the marsh, shorebirds flew up in dark commas. Bing had kicked me out of the Spencer-Jackson House. If he knew I was headed there now, he'd rise from the mortuary slab and haunt my ass.

When I turned onto East Bay Street, the "For Sale" sign gleamed in the afternoon light. I parked at Adgers and got out of the car. I hurried across the street and unlocked the entrance gate, trying to shake the feeling that something was off kilter.

T-Bone's nails ticked over the floor as he ran into the hall, trailed by Coop and Red Butler. Both men gazed up at the curved staircase. "Nice digs, girlie," Red Butler said.

I dropped my keys into the bowl. "It's the funniest thing," I said, "but the keys to this house went missing the other day. I'd put them right in this bowl. But after the air conditioning men left, the keys were gone."

"You think the HVAC men got them?" Red Butler asked.

"No. Maybe." I looked at the staircase. Saffron light fell through the arched window and hit the paintings, throwing shadows over the frowning women. What had disappointed them? Bad hair days or bad men in their beds?

"You see that beige Camry down the street?" Red Butler pointed to the window. "Two of Charleston's finest are on a stakeout."

"I don't like this," Coop said. "Why don't I leave T-Bone with you?"

"I'll be fine," I said, hoping I sounded brave.

"Plus, I'll be in my van," Red Butler said. "I'll keep an eye on your girlie."

"I'm only fifteen miles away." Coop picked up my hand. "I'll call when I get home—wait, what's your number?"

"Don't call," Red Butler said. "Line's tapped."

"Give it to me anyway."

I found a notepad in the hall table and wrote down my number.

"While you're at it, here's mine." Red Butler handed me a business card. RED BUTLER HILL, PRIVATE INVESTIGATING SINCE 1980. "Just let me check the house for little green HVAC men, and I'll be off."

"Wait." I tore off a piece of paper and started to write down my number, but he waved. "Got it already. Thanks."

He headed upstairs, presumably to check closets and under the beds. Coop opened the back door and peered into the garden. T-Bone loped over the grass. Coop whistled but the dog wouldn't come.

"Don't worry, he can't get out," I said. "The garden is walled. Wait, there's a gate in the back. Just let me check and see if it's shut."

"Hold on." Coop put his hand over mine. He pulled me into the garden, around the hydrangeas, into a shadowy corner. "When this is over, I'm taking a long break," he said. "Let's stay in bed for a month."

He pressed me against the stucco wall. It was still warm from the scorching heat. His hands moved under my hair, up to my face, and he kissed me. His belt buckle pressed into my stomach. We broke for air, then he covered my lips with short, sweet kisses, each one ending with a satisfying smack. The sounds floated around us like tiny peeping birds.

T-Bone nuzzled between us, his tail thumping against my leg. I heard whistling. It was coming from the second floor. I glanced up. Through the dense net of branches, I saw movement, and a corner of the iron balcony railing.

"Anybody down there?" he called.

Coop pulled back.

"Hey, T-Bone," Red Butler called. "Where's the boss? He down there?"

Coop tilted his head. "Can't you see us?"

"No," Red Butler said, leaning farther over the rail. "Sheesh, you better not be bumping no-no parts."

Coop pulled me against his chest and kissed all around my mouth. I laughed.

"He can't see us," I whispered. "We're invisible."

Above us, the balcony door creaked shut. I leaned against Coop. "We've got less than a minute to do the no-no thing."

I slipped my tongue into his mouth. He tasted so sweet. My hands moved up to his ears, into his hair. He broke the kiss and pulled back.

"He's coming down the stairs." Coop took my hand and we walked back to the house.

"House is clean," Red Butler said. "No boogeyman. And stop holding hands."

T-Bone trotted into the foyer, and Coop shut the door. "Do you have an alarm?"

I nodded.

"Use it."

"You better shove off, Boss. And take the dog. Or the dicks will wonder if you're banging her. That's never a good thing, having them wonder."

"Dicks?" I asked.

"Cops." Coop squeezed my hand. "I'll see you in the morning."

"Bring coffee," Red Butler called.

I walked them into the brick corridor. They stepped past the iron gate and split in different directions. T-Bone trotted next to Coop as they walked by the beige Camry. I locked the gate and went inside. I rushed around the first floor, closing the wooden shutters. I felt gritty from the beach but was too scared to take a shower. Visions of *Psycho* kept running through my head. I was glad Hitchcock had made that movie in black and white.

I went upstairs and looked out the hall window. The white van was parked at the end of the block—illegally, if Miss Dora had been right about the prepaid parking spaces in this posh neighborhood.

The beige Camry hadn't moved. Police didn't have to worry if they took a rich person's slot. If I were rich and saw Red Butler in my parking space, I'd let him stay. You wouldn't want to get on his wrong side. But I was. He didn't like me; I could tell.

The street was filling with blue twilight. Over the rooftops, I saw the harbor, but I was too tired to enjoy the view. I walked to the pink toile room and patted the coverlet. I hadn't thought I'd ever see it again. I thought about calling Miss Dora, but if my phone really was tapped, it could get ugly. She'd give the police an earful of anti-Bingisms. I'd just wait till tomorrow and pay her a visit, explaining about the tap and asking her to write a note that made it legal for me to stay at the Spencer-Jackson House.

I shut my eyes and tried to make my mind relax but it twirled. My girlish heart had loved Cooper O'Malley forever. This was punishment, a karmic bitch slap for not loving Bing and Aaron the way I should have. A crazy logic was at work, and it had caused me to sleep with the wrong men because I'd abstained from sleeping with the one I'd truly wanted.

But I'd fixed that, right?

Coop phoned twice. Both conversations were short and bland, just a lawyer checking on his client. When the phone rang a third time, I was almost asleep. "Hey," I said.

Silence.

I sat up, my elbows digging into the mattress. "Hello?" I said. I heard traffic noises in the background. I glanced at the phone. It didn't have a caller ID display.

"Anyone there?" I said, trying to sound tough. The line clicked. Red Butler and the police were watching the front door, but anybody could sneak into the backyard. I thought about getting up and cooking something called I Didn't Kill My Boyfriend Cake with I'm a Suspect Icing. I crept out of bed and pushed a dresser in front of the door. Not that it would help, but if someone broke in, they'd make a world of noise.

If you really and truly wanted to kill someone, all you had to do was stick a cigarette up their rear end. No kidding. I saw this on Discovery Channel. The nicotine causes a skippy heartbeat, and the victim stops breathing. Another way to kill someone is with bacon deviled eggs made with homemade mayonnaise. I'd learned this at Food Lion. Botulism can take hours to grow. It causes a toxin, I forget what it's called, but the victim suffocates. It's the same thing as Botox, which just goes to show that a good thing can be a bad thing. It just depends on how it's served.

twenty-two

The following morning, I put on a blue plaid sundress and brushed my hair into a ponytail. I wanted to look extra sharp because I was picking up my bulldog. I'd need to buy a leash, dog food, and treats, but I was running low on cash.

I called Bonaventure Savings and Loan and had my honeymoon money—$2,500.67, to be exact—transferred to First Charleston Bank. But I was stuck in South Carolina until December, and my savings wouldn't last that long. I had no choice but to sell Aunt Bluette's farm. I called Lakeside Realty in Bonaventure and asked for Betty Masters. She'd belonged to Aunt Bluette's sewing-and-prayer circle and she wasn't the type to ask questions. When Betty picked up, I almost burst into tears. To distract myself, I pinched my arm.

"I'd like to put the farm on the market," I said.

"I figured you would, seeing as you're getting married and all," she said. "But the farm is in bad shape. It'll take a while to sell in this economy. You might have to take a rock-bottom price."

"All right," I said, wiping my eyes on my shirt. Selling the farm at any price was enough to give me the heebie-jeebies. "But I'm stuck in Charleston. Can you mail the contract?"

I made a cup of tea. A little while later, Coop showed up with a bag of McMuffins.

"How'd you sleep?" he asked.

"Better than I thought." I reached for a McMuffin. "But I did get a hang-up call."

"Could be a wrong number," Coop said. "Are you still wanting to pick up your bulldog?"

"I was just fixing to go."

"I'll take you."

"I can drive myself."

"I'm not questioning your ability, Teeny. Whoever murdered Bing was in his house when you showed up. I've got to assume they're running loose around Charleston. Maybe he—or she—is getting paranoid. Maybe he's worried you saw him."

"I wish I had."

"Before we get Sir, let's stop by Miss Dora's," he said. "I'd like to get a written statement from her. Otherwise, you can't stay in this house."

We drove up to Queen Street. Coop parked around the corner, and we walked to Miss Dora's house. The hipped roof peeked through the trees, and the sun hit the copper chimney pots. As Coop and I got closer, I saw scaffolds on the pavement. A painter squatted by an olean-der tree, mixing paint. The iron gate stood open, and I could see into the corridor. It was just like the one at the Spencer-Jackson House, but the red walls made it darker.

I was mindful of the Camry nosing along the sidewalk, so I didn't grab Coop's hand. I stepped into the narrow passage and two words blinked behind my eyes: criminal trespassing. Never in my life had I worried about breaking the law—I'd been a Baptist teenager and had grown into a lie-counting adult. Now I questioned everything.

I stopped one of the painters. "Is Miss Dora home?" I asked.

"Is she ever," he said.

Coop and I passed into the courtyard with its cherub fountain and iron patio furniture. At one end of the house, the French doors stood open. Miss Dora's shrill voice rose up and she strode into the hall, her rosy silk caftan billowing. She was trailed by Estaurado and a painter with bushy eyebrows.

"Pink!" she said. "For the last time, pink!"

The painter scooted ahead of her. "But Mrs. Jackson, pink's bad for resale."

"You say pink like it's a four-letter word," she said.

"You need permission from the historical foundation to change your colors," he said.

"Pshaw. Those hysterics can jump in the harbor." She whirled. Her eyes widened when she saw me. She flung open her arms, and her bracelets clinked. "There you are! I've been worried sick."

She air-kissed my cheeks and gave Coop an admiring glance. "Sorry for the mess and confusion. I've decided to sell this grand old dame. But it's going to take a whole lot of cosmetic surgery."

"But you love this house," I said.

"I do, but it's just too big. It cries out for a large, rambunctious family. At my age, I need a little pink cottage overlooking a marsh. No yard, no upkeep. No worries. No committee picking my color scheme. It's the wrong time to sell, but I'm old. I can't wait for the economy to improve."

"Miss Dora, I wanted to thank you for posting bail."

She waved her hand, setting off another series of jingles. "The least I could do. Did you go back to the Spencer-Jackson?"

"Can we talk?" I looked around and lowered my voice. "In private."

"Oh, dear. This sounds serious." She crooked her finger. "Come this way, duckies."

Coop lagged in the hall, shuffling his feet. "I'll just stay here, if you don't mind."

"Suit yourself, darlin'." She took my arm. "This is getting more mysterious by the second."

She led me into the kitchen. It was a formal, majestic room. A crystal chandelier hung from a pink ceiling, casting rosy light on the marble counters and tall white cabinets. She reached for a carton of eggs.

"Estaurado bought these at a farm in Summerville. I was just going to make an omelet. Are you hungry?"

"I just ate."

"This won't take a second. Talk to me while I cook." She opened the carton, but it was empty. "That Spanish bastard got to them first. Estaurado! Get in here, pronto."

He appeared in the doorway, his face pinched and sallow.

"Estaurado, I'd planned to eat your damn *huevos*. Give them to me now."

"No, no," he cried and spread his hands over his privates. "*No comas mis huevos!*"

The painter walked up, laughing. "Miss Dora, you just told him you were going to eat his testicles for breakfast."

"Oh, for heaven's sake," Miss Dora cried. "Estaurado, don't flatter yourself. Come with me, Teeny."

We walked into the drawing room, which was all done up in raspberry chintz. She closed the pocket doors, then sank into a plaid chair. "Between the painters and Estaurado, I just don't know how much more I can take. But never mind me. Tell me everything that's going on, and I do mean everything."

"I'm back at the Spencer-Jackson. Coop was wondering if you could put it in writing that I'm house-sitting your antiques and I have your permission to stay."

"My pleasure." She walked over to her French desk and pulled a sheet of pink paper from a drawer. "After all, that house is part of the Jackson estate, and I *am* a Jackson."

"Detectives are watching me," I said. "They followed me here. And my phone is bugged."

"The police are fools. I'm not scared of them one bit." She scribbled a note, signed her name with a flourish, and stuffed the page into a pink polka-dot envelope. She added a thick stack of money and pressed the envelope into my hand.

"Oh, no, ma'am." I pushed the envelope back. "You've already been way too generous."

"Take it. You're broke." She spread her arms. "Broke, broke, *broke!*"

"That's what Renée Zellweger said in *Jerry Maguire.*"

"And she was right, wasn't she? Old Jerry Maguire was broke. So are you. Take the money, darlin'. It's not that much, just a few hundred. Bake me a key lime pie, and we'll call it even."

"I'll be happy to bake you a pie, but I won't take your money."

"Yes, you will." She fit the envelope inside my blouse.

"Miss Dora, why are you so good to me?"

"Well, first of all, I feel terrible that I didn't warn you about Bing. That boy never treated you right. Second, you are Gloria made over. I always took care of Sister, and I want to take care of you, too." She patted my cheek. "So just let me do my thing. I know you're proud and want to pay your own way. But I can help there, too. I'll make a few job inquiries. I know you're worried about your phone having a bug, but if I hear anything, is it okay to call?"

"If it's about a job, sure."

She stood. "Where you off to?"

"I'm fetching Sir. He's at the pound."

"Give him a big old hug from me."

Coop spent the day with me. First, we picked up Sir, who smelled like pine needles. Then Coop invited me to his house for dinner. We headed over to Isle of Palms, losing the Camry in the bridge traffic. We stopped at the Red & White Grocery to buy steaks and dog food, taking care to leave the windows cracked.

The store was crowded with weekend shoppers, most of them wearing sunglasses and flip-flops. Coop pushed the cart over to the meat counter. "Why don't you let me cook supper tonight?" he asked.

"You cook?" I smiled.

"I get by." He leaned over the case and shuffled through packages. "You like T-bone or New York strip?"

"Both."

"Maybe you can share your cooking secrets?" He grinned and looked past me. His eyes rounded, and the smile morphed into a frown. I turned and saw a woman with long, glossy brown hair that fell past her shoulders, straight except for a slight curl at the ends. She was tall and thin, with curves in the right places.

"Hello, Cooper," she said in a British accent. She angled her cart next to his. She wore beige slacks and a crisp white blouse that showed a hint of cleavage. "Having a cookout, are we?"

When he didn't answer, she lowered her sunglasses, showing bluish green eyes.

"Yeah," he finally said.

"You always were gifted with charcoal," she said. She reached past him, into the meat case, and grabbed a filet mignon. "You shaved your beard. I rather like it."

Coop tossed two steaks into our cart. Without looking up, he said, "When did you get back?"

A loaded question, to be sure. I tried my best to analyze it. It could mean, *I thought you were visiting your sick mother in Greenland.* But I hoped it meant, *What part of I never want to see you again did you not understand?*

"Not too terribly long ago," she said. "I'm staying on Sullivan's Island."

I was praying she'd add, *with my cute lover.*

"Staying long?" Coop asked.

Her eyes cut to me, then to Coop. "Indefinitely," she said.

He looked down into our cart. I looked, too. Food defines people just as clearly as their taste in clothing and their interior design. Miss

Dora and I had discussed this a lot. Our cart overflowed with carby things: garlic French bread, potatoes, fresh corn, and a bakery sour cream cake that I planned to turn into a trifle. To our credit, we had a box of strawberries for the aforementioned trifle.

Quick as a flash, I looked into the British woman's cart. Two lemons. Bottled water—not in plastic containers but in dark green, foreign-looking bottles. A bag of lettuce, and not just any lettuce but a Euro blend with bitter endive. I swallowed around the lump in my throat. Damn this woman and her bitter greens.

She extended her hand. "I'm Ava."

"Teeny." I shook her hand, but it took all my strength not to give her the stink eye.

Her eyes swept from my hair to my feet and back up. With that one look, I could tell that she'd eliminated me as competition. Please let her be his long-lost sister. It didn't seem likely that he had any relatives in England, or I would've heard about it. Although, back in Bonaventure, the O'Malleys had celebrated their Irishness with huge St. Patrick's Day parties.

Coop's silence told me all I needed to know. Please let her be a bitch. A man-eating, out-for-herself, doesn't-wear-panties bitch. She wore a ring, but not on the married hand. It wasn't a diamond, but a twisty gold ring with pearls, something an evil fairy godmother would use to gouge people's eyes out.

"Are you still enjoying the beach?" she asked.

"Yes," he said.

I tried to control my face, but from the way Ava was staring, I knew I'd failed. This was my cue to gather up my dignity and leave, tossing out a comment like, I'm out of here, the stakes are too high.

All the bits and pieces of my personality began to talk at once. My logical self said, *Fight or flight, what's it gonna be, Teens?* Thanks to my criminal record, and my undecided punishment over trespassing, fight wasn't an option. Nor was flight.

Ava looked away from me and smiled at Coop. He stared back, and I could have sworn that the store's overhead lights dimmed.

"We're in a rush," Coop said. "Take care."

He steered the cart away from the meat counter, down the baking aisle. I shot her a final glance, but she wasn't looking at me. Her eyes were latched onto Coop. I strode ahead and started piling items into the cart. Flour, sugar, vanilla, baking chocolate, confectioners' sugar.

"I guess you're wondering who she is," he said, eyeing me warily.

"Not really," I said and tossed in a Betty Crocker cake decorating kit. I turned. Ava was still staring. I grabbed a brownie mix and a bag of chocolate chips. I felt an urgent need to make triple-layer brownies, just the thing for sour thoughts and a worried mind.

Coop leaned forward and rested his arms on the cart, watching me toss in items. "What're you fixing to cook?"

"Sweetness," I said. "Lots and lots of sweetness. But I need cream cheese."

"I'll get it," he said. Before I could protest, he walked to the end of the aisle, where Ava was still standing. He took a sharp left toward the dairy department. I fought the urge to scurry after him. A homegrown girl like myself couldn't defend him against a goddess.

He caught up with me at the checkout. I was flipping through a fashion magazine, scanning articles: "Lose the Belly Fat!" "Do Cellulite Creams Work?"

"I can explain," he said.

"Not here." I tucked the magazine into the rack and loaded our items onto the conveyer belt with excruciating slowness. Ava glided into the next lane. With her few items, she checked out in a heartbeat and didn't look at us as she started toward the exit. A hush swept through the grocery as she carried her plastic bag, the two lemons hanging low in the bottom like she was carrying a man's balls. The electronic doors parted, and she floated through.

I was on fire with curiosity, but I tried to act nonchalant as we piled our bags into a cart and hurried out of the store. My poor dog was standing in the window, ears perked forward, watching for me. Two rows over, I saw Ava sitting on a motorcycle, tucking her hair into a helmet. Her puny shopping bag was nowhere to be seen. I bet if I stripped her down, I'd find all kinds of tattoos—*I Ching* symbols, hieroglyphics, or naked Mayan figures. Maybe she even had a heart on her ass with COOP written in the center.

She revved the engine. The motorcycle blasted across the lot.

Coop and I climbed into the truck, and Sir began to squeak with delight. My plan was to act calm, no questions, just let him talk. Instead, I blurted, "Take me home. I'm not feeling good."

He turned toward his house.

"Coop."

"Just hear me out," he said.

Lord, this sounded serious. *Hear me out* was what men on death row said before the lethal injection. I hugged Sir. Part of me wanted to listen, but another part craved silence. One thing was certain: I didn't want to be trapped at his house after he admitted his relationship with this she-wolf.

I wanted her to be a one-night stand, not someone he'd loved.

But what had she meant about him being good with charcoal? No, she'd said *gifted* in a way that hadn't meant food.

A pensive look crossed Coop's face as he pulled into his driveway. He shut off the engine and stared out the windshield, rubbing the top of his head. Through the windshield, the sea oats moved back and forth.

"Just spit it out," I said.

"Ava is my wife," he said.

twenty-three

I grabbed my dog, climbed out of the truck, and started toward the house. Fine, I'd just call a taxi. I wasn't mad; I was scared. History was repeating. Only Coop wasn't going back to his old girlfriend, he was being reined in by his beautiful wife.

Behind me, I heard his door slam. The wind was picking up and the sea oats ticked. Dark, bruised clouds piled over the water.

"Teeny, wait. It's not like you think. We're separated."

I stopped walking and turned. "For how long, O'Malley?"

"Almost a year."

"Why didn't you tell me? And please don't say 'I was going to.'"

"But I *was* going to."

"Sir's getting hot," I said. "He can't breathe in this heat."

"Hold on, I better put T-Bone on the screened porch," he said, unlocking the door. "He likes other dogs, but he's mighty big, and you just never know."

He went to find T-Bone. I carried Sir into the hall. For a teenaged bulldog, he was a tad on the heavy side, almost sixty pounds, and I was breathless when I reached the kitchen. I set him on the floor and started looking in cabinets for a bowl. I could hear Coop talking to T-Bone, telling him to be gentle with Sir. Then he put the enormous beast on the porch with a large chew bone and shut the door.

When Coop stepped into the kitchen, I was still looking for a bowl. I'd never seen so many cabinets in a kitchen. Not even the Spencer-Jackson House had this many.

"What you need, babe?" Coop asked.

"A dog bowl." I pulled off my shoes and set them on the floor. He opened a bottom cabinet, grabbed a metal dish, and filled it with water. He set it on the floor next to my shoes. Sir began to drink greedily.

Coop leaned against the counter. "The marriage is over, Teeny. I wasn't hiding anything."

"Why does it feel that way?" I asked.

"I'm sorry."

"I thought you were all about the truth. Is there anything else you've forgotten to tell?"

"No."

"But you were surprised to see her."

"She's been on a dig in Sudan." He paused. "It's a dangerous region." So he cared. "A dig?" I asked.

"She's an archeologist. We met in England. She was a protester when ground was broken for terminal five at Heathrow Airport."

"What was she protesting?"

"It's an important archeological site. I was on her defense team."

"It took a whole team?"

"She wasn't the only protester." He folded his arms. "She has nothing to do with us, Teeny."

"I need air," I said and walked to the living room. I opened the French door, stepped across the deck, and ran down the steps. The walkway was so hot, it burned my feet as I raced to the shoreline. I crossed my arms and gripped my elbows, concentrating on the exact point where the sky and water blurred together.

"Teeny!" Coop yelled.

I turned. He sprinted toward me, kicking up sand. My thoughts moved in circles. He'd dropped Barb and took up with me. Then he'd dumped me for Barb. She got left behind and years later, he hooked up with Ava. Had he left her, too?

His hand closed on my arm. "A storm is coming," he said. "Let's get inside."

"You go." I pulled away.

"I'm not leaving." His hand moved again toward my elbow, and I stepped back. Lightning zigzagged across the sky, dividing it in half. Then it began to rain. Fat stinging drops hit my arms and shoulders and gouged the sand all around us. My sundress felt cold against my bare skin, but I couldn't move. I bowed my head, and my hair swung forward.

"Teeny, come on."

The rain fell at a slant, sweeping across the beach. The waves rounded, tipped with foam, and exploded against the sand. A tall wave slammed into my hips, pushing me against him. Coop grabbed my shoulder, and I jerked back. My teeth clicked, not from the sudden cold but because I was going to cry. I bet Ava never cried.

"I'm not in love with her," he said.

"Then you should've told me about her."

"I was going to. But I didn't want to ruin things." Water dripped off his chin. He was so drenched, I could see his skin through his shirt. He grabbed my hand and pulled me against him.

"I'm falling for you all over again, Teeny."

I wanted to believe him but couldn't. I didn't want to spend the next decade mooning after him. I squirmed away. "Your groceries are melting," I said and walked back to the house. As I approached the kitchen, Sir skidded around the corner, jowls flapping, and slid to a stop. Poor little fatherless bulldog. Bing had loved him truly. The dog stood on his hind legs and licked my hands—right hand, left hand, back to the right.

By the time Coop returned, I'd found towels in the laundry room.

I set one on the counter for him. He put down the groceries, lifted the towel, and rubbed it over his head.

T-Bone was still on the screened porch off the dining room. When he saw Sir, he stood on his hind legs, revealing a furry white belly. He looked more like the abominable snowman than a dog.

I sat on a bar stool. The house was chilly, and my wet clothes made me shiver. I rubbed my forehead. I'd jumped in bed with him too fast— the exact opposite of what I'd done in the old days. Back then, I hadn't jumped fast enough.

"Who left who?" I blurted, wondering if I should've said who left whom?

"It's not that simple, Teeny." Coop ripped the plastic off the steaks and set them on a wooden board.

I waited for him to continue. He opened a cabinet and pulled out jars and boxes. Sea salt, pepper, meat tenderizer.

"You got any espresso beans?" I asked. "If so, I'll make a rub."

"Sure." He looked relieved because the topic had shifted to food preparation, but he didn't know me. If I didn't chop, fry, or dice, I'd have a conniption fit. Cooking was the only way to calm down. I'd witnessed Aunt Bluette's gentle guiding hand with Mama, controlling her excess energy through productive kitchen work, so it was only natural that I would use food as a stress-reduction tool.

He moved to another cabinet and pulled out a bag and a grinder. I opened the bag and sniffed the beans. I thought I detected a fruity aroma. "Are they flavored?" I asked.

"No." He laughed. "Why?"

"Raspberry espresso makes a horrid rub."

"The beans came from Ethiopia," he said.

I thought of Ava and her Sudanese dig as I ground the beans and shook them into a glass bowl. "I need chili powder and Hungarian paprika, if you've got it." I paused. "So, why did you and Ava separate?"

"We grew apart."

"Why?"

"You ever ask easy questions?"

"Not when you're answering my questions with a question." I paused. "Did she have a lover?"

"What makes you think that?"

"She looks the type."

"No. At least, I'm pretty sure she didn't."

"Did you have a mistress?"

"Hell, no. How can you ask that?"

"Easy. You're married to her and you're screwing me." Just like he'd been dating me and screwing Barb.

I poured the spices into the bowl and stirred them with a fork. I pointed to the meat. "While I'm doing this, could you rinse the steaks and pat them dry with a paper towel?"

"Why? To make the rub stick?"

"Well, yes, but it just freshens up the meat. Washes off the grocery goop. So, if nobody was unfaithful, what went wrong? And don't say 'we drifted.' It's got to be more than a drift." I blinked. "Where's your sugar?"

He kissed me.

"Not that kind," I said.

"I love how your mind works, Teeny. Like a bird hopping from twig to twig, never losing sight of the worm." He handed me a twisted bag of brown sugar. I shoved a spoon inside. I hated being compared to a bird. Bing hadn't liked my brain. He'd accused me of being simple, but I could focus when I had to. Like now. I wanted to know more about Coop's marriage and his dashing, motorcycle-riding bride.

"Tell me about Ava," I said. "Tell me everything."

I added a pinch of sea salt and a grind of pepper. Then I dragged the fork through the seasonings. Coop pulled up a stool and leaned against the counter.

"Can we talk about this later? Because I hate to go from making sweet love to you to my problems with Ava."

The way he said "problems" gave me hope. My mind filled with wildness. Maybe Ava smoked crack, suffered from bulimia, or followed a strict macrobiotic diet. You couldn't be that thin and eat much.

"You're going to have to tell me sooner or later." I lifted a steak and dredged it in the bowl, patting the mixture into the beef.

"I wanted to practice law here in the Low Country, and she wanted to live in England. So we shuffled between her house in Wiltshire and Charleston."

"And the Wiltshire house was filled with her obnoxious relatives?" I smiled.

"No, they're all dead. It was me and her and sixty-three rooms."

"Wow. So, she's rich?"

"Yes."

"I was kinda hoping she was a gold digger."

"Her cousins thought I was."

"And they drove a wedge between you?"

"No."

"Then what?" I flipped the steaks, sending up a cloud of rub.

"This is embarrassing." He rubbed his forehead. "She expected me to sit home and shoot clay pigeons while she skipped from one dig site to the next."

"Why didn't you go with her?"

"Oh, I tried. For a while. At first, I liked it. All of that history. Then the novelty wore off. I broke her concentration."

"You were in the way?" I was thinking along the lines of, Please god, let this be it, even though I was having trouble seeing him as a long-suffering husband.

"It felt like that, yes. When she was working, she gave it her full attention. I went back to Wiltshire."

I couldn't imagine a hot-blooded man like Coop sitting beside the fire with hunting dogs, playing cribbage with the butler. "Are you sure you didn't fool around?"

"Never came close."

"Because you loved her, right?"

"Yes." His brows came together. "Then Uncle Ralph died. Ava and I flew home. We stopped off in Charleston for a few days. I ran into a friend from law school, and the next thing I knew, I'd agreed to work part-time—in Charleston. Ava pitched a fit, but it seemed like a good solution for us both. She could play in the dirt and I'd play with torts. And I could plan my schedule around hers so we could play together."

"And y'all broke up?"

"Not right away. She flew in and out of Charleston. We rented a place at Seabrook."

I nodded. A picture was forming of a posh, la-di-da she-explorer who refused to give up her career for love—or the man who'd done backflips to please her.

"I practiced law in Charleston," he said. "She stayed at the resort, golfing and horseback riding. She learned to sail. She enrolled in a fire-arms class. And she took flying lessons."

On a broom, I thought spitefully.

"She got her pilot's license. We went to parties and art galleries and restaurants."

"Sounds heavenly."

"The social scene bored her. She called Charleston the land of deep-fried magnolias." He shook his head. "She thought my friends were pretentious and shallow. Funny, I'd thought the same thing about the crowd she ran with in Wiltshire and London. But it was more than that. She missed the dampness of England."

"It's wet in South Carolina," I said.

"Yeah, but England is home. The wetness over there is more like a glaze. Perfect for her roses. She tried to grow them here, but the thunderstorms beat them to a pulp. So she got bored and went to the desert."

"To punish you?" I asked. "Or does she like contrasts?"

"Both, I think."

"Oh," I said, but I thought, Please, if there's a god in heaven, let her have a bedouin lover. A dark Biblical guy with a beard and a robe.

"Now you know the gist of it," Coop said.

"Does gist mean all?" I glanced over the counter, into the dining room. Sir was licking one side of the glass door, and T-Bone was licking the other.

"She flew back and forth, from Charleston to wherever."

"And?"

"I got tired of it. One of my pretentious pals drew up divorce papers. She came home all lovey-dovey, and refused to sign. I thought maybe we had a chance. Then she was gone within the week."

"And now she shows up at the Red & White Grocery, when there are perfectly nice supermarkets on Sullivan's Island," I said.

"She likes to charge full bore into everything—even a divorce. See, whatever she's doing at the moment gets 100 percent of her attention."

"You said you wanted me to know everything."

"And I do."

"Keep talking." I dredged the other steak in the rub. He still wasn't telling everything about him and Ava. He was telling me what he thought I could handle. I refused to get all bent out of shape over his love life. What kind of crazy logic was at work here? Quirky astrology, stars in the wrong places, or bad luck? Sure, I was talking trash. Aunt Bluette would be so disappointed, but I needed to get it out. If I didn't, I'd swear to god I'd burst into flames.

"Would you have told me about Ava if we hadn't run into her?"

"Yes."

"She wants you back."

"It's impossible to know what Ava wants."

"What do *you* want?" I understood the why of his marriage. I understood the why of their separation. I got all that. Two gorgeous, highly educated people from good families—hell yes, they'd fall in love.

"Like I said, you ask hard questions." Coop smiled.

"You're sopping wet," I said. "You'll catch your death if you don't put on dry clothes."

"You're wet, too." He held out his hand. "Come with me?"

"I need to cool off." I kept dredging the steaks. When he left the room, I spread my hands across the counter and knocked over the salt shaker. Mama used to say if salt spills, it means evil is nearby. At the very least, you'd cry one tear for every grain you'd spilled.

I flipped a few grains over my left shoulder. Okay, fine. He had a wife, sort of. But it was over. I found a frying pan, set it on the burner, and added a pat of butter. Just because I was a "more is more" girl, I threw an extra pinch of salt over my shoulder.

twenty-four

It was still raining when Coop drove me back to the Spencer-Jackson House. He walked me to the door, acting proper for the benefit of the detectives, but he gave me long, meaningful stares. Since I was facing the unmarked car, I clasped my hands behind my back to keep from pulling Coop into my arms.

"Call if you need me," he said over his shoulder as he headed back to the street.

I went inside and shut off the alarm. Then I ran to the window and watched his taillights move away from the curb. Would he call Ava, or let it slide?

After I set my keys in the bowl, I walked to the kitchen and turned on the little television that sat on the counter. *Dragonwyck* was playing, and Vincent Price had just added deadly oleander to his first wife's cake.

While I watched the movie, I flipped through Uncle Elmer's *Joy of Cooking*. There wasn't a single recipe that suited an almost-ex-wife. I'd just have to write my own anti-Ava recipe. I opened a kitchen drawer, grabbed a pen, and found a blank page in the back of *Joy of Cooking*. Then I jotted down a recipe called Skewer Your Ex Kabobs. I imagined cubed pork, chicken, pineapple, kiwi, and peaches, along with thick slices of red and green bell peppers.

Find a bowl and mix olive oil, peach wine vinegar (or bottled salad dressing), and salt and pepper to taste. Pull on disposable gloves and make a skewer, using two oleander branches. Strip the leaves and add to olive oil mixture. Steep at least three hours to mingle flavors, and to infuse oleander. Baste fruit, vegetables, and meat with olive oil mixture. Sprinkle with kosher salt and pepper. Assemble kabobs, alternating meat, vegetables, and fruit, taking care to alternate the colors. Grill until browned. (Spread tinfoil over surface of grill to prevent unintentional seepage of oleander marinade.) After the meal, gather the skewers, serving plates, and any leftover marinade. Place into paper bag. Bury the bag.

Miss Dora showed up early the next morning. I led her through the brick corridor into the garden. "Hope I'm not disturbing you, but I was horrified to call," she said.

"I was just fixing iced tea—would you like a glass?" Sir was stretched out in the grass, watching Miss Dora with interest.

"No, no, I'm fine. I stopped by because I've found you a sort of job. And you won't even have to leave you. First, I've found you a sort of job. And you won't even have to leave home. I know the owner of The Picky Palate. Jan's got terrible taste in furniture, but she's got a business mind. She can't be beat making pâté, either. She needs a ghost baker."

"You've lost me."

"That's a hired cook who bakes dishes for money. The restaurant—or, in this case, Jan—pays the cook and takes credit for the dish. Apparently, The Picky Palate is overwhelmed with special order desserts. That's where you come in."

I tilted my head, trying to imagine such a job.

Miss Dora barreled on. "Like I said, you don't have to leave home. Jan will give you the orders. Y'all can discuss how much she'll pay you. 'Course, you'll have to supply the ingredients and all. Don't tell her I said so, but Jan's desperate. A lot of cooks don't like this setup because it's advantageous to Jan. She'll charge her customers twenty-five dollars for a layer cake, but she'll pay the cook fifteen dollars. If you've put a dozen eggs into that cake, and fresh Meyer lemons, you'll lose money."

"Sounds dicey."

"Could be. But if you're a smart shopper, you might turn a profit."

I nodded. This wasn't perfect. A fifteen-dollar cake wouldn't buy gas money for Coop's Mustang, much less pay the electric bill for this humongous house, but it was a start.

"Fabulous," Miss Dora said. "I'll take you to meet Jan right before the funeral."

"Funeral?"

"That's the second part of my news," she said. "The coroner released Bing's poor old body. The funeral is tomorrow at noon. I would've consulted you about the flowers, but child, I didn't know where you were. Not to pry, but where *were* you? With that Cooper fellow?"

"Yes."

"He's sticking to you like a seed tick."

"We picked up Sir. Then we cooked steaks."

"Your fiancé isn't in the ground and you're out gallivanting with your lawyer. That's not like you, Teeny. Not like you at all." She stepped closer. "I know it's not my place to offer advice. But I'm just worried sick. The gossips will paint you as a wicked harpy."

I reached down to pet Sir's wrinkled head. "Harpy fits," I said, "but not wicked."

We walked into the foyer, and Miss Dora stopped beside the table. She leaned over to examine the crystal bowl, then ran her finger over the rim. "Did you ever find that key, darlin'?"

"Not yet."

"And I don't guess the police returned your clothes?"

I shook my head.

"Don't those idiots know a thing about a woman and fashion?" She looked up from the bowl. "You'll need a sedate dress for the funeral.

And not that ugly brown sack you wore in court. The service will be graveside. The Episcopal priest will say a few words. Don't be shocked if Bing's girlfriend shows up. Trash like that always makes a scene. Just ignore her."

"Yes, ma'am."

"I'll pick you up tomorrow morning. Oh, say, around nine?" She frowned. "And please make your cute lawyer stay home—unless you want the gossips to think you killed Bing for a handsomer man."

Later that morning, I drove the Mustang to my favorite thrift shop. The beige Camry followed at a discreet distance. I shot them a glance as I opened the door. With Ava's supermodel attire firmly in mind, I found a simple black dress for five dollars. I also found a white blouse and straight black pants, two dollars each.

Next, I went to the big dollar store and bought baking staples for my ghost cooking job, along with cute black-and-white shoes. Then I hit the condiment aisle, loading up on cooking oils, spices, and extracts.

As I drove toward the Battery, I felt the pull of the Spencer-Jackson. The house was creeping up on me, seducing me with iron curlicues, secret alleys, rose petals on cobbled walkways, and the tolling bells of St. Michael's.

Lord, I loved it all. I loved the play of light on the stucco and how it changed from ice pink to peach to Pepto-Bismol. I loved the buildup of purple clouds over the harbor. I imagined myself coming down the oval staircase in a white, frothy gown with Coop waiting at the bottom. I could raise a family here, and I could almost hear the light, tapping footsteps of children and dogs as they ran across the heart pine floors. It was straight out of a forties movie. Girl meets house, girl loses house, girl falls in love. *Miss Templeton Finds Her Dream Home.*

I set the groceries on the island and stepped into the garden for lavender. Uncle Elmer had installed speakers all over the house, even on the patio, and the doorbell was hooked up to it. Now, it rang with a vengeance, with gongs reverberating all over the yard. I liked those bells. No one could sneak up on me. Sir tipped back his head and howled.

Still holding the lavender, I ran back into the house, grabbed my keys from the bowl, and hurried into the brick corridor. It was always cooler out here. A breeze rippled over my blouse as I walked toward the iron gate.

A woman with long brown hair stood on the other side. She reached up to adjust her floppy white hat. The draft caught her dark hair and blew it away from her shoulders. It was Ava.

twenty-five

I stared through the iron bars into Ava's face. God, those cheekbones. I'd been hoping a sandstorm had come up in the night and buried her house. Despite the heat, my arms broke out in gooseflesh.

"Hello, Teeny," she said with a cut-glass English accent. The wind lifted the edges of her long white linen dress, showing firm, tanned legs. She lowered her sunglasses and smiled. Despite the noon heat, she looked like a bride who'd just emerged from an air-conditioned limousine.

I unlocked the gate and stepped onto the sidewalk, blocking the corridor.

"You don't remember me, do you?" she asked, looking amused.

"You're Ava." I glanced down the street but didn't see her motorcycle.

"Is this a good time for a sit-down?" she asked. Her accent cut through me like a pâté knife slicing into foie gras. Miss Dora had served that at the engagement party, and Bing had explained what it was and how to pronounce it. I'd spit it out when he wasn't looking, thinking of the duck that had sat in a cage, force-fed until its poor liver swelled, only to end up at Miss Dora's party.

I blinked at Ava, certain that she suffered no food qualms. Her full lips parted, showing straight white teeth. Even if she'd had pancake lips and eyes no bigger than capers, she'd still be gorgeous. I drew my lips over my teeth, mindful of the gap, which now seemed like the Grand Canyon of dental flaws, and wondered how I could get rid of her—not a literal riddance, like with rat poison, just a temporary one.

"Can I take a rain check?" I waved at the corridor, as if chaos lurked behind the stucco walls. Even to my ears, I sounded rude but I didn't care.

"It's frightfully important," she said.

As she strode past me, I smelled musk and mock oranges with a touch of lily of the valley—a potent poison, by the way, even in minute quantities. She tossed her hat onto a bench. Her face was all eyes and cheekbones, the lips full and natural, with a hint of gloss. She had what Aunt Bluette used to call "presence."

I sighed, wondering if I should show her to the pink living room, with its cushy chairs, or into the kitchen. The kitchen, definitely. I opened the pocket doors and led her into the dining room, past the sun-slashed walls, into the butler's pantry, with its tall white cabinets filled with china, every imaginable serving piece. I opened another pocket door and walked into the kitchen and set the lavender on the counter.

"I just got back from the grocery," I said, waving at the mess on the island.

Ava peeked into a bag and lifted a bottle of olive oil. "Two dollars for extra virgin?" Her right eyebrow moved up. "You're quite the bargain shopper, aren't you?"

So, this was how it was going to be. I pulled the bottle out of her hands. She stared at her empty palm, then at the bottle, as if she could mind-bend it out of my grasp. In the back of my head, I could hear Aunt Bluette clucking her disapproval, reminding me that Jesus not only forgave His enemies, He fed them.

"Can I get you a cold drink?" I set the jar on the counter.

"Whiskey would be lovely."

A drinker, I thought gleefully. I opened a cupboard and poked around. "I may not have any alcohol," I said. "I haven't lived here long. Care for a Diet Coke instead?"

"May I have a glass of water?" She pronounced water like "porter." Her bracelets tinkled as she leaned across the counter. Her arms were toned and tanned. I imagined her lying on a striped beach towel, the wind streaming through her hair. Then I imagined her wearing a halter top, digging her way from Egypt to South Carolina.

Now what? A heart-to-heart about Coop or a discussion about extra virgin oil versus regular? I looked past her, at the French door, where Sir was pawing the glass. "Are you enjoying Sullivan's Island?" I walked to the door and opened it. Sir ran to his water bowl.

"Quite." She smiled at the dog.

Quite? What kind of badass, short word was that? I dumped a bag of flour on the counter, and white powder drifted up. "How did you find me?"

"Don't look so frantic. I haven't stalked you. Well, perhaps a little. Red pointed me in your direction."

She got to call him Red?

"Please don't be annoyed," she continued. "He and I are old friends."

I could've guessed that. Her reflection floated in the granite counter.

"Mind telling me why you're here?" I asked.

"Well, since you asked." She smiled. "Are you shagging my husband?"

"Why don't you ask him?"

"Well, I could, but Cooper hates emotional chitchat. It took him forever to admit he loved me. I don't imagine he's professed his devotion to you, has he?"

I shoved a bag of frozen peas in a cabinet, then I pushed a flour sack into the freezer.

"Didn't think so." She folded her hands, her fingers moving like a daddy longlegs. "By the way, is there a reason you keep frozen peas in the cupboard?"

"They're defrosting," I said. Lie number fifteen.

"And the flour?" She traced her finger along the counter.

"Keeps the bugs out." Not a lie, but I marked it up as one anyway. Number sixteen. She was baiting me. Anything I said would be used against me; then it would be used to hook Cooper. It was awful tempting to give a few X-rated details, but Aunt Bluette had taught me the value of silence. She used to say, "Loose lips sink ships."

I stared back at Ava and smiled a mysterious smile. Let her stew, let her wonder.

"Possum got your tongue?" she said in a faux Southern accent.

"Not in a while," I said. She looked like the type who'd crush a man's balls and replace them with neuticles.

"Have you known my husband long?" she asked.

Soon-to-be–ex-husband, I almost said but caught myself in time. "All my life," I said. "I grew up in Bonaventure, Georgia."

"Are you the majorette?"

"Nope," I said. "Wrong girl."

"Glad we got *that* sorted." She pushed away from the counter. "If you're shagging him, don't worry. I won't break your knees. Or throw fruit."

"That's a relief." I blinked. So, she knew about the incident in Bing's yard. Damn Red Butler Hill and his big mouth.

"Although the idea of throttling you *has* crossed my mind," she said.

"Back at you."

"Backatyou?" She looked puzzled.

"Ask Red Butler. He'll know." I paused. "Let's be really real. Why are you here?"

"I want to save my marriage."

"You're talking to the wrong person."

"No, I'm not." Her eyelids fluttered. "The Bar Association frowns on attorney-client shagging, doesn't it?"

"You should know."

"You're a bright spark. I see why Cooper likes you." She winked. "This could end with handbags at dawn."

"Excuse me?"

"It's a British saying. A duel of sorts." She pushed away from the counter. "Surely it won't come to that."

"Hope not." The bitch was scaring me.

"If you cross me, I'm a formidable enemy." Her eyes narrowed for an instant. "I never lose."

That afternoon, I found a broom and swept the corridor, wishing it was this easy to push Ava from my mind. I was just getting into a rhythm when a masculine voice called, "Yodelayheehoo."

I looked toward the gate. Red Butler stood on the other side of the iron bars. I set the broom aside and started toward him.

"Have you noticed that Winnebago?" he asked and pointed over his shoulder at a huge RV with a bumper sticker that read MY CAT IS SMARTER THAN YOUR HONOR STUDENT.

"Once or twice," I said.

"It was parked on East Bay last night," he said. "Know who it belongs to?"

"No." I unlocked the gate and we walked into the house.

"Hey, girlie," he said. "Your ex's funeral is tomorrow."

"I know."

"You going?"

"Of course." I opened the pocket doors and stepped into the kitchen. While I found two mugs, he started lecturing about funeral protocol, insisting that I should act proper and ladylike and not make a scene.

I was so insulted, I couldn't keep my hand steady as I poured coffee. But if I blasted him, I'd prove I was uncouth. Aunt Bluette hadn't raised me to be ill-mannered.

I set out cream and sugar and sliced some coffee cake. Red Butler reached for a hunk and chomped down. When a man is chewing, he's almost as vulnerable as when he's making love. I decided to pounce.

"Ava stopped by," I said. "But I guess you know that."

He swallowed, then tipped the sugar bowl over his mug. "I figured she would," he said.

I slipped a small bite of cake into my mouth and tried to frame my words. I knew they'd be repeated to Ava, but I couldn't control myself. "Why is she in town?"

"Ask her yourself." He set down the empty sugar bowl and reached for the cream. "Any more questions, girlie?"

I stuffed a bigger piece of cake into my mouth to keep from asking if Coop still loved Ava and if I should just give up and find me a kick-ass woman lawyer who wouldn't hire a biased gumshoe to watch over me. I washed down the cake with a swig of coffee, then I said, "Tell me about Ava."

"You're the PD's top person of interest, and you want to know about another woman?" He laughed. "She's not one of them women who say, 'What are you thinking? Are you mad at me? Do you love me?'" He lifted his mug. "You that kind?"

"You don't like me, do you?"

"Why you think that?"

"You don't call me Teeny. You call me girlie."

"I'd like you a whole lot better if you'd quit tempting the boss with your no-no parts." He dumped cream into the mug. "He's a damn good man, and a sharp lawyer. I don't want him disbarred because of a cute lawyer-banger."

"Is that what you think?" I lowered my mug.

"You jumped into his bed, and you barely know him." He studied the back of his hands. "Plus, you got over Bing Jackson mighty fast."

"I have a history with Coop."

"Yeah?"

"We grew up together in Bonaventure, Georgia. He was my first love."

"And your first lover?" Red Butler's eyebrow went up.

I shook my head.

"So, he was the handsomest man you never fucked?"

"That's a crude way of putting it."

"I don't care if you was blood brothers," he said. "Quit messing with him."

"I don't take orders from you."

"Do what you want. I'm out of here. And by the way, girlie, your coffee ain't worth a shit." He slammed his mug on the counter and walked toward the pocket doors. From behind, his broad chest tapered to narrow hips.

Just like a bulldog, I thought. "Hey," I called. "Was it something I said?"

"Fuck you," he said over his shoulder.

"Not even if you begged," I called back. He answered by slamming the door.

twenty-six

The next morning, I lay in bed, staring at the toile wallpaper. Then I pushed the covers aside and got ready for Bing's funeral. My thrift-shop outfit was a far cry from the brown dress that I'd worn in court. I put Sir in the upstairs bedroom with his KONG toy and walked downstairs. I went through the rigmarole of locking the doors, but these precautions were useless if someone had stolen the key chain.

I tried not to think about crazed repairmen as I walked outside and waited for Miss Dora. The RV was parked across the street. The top of the vehicle was crammed with camping gear, all of it tied down with rope. The sun glanced off the chrome and sent up a blinding glare. One large bumper sticker caught my attention. It showed an X-ray and the large caption read HERE'S WHAT DECLAWING WOULD DO TO YOUR HAND.

The driver's seat was empty, but the RV gave off plaintive meows. I was relieved when Miss Dora's Bentley pulled up. I climbed inside. The chilled leather felt good against my legs.

"Sorry I'm late," she said. "But you wouldn't believe the mess at my house. Those painters are evil. Everywhere they go, they leave spatters. They're like having birds flying loose in a room. You doing all right, darlin'?"

"I've been better. I don't like funerals."

"It'll be over in a heartbeat. I just wish the painters worked as fast."

She drove through Rainbow Row and cut down Water Street. Then she shook her head, as if pushing away images of parakeets bombing her silk curtains, and glanced at my dress. "You look precious."

"So do you," I said. Although precious wasn't the right word. She was the epitome of style, but cute. Her black silk suit was elegant, but the pink and black polka-dot blouse was pure fun. On her tiny feet were black pumps with pink dots.

"The funeral's not for an hour," she said. "We've still got time to swing by Jan's store."

She turned onto Meeting and drove to Broad. Then she pulled into a lot next to The Picky Palate.

"You'll just love Jan," she said. "Who knows? This may be the start of a fabulous food career."

"I can't think about the future too much."

"Oh, yes you can. That's why I brought you here—to smother your inborn pessimism and to plant a few seeds of hope in that dry-as-dirt heart of yours."

As we stepped into The Picky Palate, Natalie stepped out, holding a sunflower and clear plastic box. Salad. What else? Miss Dora saw me staring and said, "What's the matter?"

"That's Natalie."

Miss Dora turned all the way around to stare. "Why, I don't see a thing but a giant tart. After all, this *is* a bakery."

Our footsteps slapped on the rough wooden floor. The walls were lined with shelves that overflowed with raffia-tied jars—gourmet jellies, lemon curd, pickled okra. Interspersed among the shelves were bins of fresh flowers, sea-grass baskets, modern pottery mugs, and boxed mixes for cheese straws. Along the back wall were glass cases where people

were lined up. A sign on the wall read TODAY ONLY: FRIED GREEN TO-
MATO SALAD WITH CORNBREAD CROUTONS.

Jan Hightower-Lowe was a skinny, windblown woman with a freck-
led face and red hair pinned into a bun. She wiped her hands on her
apron after Miss Dora introduced us.

"Glad you stopped by," Jan said, shaking my hand. "I was going to
call you later. I've got a backlog for special-order cakes."

She turned to a desk and pushed aside food catalogues and old
issues of *Saveur* and *Bon Appétit*. She grabbed a legal pad and thrust it
into my hands. The page was divided into three columns. Each one
listed a type of dessert, due date, and the customer's price.

"Since you're new," Jan said, "I'll give you an easy assignment."

"Okay." I nodded. I could handle easy.

"I need two dozen red velvet cakes by tomorrow afternoon." She
raised her red eyebrows at Miss Dora, as if to say, We'll see how she works
out before I put my reputation on the line.

Twenty-four freaking cakes? I didn't have enough flour or pans, not
to mention food coloring. I'd have to stock up at the dollar store.

"Can you handle it?" Jan asked.

"Yes, ma'am. And thanks." Translation: If I have to stay up all night,
I'll bake you the best damn red velvet cake you ever tasted.

"Your cut is six dollars per cake."

"But . . ." I looked at Miss Dora, then at Jan.

Jan shrugged. "I know it's not a lot. But I'm only charging twelve
dollars per cake. I'm giving you half. If your cakes are suitable, I'll think
about doing sixty-forty."

"Oh. Okay." Suitable? Did that mean no artificial vanilla? I reck-
oned it did. If I cut corners, I'd be out of a job.

"You'll need to box the cakes." Jan handed me two dozen white card-
board sheets. "They're not hard to put together. Any questions?"

I shook my head.

"Great. See you tomorrow." Jan smiled. "Glad you're a part of my team."

Miss Dora steered her car into the shady cemetery. Cars were parked on both sides of the lane. When I spotted the hearse, a cold clammy feeling started in my chest and moved down to my feet. I cracked open the door and a blast of pine-smelling heat swirled into the car.

Miss Dora climbed out of the Bentley and walked around to my door. She opened it wider. "Come on, darlin'," she said. "We can't put this off."

I started to get out of the car and the ground spun.

"You all right?" Miss Dora cried. "Because you look ghastly."

"I'm okay." I sat back down.

"You sure?" She grabbed my hands. "You're freezing."

"Just give me a minute." I shut my eyes, thinking of Aunt Bluette's funeral and how Bing had stood off to the side, his eyes hidden by designer sunglasses. Now he was going into the ground.

"Darlin' girl, don't be so gloomy." Miss Dora patted my shoulder. "I wanted to spare you from the uncomfortableness of a funeral. I tried to have the body cremated, but Mr. Turner acted like I'd stripped naked and was getting ready to do a lap dance. Mr. Turner's the mortician. So I opted for a simple graveside service. Just try to get through it, because all eyes will be on you."

"Yes, ma'am." Just what I needed to hear. I dragged myself out of the car, wishing I'd bought a wide hat with a veil. I didn't even have sunglasses. I'd left them at Coop's house. I picked my way through the grass. Straight ahead was a maroon tent. A few people were sitting in metal chairs. They gaped up at me as I walked inside. I was going to sit in the back, but Miss Dora grabbed my elbow and steered me to the front row, dead center.

"Be a brave girl," she whispered, stretching out the *a* in brave. She patted my shoulder. "Stay right here. I'm just going to speak to the priest."

Father Williamson's crinkled face lit up when he saw Miss Dora bearing down on him. Behind me, the mourners shifted in their chairs. More people arrived, real estate agents mixed with upstanding citizens with three last names. They seemed unsure of the protocol, whether it was proper to treat me like Bing's girlfriend, offering heartfelt platitudes and a slew of "I'm so sorry's," or whether I should be shunned as a murderer. They just offered polite nods and moved down the aisle. This was Charleston, by god. The people might have lost the war but not their manners.

In the distance, I saw Estaurado drive by in an old finned Cadillac. Miss Dora gave me a cheer-up nod as she made her way down the aisle, thanking people for coming. She had a way of putting people at ease, and I could feel them loosening up. Several conversations started at once. Nothing about death or homicide, just banter about children and grandchildren, tennis games and book club meetings, parties in the past and parties in the future. They weren't being disrespectful. Their voices were a gentle reminder that death was part of life, and life moved along, whether or not we were ready.

A hush fell when Natalie walked up looking glamorous in sunglasses and a floppy hat with black netting. She clutched the giant sunflower from The Picky Palate and made a big show of setting it on top of the casket, which already had a tasteful pink spray.

Natalie gave me a wide berth and cut around to the back of the tent. Had she loved Bing? What if they had been made for each other, and I'd just been a fool in the way?

Estaurado walked up, looking positively scary with his pointy beard and shiny black suit. The fedora had been replaced with a black, broad-brimmed hat. He tipped it at Miss Dora, then took his place in the back where there was standing room only. All the metal chairs were taken, and the crowd spilled out of the tent onto the grass.

Even Red Butler showed up. He leaned against a loblolly pine, near a throng of Mount Pleasant and Charleston detectives. Bing would've been proud at the turnout. The breeze wafted over the many wreaths and flower baskets that circled the casket. Even that damn sunflower would have made him smile. I glanced over my shoulder at the mourners' calm faces and squeezed my purse, wishing it included a self-destruct button.

"Oh, my god," Miss Dora said.

I turned, half expecting to see a body rising from the casket, an undead Bing with fangs. But the coffin was sealed tight, and the floral spray was intact, as was the sunflower. Nevertheless, Bing was headed straight toward me—not a vampire Bing, but Bing in drag.

A straw boater cast a shadow over his face as he surveyed the crowd. He stepped forward, and his tight black dress lifted over his nubby knees. It was the sort of edgy dress a preteen might wear, but way too small. A dress like that cried out for spiked heels, but Bing's feet were stuffed into Birkenstocks. In each white-gloved hand, he gripped a huge black patent duffel bag with mesh sides. One of the bags meowed; the other bag twitched and then emitted a lower, raspy meow.

Behind me, people were whispering. Apparently I wasn't the only one who'd thought Bing had risen from the dead and brought cats to his own funeral. I slid down in my seat—not because I was going to faint, but because I didn't want him to see me.

Miss Dora grabbed my hand. "Don't act foolish," she whispered. "It's Eileen, Bing's sister."

The meowing got louder as the sister walked toward me. When she stopped, she set the cat cases on the ground and began tapping her fingers together, starting with the thumbs and working to her pinkies. Then she reversed the order. After she did this three times, she started in with her eyes, shifting them three times to the right, three to the left.

I thought of a man in Bonaventure who did this sort of thing—he'd suffered from obsessive-compulsive disorder, only he washed his hands umpteen times a day. I looked at the woman's gloves. I'd bet you good money her hands were red and chafed.

"Howdy do, Dora poo," the woman said.

"Eileen," Miss Dora said with a curt nod.

"Don't rush off after the funeral, Dora." She tapped her fingers again, then reached for the cat cases. "You and me, we've got unfinished business."

"I'll try," Miss Dora said.

"Try hard." Eileen nodded at me.

"You must be my brother's murderer."

"Lower your voice," Miss Dora said, glancing over her shoulder.

Eileen gave me a malignant stare, then drifted down the aisle accompanied by plaintive mewing. She stood in the rear, next to Estaurado.

"She's mentally ill," Miss Dora whispered out the side of her mouth. "I'll tell you all about it later."

A bumblebee floated over the casket while Father Williamson delivered the eulogy. His words were bland as unsalted soup, without any mention of young lives being cut short. That was a relief. When the service ended, the man from the funeral home shuffled over to me and Miss Dora and escorted us out of the tent. I could see Eileen struggling to reach us, but her giant cat carriers had caused a logjam.

"We've just got one more thing to do," Miss Dora whispered. "We've got to see Bing's estate lawyer; then you can put this day behind you."

"What's the dirt on Eileen?" I asked after we settled in the car and she started the engine. I aimed the air conditioner vent in my direction and leaned toward the cool air.

"Oh, honey. That could take years." Miss Dora leaned over and adjusted the vent, returning it to the original position. "Eileen has OCD—you know what that is?"

"Yes, ma'am."

"I guess you saw her tapping her fingers? And those gloves? Well, she's a washer—she has scrubbed the hide off her poor hands. Not only that, she's a checker, a counter, an arranger, and a hoarder. She's got that

RV packed with newspapers, back issues of *Cat Fancy*, and a thousand dresses that no longer fit her. Mostly she hoards cats. She gets obsessed with a breed and goes on a mission to find one. The minute she gets it, she's off to the next breed. She's got Siamese, Persians, Maine Coons, and the hairless Sphynxes. 'Course, that was years ago. Who knows what she's got now?"

"What does she do with them?"

"Goes to cat shows. Last I heard, she was breeding show quality Siamese. But I don't see how she can live in that damn Winnebago with a million cats. There it is, under that oak tree."

She pointed at a white RV plastered with familiar-looking bumper stickers. This was the same ratty RV that had been parked on East Bay Street. I started to mention it, but she cut me off.

"You can just imagine the filth. You can't get cat pee out of anything. But that's not why Rodney Jackson disowned her."

"What happened?"

"It didn't take a whole lot to make Rodney Jackson angry—Bing was the same way, as you found out." She pursed her lips as she drove around the hearse. "Eileen fell in love with an oyster shucker named Benjamin Dover. He was an ex-con: manslaughter and bank robbery. The shock of it nearly sent Rodney into the hospital. He couldn't have his only daughter marry a criminal with an unsuitable name. Why, the shame of it made him crazy."

"How can a name be unsuitable?"

"Think about it, darlin'. Ben Dover? Eileen Dover?" She lifted one eyebrow. "Rodney Jackson said it was a disgrace. He said she'd be the laughingstock of Charleston, unable to have personalized stationery. I had to agree with Rodney. How in the world could Eileen send engraved party invitations? Mr. and Mrs. Ben Dover cordially invite you to a party? I don't think so. Rodney demanded the boy change his name, but Ben was proud of his lineage. He claimed he'd traced his people back to the famous White Cliffs of Dover. Not that Rodney believed that for a second."

"But if Eileen loved him, why did Mr. Jackson care about something so trifling?"

"Because it wasn't trifling to him. The ex-con part was frightening to us all. But Rodney was a petty man. He put a great store in appearances. I took pity on the girl and sweet-talked Rodney into letting the girl get married. It took some doing, but Rodney finally agreed. We cleaned Ben up—shaved his beard and put him in a Thomas Pink shirt. Then Rodney got the boy a job at the real estate firm—doing what, I've no idea."

"So they got married?" I asked.

"Yes, but not the way we'd imagined," Miss Dora said. "Eileen and I planned a Valentine's Day wedding at the French Huguenot Church. Everything would've been fine if Eileen had wanted bridesmaids. But she wanted to lead her goddamn cats down the aisle. She promised it would be tasteful. She even had white satin harnesses made for the felines. When I told Rodney, he canceled the wedding. Eileen and Ben eloped."

"Surely Mr. Jackson didn't kick her out of the family for that," I said.

"That happened later. After Eileen got sent to jail."

"What did she do?"

"Ben robbed a 7-Eleven and she drove the getaway truck. Well, that was it for Rodney. He called the estate lawyer. Knocked his own flesh and blood out of her rightful inheritance. And left it all to Bing. Now, the crazy cat lady is back in town." Miss Dora glanced at me. "Just take care of yourself, Teeny. No one is safe around Eileen."

twenty-seven

The sun was dipping behind the trees when we drove past The Citadel and pulled up to the lawyer's office.

"You're a great driver, Miss Dora," I said. "How did you learn your way around Charleston? I've been here nearly six months, and I still don't understand the one-way streets."

"It's easy to find your way, darlin'. Charleston is shaped like a giant pecker, and North Charleston is the tight little ball sack. Once you figure that out, driving is a snap."

We stepped into the building. The sign in the lobby had fifty thousand surnames. Miss Dora drew her finger under QUENTIN K. UNDERHILL and led me down the hall. The secretary escorted us to a conference room with a long table.

"Mr. Underhill will be with you momentarily," she said and shut the door.

"This decor is making me nauseous," Miss Dora said, glancing at the navy blue walls. They were covered with old maps of Charleston. We sat down. A moment later, the door swung open and a spidery, middle-aged man walked in. His narrow face was dominated by thick tortoiseshell eyeglasses. His brown summer suit waffled on his thin frame as he strode toward us. He set down an accordion folder and shook Miss Dora's hand.

"So sorry for your loss," he told Miss Dora.

"Thank you, Quentin," she said.

He gave me a long stare and sat down at the other end of the table. The accordion folder creaked as he pulled out papers. "Is your name Christine or Teeny?"

The way he said my name, you'd think it was toxic waste. "Teeny is my nickname," I said.

"Are you going to do a reading of the will?" Miss Dora asked.

"Lawyers don't actually read wills unless the family requests it. We mail them. Anyway, Bing didn't have a will. He had a revocable living trust, just like his daddy did." Mr. Underhill turned to me. "But I assume you know this?"

"No, sir." I shook my head. "I don't know what that is."

"It was set up to avoid probate." Mr. Underhill handed me a thick document. "Bing designated you as the trustee, along with the First National Bank of South Carolina as the successive trustee."

Miss Dora crossed her legs, the pantyhose swishing. "What does that mean?"

"That she inherits everything," Mr. Underhill said. "Bing had properties from North Carolina to Georgia, mostly along the coast. Now they belong to you, Miss Templeton. Well, except for one property. The Spencer-Jackson House on 99 1/2 East Bay Street. Just before Bing died, he sold that property to Miss Natalie Lockhart. She submitted a copy of the sale contract."

"Sale contract?" Miss Dora blinked. "For what?"

"For the Spencer-Jackson House," Mr. Underhill said. "As you can see," he added, "it was signed by Bing and Miss Lockhart on June fifth."

"The day after I hit them with peaches," I whispered.

"Pardon me?" Mr. Underhill leaned forward.

"Never mind that," Miss Dora said. "I'm all confused. Surely you're not saying that Bing sold the Spencer-Jackson?"

"I was surprised, too, but apparently he changed his mind." Mr. Underwood showed her the contract.

"I don't believe it." Miss Dora reached into her bag, pulled out a pink Kleenex, and dragged it over her forehead. "Bing would never sell that house. Never."

"Well, he did." Mr. Underhill blinked. "And the paperwork is in order."

"Let me see that document," Miss Dora said.

"It's notarized," he told her. "You can view the original at the Register of Deeds office. I've spoken with Miss Lockhart, and she has graciously allowed Miss Templeton to remain in the house for thirty days—or until the house sells."

"Graciously? Here we go again." Miss Dora rolled her eyes. "May I ask how much Bing sold the house for?"

Mr. Underhill's cheeks reddened. "$500,000."

"That's absurd," Miss Dora cried. "Even if Bing *had* changed his mind, he wouldn't have sold that house for a bargain-basement price. It's worth millions."

"I don't suppose we'll ever know the true story." Mr. Underhill folded his hands and pressed them against his chin. "Bing had scheduled a meeting with me next week, presumably to change his trust. But he was murdered."

"Maybe that woman sweet-talked him into selling the Spencer-Jackson House," Miss Dora said. "Or she got him drunk!"

"Do you have proof?" Mr. Underhill asked.

"Well, no, but—"

"If you find evidence of wrongdoing, I'll be happy to help you."

"I'm sure you would." Miss Dora glared at him. "Just make sure that an allowance is made available to this young lady. She's practically destitute. And she's fixing to start a cake baking business."

"It was my understanding that Miss Templeton is a suspect in Bing's murder. The trust can't be settled until her name is cleared, or until—"

"So, she won't get a dime until the police find who really killed Bing?" Miss Dora cried.

"I'm sorry."

"No, you're not," Miss Dora said. "What happens if she's found guilty?"

"The bank will be the sole trustee."

"What if she's found innocent? What then?"

"If this should happen, Miss Templeton would be a wealthy woman. A monthly allowance would be set up, of course. And if she wished to purchase property, she'd have to discuss it with the bank. They would, of course, help her manage the entireties."

"Entireties?" I asked. "What's that?"

"The Jacksons' properties," he said. "Strip malls, beachfront condos, office buildings."

"What's she supposed to live on until the trust is settled?" Miss Dora asked. "Can't you give her an advance?"

"That's up to the bank," he said. "And the justice system. But there's another problem."

"What?" Miss Dora rubbed her forehead.

"Mr. Jackson's sister is challenging the trust."

"Oh, come now, Quentin," Miss Dora said. "We went through this after Rodney died. Eileen challenged his trust—and you told her to ske-daddle."

"I'm merely advising you that it may be a while before the trust is settled."

Miss Dora and I got up to leave. On our way out the door, Mr. Under-hill said, "Remember, Miss Templeton. You can only stay in the house thirty days or until it sells."

Since Mr. Underhill's office was near the Ashley River, Miss Dora in-vited me to lunch at the Crab House. During the drive across the bridge, she was uncharacteristically silent, touching her pink nails against the steering wheel the way Eileen had tapped the cat carriers. Behind us, the beige Camry hovered at a distance.

We caught the Wappoo drawbridge when it was down and drove over the creek. Finally, she pulled into the Crab House parking lot. So did the Camry.

A waitress seated us next to the window. We ordered coconut fried shrimp with she-crab soup. Miss Dora's phone kept ringing, and she barked orders to her painters. "They did what?" she cried, and her face tightened. "Oh, for pity's sake. We'll discuss this later."

She threw the phone into her purse and grabbed the waitress's arm. "Darlin', bring me a pomegranate martini. Teeny? You need something?"

"I'm fine."

"Well, I'm not," Miss Dora said as the waitress bustled off. "The hysterical society is raising holy hell over my paint colors, inside and out. I should be allowed to paint my house purple if I want. Don't you agree?"

"Yes, ma'am."

"Life isn't like a box of goddamn chocolates, Teeny. It's more like pasta—curly as rotini, versatile as tortellini."

I dipped my spoon into the she-crab soup. It was thick, with orange roe and a hint of sherry. Almost every restaurant in Charleston offered she-crab soup on the menu, but the Crab House version couldn't be beat. I took my time, savoring each mouthful. If I had their recipe, I'd die a happy woman.

We shared key lime pie for dessert. As we were leaving, a sailboat bobbed toward the bridge. We got into the Bentley. Miss Dora hit the gas and swerved onto the road, shrouding the Camry with exhaust fumes.

"Let's lose those nitwits," she said and pointed at the bridge. "I bet I can beat that sailboat."

I wasn't so sure. I stared up at a yellow light and the drawbridge sign. The yellow light turned red, and a pole started to drop over the road.

"Oh, bother," she said and pushed her foot against the gas pedal.

"Miss Dora, no!" I cried.

"Oh, poo," she said and mashed the pedal harder.

In the opposite lane, traffic had stopped as the pole continued to fall. A red light flashed in Miss Dora's sunglasses as she sped under the barrier. The sailboat was almost to the bridge.

"Hit it, Bessie!" she yelled to her car and squeezed the steering wheel. I muffled a scream as the bridge cracked apart and started to rise. The Bentley zoomed up one half of the bridge, the tires singing on the metal seams.

"Stop!" I cried. "I'm getting out." My heart whooshed in my ears, and my lunch was trying to come up. I grabbed the door handle, ready to jump.

"Too late now." She hit the power lock. "They won't arrest me."

"Arrest? We could die!"

"Not with me behind the wheel."

"But—"

"Hush now, and let me drive."

Each half of the drawbridge inched up and up. My fingers dug into the leather seat. The Bentley rose into the air, leaped over the gap, and shuddered when the tires hit the metal on the other side. I shut my eyes as she drove down the still-rising ramp.

Her front fender broke through the pole. The pieces flew over the car and shattered against the pavement. "Tra la la," Miss Dora sang as she sped off the bridge.

"See?" She twirled one hand in the air. "Easy peasy. Sorry if I frightened you. But I lost your police escort."

"They'll catch up."

"They aren't the only reason I'm rushing," she said. "My supper club meets tonight at six thirty sharp. You just don't know how compulsive Mary Martha is."

"Mary Martha?"

"Supper club meets at her house tonight. Last year, her own husband

showed up late to the dinner. Dessert was being served, and she flat refused to seat him. He had to eat cake in the kitchen, and he's a big-shot
banker. So I wouldn't like to think what she'd do to me."

It was only one thirty, plenty of time to make that dinner, but I
didn't dare say so. Miss Dora wasn't a Charleston native, and she felt
as if she had to try extra hard to fit into the world she'd married into.

While she talked about the members of her supper club, rating their
decor, she headed back to Charleston. Minutes later, she stopped in front
of the Spencer-Jackson House. I looked everywhere for Eileen's Winnebago, but I didn't see it.

"Toodle-loo, darlin'," she said. "Have fun baking."

"I'll try," I said. For once I was glad to be climbing out of the Bent-
ley. My legs were still a little shaky from our race with the drawbridge.
I walked toward the palm tree, where the Jackson Realty sign jutted up.
When I got closer, I saw a red sticker: SALE PENDING.

twenty-eight

Miss Dora jumped out of the Bentley, leaving the motor running, and joined me beside the palm tree. We gaped at the Jackson Realty sign like it was roadkill.

"We need to find out the closing date," she said.

"What does it matter?" I shrugged.

"Because if they're closing soon, you don't have thirty days. Why, you'll barely have time to find an apartment. Although Bing has tons of rental property. Don't worry. I'll help you decorate your new place."

I nodded, but paint colors were the least of my woes.

She tapped her chin. "Maybe you should call your lawyer."

"Why?"

"He might know how to fix this. You know, delay the sale—at least until you're settled elsewhere."

She pushed her cell phone into my hand. I reluctantly dialed SUE-THEM and got a recording saying that Mr. O'Malley would be out of the office until next week.

"Well?" Miss Dora said. "Did he answer?"

"No."

"Let's go to his house. Get in the car, darlin'." She grabbed the phone. I'd never seen her this flustered. "Where does he live?"

"Isle of Palms."

"Maybe he'll be home."

"I don't want to go."

"Is there a problem?" Miss Dora asked.

"Well, no, but—"

"But what, darlin'?"

"He's probably not home. We shouldn't barge in."

"You're paying him. That means you're calling the shots." She steered the car with one hand and punched the cell phone's keypad with the other.

"Is this Billy Lee King's answering service?" she said. Billy Lee was her personal lawyer, a partner of the gin-rickied Mr. Bell.

"I don't care if he's boating," she cried. "You tell him it's a legal emergency and to call Dora Jackson or I'll hunt him down. You tell him that, you hear?"

Miss Dora hung up and made another call. I thought she'd wear out the keypad before we made it across the Ravenel Bridge. I was just thankful the old bridge was gone. The Old Grace had been the scariest bridge in the Carolinas, if not the world, with its two itty-bitty lanes. I had a deep fear of bridges, but the Ravenel wasn't scary. You wouldn't know you were on a bridge. Joggers and bike riders sped down a separate lane. The graceful white cables swept by, two diamonds glinting in the sun. Now that I was in a love triangle, I saw them everywhere.

We drove across the bridge, toward the Isle of Palm Connector. I stared out at the spartina grass and palmettos. A broad view opened up, and I saw homes on pilings and a wedge of blue ocean. I couldn't stop thinking about the trust. I didn't want a thing to do with it. Bing had died before he could change the trustee, and only the Lord knew who that would've been.

"Don't look so glum, Teeny. Frowning causes premature wrinkles." Miss Dora shook her head. "But you've got a right to be upset—Bing's whore has sold the house. And in this market!"

I could believe it. Shelter was a requirement even in the animal kingdom, and the Spencer-Jackson House was a real fine example. I could see why it would sell.

"How much farther is Coop's house?" Miss Dora asked.

"Once you get to the pier, it's a half mile."

"You've been here a lot?" She grinned.

"Here's the turn off," I said.

She pulled into his sandy driveway. His truck was parked at an angle, in front of Ava's motorcycle. "You didn't tell me he was a biker," Miss Dora said.

"I wish. The motorcycle belongs to his wife."

"His what?" She hit the brake. Sand filled the windshield, blotting out the house.

"They're separated," I said.

"Teeny, I'm shocked. Couldn't you have picked a single man for your lawyer?"

"Miss Dora, married men don't give off a smell. I thought he was single."

"I hope he's better at the law than he is with relationships." She pulled off her sunglasses and squinted at the motorcycle. "Look how close she's parked to his truck—not much separation. She's got him blocked. He couldn't leave if he tried. And if they're separated, why is she here?"

"'Cause she wants him back."

"Well, that's obvious. I hate to say this, but could he be a ladies' man?"

"I don't think so."

"Where does the wife live?"

"Sullivan's Island."

"I'll just bet her house is gaudy."

"I bet it's not."

She reached for her purse. "Should we go in? It's your call."

I was curious about Ava, so I climbed out of the Bentley and picked my way through the hot sand. I climbed the stairs, rapped on the door, and squinted through the glass panes. The foyer looked empty. My breath caught a little when Coop walked around the corner in tan shorts and a gray striped shirt. He looked scrumptious.

He opened the door and smiled. "Hey, I've been calling you," he said.

"And we tried to call *you*," Miss Dora called from the bottom of the stairs. "Teeny dialed SUE-THEM."

She looked at me and raised her eyebrows, as if to say, *major player*. Then she turned back to Coop and extended her hand as she climbed the stairs. "It's so nice to see you again, young man."

"Nice to see you, too," Coop said. "Come on in, ladies. Get out of this heat."

T-Bone suddenly appeared next to Coop, followed by Ava. She leaned against the doorjamb, arms folded. A tight little smile creased her face. She looked spiffy in a sleeveless black top and tight pants. She wasn't wearing shoes, and her toenails were painted a violent shade of red. Barefoot—my Lord, not a good sign.

Coop made the introductions. Ava shook Miss Dora's hand, then she smiled at me. "Lovely to see you again," she said.

Miss Dora dragged a pink tissue over her forehead. "I hope we didn't catch y'all at a bad time."

"Not at all," Coop said.

Miss Dora sashayed into the foyer. I shuffled behind her, trying to ignore the tightness in my chest. The house smelled feminine and sweet. When I passed by Ava, I recognized the source of that aroma: lilacs and ylang-ylang, with a hint of orange.

Miss Dora pointed to the tiny square windows. "Hugh Newell Jacobsen designed this house, didn't he?" she asked.

"I wouldn't know." Coop shrugged. "It's a rental."

"Yes, but with great style. Jacobsen is an architect. And *those* are his signature creations." Miss Dora pointed to the white bookcases in each end of the foyer.

"Love your black-and-white pottery," she added.

"It's his signature color," Ava said.

Coop shot her a look, then he smiled at me and Miss Dora. "Could I get you ladies something to drink?"

"Something with alcohol would be divine." Miss Dora dabbed the Kleenex over her chin. "And get Teeny a drink, please. My driving has scared that poor girl to death. But I managed to evade those policemen who're watching her."

"How'd you do that?" Coop laughed.

"I had a little help from the Wappoo drawbridge."

Coop led us into the living room, then disappeared into the kitchen. Ava cut around me and sank down on the leather sofa, tucking one long leg beneath her hips. The dog settled at her feet; his head level with hers.

"Pottery Barn," Miss Dora said, dismissing the sofa with a wave, then she sat down and smiled at Ava. "We've had a day and a half. Funerals, lawyers, and lunch. Have you ever been to the Crab House?"

"Many times," Ava said.

I perched on the edge of a chair and tried not to look at Ava, or how she was looping her long fingers through T-Bone's fur. Coop stepped around the corner, holding a tray with four wine glasses, the dark red liquid swaying. He handed one to Miss Dora, then stopped by my chair. Our eyes met. He winked and turned back to the sofa. Ava reached for her glass and thanked him. He sat down on the ottoman.

Ava lifted her glass. "Shall we make a toast?"

"Honey," Miss Dora said, "this isn't a toasting matter. Teeny's being kicked out her house again. And Bing's greedy sister is going to contest the trust. Is that what it's called—contest? Well, that's what Eileen's going to do. She's still upset because her daddy left his fortune to Bing. And now Bing has left it to Teeny."

"But he didn't mean to leave me anything," I said.

"It's not your fault he got murdered before he changed the trust," Miss Dora said.

Coop set down his glass and ran his hand over his hair. "I better call Red."

"Young man, this isn't the time to make phone calls," Miss Dora said. "You better find a damn loophole so Teeny can get her money. Or better yet, maybe you can get the judge to let her move back to her aunt's peach farm. That would solve all her problems."

"But it's out of state," Coop said, rising to his feet.

"Barely," she said.

A few days ago, I'd thought along these lines. I'd been hell-bent on going back home. It was that whole "I've got to get back to Tara" thing—fight, flight, or freeze. But I hadn't been thinking clearly. Returning to Georgia wasn't an option. Not only would I violate the terms of my probation but the farm was in bad shape. I couldn't bring in a peach crop this year or next. I'd have a roof over my head, but I'd still need five jobs to pay the utilities. Even if Bing's murderer was caught tomorrow, I wouldn't leave Charleston. I was in love with Coop, and I truly liked the Spencer-Jackson House.

"I'll just be a minute," he said and went to the kitchen.

"Where is he going?" Miss Dora twisted around in her chair.

"He's calling Red Butler," I said.

"Who?"

"His PI," Ava said.

"I hope he's a good one. But with a name like that, I can't help but wonder." Miss Dora drained her glass and looked at Ava. "Would you be a dear and get me a refill?"

"I'll get it." I rose from the chair, lifted Miss Dora's glass, and hurried to the kitchen.

Coop sat at the built-in desk, talking on the phone. "How soon can you get here?"

The wine bottle sat on a black slate island. I tilted the bottle over Miss Dora's glass, trying to eavesdrop as she quizzed Ava up one side and down the other. She was doing what Southerners do best, "placing" Ava in the small pond of the Low Country.

"Oh, I'm not a native," Ava said.

"Honey, I figured that out ten minutes ago," Miss Dora said. "What with your strange accent and all."

"*I* have a strange accent?" Ava laughed.

"Well, I shouldn't say strange," Miss Dora said. "More like an alligator's love call."

I didn't hear Ava's reply because Coop hung up and faced me. I half expected him to give me a real kiss, but he walked over to the sink and gazed out the tiny window. "Ava just showed up," he said.

"You don't have to explain." I refilled the glass.

From the great room Miss Dora called, "Teeny? Forget the refill. I've got to skedaddle."

I lifted Miss Dora's glass and took a sip of wine. Then I followed Coop to the living room.

Miss Dora stood. "I hate to drink and run, but I've got a million things to do before my supper club. Teeny, darlin', you ready?"

"Sure." I looked back at Coop. "Unless you need me for something?" Then I cringed. Damn, that hadn't come out right. I tried again. "I just meant, if you needed me to explain anything to Red Butler about the trust."

"That would be helpful." Coop nodded. "I can drive you home."

"I can take her," Ava said.

"No, ma'am," Miss Dora said. "She's not getting on the back of a motorbike."

"I'll see that Teeny gets home," Coop said.

"Personally?" Miss Dora tilted her head.

"Yes, ma'am."

He escorted Miss Dora to the Bentley, leaving me alone with Ava and T-Bone. She kept tracing her slender fingers over the sofa, drawing patterns in the leather. The silence made me nervous. I sipped Miss Dora's wine, then I said, "I've got to get home and bake two dozen cakes."

Ava made no comment. I took another sip of wine. "They're due tomorrow," I added.

"Sorry, you've lost me." Ava flipped her hair over her shoulders. "What's due?"

"Cakes," I said.

"What a relief." She laughed. "For a moment I thought you said conjoined triplets were due tomorrow."

Bitch, I thought and dug my nails into the leather chair. Why had I told her about my cakes? Why couldn't I keep my mouth shut? She didn't need the inside scoop on what I was baking or thinking; but after her crack about the triplets, I felt compelled to explain.

"The trouble is, I don't have a decent recipe for red velvet cake," I said. This was totally true. Now that I was faced with baking two dozen freaking cakes, only one cookbook would do, and not because I needed the recipe—I needed *Templeton Family Receipts* so I could go back to the Spencer-Jackson and make up another recipe about Ava.

Ava gave me a "Who Gives a Shit" stare. I glanced over my shoulder. Where was Coop? Still talking to Miss Dora? When I looked back, Ava was studying me like I was a clay shard she'd pulled from the dirt.

Careful, Teeny. Careful. She's not your friend. She's your rival. Tell her too much, your butt is going to jail. Just change the subject. Instead, I blurted, "See, I left all my cookbooks at my fiancé's house? One of them is an old family cookbook. I really, really need it."

I paused, wondering if I should mention the key I'd found at Bing's house. No, probably not. She gave me a penetrating stare. "Isn't your fiancé's house a crime scene?"

"It's kinda hard to explain. I really need that book. See, I'm making the cakes in bulk. Not all recipes double real good." I smiled, grateful she couldn't translate Teenyisms into regular English. I needed that book because it was full of make-believe evilness, penned by a whole slew of

Templeton women trying to improve their moods with pounded peach seeds and foxglove. I needed that damn book because, if the police found it, they'd use the recipes against me in a freaking court of law, even though I was totally innocent.

"What if I went with you to your fiancé's house?" Ava asked.

"You?" I tried to keep my face blank. Why would she go out of her way to help me?

"Why not?" She stretched her arms over her head. Long, lithe, tanned arms, not the least bit jiggly. "I haven't had an adventure in a while. I'm getting antsy, as you Southerners say. I'd love a little old-fashioned breaking and entering. And a crime scene!" She clasped her hands together. "I love it."

"One problem," I said. "The police are tailing me."

"That *would* be dicey." She ran her long fingers down T-Bone's neck.

I was having second thoughts. "Maybe Coop knows a way to get my books," I said.

"Don't ask him yet," she said. "He's such a law-abiding citizen. He'll go through legal channels, and by then, your cakes will be baked, right?"

"True," I said. And the baker will be in jail.

twenty-nine

After Coop returned, he made a red pepper omelet. Ava stared out the window and did little gestures with her hand, as if she was having an argument with herself.

Her concentration seemed to dim when Red Butler Hill showed up. His combat boots left sandy footprints as he walked across the room and set a six-pack of beer on a desk. He straightened his tuxedo jacket, then reached for a bottle.

"Love your outfit," Ava said. Instead of wearing formal trousers, he'd opted for cutoff denim shorts.

He gave her a two-finger salute and sat down beside her. "Hey, beauty," he said, pointedly ignoring me.

Coop stepped out of the kitchen, holding a spatula. "Hey, Red. You hungry? I fixed an omelet."

"I never turn down food," Red Butler said.

"Or anything else." Ava smiled.

"You know me too good." Red Butler winked.

During the meal, I couldn't stop thinking about *Templeton Family Receipts*. If Ava chickened out, I'd have to return to Bing's house by myself. Me, who wouldn't drive her Oldsmobile if a brake light was out. It was amazing how being accused of a crime could change your whole outlook. I wasn't 100 percent sure the police, or the district attorney, would look in my cookbook. But I couldn't risk it.

I nibbled on the omelet. It was the perfect texture, filled with bacon, peppers, mushrooms, and ham—more like a deep-dish frittata, since Coop hadn't folded it in half.

"Tell me about the trust, girlie," Red Butler said.

I told him a quick version, finishing with the pending sale of the Spencer-Jackson House.

"Do you have a copy of the sales contract?" Red Butler asked.

I took the documents out of my purse and put them on the table. "The lawyer said I'd have to get a copy of the new deed at the courthouse," I told him.

Coop and Red Butler bent their heads together and flipped through the pages I'd given them. Ava peered over Coop's shoulder. What did an archeologist, or whatever kind of -ologist she was, know about the law? I didn't want her digging through my papers.

"Everything's in order," Coop said. "The real estate contract's notarized. Signed by both parties."

Red Butler shoved the sale document into the envelope.

"Let me see the signatures again," Ava said.

He pulled out the papers. She leaned over, her eyes switching from the trust to the sale contract. "Something is dodgy."

"You can't be serious," Coop said. He bent over the documents.

I got up to see what they were talking about. The documents were side by side, with Ava's red fingernail under each signature, *Rodney Bingham Jackson III*.

"They look identical," Coop said.

"They're not," she said. "Look at his signature on the trust. The bottom loop of the J is open. See? But it's closed on the sale contract. And look at the *B*s and *g*s in each Bingham. They're different, too. The Roman numeral isn't consistent. One has gaps, the other is tight."

Coop glanced at me. "Do you have samples of Bing's handwriting?"

"No. But there are plenty of examples at his house. He kept all his important papers in a closet."

"Maybe the police have them," Ava said.

"Not likely," I said. "The closet is hidden. It's behind paneled doors."

"I'm assuming this is the house where your cookbooks are?" she asked.

"The whole shebang." I sat back down.

"Let's go get them," she said.

"Get what?" Coop frowned.

"Haven't you been listening?" Ava raised her eyebrows. "You need signature samples. Teeny needs her cookbooks. I hope you still have a key."

I nodded.

"Brilliant." Ava clapped her hands.

"Hold on, you two," Red Butler cried. "Which house you talking about? 'Cause if you're referring to the murder scene, don't even think about going there."

I tried to explain about my aunt's especial cookbook, carefully skirting the part about the poisoned recipes and my paranoia. Before I finished, Coop shook his head.

"No way," he said. "You can get the books when this is over."

"I knew you'd put a damp blanket on this," Ava said. "That's your whole problem. You won't ever take a chance."

"No, not on illegal activities," Coop said.

"Not on anything," Ava said.

He flinched—not a jerk, just a little eyelid flicker and a stiffening in his shoulders. But I knew she'd pricked his ego. And I knew that this was at the heart of their separation. She was audacious, and he followed rules. No exceptions. Ever.

Ava slid a paper in front of me. "Teeny, could you draw a map to the hidden closet?"

"It's tricky. I'd almost have to show you."

"Not to worry. When I get there, I'll ring you. And you can talk me through it."

"You ain't talking her through nothing," Red Butler cried. "For all I know, the boss's phones are tapped."

"You're a ruddy fool. Teeny, come with me." Ava grabbed my hand. "I'll be careful. I won't let the police get you. I've got a plan all—"

"Won't let the police get her?" Red Butler sorted. "Hell, you'll deliver her on a silver platter. She's being tailed. They'll follow her straight to the murder scene."

"They're not following me," Ava said. "In fact, I'm the only person in this room the police aren't following."

"Bad idea, Ava." Coop squeezed her arm.

"I'll be careful." She looked up into his eyes.

That did it. I got to my feet. "I'm coming with you."

"Right," said Red Butler. "Just hop on the bike. Wink at the cops when you pass by. Show some leg. Sheesh."

"You can't do it," Coop said.

I wasn't sure if he was addressing me or Ava, or both of us.

"Look the other way, Dudley Do-Right," Ava said.

"You bitches are crazy," Red Butler said. "I don't want no part of it."

"Have I asked for your help?" Ava asked. "If we have copies of Bing's signature, Cooper can stop the sale of the house. That will buy Teeny some time. And the girl needs her books. How is this crazy?"

"Because it's a fucking crime scene," Red Butler said.

"And it's against the law," Coop said.

"You haven't changed and you never will," Ava told him. "You're inflexible and dogmatic. You won't take risks."

"So you keep reminding me," he said. All the color left his face. I knew exactly what she was doing. Sure, his ego might be smarting, but if she brought back the signatures—and they ended up proving that Natalie had done something illegal—then Ava would be the hero. And here I was, wallowing in faulty thinking and practically eating my own hair over recipes that may or may not ever be found. Meanwhile, Ava gets the guy by being plucky and fearless. But if that cookbook was found, I'd not only lose the guy, I'd lose my freedom.

"He will, too, take risks," I said. "He saved a drowning girl in Lake Bonaventure. Boats were cutting in too close. But Coop wasn't worried for himself. He just plunged in and saved the girl's life."

"I'd forgotten that," he said.

"That's not the kind of risks I meant." Ava pushed back her hair. "Are you staying or going, Teeny?"

"How she gonna slip past the tails?" Red Butler asked.

"Simple." Ava turned to me. "Teeny, exit by the back door and walk to the pier. And take your mobile phone."

"I don't have one."

She reached into her purse. "Here, take my mobile. Go to the beach. Walk toward the pier."

"Why does she need a freaking phone?" Red Butler asked.

"Haven't you been listening?" Ava asked. "If the police see her, I'll ring her. Simple."

I pulled off my shoes and tucked the phone into the right toe.

"You're certain you're up to this?" Ava asked.

"Yes." And I was. This was my chance to break the mold and be daring. I looked at Coop for a split second, and his sad eyes broke my heart. Red Butler's face was dark purple, with veins popping on his forehead.

The wind kicked up the hem of my dress as I walked onto the deck and hurried down the back steps. The sky was the color of blueberries and spilled into the ocean. I had serious doubts about Ava's plan. She'd all but said she was an adrenaline junkie, but she also wanted Coop. If she had a chance to undermine me, wouldn't she take it?

I walked down the beach toward a three-story white house with blue shutters. A clump of sea oats grew behind a wavy wooden fence and blocked my view of the road. I heard a shrill ring. I reached into my shoe and lifted the squawking phone.

"Teeny?" came Ava's clipped voice. "Are you there?"

"Yes." I glanced back at Coop's house. It was a tiny gray speck, no bigger than the head of a match.

"Your escorts haven't moved," she said. "Meet you at the pier."

thirty

The ride to Bing's house was even more terrifying than Miss Dora's speed-a-thon over Wappoo Creek. Ava turned into the subdivision, zooming past empty lots into the cul-de-sac. Just as I'd expected, the driveway was blocked with yellow tape.

Ava switched off her light and drove into an empty lot, the weeds and palmettos whipping against her tires. She parked behind an oleander bush and removed her helmet. I slid off the bike, and the weight of my helmet almost tipped me forward.

"Steady." Ava grabbed my arm. She unsnapped my helmet and slung it over the back bar. Then she opened the carrier compartment and pulled out a snub-nosed revolver.

"What's that for?" I stepped back. I should have guessed; she was totally going to shoot me.

"Self-defense." She grabbed a slender flashlight and tucked it into her pocket. "Lead the way, Teeny."

I didn't like the idea of walking in front of her, so I ran through the waist-high weeds. I was out of breath when I reached the peach tree stump. I started past the badminton net when I saw car lights sweep through the trees.

"Down!" Ava tugged my arm. We crouched behind the azaleas and tracked the lights. They moved over the trees and circled back as the car made a U-turn and left the cul-de-sac. We waited a moment longer, then crept to the patio.

Ava reached for her flashlight and aimed it at the door. My hand shook as I fit the key into the lock. The day Bing had been murdered, this same door had stood open. I'd taken the key, meaning to set it on the counter; instead, I'd picked up Sir and put the key in my handbag. But who'd left the key in the lock? Had I been meant to find it?

All these questions swirled as I opened the door and led Ava through the den, into the foyer. We climbed the curved staircase and walked to the guest room. She moved to the window, shut the curtains, then clicked on her flashlight. The beam hit the far wall, illuminating the gilt trim on five antiqued wooden panels. Pictures of old-timey ships hung on each panel. I moved to the third picture, flattened my hand below the frame, and pushed against the wood. The disguised door swung open. I flipped a switch. A fluorescent hummed, casting green light over the small room.

"Find what you need and let's go," she said.

I opened a file drawer. Bing had been meticulous with his records. Every folder was labeled and dated. According to Mr. Underhill, Bing had sold the Spencer-Jackson House the day after I'd attacked him. I opened a folder marked "June" and riffled through the papers. I didn't see any document that remotely looked like a sale contract. But I saw a dozen papers with his signature.

I tucked the folder under my arm and squatted next to the metal safe. Bing had used his date of birth for passwords and secret codes. I unlocked the safe and opened the door. I saw DVDs with girls' names written on them in Bing's handwriting. I grabbed those and leaned inside the safe. I found the deed to this green stucco house and the deed to the Spencer-Jackson. A thick pile of other deeds were wrapped with a rubber band. I grabbed those, too.

Ava saw me grappling with the DVDs and got a pillowcase. I dropped everything inside, then I shut off the light and stepped out of the room. As I shut the panel, the picture tilted. I reached up to straighten it.

"Let's go," Ava said.

Halfway down the stairs, a beam of light speared through the front door. Ava and I ducked behind the railing just as the light passed over our heads. It moved past the staircase, across the walls, and snapped off. A few seconds later, it appeared in the dining room window. The light flowed over the walls and disappeared.

"We can hide in Bing's closet," I whispered.

"You go." She stood. "I'm not afraid."

"What if it's the police?"

"What if it isn't?" She pulled out the revolver and flipped off the safety. She crept down the stairs and flattened herself against the wall. I was right behind her, my heart thumping. I'd left my inhaler with the motorcycle, so I forced myself to take slow breaths.

Holding the gun in both hands, she inched her way into the hall and turned into the den. The windows along the back of the house resembled black lozenges. Farther out, in the backyard, a ribbon of moonlight sliced through the trees.

A wobbly beam hit the glass door. Behind it, a large shape rose up. The knob rattled and spun around. The door opened and the light hit me in the eye.

"One more step, and I'll shoot," Ava called.

The figure raised its arms. "It's me," Red Butler said.

"You bloody bastard." Ava lowered the revolver. "I almost shot you. What are you doing here?"

"Checking on y'all."

I started for the bookcase, and Ava called, "Where are *you* going?"

"To get my cookbooks." I reached for *Templeton Family Receipts* and my fondant icing book. I hated to leave the rest of them, but I couldn't ask Red Butler to tote my entire collection. I glanced at the volumes and held a little funeral for them.

"I can take some books in my van," Red Butler said.

For once, I could have kissed him. I dumped a load into his arms and went back for another stack. Then Ava and I followed Red Butler to his van and set the books in the rear compartment. All the seats had been ripped out, and boxes of surveillance equipment were strewn about.

"I've heard of crazy bitches," he told me, "but you're the world's first crazy cookbook bitch."

We walked back to the house. Red Butler pointed to the empty shelves. "The crime boys prolly videotaped this room," he said. "They gonna notice the shelves been messed with."

"No, they won't." I opened the bottom cabinet, pulled out encyclopedias, and shoved them into the empty slots.

"Brilliant," Ava said, lifting a pile of books.

Red Butler shuffled his feet. "It looks okay," he said. "Let's get out of here."

"Got everything?" Ava asked me. "Keys? Documents? Flashlight?"

God, she was thorough. I nodded and slipped *Templeton Family Receipts* into the pillowcase.

"Red, lock the door on your way out," Ava said over her shoulder.

"You would've made a good general," he muttered.

"See you at Cooper's," she said.

"We're going back to Coop's?" I asked

"Where else?" Ava pushed back her hair. "Remember, the police didn't see you leave. They believe you're with him—alone."

"If the police think I'm with Coop, they're going to freak when they see me drive up on the back of your motorcycle."

"They won't."

"But how will I slip past them?"

"Same as before," she said. "You walk."

thirty-one

Halfway to Coop's house, it began to drizzle. By the time I slogged onto Coop's deck, I was pretty sure my hair looked like Tina Turner's "Private Dancer" wig, one that had been plunged into a toilet and drip-dried on a mop handle. I was sopping wet.

Drowning was the least of my problems. When I walked into the house, I found the three of them in the dining room, having a party. Coop was wedged between Red Butler and Ava, laughing and digging into a pepperoni pizza. The boys seemed to have sufficiently recovered from Ava's criminal activities. Coop shoved a wedge of pizza into his mouth. His eyes widened when he saw me.

Ava smiled. "Cooper, where're your manners? Get the poor girl a towel."

My sweetheart rose from the chair and shot into the kitchen. I heard the clothes dryer open and shut.

"Sorry I'm late," I said. "I fainted five times and got attacked by sand fleas."

"Get you some pizza." Red Butler pointed to the boxes.

Coop returned and put a towel over my head. I sat down and Ava's smile broadened. I dragged the towel over my possum hair.

"Red?" Ava smiled. "Would you open another bottle of merlot?"

"'Get me this, Red,'" he said in a fake British accent. "'Get me that.'"

Ava emptied the pillow case onto the table, then she spread out the documents and studied Bing's signature. "Whoever Natalie Lockhart is, she's not a clever forger. She's sloppy."

Coop lifted a DVD. "Why are they labeled with names? Barbara Jo, Faye, Amber."

"I'm not sure." My breath caught a little when I saw *Natalie* written in Bing's script. I handed it to Coop. "Do you have a DVD player?"

"Sure do." He walked to the great room and slid the disc into the machine. The television screen filled with grainy static, then a bull's-eye came up with a count down. 3, 2, 1. The screen flickered and showed a hairy thigh in black and white. The date and time were stamped on the bottom of the screen. Exactly one week after we'd gotten engaged.

"What a cheap fucking video camera," said a man with an intense coastal drawl. Bing.

The camera panned down to his crotch, showing his fully inflated manly parts. The camera jerked up, and Natalie came into view. "God, you're sexy," Bing told her. "Come over here and suck me, you beautiful bitch."

My legs wobbled, and I sank into a leather chair. Coop pulled out the footstool and perched on the edge. He looked away from the television, back to the pile of DVDs. "These are sex tapes," he said.

"Crappy, homemade ones," Red Butler said.

"Can they be used as evidence?" Ava asked.

"Of what?" Coop asked.

"That Teeny was engaged to a man-whore," Red Butler said. "No way. We'd have to explain how she found them. Plus, it's inadmissable evidence."

Red Butler grabbed another slice of pizza and crammed it into his mouth. He chewed thoughtfully a minute. "So, all you got is video evidence that her boyfriend was a revtard?"

"What's that?" I frowned.

"A guy who can't add two plus two, yet he's knee-deep in pretty women. A total babe magnet."

Revtard, indeed. I couldn't listen to the commentary—or Bing's tape—another second. I rose from the chair and hurried to the bathroom. I leaned into the tub, turned on the faucet, and rinsed sand off my feet, wishing it was this easy to remove the last six months.

When I returned, Coop and Red Butler were arguing about who should drive me home. I leaned against the wall and crossed my arms.

"The less you and her is seen together, the better," Red Butler said. "Besides, I've got her damn cookbooks in my van."

Coop held up his hand. "I don't want to hear about those books."

"Relax," Ava said. "You've got enough evidence to clear Teeny."

"Illegally obtained evidence." Coop rose from the footstool. His eyes met Ava's, and something seemed to pass between them. He sat back down.

"But I thought you wanted the signatures," Ava said. "Stop fretting. Let's compare the handwriting, shall we?"

"I'm not a graphologist," Coop said, his voice full of angry edges. "Neither are you." He pointed at Ava, but he was really pointing at both of us, at our bad behavior.

"I'm sure you can find a qualified person." Ava reached for her purse. "If the expert thinks the signatures are dodgy, you can follow the law to your heart's content. Go through proper channels. Bring in your expert witnesses. I've no doubt you'll successfully argue your case. The police will stop hounding Teeny. Then she can go back to her life."

Her unspoken words hung in the air, *Teeny can go back to Georgia*.

"It's not that simple." Coop shook his head.

"It could be." She stared at him for a long moment, then she patted T-Bone and headed for the door.

"Hey," Red Butler called. "Where you going?"

"Home," she said over her shoulder. "I've had quite enough for one night."

"It's raining." Coop got up again and stepped toward her. "Be careful."

"Not to worry, I like a challenge." She walked out. No "Good-bye, Coop." No "See you later." That was a good sign.

Coop ran his hand over his hair. "You shouldn't have gone back to the house, Teeny. It was irresponsible. Absolutely reckless."

"I really needed those cookbooks."

"Why?" He lowered his eyebrows.

"I've got a job." I paused. Was this a lie? No, just an evasion. I explained about The Picky Palate. "The cakes are special order," I added. "They're due tomorrow."

Coop's gaze softened. "Teeny, you're going to work yourself to death."

"It's not work." I smiled. "Baking relaxes me."

"If you say so." He glanced at Red Butler. "Could I have a moment alone with Teeny?"

"What for?" Red Butler asked.

"It's private," Coop said.

Red Butler grabbed another slice of pizza. "I'll be in the van, girlie."

The front door slammed. Coop drew me into his arms. I was all set to push him away, but my traitorous arms slid over his shoulders.

"I'm crazy about you," he said.

"You better be, O'Malley." I stood on my toes and kissed him. It was the first time we'd kissed since Ava had shown up. I cast aside my scruples about kissing a married man and flitted my tongue against his lips. I was just about to ask him to come back with me to Charleston when a horn blared in the driveway.

Coop pulled back a little and kissed the tip of my nose. "Your chariot awaits," he whispered.

Some chariot. I thought of the movie *Troy*. Red Butler put me in mind of Achilles, relentlessly circling the city walls. "Your detective doesn't like me very much," I said.

"He just doesn't like driving on a rainy night," Coop said.

The rain stopped when Red Butler turned onto the Connector. I stared out the window, watching the headlights cut through the fog.

"Hey, girlie. Did you make a sex tape with your boyfriend?"

"No, indeed not." I frowned. I was so insulted, I couldn't think straight.

"Just asking," he said. "Wouldn't want one to surface during the trial."

"My trespassing trial?" I sighed. I was too heartsick to carry on a conversation, and I wasn't above telling him to stuff it.

"No. The one that's in your future. You got to know where this is headed, girlie. They goin' bring you down for first-degree one way or another. If a sex tape fell into the wrong hands, the DA would cream his panties."

"Bring me down?" I made a fist. I pushed all thoughts of Coop from my mind and went on the attack. "I haven't done anything. And since you brought up the tapes, tell me why it's okay for a man to videotape his sexcapades, and when I find the tapes, I look guilty."

"Like the boss said, it's all about motive. You seen the tapes and wanted revenge. Women do it all the time."

"I didn't know they existed."

"Right, so you broke into your dead boyfriend's house and found the tapes."

"I was just looking for his signature. I didn't know what was in his safe."

"All this time you was engaged to this douche nozzle, it never occurs to you to poke around his secret room and take a gander in his safe?"

"I didn't think he had anything to hide."

"Sure. Whatever. He just had a secret room. I rest my case."

"I'm a real imperfect person, but I'm not a liar. I say pretty much what's on my mind. And what I don't say is written all over my face. This may be hard for you to believe, but I don't always recognize trickery until it smacks me upside the head."

"That don't mean you didn't look in his safe."

"After Bing and I got engaged, he showed me how to open the panel to his room and he gave me the combination to his safe. He asked me not to open it except for an emergency. And I didn't."

"All women are snoops."

"I'm not. I didn't have much privacy when I was growing up."

"What kid does? My sisters hogged the bedrooms, and I had to sleep on the den sofa."

"I lived in a car, okay? A station wagon. Mama got the front seat, I got the back. She was real clear about our territory. She used to say, 'Don't you mess with my stuff, and I won't mess with yours.'"

I crossed my arms. I thought about Mama all the time, but I rarely talked about her. An image rose up and I pictured my old Roi-Tan cigar box. Inside it still smelled faintly of Donnie's tobacco. He'd given it to me to keep my special things: a piece of blue ribbon, my cursed inhaler, a peach pit, and the boot from a Monopoly game. Far as I knew, Mama hadn't looked inside the box.

"Your mama still living?" Red Butler asked.

"Who knows? She ran off."

"That's too bad. How much are you inheriting from your dead boy-friend's trust?"

"I don't want it. Let his sister have it."

"Right." He rolled his eyes.

"It's blood money."

"Yeah, but it's still money. Why would you give up a fortune?"

"I told you. Plus, Bing wouldn't have wanted me to have it."

"It don't matter what the dead want."

"It matters to me."

"It shouldn't. You act like money's a bad thing."

"There's not a thing in the world wrong with it. But I just know myself. I cut my own hair and do my own nails. I'm a drip-dry girl. I like cotton, not silk. I like plain white dishes and don't care if they match."

"Okay, okay, I get it. You ain't a material girl."

"I want to forget how Bing looked when I found him in the kitchen."

"So go to a hypnotist."

"I ought to split it with his sister and give my half to charity."

"Is his sister the dame who brought cats to the funeral today?"

I shrugged.

"You can't let the dude's money go to support cats."

"Maybe I'll just give the trust to you," I snapped.

"Well, I wouldn't hand over perfectly good money to a bunch of yowling cats." He turned down Adgers. As I glanced out the side window, a Winnebago sped by. It was too dark to see the driver, but I recognized the distinctive boxy shape.

"There's that RV again," I said. "It belongs to Bing's sister. Maybe you should chase it."

"Why?" Red Butler shrugged. "She ain't done nothing wrong."

The van's headlights swept over the damp cobblestones. Red Butler parked, then reached in the back of the van and grabbed a stack of books. "Let's just take in a few tonight," he said.

"But I need them all."

"The dicks might notice. I don't want no trouble over some recipe books."

I crawled into the back of the van and grabbed as many books as I could hold. Red Butler and I walked in silence back to East Bay. Down by the brick wall, I saw the Camry trying to nose into a tiny slot. When I passed the Jackson Realty sign, I repressed an urge to spit.

Red Butler held the books while I unlocked the iron door. I hurried into the corridor, opened the gray door, and shut off the bleating alarm.

From upstairs, I could hear Sir's frantic barks. I started for the staircase. Above me, the chandelier prisms tinkled, and a shadow moved back and forth. I glanced up. A long thick rope hung from the chandelier, and dangling at the end was a bulldog.

thirty-two

My brain couldn't reconcile the dog's body swinging back and forth to the barking that was coming from upstairs. "It's a stuffed dog," Red Butler said. He threw down the books he was carrying, reached under his tuxedo coat, and pulled out a gun. With his free hand, he tossed me his keys. "Go back to the van and lock yourself inside."

"You think whoever did this is still here?"

"Just go."

"Let me get my dog."

"Go!"

I ran into the corridor, through the open gate, and cut across the street. Earlier today, before the funeral, I'd locked both the gray door and the gate. Someone had been in the house and hadn't tripped the alarm—*because they knew the code.*

I jumped in the van and hit the auto lock. I watched the side mirror so nobody could sneak up from behind. I still had to bake twenty-four red velvet cakes. I'd hoped to fix one batch tonight and finish the rest before lunch tomorrow.

A few minutes later, Red Butler rapped on the window. Sir squirmed in his arms. "All clear," he said.

I climbed out of the van and he dumped Sir into my arms. I sagged beneath the sudden weight and started checking Sir for wounds or blood, but Red Butler shook his head.

"He's fine."

We walked back to the Spencer-Jackson House, and I glanced at the Camry. The car stayed the same, but the detectives changed on a daily basis.

"Should we tell the police?" I asked Red Butler.

He pulled out his phone. The keypad beeped as he punched in a number. It was way too long for 911. I gave him a questioning stare, but he held out his hand to shush me.

"Coop? We got a problem here. Somebody hung a stuffed bulldog from Teeny's chandy." He paused, his eyes switching back and forth. "Yeah, they're up the street, but—" He paused again. "Okeydokey, Boss. Will do."

Damn, I didn't want to see Coop, not until I'd eaten my way through a pound of Market Street pralines. A sugar fix would go a long way to calm me down.

Red Butler guided me into the corridor. "Go inside. I'm getting the dicks."

I stepped into the house and looked up at the stuffed dog. I was shaking so bad, Sir nearly fell out of my arms. I wobbled over to the stairs and sat on the bottom step. Sir's flat nose pushed into my ear. The stuffed dog was a warning. Natalie had a key to the house, and she knew the alarm code. If she hurt my dog, I didn't know what I'd do, but I was pretty sure it wouldn't be legal.

Red Butler returned with the detectives. One was prematurely bald and wore a white t-shirt with USC printed on the front; the other guy was about my height with brown eyes and needed a haircut. They looked past me, to the chandelier. The man in the USC shirt called for backup, and the short man bent to examine the door.

"Don't see any sign of forced entry," he said.

"There wasn't," Red Butler said. "And the burglar alarm was set."

The short man rubbed his face and gave me a "maybe she did it herself" look. "Any workmen been here?" he asked me.

"Yes. The upstairs air conditioner went out."

"And her house key went missing," Red Butler added.

"Name of repair company?" asked the tanned guy.

"Coastal Electric and Air."

"You didn't change the locks?"

I wasn't sure how to answer. Red Butler beat me to it. "No, she was staying here on a temporary basis. And if you was doing your homework and been watching her house instead of sitting at the beach and pissing in the sea oats, you'd know who done this."

At that moment, I almost loved him. "The house next door has security cameras," he added. "Maybe their tape will show something."

I heard sirens, and police cars swarmed down East Bay, parking at angles. Blue lights washed over the windows like spilled food coloring. I went into the corridor and sat beside the far gate, holding Sir in my lap.

Coop stepped into the corridor and walked over to me. His hand moved to my face, as if he were going to brush hair out of my eyes, but the short detective walked by and said, "Hey, O'Malley. Didn't know you had a dog in this fight."

Coop ignored him. "You okay, Teeny?"

"Been better."

"You shouldn't be out here." He glanced at the policemen who were standing at the end of the corridor and helped me to my feet. We walked through the door, into the hall. A policeman was taking pictures of the stuffed dog from various angles.

Coop started talking to the detectives. I put Sir down, gathered up the spilled cookbooks, and walked to the kitchen. I dumped them onto the small built-in desk and pulled out *Templeton Family Receipts*. The stiff pages grazed my fingers as I leafed through the book, pausing to look at handwritten notes in the margins. A few recipes were written in minuscule print, compressed between the lines of the printed church recipes. It was impossible to know who'd written them—Granny Templeton, Mama, or Bluette and her sisters.

In the middle of the book, I found a recipe for red velvet cake that called for vinegar, cocoa, buttermilk, and a whole bottle of red food coloring. Aunt Bluette had written in the upper corner: *dense and moist, the best cake you'll ever put in your mouth, but doesn't double good.* In the weird alchemy of cooking, "doesn't double good" meant to bake one cake at a time, not in bulk.

I propped the book open on the island, then I knelt in front of the lower cabinets. Since I hadn't made it to the dollar store, I didn't have enough pans. I'd just have to make do.

After I turned on the oven, I plugged in the KitchenAid mixer and started the first cake. I poured batter into pans and slid them into the oven.

Red Butler came in and sniffed. "You're not cooking, I hope?" he asked like I was smoking crack.

"This is a kitchen. It's perfectly legal to bake."

Sir barked, then he started wheezing. I bent down to pat him.

"You're just like the mutt," Red Butler said. "Neither one of you can breathe. Do they make inhalers for bulldogs?"

I ignored him and smoothed the wrinkles on Sir's head. "Where's Coop?"

"Talking to the dicks. Get me a apron, and I'll help."

"I'm making these cakes for The Picky Palate." I stood. "They've got to be perfect."

"You're not the only one who can cook, Teeny. I know my way around a kitchen."

I gave him a side-eye glance. He'd called me by my actual name.

Repressing a smile, I opened a drawer and found a red-and-white checkered apron, still in the cellophane package. "Will this do?"

"Give me it," he said. He pulled off his tuxedo jacket and put on the apron. I watched as he sifted flour into a glass bowl. He pressed his tongue against his upper lip as he filled a measuring cup and leveled the top with a knife, taking pains not to compact the powder. So, he really knew how to bake.

The pocket doors slid open. Coop looked at Red Butler and nodded, as if he saw him every day in an apron, then he waved at me.

"Teeny, when Miss Dora picked you up this morning, did she come inside?" he asked.

"No. Why?"

"I was hoping she could tell the police that nothing was hanging from your chandelier."

"But I already told them," I said.

"They think you did it."

"Me?" I drew back. "I was gone all day. Even with a ladder, I'm not tall enough to reach the chandelier."

"I know. That's why I need you to climb the ladder," Coop said. "Just to demonstrate that you couldn't have hung that rope."

"Sure."

The detectives stood in the hall with two policemen. They'd already found a tall ladder and were setting it up under the chandelier. Coop tilted back his head. "How high is that light fixture?" he asked a uniformed cop. "Twenty-five feet?"

"Nearbouts," the policeman said.

Coop turned to me. "Teeny, climb."

My black dress swirled around my knees as I took a step. The detectives came over to the ladder and tried to anchor it.

"Keep going," Coop said.

"I don't like heights," I said.

"Hold tight. I'm coming up."

The policemen held the ladder while Coop climbed behind me. Red Butler came into the hall to watch.

"Okay," Coop said. "I'm right here. Take another step."

Even though I felt safe with him behind me, I wasn't steady on my pins. If I slipped, we'd end up in the hospital, for sure. I pushed that thought from my mind and bent my leg at the knee. My bare foot slid onto the rung. I climbed one more and stopped when the ladder trembled. The cops stared up, their faces tense.

"You're doing good, Teeny," Coop said. The ladder wobbled as he moved right behind me.

When I got to the top, Coop said, "Teeny, stretch out your hand."

I squeezed my eyes shut and lifted my arm, spreading my fingers wide apart. I cracked open one eye. The chandelier was miles over my head.

"Okay, Teeny," Coop said. "Now climb down. That's it, take it slow."

I felt his hands on my calves, then on my waist. When I got to the bottom, he pointed up at the chandelier. "This woman is innocent," he said in a hard-ass voice. "Somebody's trying to scare her. Quit focusing on her and find the person who hung this toy. Then you'll find who killed Bing Jackson."

The detectives didn't look impressed. They were too busy making faces at Red Butler, who was standing next to the pocket doors. "Nice apron," the short detective called.

"Fuck you, Boudreaux." Red Butler lifted his middle finger. "Hey, did the security tapes show anything?"

"Nothing," the short detective said. "We seen Miss Templeton leave at 9:00 a.m. and get into a silver Bentley. After that, foot traffic until you and her came back at nine forty-five tonight."

"Did you check the back door for signs of forced entry?" Coop asked.

The detectives exchanged glances, then they all went over to the rear door to examine it. A policeman climbed the ladder and cut down the stuffed dog. He lowered it to another policeman. A sick feeling went through me as the dog went into a giant evidence bag.

Evidence of what?

On the other side of the room, Sir tucked his paws under his jaw. His eyes switched from the dog to me, as if to say, *I'm next.*

thirty-three

Coop was back from going door to door, asking the neighbors if they'd seen anything unusual. Red Butler had given him the description of Eileen's RV, then he'd stayed in the kitchen and helped me bake. I'd had enough flour left over for one more cake, and seeing as Red Butler had helped, I'd made one specially for him.

"Miss Loonhart prolly hired some dude to hang that dog," he said.

"Quit scaring her," Coop said. "Natalie just wants Teeny out of the house."

"You better hope that's all," said Red Butler.

"You shouldn't be alone tonight," Coop said.

"I'll be here," Red Butler said.

"I'm staying, too," Coop said. I set the alarm and showed Red Butler to a room with paintings of ships. Then I took Coop to a pale green bedroom that faced the harbor.

"I'm glad you're here," I said, lingering in the doorway. Sir trotted between us.

"Me, too." His cheeks dimpled. "Where's your room?"

"There." I pointed to the door at the end of the hall. I touched his hand. "Can you fix it so Bing's sister gets the trust?"

"I can set you up with an estate lawyer—unless you want to use Mr. Underhill."

"He doesn't like me much."

"He doesn't like anyone."

"Red Butler says I'm crazy for giving up the trust. But you understand, don't you?"

"It's your fortune to lose. You can do what you want." He squeezed my hand. "Holler if you need me."

"Night." I walked to the pink toile room. I didn't push the dresser in front of the door and didn't shut the curtains. A car rumbled down the street and I peeked out the window. Red taillights shone on the damp pavement. If a bank robber had been speeding off, I couldn't have given the police a description. A fine eyewitness I'd be. *What was the make?* they'd ask. Don't know. *Color?* Dark. *Get a license number?* No way.

I stepped out of the funeral dress and found a ragged Edisto Island shirt in one of the drawers. I lifted Sir onto the bed and smiled as he turned around and around. Finally he plopped down with a satisfied grunt. I didn't realize how tired I was until I stretched out. I fell asleep in an instant.

Sometime during the night, Sir woke me with a low growl. Outside my door, the floorboards creaked. I glanced at the clock. 2:00 a.m. My door opened and a tall shape stepped into the room. Sir's tags jingled and his growl deepened.

"Teeny?" whispered a familiar voice. Coop.

"Yes?" I patted Sir's head and he stopped growling.

Coop walked to the bed, moonlight rippling over his t-shirt and boxer shorts, and he knelt beside the bed. I couldn't see his eyes, just the outline of the face I'd loved all my life. I still did. And I couldn't explain why any more than I could explain why peaches grow on trees. I loved how he squatted by T-Bone and talked to him like the dog could understand. I loved the plants in his spare room and the way his eyes squinted in the corners when he laughed. It wasn't just his handsomeness, although that was a plus, it was his selfless streak that made him dive into the water to save a drowning swimmer, not waiting for someone else to act or thinking of his own safety.

A car sped down the street and its headlights passed over him, briefly illuminating his eyes. He didn't move. Silence curled between us the way the scent of baking bread moves through a room. I tucked my hand under the pillow. He leaned closer and smoothed back my hair.

"I dreamed about you during the night," he whispered. "Then I woke and had to make sure you were okay."

I nodded. I wasn't scared as long as he was here, but it made me sick to think that someone had slipped unnoticed into the house—not to steal the antiques but to hang a stuffed replica of Sir. It was a warning to get out of this house, and soon.

Coop leaned closer and his tongue slipped past my lips. His whiskers grazed my chin, and I reached up and felt the cleft. My breath came in sharp gasps, but I didn't need my inhaler. I breathed in the scent of his shampoo as he moved his chin down my chest and rested his face against my t-shirt. His breath stirred the thin fabric and scattered, warming my nipples.

I moved my hand under his shirt, brushing over the fine hairs on his chest, and pressed lower. My palm brushed the elastic band of his boxers.

"I want you so much," he said.

"I want you, too." I pulled my shirt over my head, wound my arms tightly around his neck, and drew him against me into the warm blankets. His lips moved up to my neck, and he bit my earlobe. I traced my hands over his shoulders, feeling the hard curve of his muscles. I was keenly aware of the infinitesimal space between us and moved closer.

"So sweet," he said and inched down his boxers.

I couldn't wait another second and tried to pull him to me.

"Not yet," he said. His hand slipped between my thighs, nudging them farther and farther apart in excruciating slowness. He kissed me again, and his hands moved down. Then he drew back.

"Please forgive me for not telling you everything," he said.

"We'll . . . discuss this later," I said.

He rolled over and braced his elbows on the mattress. I wrapped my legs around him and felt him enter me in one long pulse, then another and another. I couldn't hold still. His touch was an ocean. I moved like a swimmer, pushing through the slippery blue. His kisses pulled me under, powerful as a current, but this time I didn't hold my breath. I was breathing underwater.

Sunlight trickled through the curtains and moved in dizzy patterns on the floor. I rubbed my eyes. Coop's side of the bed was empty. I rolled over and felt a vague soreness between my legs.

I couldn't stay in bed another second. I had to see him. I slipped out of bed, walked to the closet, and pulled the sale tags from the thrift-store outfit. I buttoned the white blouse, then stepped into black pants.

Sir's toenails clicked behind me as I walked into the hall. The door to Coop's room stood ajar, and the bed was tidily made. I went down the stairs, turned off the burglar alarm, and opened the back door. Sir waddled out and stretched his stubby hind legs. I leaned against the door jam and waited while he did his business.

Red Butler came into the hall, holding a coffee mug. "Morning," he said. "I already cut into that cake you made me."

"Was it good?"

He touched his thumb and finger together, making an OK sign. I whistled for Sir, and he trotted into the hall, wiggling against my ankles. I patted his broad, flat head. His fur felt warm, and he hadn't been out there a minute. It was going to be another hot day in Charleston.

Red Butler walked to the door and stepped onto the patio. His head moved from side to side as he scanned the yard. He looked just like a human bulldog. "Teeny, does anything look out of place?" he asked.

"No."

"Best I can figure, the dude came through the back gate." He pointed toward the brick wall.

"Where's Coop?" I asked.

"Kitchen."

I hurried through the pocket doors. He was leaning against the counter, sipping coffee. "Morning," he said and turned back to the sink, as if he felt embarrassed to look me in the eye. At the very least, I'd expected a kiss, but something in his voice worried me. I flashed back to that long-ago day when he'd come to Aunt Bluette's farm to break up with me.

"You been up long?" I asked, keeping my voice light and casual.

"A little while. Red Butler's staying with you today."

"Great." I shook kibble into a bowl and set it on the mat. Sir grabbed a nugget and carried it away from the bowl. He chewed fiercely, then darted back for another morsel.

"Teeny, we need to talk," Coop said.

"Sure."

He still wouldn't look at me, so I squeezed past him and poured a cup of coffee. Then I leaned against the counter and waited. But he kept staring at the floor.

"So, talk, O'Malley," I said.

Red Butler walked into the room. "I checked the back gate. It's shut, but it needs a chain and padlock. Even though you ain't gonna be staying here long, you still need to take precautions."

Coop took a sip of coffee and turned to me. "I'm taking the documents to a forensic expert in Columbia. If he thinks the signature is fishy, I'm calling the state attorney general's office." He touched my arm. "I'll stop by later."

I looked up into his eyes. Was this what he'd wanted to talk about?

"Not a good idea, Boss. The DA is after your ass."

"I thought he was after me." I laughed.

Cooper set his mug on the counter. "Red, can I have a few minutes with Teeny?"

"Make it snappy," Red Butler said and walked off.

Coop reached for my hand. "I'm in a little trouble."

"You?"

He nodded. "The DA called. Someone sent him a picture of me and you."

"I don't understand." I felt dizzy. Where was my damn inhaler?

"Remember the night at McTavish's?" he asked.

"You drove me home."

"And we kissed." He paused. "Someone took a picture. They mailed the photo to the DA. He's going to report me to the Bar unless I cool it with you."

"Who would take our picture?" I cried.

"That's not the point, Teeny. Someone has been following you."

Or you, I thought. "Is that the only reason you're cooling it?"

"Isn't it enough?" His eyes widened. "I can't be your lover and your attorney."

Tears pricked my eyes, but I struggled to compose myself. "You didn't mind last night."

"I didn't know about the photograph then. Teeny, please don't cry."

"I can't help it." I wiped my cheeks. "Why did you go to that pub in the first place?"

"I go all the time. They have authentic British food. I'm addicted to their fish and chips."

"Oh."

"I want to be with you. I want it more than anything. You've got to know that." He started to take my hand, then stopped. "But for now, we need to keep our relationship professional."

"I wouldn't get you in trouble for the world." My shoulders sagged. I felt utterly defeated. I'd gotten over him once; I'd just have to do it again.

"We'll still see each other," he said. "We just have to keep it professional."

Right. Whatever. I dabbed my eyes on a dish towel.

"Teeny, it's only till this case is over."

Sir trotted away from his bowl, and a moment later, Red Butler stepped into the room. "Get out of here, Boss. I'll watch her good."

"I'll stop by tonight and see how y'all are doing," he said, then he walked out the kitchen. A few moments later, the front door shut.

"When you got to deliver these cakes?" Red Butler asked.

"This afternoon."

"We better get busy."

He drove to Sam's Club for flour and disposable cake pans. I pushed Coop and the DA out of my mind. Red Butler and I baked all morning, and by one o'clock, twenty-four cakes were boxed and waiting on the counter.

"I been watching *Top Chef* and *Man v. Food*," Red Butler said. "I like Rachael Ray, too. She makes it look so damn easy. Doesn't always measure, just eyeballs ingredients."

He brought his van around front and we loaded the cakes. I was relieved not to see the catmobile. I put Sir in the bedroom with a piddle pad and a KONG toy. Just as I was punching in the alarm code, the gray front door flew open. I gaped into Natalie's startled face. Behind her was a stumpy man with thready brown hair combed sideways over a bald spot. His muscular arms bulged in a green striped polo shirt. Standing next to him was a pretty honey-blonde, her curls floating around her chin.

"I didn't know you'd be here," Natalie said. A key was in the lock, with a tag that said Spencer-Jackson House.

"Hold on." I canceled the alarm, fingers trembling. I looked past her, at the couple. I guessed they were the buyers. "This is sort of a bad time," I said, twirling my key chain. "Can you come back later?"

"Leave." Natalie shrugged. "I've got a key. I'll lock up."

"But my dog's in the bedroom. Someone could accidentally let him out."

"I'll be careful."

"Sorry, I can't be too careful with my dog. Come back in an hour." I paused. "Or three."

The couple glanced at each other. Natalie pushed her sunglasses onto her head. "I don't think you understand. This isn't your property. I'm letting you stay out of the goodness of my heart."

If she had a heart, and she didn't, I'd be tempted to drive a stake through it. Better yet, I should serve her pie and coffee. I would serve key lime, with a few Templeton variations. I'd make the usual filling, but I'd add a nut crust, lots of chopped almonds and macadamias, with a handful of Barbados seeds. If a 120-pound woman ate two slices of pie, she'd be dead in thirty minutes. Tiny amounts only caused a laxative effect, but it was a powerful one and most unromantic.

She strode past me into the dining room, with her entourage right behind her. Their footsteps clattered as they stepped into the kitchen. My nerves were already frayed, so I followed them, ready to kick them to the curb. When I reached the kitchen, Natalie was reading *Templeton Family Receipts.*

"Poisoned vanilla peach pecan coffee cake?" she cried. "What kind of cookbook *is* this?"

The back cover tore when I jerked it out of her hands. I hugged the book to my chest. "You better leave."

"Says who? The owner of the house, or the dwarf with a poisoning cookbook?"

I heard footsteps in the dining room. Red Butler appeared in the doorway, looking from me to Natalie. "What's going on?"

"She wants to show the house," I said. "I asked her to come later."

"So do it," Red Butler said.

"Excuse me, but who are *you?*" Natalie's nostrils flared.

"Her fairy godmother."

"I own this house, and I'm going to show it to the new owners," she said. "And if you try to stop me, I'll call 911."

"I am a cop, lady. Want me to call?"

"Look, I've been more than gracious. *I* have every right to be here."

"Yeah, you're the picture of Southern hospitality," Red Butler said.

"It *is* my property, you know." Natalie waved at the couple. "The Randolphs are buying this house. Closing is next Friday. Teeny, you'll need to be out by Thursday at midnight."

"No problem," Red Butler said. "She'll be gone. Until that happens, if you want to barge in, you either make an appointment with Teeny or wait till closing day."

"Well, Mr. Whoever You Are, I'll come when I please. And so will my buyers."

"Were you here yesterday?" I asked.

"No." She flashed an icy stare.

"I think you were," I said. "And you left me a present."

"No way." She laughed.

"Someone hung a stuffed bulldog from the chandelier," I said.

"I hope you aren't accusing *me* of anything." Natalie looked at the Randolphs as if she wished they weren't there. "I'm not the dangerous one. Ask Teeny to show you her book. I pity her lawyer. Poor thing is rushing around like a cat, covering up her shit."

The curly-headed woman squeezed Natalie's arm. "Let's go have a latte and come back later."

"We'll do no such thing," Natalie said. "Besides, your decorator is on her way. Teeny and her fairy can't do a damn thing to stop us."

"I guess you're right," I said. "But you won't be able to do a damn thing to stop me from playing your sex tape on the TV while you're here."

"What?"

Red Butler stepped between us, his eyes bugging. "Teeny, stop right now."

"Somebody should've stopped her before she made a sex tape with my boyfriend," I said. "I saw the tape. You and Bing. Gosh, if something like that got into the wrong hands, you could end up all over the Internet."

"You are a liar," Natalie cried.

"No lie. Just the truth."

"I'll sue you for defamation."

"Do it!" I glared. "You're in lots worse trouble. The signature on the deed isn't Bing's." I turned to the couple. "There could be a problem. I wouldn't call in a decorator just yet."

Natalie whirled and pushed past the couple. Her high heels clicked frantically down the corridor. Red Butler put his hands over his eyes. I turned back to the couple.

"Can I give you a lift?"

thirty-four

During the drive to The Picky Palate, Red Butler gave me a crash course in slander. "Sheesh, you did it in front of witnesses! You can't go round accusing Natalie of forgery or hanging stuffed dogs from chandys."

"I never said forgery."

"You said everything but. That's still slander, okay?"

"If she didn't hang that dog, who did?"

"That's for the police to decide. But you—you're in big trouble. You're on probation, for Christ's sake."

"It won't happen again." If only I'd just called her an asshole.

"Too late for promises. If she's guilty of faking Bing's signature, you just tipped her off. She'll have time to cover her tracks."

The Picky Palate was empty when we arrived. Jan opened a box and sniffed the air over the cake. "Nice," she said and pressed her finger against the surface. I stared, awestruck that she was handling food that she intended to sell. She glanced up, as if she'd heard my thoughts. "This cake is mine," she said.

She cut a thick slice and held it up to the light. Her eyes closed as she fit a morsel into her mouth. There was no way of telling who'd baked this particular cake, me or Red Butler. We fidgeted while we waited for the verdict.

Jan nodded and swallowed. "Oh god, this is good. Can you deliver six Italian cream cakes by 10:00 a.m. tomorrow? Your cut will be fifteen dollars each."

"You can count on me," I said.

Red Butler drove me to the farmer's market for organic eggs, then we hit the dollar store for staples. Despite Coop's pledge to keep things professional between us, I wasn't letting down my guard. When Red Butler wasn't looking, I grabbed a lacy white bra and matching panties. Then I got three sheer nightgowns. I shoved the delicate items into the cart, under the flour and confectioners' sugar. I drifted to the sale rack, where I found sophisticated blouses that reminded me of Ava. Two dollars each.

I piled them in the cart, one in each color—cream, raspberry, lettuce, pear, grape—then I froze. The colors were too loud. Just because my aunt Goldie was a clown didn't mean I couldn't dress anemic like Ava. I put back the blouses, except for the cream, and threw in white denims.

Red Butler let me out in front of the Spencer-Jackson and drove back to the parking lot on Adgers. I'd no sooner unlocked the gate, when I felt a tap on my shoulder. I spun around and looked up into Eileen's broad face. She smoothed her gloved hands down a yellow jumpsuit with paw print appliqués. A yellow headband held back her bushy, dark blond hair, and a patent leather cat purse dangled from her arm.

"Do you remember me?" she asked.

"You're Eileen, Bing's sister," I said. "I remember you from the cemetery."

"You've got a good memory." Eileen tapped her fingers five times, then she rolled her eyes.

"Where're your cats?" I asked.

"In the RV. I left the air conditioner running full blast. So if you're thinking of calling the Humane Society, think again." She glanced past me, into the corridor. "May I come in?"

"I'm waiting for someone." I looked over my shoulder, hoping to see Red Butler standing on the corner of East Bay and Adgers.

"I'm not stalking you, I swear." She adjusted her gloves. One edge stuck up, and I saw her red wrist. "Although I had been," she added. "But only a little. I wanted us to have a heart-to-heart. But you're never alone. Honey, I don't know what scheme you're into, but it must be good. You've got men coming and going."

"They aren't my boyfriends," I said.

"Sure." She chuckled. Then she tapped her feet twenty times. "Don't bother calling for help. I'm not going to stay long. I talked to Bing's lawyer. He says you're getting all my daddy's properties."

"Bing's properties," I said. I couldn't resist.

"I'm sure you're just itching to buy a private island somewhere, but I wouldn't advise it. 'Cause I'm going to tie you up in court for years. I'm hiring me a heavy-hitting litigator—that's a people version of an alligator. I'm not kidding. I'm contesting on grounds of undue influence. You put the squeeze on my brother."

"It was the other way around, Eileen," I said. "You'll be gray-headed when you get that money."

"I know it's not easy to contest a trust," she said. "I've been through this after Daddy died. He wanted a dainty debutante, but he got me. Even so, he wouldn't have cut me out of the trust if Miss Dora hadn't egged him on." She licked each gloved fingertip, then tapped her feet together. "Look, Miss Templeton. I'm the last of the Jacksons. I'm sure you're nice and all, but I can't walk away from that trust. Besides, if the lawyer works pro bono, what have I got to lose?"

"Just your time. But I've been thinking. If I end up with the trust, I'd like to split it with you."

"Split it?" Eileen looked suspicious. "What do you have in mind?"

"You take half, and I'll give the other half to charity."

"Charity?" Her face turned white. "Why would you do a fool thing like that?"

"Bing had goodness in him, and I want to set up a foundation in his name, to remember that goodness."

"Are you shooting me a line of bull poop?" She snorted. "Because if you are, I'll put a hex on you."

"It's the truth."

"Well, I'm not buying it." Her eyes switched back and forth. "You might go to jail. Then I'll get the whole thing."

"Maybe you will. No matter what, I don't want it."

"Why the heck not?"

"If Bing had lived, he would've named a different trustee."

"But he didn't live. I deserve the whole estate. Not a penny should go to charity." She peered into the corridor and frowned. "I wouldn't want to live in this house—it's a death trap for cats. If I did agree to a split, I'd gladly give you this pink monstrosity."

"Why don't you give me your phone number, and I'll have my lawyer call you?" I glanced anxiously toward Adgers. Where the heck was Red Butler? Why wasn't he coming?

Eileen opened her cat purse. I edged into the corridor while she scribbled on a piece of paper that had pictures of cats on it. She saw me looking and said, "Isn't my scratch pad cute?"

She handed me the slip of paper and turned to leave. Then she whirled.

"You haven't heard the last from me," she said. "I'll chase you off yet."

"Whatever," I called. Despite the 92-degree heat, gooseflesh broke out on my arms. Eileen was tall enough to hang a stuffed dog from a chandelier. Had she sent that photograph of me and Coop to the DA?

Eileen lifted one hand, drew her fingers into a claw, and scratched the air. Her eyes narrowed for an instant, then she crossed the street to her RV. By the time Red Butler lugged our shopping bags up to the house, Eileen was gone.

"You just missed Bing's sister," I said.

"Did y'all have a cat fight?" Red Butler laughed. "Sorry, couldn't resist. What'd she want?"

I grabbed one of the bags. "Come on inside, and I'll fill you in."

I carried a tall glass of ice water to the garden and sank into a chair while Sir watered on the bushes. The bells of St. Michael's pealed in the distance. I looked up into the canopy of the live oaks. The garden was a tiny pocket of isolation in a world of noise. I couldn't say why, but I felt utterly safe here.

Red Butler wandered out and hooked a lock to the gate. He hadn't said much about Eileen's visit. In fact, he seemed downright pensive. He didn't glance up as Sir romped over the grass, chasing a yellow butterfly.

I pressed the cool glass against my forehead and thought about Coop. If Eileen hadn't taken that photograph, who had? Who would benefit other than Ava?

I saw a flicker of movement along the brick wall, where the ivy spilled down. A Carolina chickadee flew to the grass and swooped back up to the wall. The bird's movement soothed me. Surely no evil would happen where a chickadee played. Until I'd seen that stuffed dog, I'd never dreamed that anyone would want to hurt me or Sir.

Whoever had hung that stuffed dog had probably come through the garden, creeping through hedges, jumping over the wall. It would have to be an agile criminal, that's for sure. I got up and barely made it to the tiger lily bed before my water came back up. My heartbeat ticked in my ears, blotting out the gagging sounds. Too bad my safe feeling had only lasted a few minutes.

"You okay?" Red Butler called.

"Fine." I rubbed my arms, feeling the gooseflesh. If I was this scared in daylight, what would happen after dark? I wanted to be brave, but I didn't want me or my real dog to end up hanging from a chandelier.

I held out my hand. It trembled. No one in my life had wished me ill, nor had they coveted what little I had. Tonight I'd just stay awake for as long as I could and if I saw anything scary, I'd call 911. The police were only down the street and didn't have far to come.

I balled my hand into a fist and pushed it into my chest. Get you some gumption, I whispered to myself. Maybe if I laced barbed wire thought the ivy, twisted it around and around, I'd trap the evildoer. Take that, you bad man, and get you a tetanus shot while you're at it.

Red Butler walked up. "Something happen between you and the boss?"

"Why do you ask?" I narrowed my eyes. Was I truly that transparent?

" 'Cause you're mooning like a love-struck kid."

"I'm not."

"Yeah, you are. You got it bad. The boss really was your first love, wasn't he?"

"I wish I hadn't told you that."

"So, you're thinking you and him reconnected by happenstance? Or for a reason, like y'all are meant to be together?"

I had thought that, but I gave him a hard look.

"Girlie, you're making too much out of this. Don't you understand the psychology behind a first love? It ain't who the person is but what they represent. It was the first time you probably felt strong emotions for someone other than blood kin. You follow me?"

I nodded.

"See, the heart is tight and virginal. A first love makes you bleed. It opens the heart fully. That's why people can't forget their first loves. They show us just how deep the love can go. That's my take on it, anyway."

"You could give Dr. Phil a run for his money."

"Who'd want to?" He grinned.

I fixed a red-potato frittata, adding chopped bacon and onions. Since I was in a cooking mood, I made a corn and tomato salad with sweet mayonnaise dressing. I set the patio table with blue-and-white floral dishes, added a vase filled with hydrangeas, and called Red Butler to the garden.

He ate in silence, scraping his fork over the plate. I cut another wedge of frittata and slipped it onto his plate. He dug in greedily. "Damn, this is good," he said.

"Save room for your cake," I said.

"Answer me something, Teeny. What if you don't go to jail? What if you find some guy and get married? Have lots of kids. Would you keep baking cakes and selling them, or would you kick back and take it easy?"

Some guy? I repressed a smile. Now that I'd eaten, I was in a better mood. I clasped my hands and stretched them over my head. "I'll always bake," I said.

"Even if you don't have to?"

"The whole process just tickles me," I said. "I like matching food to people and filling up their empty spaces."

"You sound like my daddy. He was all eat up with food. Back when Charleston had a chef school, he wanted to go, but it cost a fortune. So my daddy, he taught himself how to cook." He pointed at the frittata. "Something like this takes skill."

He moved on to the cake. If I'd had time, I would have made crème frâiche. An iced cake is always tastier with something dense and slightly sour. If you want to cook good food, you have to think like a cook. It's messy. Cooking isn't a clean activity. It's not a stage set on Food Network, where ingredients are waiting in clear bowls and everything follows a script.

Every now and then, you must deal with dough that just won't rise. Do you start over? Knead the dough, cover it with a warm, moist towel, and hope for the best? Relationships are the same way. You can think you are following a recipe, you can do everything right, and your product might turn out indigestible. If it smells like bread, it may not be bread.

After Red Butler finished his cake, he loaded the dishwasher while I put my cookbooks onto the shelf above the desk. The phone trilled. It was decorative, made to look French. It even rang French. I picked up, hoping it was Coop. "Hey."

Silence.

"Is anyone there?"

"Die," a voice said. It was female, but I couldn't place it.

I banged down the receiver like I was crushing a wasp and stepped back.

"Damn, what'd they say?" Red Butler asked.

I put my hand over my mouth. It took me a few seconds to compose myself. "They said, 'Die.'"

"Man or woman?"

"Woman."

He lifted the phone. It jangled when he turned it upside down. "You got caller ID?"

"No."

"The police have this number tapped. Maybe they heard. Has this fucker called here before?"

"Once. But she didn't say anything."

"Where's your gate key?"

"In the bowl."

He walked into the dining room, into the hall. I heard the front door open, heard his footsteps clap over the bricks. I ran to the kitchen window and saw him bearing down on the stakeout car. He rapped on their window. It inched down, and I saw the short, gray-eyed cop's forehead. Red Butler yelled, thick cords standing out on his neck. His left arm flew into the air and he shook his fist. Then he hurried back to the house and slammed the door. "Bastards!"

I pushed away from the window and ran into the hall. "What's wrong?"

"They're checking it out." He looked at me from under his eyebrows. "Why didn't you tell me about that other call?"

"I told Coop. He thought it was Natalie. So did I."

"It prolly is, but you don't know for sure. People are meaner and crazier than they used to be. 'Die' is a big fucking deal. It's a threat."

"You're scaring me."

"You should be scared." He pointed at me. "Don't you keep nothing from me again. *Nothing*. Your life may depend on it."

thirty-five

At five o'clock, I went upstairs to take a bath. The room was larger than Aunt Bluette's living room and reminded me of a chessboard, with black-and-white tiles on the floor and walls. Monogrammed towels hung from silver rings, *EJ*, for Elmer Jackson.

I leaned into the claw-foot tub, pushed the stopper into the drain, and switched on the faucet. While the tub filled, I opened the linen closet. Towels were stacked on one shelf, toilet paper on another. I pulled out a black plaid towel and saw the top of a ziplock bag. I bent closer. The bag was filled with dried oregano and a glass pipe. Except I was pretty sure this wasn't a cooking herb. I blinked. Had Bing's late uncle been a doper?

I undressed, then eased down into the steaming tub and thought about Uncle Elmer. I'd never met him. Prior to his death, he'd been something of a recluse because of Alzheimer's. He hadn't attended Miss Dora's party, and she'd told me not to take offense, that poor Elmer never went anywhere. Yet he'd left this house long enough to buy drugs. Or, maybe they'd been delivered.

I made a note to tell Coop about the marijuana, then I climbed out of the tub and reached for the towel. I didn't want to put back on the clothes I'd worn all day, so I tucked the towel at my breasts and stepped across the hall to my bedroom.

I didn't have perfume: a little vanilla extract on my pulse points would have to suffice. The dollar store underwear and bra fit nicely. I put on the cream shirt and rolled the sleeves above my elbows. The buttons started at my breast bone, and I wished I had Aunt Bluette's long cameo necklace. That would have been a nice touch.

I removed the tags from the white denims I'd bought and slipped them on. A perfect fit. I'd have to quit spending money on clothes. I needed other things. Even a cheap apartment would require a deposit. I could do without furniture, but not electricity and water.

Of course, I had a good chance of ending up in jail. While my utilities would be covered, I couldn't see Coop and me talking through a partition, heating the air with heavy breathing, drawing I ♥ You's on the glass.

Six o'clock came and went. I didn't see Red Butler anywhere, so I took *Templeton Family Receipts* to the pink living room and curled up in a wing chair. It faced a long window that overlooked East Bay. Sir stretched on the floor, his stumpy legs splayed behind him. Each time a car went by, I jumped up and Sir scrambled to his feet.

"Poor baby," I told him. "I'm wearing you out."

I honed in on Aunt Bluette's handwriting and looked for her recipes. I found two for Italian cream cake, both with minor variations. I turned a page and ran my finger over Mama's back-slanted script. She'd jotted down Luke 23:43, plus Jimmy Buffett's "Cheeseburger in Paradise," adding a recipe for onion-bacon meat patties.

Another car passed down East Bay. I got up to look at the gold dolphin clock on the desk. Almost seven o'clock. I walked to the bookcase. In the cabinet I found a CD player and turned it on. Muse began to sing "Unintended, " a song about a man who'd found his true love, only he was still in another relationship.

Uncle Elmer must have been an interesting guy. He'd smoked marijuana, listened to alternative music, and lived in this fussy old house. He'd even let Miss Dora fill it with pinkness. I would have liked him tremendously. As long as I was the custodian of his home, I would take care of it.

The music changed to a Cary Brothers song, "Ride," which is about a man asking the love of his life to risk everything and go off with him. Coop had every reason in the world to ride away from me—if he dallied with a client, he could be disbarred. Dammit, why did everything have to be black or white? Couldn't we be friends by day and go into a gray area after dark? We could step into Uncle Elmer's dish closet, surrounded by pewter cups and silver trays, and do what we wanted.

No sooner had those self-pitying thoughts crossed my mind when the doorbell rang. Sir trotted over with a "Shall I eat them?" look in his eyes.

I set the cookbook on the cushion and walked to the corridor. Coop was waiting by the iron gate, one hand braced against the stucco wall. The gas lantern flickered over his pale yellow shirt. I unlocked the gate and studied his face. His hair was windblown and he gripped a file folder under his arm. His eyes had the tired, unfocused glaze of someone who'd been driving for hours.

"I was getting worried," I said.

"I just got back from the state lab in Columbia." He walked past me toward the gray door. No welcoming kiss, no accidental brushing of the arms. I bolted the gate and we walked into the foyer.

"I have good news," he said. "The forensic expert says the signature isn't Bing's."

"Natalie lied? I knew it!"

"She did more than lie. We'll need to do a full-bore investigation into her background. My guess is, she's no stranger to forgery. I've called the DA and the state attorney general."

I was having trouble breathing. I tried to relax as music drifted from the house.

"The police still have you under surveillance," Coop said. "We need more evidence that points to Natalie."

"The fake signature isn't enough?"

"I have to prove that she forged it." He paused. "Where's Red?"

"He was in the garden earlier." I started toward the back door and he caught my arm.

"Teeny," he began.

"What?" I had the feeling he was withholding bad news, something about the murder. Or maybe he'd gotten back with Ava. He stared until the music changed, and Coldplay began to sing "Yellow."

"Just say it," I whispered. I stepped closer. I thought he might jerk back, but his hands moved down to my hips. I stood on my toes and kissed him. And he kissed me back. He was all I'd ever wanted. If this was true love, then my other relationships had been pale imitations.

His hips moved against mine. Something hard pressed against my hipbone. I gently sucked his tongue and the taste was pure yellow. I'd never thought of love being a color, but here it was, a sweet taste in my mouth. Banana pudding, pineapple fluff, lemon ice, meringue pie.

"Yodelayheehoo!" Red Butler called.

We broke apart. Coop drew back and folded his arms. I started for the back door, wiping the edges of my mouth. I stepped into the garden, moving through the heavy night air. It smelled like rain was on the way. Coop shot ahead and grabbed one of the iron patio chairs and waved, indicating I should sit.

"How'd it go, Boss?"

"The signature was forged," Coop said. "I need you to get the dirt on Natalie Lockhart."

"Oh, I *have* been digging." Red Butler shrugged. "She moved to Charleston five months ago. Got a job at Jackson Realty."

"You talked to the other real estate agents?" Coop asked.

"They don't want to touch this while Miss Lockhart is still working at the agency. You'll have to depose them."

"What about the redhead?" I asked.

"Who?" Coop sat down next to me.

"Faye Carr?" Red Butler said. "The other naked badminton player. Teeny busted the gal's nose pretty bad. Anyhow, this Faye works for an escort service. I doubt that's her real name. But that's as far as I got. The stuffed dog incident derailed me. Plus, Teeny got a threatening call."

"Another one?" Coop asked.

"Yeah, only this time they said, 'Die.'" Red Butler bit down on a cigar. "You mind?" he asked me.

I shook my head.

Coop put one hand to his temple. "We need to file a police report."

"Relax. Already did. The dicks are looking. Should be easy peasy to see who called Teeny." Red Butler smoked fiercely for a few seconds. "But they aren't the only ones listening in to her calls. The boys found a line running down the front of the house. It went to a shitty box from Radio Shack."

"Somebody other than the police have tapped the phones?" I cried.

"Looks that way, girlie."

"Did the police remove it?" I cried.

"Not till they find out who put it there," Red Butler said. "They'll come back. If I had to bet, I'd say it's that Loonhart dame. She set you up. Now she's keeping tabs."

"We'll nail her, Teeny," Coop said.

"What if she ain't working alone?" Red Butler blew a smoke ring. "Maybe some badass guy is her accomplice."

"He'd have to be tall," I said, thinking of that chandelier. "Whoever killed Bing was there when I arrived. I got tased. Why didn't she—or he—just kill me?"

"Who knows what happened that day? Don't question the angels, girlie." Red Butler glanced at my neck. "You wasn't tased. Or you would've saw."

"Saw what?" I asked.

"It would've paralyzed you, but you would've been conscious."

"Teeny's marks were consistent with a stun gun," Coop said.

"What's the difference?" I asked.

"An 800,000-volt stun gun will knock out a man for twenty minutes," Red Butler said. "How much you weigh, Teeny?"

I gave him the stink eye. If I was on my deathbed and doctors wanted to know my weight to adjust my medicine, I'd just have to pass away. What I weigh is nobody's damn business. Not that I was fooling anyone with my vanity, but if I didn't say the numbers, they weren't real. So I changed the subject.

"Maybe the redheaded girl was involved?" I said.

"Nah, I'm thinking she was a hired whore," Red Butler said. "Brought in for your benefit. To make sure you broke up with your boyfriend. They wanted you out of the way."

I repressed a shiver. Whoever had killed Bing had planned it carefully. They were smart, and I was naive.

Red Butler leaned forward, resting his elbow on his knees. "If the redhead *was* hired, then Natalie had insider knowledge. She knew you'd catch them."

"That means she knew my cake decorating class was canceled," I said. "What if she was in Bing's house when the teacher called?"

Red Butler shrugged. "She could've checked your mail or checked the answering machine."

"Or Bing may have told her," Coop said.

"Doubt that." Red Butler said. "No man wants to get caught in a slutfest. Who else knew about your cake classes?"

"No one." I glanced at Coop.

He jiggled his car keys. Even if I was cleared, the taint would stick to me, and to him. At some point, we'd have to leave the bedroom and look for friends. Here in Charleston, coupling up was a normal thing. It was probably normal everywhere. Easy solution: move. But hadn't he already been through this with Ava?

Coop's cell phone buzzed. A female voice drifted up, British. "Wait, he killed it?" he asked, then paused. "Damn. Where are you now?"

Red Butler bit down on his cigar and tipped back his head. Coop was making sympathetic noises. "Hang on. I'll be right there."

He dropped the phone into his pocket and turned. "That was Ava."

"Who got killed?" Red Butler asked.

"A skunk. T-Bone killed it down in Edisto."

"Sheeit," Red Butler wrinkled his nose. "Did he get sprayed?"

"Yeah, big time."

"What was Ava doing in Edisto?" Red Butler asked.

"Looking at property."

"Harebrained idea, if you ask me." Red Butler waved his cigar.

What was harebrained? And why was T-Bone with Ava? I was nervous about the time line. Coop had left my house at 9:00 a.m. this morning to meet with the handwriting expert. When he showed up tonight, he said he'd just gotten back. If he'd been in Columbia all day, how had T-Bone ended up with Ava? Simple, either Coop had left a key under the mat or he'd gone home to meet her.

I was breathing too fast—where had I put my inhaler? "What kind of property is Ava looking at?" I asked, not caring if I was prying.

"She wants to build a house on the Edisto River." Coop stood and grabbed the back of the chair, his fingers curling around the iron spindles. "She's been looking for land."

Right. A house. She was putting down roots. She hadn't come back to South Carolina on a romantic whim. I pressed a hand against my midriff. My lips felt tingly, and I couldn't get a satisfying breath.

"Ava's frantic," Coop said. "I should go."

"For a dead skunk?" Red Butler snorted.

"The realtor is making a big fuss." Coop kept jiggling his keys. "Apparently the woman's married to a veterinarian. She said skunks don't come out in the daytime unless they're rabid. She started making phone calls. Now the health department is involved. Some guys showed up and cut off the skunk's head."

"Jesus on an emery stick," Red Butler said.

"They took T-Bone. Quarantined him."

"Did the skunk bite T-Bone?" I wrapped my feet around the chair's legs.

"No, but the vet is saying that rabies is transmitted by body fluids. And T-Bone bit the skunk."

"Ain't he been vaccinated, Boss?"

"Last August. It was a three-year vaccine."

"So he's covered, right?" I said.

"It's not 100 percent. Dogs are supposed to be vaccinated annually."

"A damn racket." Red Butler snorted.

"Yeah, miss one, and it's a misdemeanor," Coop said.

"Can't they test T-Bone and see if he's infected?" Red asked.

"They'd have to cut off his head."

"Screw that," Red Butler said.

"If the skunk's rabid, they'll euthanize T-Bone." Coop released the chair and stepped back. "I've got to find his health record and drive to Edisto. I'll call later."

Before I could untangle my feet and rise from the chair, he'd shot into the hall, his footsteps echoing over the hall floor. I sat there a minute, wondering if I should run after him or head to the kitchen and make Bitter Peach Pickles. It called for lots of vinegar, chopped onions, alum, and peaches, of course. I wouldn't feed them to Ava or Natalie. I'd eat them myself.

"Hey, Teens," Red Butler said. He was leaning in the doorway, giving me the eye. "Stop thinking bad thoughts."

"I'm not."

"Right. You're easy to read. You're hoping a tidal wave hits Edisto and washes Ava out to sea." He spread his hands wide. "Gone with the surf. An act of God."

"Wrong." But he'd seen the truth. If I couldn't control my tell-all face, I'd just have to wear a mask. I started into the house, but he was right behind me.

"Boss can't help this. He and Ava worship that dog and vice versa. She's T-Bone's mama. And Boss is the papa."

"I know that. I like T-Bone, too."

"I'm glad to hear it. But if you want the boss, you better get with the program."

"What program?" I said irritably.

"You don't know what you're up against," he said. "You better get a strategy."

"For what?"

"Ava is a beautiful pain in the ass. Competitive, impulsive, exciting. Going in fifteen directions at once. Boss is a rock. She needs his stability. The way he follows the rules and thinks things through. If she's with a man like herself, it's a disaster. She can't be with nobody but the boss."

"What about him? Can *he* be with anyone else?"

"Jury's out on that one. You're the first woman he's dated since they split up."

I blinked, trying to decide if this was due to heartbreak or lack of time.

"Boss ain't perfect. He won't take risks. Just once Ava wants to see him put his neck on the line for her. But he won't."

"Yes, he will. He saved that drowning girl."

"But that girl wasn't Ava. You can love someone and not give them what they want."

"How do you know all this? Did Ava tell you?"

"Lots of times. I don't know what it is about me, but women tell me their problems. Always have. I 'get' them. I know how their freaking minds work."

"How does Ava's work?"

"She's a man's wet dream. She flies planes and digs up thousand-year-old bones. A little on the skinny side, but her tits make up for it." He gestured at his chest. "And you're the homegirl. Cute. Not too skinny. Great hair. Big heart. Not too educated. Homegirl talks tough, but she's a softie. A little frightened on the inside but tries like hell to hide it. Men need a homegirl. She'll watch your back. She'll be there for you."

"Right now, I've got to be there for The Picky Palate." I walked past him, into the kitchen, and began setting out flour, sugar, and a bowl. I was stirring the batter when Red Butler appeared in the doorway, his thumbs tucked under his armpits.

"The boss is pulled between you and her. He's attracted to the differences. Ava's brave. You're skittish. You can cook. She eats men. You're local. She's foreign. Which girl gets the happy ending?" He shrugged. "It's a tough call."

"Ava wants happiness, too."

He pointed to the mixing bowl. "You're crying in the batter. You're gonna ruin the cake and your life. Hand me the spoon and go wash your face."

thirty-six

The worries took hold with a vengeance while I baked and iced those cakes. History was repeating. I understood what was happening much better this time around, but a part of me was still seventeen years old, sitting on Aunt Bluette's porch swing, planning to bake a sunflower cake for Coop, and dithering over the icing. I struggled to move beyond my selfish heart. What if Coop hadn't found T-Bone's health records? The state would hold the dog. I worried that the skunk was rabid. If so, Red Butler said everyone who'd come in contact with T-Bone after his encounter with the skunk would get rabies shots—and T-Bone would be put to sleep.

The next morning, I still hadn't heard from Coop. Red Butler and I made a delivery to The Picky Palate. Jan gave me an order for a dozen more red velvet cakes. "They're for one person," she said. "Apparently they had a fit over your other cakes. Can you have them ready in forty-eight hours? If you can, I'll do sixty-forty."

"Deal," I said.

Red Butler parked on Adgers and I dragged a laptop computer from his van. He grabbed another armful of cookbooks. When we reached the intersection, I spotted Eileen's catmobile at the corner. For all I knew, she'd tapped my phone and hung the stuffed bulldog.

"Bing's sister is back," I said.

He dropped the cookbooks and took off running. The Winnebago's brake lights turned bright red and a plume of smoke drifted from the tailpipe. The RV blasted toward the Battery.

He came back and showed me numbers he'd written on his hand. "I got the bitch's license number. You got wireless Internet?"

"I think so. If not, there's a phone jack below the desk. What you looking up?"

"First, I'm going to find this cat fanatic. Then I'm doing a background check on Natalie."

He set up his laptop on the kitchen desk. I leafed through my books and found a red velvet cake recipe that could be doubled. I wanted to make good use of Uncle Elmer's double convection ovens before I had to move. I mixed the ingredients, poured the batter into six greased pans, and slid them into the ovens.

"I hope you find plenty," I said.

"Before Miss Loonhart moved to Charleston, she lived in Savannah. Worked at a bank. Divorced in 1998 from a used car salesman. He claimed she tried to kill him, but the charges didn't stick. Anyways, she got herself another bank job, a loan officer. Started fooling around with one of the married VPs. Big scandal. He got divorced and married Natalie. A year later, he died in his sleep."

"How old was he?"

"Fifty-two."

"That's young."

"She could've screwed him to death. The Savannah coroner said it was a heart attack. But get this, the banker had a $500,000 life insurance policy. Natalie went to live with her aunt. Alice E. Wauford. I'm checking her out next."

The doorbell chimed. I patted Red Butler's shoulder. "Maybe that's Coop. Keep an eye on my cakes?"

"You betcha."

Sir was right on my heels as I grabbed the key and stepped into the corridor. A man and woman stood on the other side of the iron grille. "Can I help you?" I called, folding my arms. Sir must have picked up on my tone and body language. He ran to the gate and barked.

"Sorry to disturb you," the woman said, "but we're the Randolphs. We met the other day? We're buying the Spencer-Jackson House?"

"I remember you," I said.

"The closing date is around the corner, and I wanted my designer to have a look."

I lifted Sir and unlocked the gate with my free hand. "Come on in," I said. Mr. Randolph shuffled his feet, looking embarrassed, but his wife stepped through, followed by a perky woman with auburn hair. A low rumble started in Sir's throat.

"He won't bite, will he?" The auburn-haired woman put her fingers in her mouth.

"He never has." I stroked Sir's head. "I'll just put him in the kitchen. Y'all look around all you want. The door's open."

I walked down the corridor, into the hall. The designer was eyeing the baseboards. "Is the puppy housebroken?"

"Housetrained." I crossed the hall, into the raspberry dining room, into the butler's pantry, and reached out one hand to shut the pocket doors. "Be nice," I told Sir when I set him down. He looked up at me and growled under his breath, his stubby tail wagging. I turned into the kitchen.

Red Butler swiveled in the chair. "The boss here?"

"No, it's the couple who bought the house." I shrugged. "Their decorator came with them."

"That's some nerve." He shook his head. "No way that sale is going through."

"I didn't want to bring up the forged signature," I said.

"You trying to give me a heart attack? Anyhow, it's alleged forgery. If the DA proves that Natalie did it, she'll go to the pokey. We're talking murder, grand larceny, and criminal possession of a forged instrument."

"The new buyers are closing next week. The law can't fix this by then."

"The boss knows how to slow things down."

"Boy, does he ever," I said. A soothing vanilla smell wafted from the ovens. I took a breath, then found a clean bowl and began mixing ingredients. The sound of feminine voices echoed along the high ceilings. The pocket doors banged open, and the decorator strode into the kitchen, trailed by the couple.

"I see a terra-cotta ceiling," the designer said, waving her hands. "Let's jerk out the granite. It's so passé. We'll replace it with concrete."

"Concrete?" Mr. Randolph looked shocked.

"Concrete," the designer said with a decisive nod. She faced the old brick wall behind the cooktop and made a scrubbing motion with her hands. "The bricks are old, but they're probably not original. So, let's get rid of them."

"I kinda like them," said Mrs. Randolph, and her husband nodded.

The decorator wrinkled her nose, as if she'd caught the scent of dead mice in the walls. "You can try painting them. I'd go with black. It'll make those white cabinets pop. But honestly? I'd get a demolition crew in here and knock out those bricks."

"And replace them with what?" Mrs. Randolph asked.

"Copper. I see copper." The designer's heels snapped over the floor as she bustled around the room. She opened the dishwasher, peered inside, and moved to the warming oven. "Do the appliances work?"

"Yes." I nodded.

"That's too bad, they're kinda generic. I'd prefer a Wolf range, Sub-Zero fridge, and Asko dishwashers—two of them will be perfect for entertaining. Are those ovens Thermador?" The designer stopped by the ovens and started to open the top door.

"No!" I shouted.

She jumped back, her hair swinging. "What?" she cried.

"My cakes," I said. "They'll fall."

Sir growled again and scooted under the desk. He rested his head on his paws. The designer frowned. "I don't really like animals," she said. "Are you sure he isn't doing poo-poo all over the floors?"

"He's not. I promise."

"Who decorated the kitchen?" asked the designer.

"I'm not sure. Dora Jackson did the other rooms."

"That explains a lot." She glanced into the dining room and smirked. "That woman is in the wrong profession. If she likes pink things, she should've been a gynecologist. "

I crossed my arms, ready to defend Miss Dora with my last breath, but the designer smiled. "Do you know the history of the house?"

"No, ma'am."

"You don't have a file? No research?"

"I'm sure Natalie Lockhart will know," I said. From the desk chair, Red Butler turned and gave me a warning glance.

"It would be lovely if we knew the original colors," the designer continued. "I like to keep things authentic." She opened a cabinet and pulled out a china plate with a bird pattern. "Do the contents come with the house?"

"I'm sure it's all laid out in your contract," I said, glancing at the cookbooks above Red Butler's head. If I had to steal them again, I'd have no qualms. I thought about Uncle Elmer's homemade music CDs, his extensive dish collection, and his secret stash of pot. Who *would* be the recipient of his belongings?

The designer turned to the Randolphs. "You might consider selling the art and accessories. I know antique dealers who'll give you a pretty penny."

"I like some of the stuff," Mrs. Randolph said.

"The pink needs to go."

"But the outside of the house is pink," said Mrs. Randolph. "It matches."

"A pink facade is one thing," said the decorator, "but inside? An abomination."

The designer faced me. "When will you be out?"

"Thursday at midnight," I said.

The designer walked over to the French doors. "A harvest table should go right here," she said, then glanced out at the garden. "Mind if we go outside?" she asked.

"Sure." I waved.

The Randolphs followed the woman down the steps, onto the patio. The phone trilled, and Red Butler answered with a gruff hello. He sat up a little straighter. "Hello?" he said again. His face softened. "Oh, okay. Just a minute." He held out the phone. "It's for you, Teeny."

Judging from his baffled expression, I didn't think Coop was calling. And Miss Dora knew about the tap, so most likely it wasn't her, either.

"Who is it?" I whispered.

"A woman." He shrugged.

Frowning, I took the receiver. "Yes?"

"It's Natalie," said a breathless voice. "Is this phone tapped?"

I caught Red Butler's eye and said, "It's not tapped, Natalie."

He nodded and made an OK sign.

"Fine." Natalie released a theatrical sigh. "We need to talk. I know who killed Bing."

"You know who killed Bing?" I tilted the phone so Red Butler could hear her reply.

"Shhh, be quiet," Natalie said. "God knows who's listening. Can we meet?"

"I'll be home most of the day," I said. "Come over."

"I can't." Her voice broke. "See, they're watching you."

"The detectives? They aren't interested in you."

"Don't you get it? The watchers are being watched. Come to my house right now."

"Watchers?" I said.

Red Butler pointed to his ear and made little circles. "Looney tunes," he whispered.

I wasn't too sure. Someone else was watching? I'd spouted off about those sex tapes and fake signatures.

"I can't come right now," I said. "The Randolphs are here with their decorator—unless you want me to kick them out."

"No!" She released an agonized sob. "Look, I'm risking my life just talking to you."

"Then call the police. Tell them what you know."

Red Butler lifted his thumb. "Perfect," he mouthed.

"If you want to talk," I said, "you'll have to come here."

"Impossible. Just come after the Randolphs leave. I'll wait. Just don't make me wait too long. I've got something you want."

"What?"

"A surprise."

Red Butler mouthed, "Get her addy."

"Where do you live?" I asked her.

"You know where Hermosa Country Club is? My house is the last one on Persimmon Lane, way back in the cul-de-sac. Peach stucco with dark green shutters. Are you writing all this down?"

"Got it."

"Be careful. Make sure you're not followed—and bring that tape." She hung up with a decisive click.

Red Butler took the phone from my hand and set it in the cradle. "It's a trap," he said. "You can't go alone."

"Her sex tape is at Coop's." I opened a drawer and grabbed a band.

"You can't get it." He popped his knuckles.

"What about the surprise?" I pulled back my hair and rubber-banded it.

"Teeny, you're too innocent. The bitch plans to shoot you."

The decorator walked through the French doors, trailed by the Randolphs, and began to outline her visions for the kitchen. I was having serious doubts about going to Natalie's. I pulled Red Butler aside.

"My phone is tapped, right?" I whispered.

He nodded and glanced at the decorator. She was going on about the brick wall again.

I moved closer to him. "So, the police heard what Natalie said?"

"You don't understand wiretapping," he said. "The po-po aren't sitting in a van, listening to your calls. Everything's taped, and it's miles away. I don't know how often the police are checking, or how efficiently. I'm still waiting to hear about the trace on your death threat call. But the Radio Shack box is another story. The device isn't taping your calls; it's sending them via a wireless connection. So, yeah, whoever did the tap could be listening."

"Bing's sister is hanging around in her Winnebago. Maybe she did it."

"Could be." He handed me his cell phone. "I'm going to talk to the boys outside. While I'm gone, call the boss. He's on speed dial. Tell him where we're going."

After he left, I scrolled through the menu, and pressed *Boss*. When Coop's voice mail picked up, I hesitated. What to say? *Come save me, Coop. My crisis is bigger than Ava's.* I hung up.

Red Butler walked into the kitchen just as the decorator was herding the Randolphs out of the house. "The boys outside are gonna follow us to Natalie's house," he said. "You talk to Coop?"

"He didn't answer."

On the way to his van, he called Ava. "Coop with you?" He paused. "You know where he's at?" Another pause. "Damn, that stinks, don't it? Listen, if you hear from the boss, tell him to call."

He hung up and said, "Ava's having a breakdown. She produced T-Bone's health records, but he's still in quarantine. The state's suffering from budget cuts. Everything moves slower. If they don't call in a few days, it means the skunk wasn't rabid. Then T-Bone can come home."

Red Butler glanced up and down the street, his sunglasses reflecting cars and buildings. Eileen's RV was parked by the seawall. As we walked toward it, I heard meowing, but I didn't see her anywhere.

I climbed into Red Butler's van. Before I could fasten my seat belt, he did a U-turn and blasted onto East Bay. He wasn't the smoothest driver, but I was glad to have him as my chaperone. Not only did he understand the city's streets and alleys, he understood the twists and turns of the heart. And if Natalie pulled anything, he was packing a gun.

thirty-seven

Natalie's stucco house sat on a half acre lot behind a thick screen of oak trees. A Jackson Realty sign was staked on the immaculate lawn. Red Butler turned up the pea gravel drive.

"Ritzy fitzy," he said and pointed to a white BMW convertible. "That her car? SOSEX-E."

"Is it ever."

"Let's go see the loon." Red Butler cracked open his door.

"Shouldn't I go alone?" I asked.

"You kidding?" He flipped his hand at the house. "Look at all them windows. She's prolly watching with binoculars."

We walked to the porch, past a concrete bunny that held a "welcome" sign. Potted ferns and impatiens spilled out of urns, making a pathway to the door, which was adorned with a fake magnolia wreath.

Red Butler peeked through the sidelight while I pressed the bell. It squawked, putting me in mind of an indignant chicken. I squinted through the sidelight, too. A stairway curved up into shadows, and paintings of nude women were staggered on the wall.

Red Butler opened his cell and punched in numbers. "It's me," he said, glancing over his shoulder at the Camry. "Miss Lockhart won't open the door."

The detectives got out of the car and headed toward us, looking grim. I stepped to the edge of the porch to get out of the way. Red Butler grabbed my arm. "Don't be scared of them," he whispered. "They're just regular dicks, okay? They got names and families. The short fellow is Boudreaux and he likes hot sauce. Baldy's name is Lennox and he's got newborn twins."

Boudreaux ran up the steps and pressed his stubby finger against the doorbell. Again, the two notes screaked. "Police, open up!" he called.

Lennox walked up and rapped on the sidelights.

"She ain't coming," Red Butler said. "Will it take long to get a warrant?" he asked.

"What makes you think we'll need one?" Lennox asked. He banged harder on the door, and the wreath fell off. "Miss Lockhart?" he yelled. "Police."

I reached down to pick up the wreath, and Red Butler grabbed my hands. "Don't touch nothing, homegirl."

The detectives split in different directions and walked around the house. Red Butler and I trailed after Boudreaux. Afternoon light glanced off a swimming pool. Lounge chairs with white cushions lined up on the pavement. Pink petunias spilled out of concrete urns, with damp circles spreading from each one. They'd been watered, and not too long ago.

We followed Boudreaux up the deck. At the far end, the French doors stood open, showing a blue and white kitchen. Boudreaux poked his head inside, then he scrambled back and called for backup and an ambulance.

"What's wrong?" I cried, and ran to the door. A pie sat on a white table. One wedge was missing. The scent of bitter almonds mixed in with the tang of rusty nails. I heard a gurgle and looked down. Natalie lay face up on the kitchen floor in a red puddle. Several feet away, next to an overturned chair, was a redheaded girl. I couldn't see her face, but

I recognized her hair. There was no blood, just broken pottery mixed with glazed peaches and pie crust.

Bile shot into my throat. I ran to the edge of the pavement and was sick. A few moments later, I felt strong hands grip my shoulders and guide me to a lounge chair.

"Sit down before you faint," Red Butler said.

"Couldn't help it." I spat. My right knee began to shimmy.

"Don't freak out," he said. "Homegirl's got an alibi. You ain't taking the rap for this."

"Are they dead?"

"The redhead is. Natalie's still got a pulse."

"What if we'd come sooner?"

"Hard to say. We might be coughing up blood, too."

The ambulance arrived, and the gurney rattled over the pavement. A policeman took my statement. Through the French doors, I watched EMTs working on Natalie. Another group of policemen arrived wearing biohazard suits.

"What's all that about?" I asked Red Butler as we walked around the house.

He didn't answer. Natalie's neighbors were standing in the cul-de-sac, and a cop was trying to push them back. Red Butler's van was blocked by police cars, so he started making phone calls. I heard him say, "Can you come to North Charleston and get Teeny?" He paused. "There's been a shooting." Another pause. "No, Ava. You got to stay with her."

Oh, crap, I thought. Not her.

"Ava's picking you up," Red Butler said. "I know you don't like her, but my van's bottlenecked."

"Why can't I just stay with you?"

"Look at you." He spread his hands. "You're a wreck. Plus, there's a murderer on the loose. You need looking after."

"I can look after myself."

"Yeah, but Ava's got a gun and she knows how to use it."

It was a steaming hot June afternoon. Still, I couldn't stop shaking. Maybe the murderer was standing in the crowd, watching and listening. Or maybe Natalie and the redhead had been in cahoots. "None of this makes sense," I said.

"Murder never does, kiddo. We may never know why Nataloon lured you here. But it's clear that somebody's after the coin. The Spencer-Jackson House is worth millions. You and Sir got squatter's rights. So, please, let Ava keep you safe, okay? I know you don't trust her ass, but she won't let nothing get you. She'll keep watch till the boss gets back."

"When will that be?"

"He'll be here when he gets here. If you love the boss, you gotta get used to long hours. He'll always be saving somebody. This time it's you. Next time, who knows?"

Minutes later, a motorcycle nosed its way through the growing crowd. The policeman ran over to Ava, waving his arms. She shut off the engine and coasted to a stop. She pulled off her helmet, and the wind caught her hair, sending the dark curls rippling behind her.

She tossed me a helmet. I missed because I was looking at her left hand: she was wearing her wedding rings. The helmet thumped against the pavement and rolled over to the policeman. He handed it to me.

My hands shook as I shoved the helmet onto my head and climbed onto the back of the bike. I barely had time to grab her waist when the engine sputtered. The crowd parted, and the bike lunged forward down the heat-waved road.

When we pulled up to the Spencer-Jackson House, I looked around for Eileen's RV. It was gone. I unlocked the gate for Ava to roll her motorcycle into the corridor. She grabbed a lemon purse from the compartment—it was nearly identical to the one I'd bought, only hers had white leather trim instead of plastic. We had the same taste in men—why not pocketbooks?

I went through the whole rigmarole of unlocking the door and shutting off the alarm, which should have comforted me but had the opposite effect. I set my purse on the bench and ran upstairs to fetch Sir. He trotted downstairs, snorting with pleasure, and scratched at the back door, pointedly ignoring Ava. I opened the door and he ran outside.

"Cute dog," she said.

"How's T-Bone?" I asked.

"Still quarantined. I've been on the phone with the health department all day." She set her pocketbook on the bench. "If we don't hear anything horrid by tomorrow, T-Bone is in the clear. And he can come home."

"I've been praying for him."

"You believe in that?"

"Yes."

She seemed pleased with my answer, but I couldn't have said why.

"I better get Sir." I stepped into the garden and broke off a few lavender sprigs. Sir darted around the hydrangeas, his jowls swaying, and ran through the door, casting a suspicious glance at Ava, as if just noticing her for the first time.

She ignored his bark and smiled at me. "Can I help you do anything?"

"Just make yourself at home. I'll be in the kitchen."

"Are you the type who cooks when she's upset?"

"Anything wrong with that?"

"You just left a crime scene. How can you be in the mood to cook?"

"If I waited for the mood to strike, I'd starve." I walked toward the dining room and turned. "Do you have to be in the mood to dig?"

She just stared.

The pine floor creaked as we passed through the dining room, into the kitchen. She leaned against the island and folded her hands. I rinsed the lavender and set it on paper towels to dry. Shortbread was the most English dessert I could think of. Plus, lavender would defuse the catfight that was brewing.

"Can you cook?" I asked.

"Would that shock you?"

It would. I set out a wooden block and a French knife. "Care to dice the lavender?"

"You trust me with a knife?" She winked. "What are you making?"

"Shortbread."

"How clever of you. Lavender, to calm the stomach and the mind."

Ava chopped the lavender into precise bits while I creamed the butter and sugar, then she watched me mix in the flour, salt, vanilla, and lavender. I started kneading the dough and she pressed her finger against it.

"Shortbread feels like a baby's bum." She licked her knuckle. "My nana used to make this."

I hoped she'd keep talking, but she fell silent, watching my hands shape the dough into a circle and prick it with a fork.

"My nana did that to shortbread." Ava pointed to my fork. "She never said why."

"Prevents air bubbles," I said.

She smiled. "You don't care for me, do you?"

Not one bit. I hate your beautiful hair and your toned thighs. I hate that Coop has made love to you. Naturally I couldn't tell the truth, but I'd told enough lies, so I decided to level with her—to a point.

"You're a great cookbook thief," I said. "I owe you a debt of gratitude."

Her smile widened. "You know why I came back to Charleston, don't you?"

"A lot of people come here. It's a beautiful city."

"I want my husband. And I might have gotten him back if he hadn't bumped into you at McTavish's Pub."

I looked up. "How did you know I was at the pub?"

"Cooper told me."

Right. Maybe she took that picture and sent it to the DA. I didn't dare mention it—wasn't that defamation? I had a sudden vision of Aunt Bluette swooping down from heaven to beat me with a switch. She'd raised me to never be hurtful. She used to say, "Teeny, there's a fine line between telling the truth as you see it—the key phrase being *as you see it*—and being a judgmental smart-ass."

"Cooper and I aren't enemies," she said. "We'll always be . . . close."

What the doodly hell was that supposed to mean? How close was close? I picked up a lavender sprig and sniffed. I was trying my damnedest not to take offense, but she was a little too direct for my taste. The sugar in me was melting, coming to a boil.

"I've upset you, haven't I?" she asked.

"Nope." I was lying through the gap in my front teeth. Prickly, bloodsucking thoughts were circling in my head. My hands shook as I put the shortbread into the oven.

"God, I could use a drink," she said, pressing the heel of her hand against her forehead, her long, elegant fingers curling inward. "I tend to be a bit hyper, if you haven't noticed."

"What about warm milk? Sometimes that's real soothing."

"Why not?" She flashed a smile, but it didn't touch her eyes.

I found a copper saucepan, poured in milk, added a vanilla bean, and turned the flame to low. "I don't have artificial sweetener," I said. "Will sugar do?"

I was stereotyping the "thin people never eat carbs" theory, but sugar was loaded with carbohydrates, and I didn't want to fix something she wouldn't like.

"I've got Splenda." She went to the hall and returned with her purse. When she unzipped it, I saw that it was filled with yellow packets. She plucked one out and handed it to me. "I have an odd habit of nicking sweetener."

"Nicking?"

"Stealing. When I'm on digs, I don't always stay in hotels. Sometimes I'm in a tent. I cook on butane—now there's a challenge for you, Teeny. But if I need to sweeten my coffee, I can't ring room service or find a minimarket."

"Miss Dora can't use anything with sucralose in it." I emptied a yellow packet into the milk. "It makes her swell up and itch."

I checked the pan. Bubbles rolled along the curved edge. I shut off the burner and fished out the vanilla bean. Steam curled as I poured the milk into two mugs. I thought of *Arsenic and Old Lace* and the aunts discussing the best way to disguise the smell of arsenic.

For a tiny moment, I indulged in a wicked fantasy, but I pushed it aside. This had to stop. I might be jealous of Ava, but I would never harm her. Maybe this was how evil started. Maybe thoughts were bridges and when you crossed over one, you passed from safe to dangerous. And once you did that, there was no going back.

thirty-eight

I cut the warm shortbread into wedges and put it on a tray with the mugs. We settled in Uncle Elmer's library. It was a cozy room, with butternut paneling and cherry antiques. Uncle Elmer's porcelain bird collection was lined up on the mantel. Pink-and-green plaid curtains hung on the windows. Through the wavy bubbled glass, I saw the garden.

I set the tray on the coffee table. Ava curled on the settee and reached for a shortbread wedge. I lifted a mug and sat down in a chair.

"Delicious," she said and reached for her mug.

I repressed a smile, but I was tickled to pieces. I wasn't looking for friendship through food, but I was looking for acceptance. I needed to know that when I cooked something, it hit the spot.

She lowered her mug. "Teeny, you're awfully pensive."

Pensive hadn't been in my word-a-day calendar, so I just said what was on my mind. "I was just thinking of Bonaventure."

"Do your parents still live there?"

"No."

"Are they still alive?"

"My mother ran off when I was eight. She didn't come back. I never knew my dad. My aunt raised me."

"You're fatherless?" She took a sip of milk.

I nodded.

"Do you have an Electra complex?" she asked.

I had a feeling she wasn't referring to vacuum cleaners. But I wasn't going to ask for an explanation.

"Are you bitter about your mum?" Ava asked.

"No, I love her. I always will. She was sick and confused. She did the best she could."

"You're far more magnanimous than I would be. I'm still angry with Father. He ran off with the au pair. It was quite scandalous. I was only ten but I felt responsible—my own babysitter." She stretched her legs. "Of all the women in the world, Cooper picks two with abandonment issues. It makes me wonder what happened in his childhood."

"He had a happy one," I said. "His parents were good people. They're still together."

"Yes, I know." She dipped her cookie into the milk. "Mrs. O'Malley is my mother-in-law."

"Sorry, I misspoke."

"It's quite all right. She likes me but she doesn't know what to do with me." Ava dropped the cookie into the milk. "I'm sure you're wondering why Cooper and I broke up."

"It's crossed my mind."

"He and I are quite opposite, if you haven't noticed. He's cautious. Mr. Straight-as-an-Arrow. His moral rectitude is beyond reproach. I'm a risk taker. He's not." She set down her mug. "Our problems reached an apex when I went caving in the Gilf al-Kebir—that's in Egypt."

"I saw *The English Patient*." No matter how many times I watched that movie, I wanted Katharine to tell her husband that Almásy was more handsome and she was running off with him.

"Then you know the desert is dangerous and beautiful." She got up from the settee and walked to the window. "I went with a group. Fifteen in all. We hired guides and headed to Egypt. The Libyan border is dodgy. Lots of drug and gun trafficking. We were taken by Sudanese bandits." She turned. "Cooper didn't tell you?"

"No."

"That's just like him—he's like Russian nesting dolls. Just when you think you've opened the last egg, there's another and another."

She pulled her hair to one side and held it up like a paintbrush. "The kidnappers held our group for ten days. Our respective governments were asked for fifteen million in ransom. We weren't treated poorly. But it was harrowing, especially when the Egyptians sent in commandos and helicopters. The kidnappers were shot. We were taken to a hospital in Cairo. No harm done. Or so I'd thought."

"I'm so sorry, Ava." I put my hand on my chest.

"Cooper flew to Egypt, of course. He demanded I give up my career, or at least confine myself to digs in Williamsburg. That's just too tame." She walked back to the settee and perched on the edge. "Here's the tricky bit. Cooper has led a sheltered life. Nothing truly awful has ever happened to him. Ever. He was more horrified by the kidnapping than I was. We had a huge row. He went back to Charleston. I went to Sudan. And he filed for divorce."

My hand shook as I lifted my mug and watched her over the rim. I'd always felt Coop hadn't told me the full story of their breakup. I was starting to understand why.

"I came back to Charleston, back to Cooper," she said. "I thought we'd sort things out, the way we'd always done. Our house at Seabrook had been rented to a family of four. Cooper had moved to Isle of Palms— and he'd taken T-Bone with him. I rented a house on Sullivan's Island. One of his friends mailed me divorce papers. I tore them up, mailed the bits to Cooper, and flew back to Sudan. I had a long while to think. At night, with no distractions, I ached for Cooper. I wanted him back. I abandoned the dig and came back to Sullivan's Island, determined to try one more time. But then I saw you and Cooper at the market."

I reached for a shortbread wedge and crammed it into my mouth.

"I was so hurt and confused," she continued. "I almost flew back to Sudan. But I finally sorted my feelings. If it takes giving up my career, I'll do it. Archeology is my life's work. I'm over the moon about dirt. I like how it smells. I like the colors and textures. I like the way it collects under my fingernails. I'm particularly fond of it when it's hiding something I want. But I'll toss it aside if that's what Cooper wants."

My mouth was full of shortbread, so I couldn't answer. But I felt the same way about cooking. I love the way dough sticks to my fingers. I love watching butter run down the sides of warm bread. I like taking something whole, like an onion, mincing it into tiny pieces and slipping it into a garlicky risotto. I don't even mind the tears.

"I know you care for my husband," she said. "But I want one more chance with him." She lifted her finger. "Just one more."

I swallowed and the cookie stuck in my throat. I reached for my mug and gulped milk, as if washing down her words. Her one chance was hampered by me. Coop couldn't give full attention to a reconciliation if he was rescuing me.

"There's no obfuscated meaning here. I've laid it out. I'm not the type to beg, but I'm begging you, Teeny." Tears stood in her eyes. "I know it's a big ask, but please let me try to patch things up. I love him beyond all else. And I'm quite aware of your history with him. The way I see it, I might lose Coop but gain a friend."

"Me?" I leaned back.

"Sometimes the best relationships are forged when we meet someone who makes us want to be better than we are."

I nodded. She was exactly the kind of woman I'd hoped to be one day. Still, I couldn't see us shopping together at Big Lots.

She extended her hand. I knew if we shook, we'd be sealing a deal like wary politicians. But I didn't want to seal it.

"I've got to think about it, Ava."

"I'll give you a day or two." She wiped her eyes. "Then I'll take matters into my own hands."

Right, I thought, and bit into another cookie. She'd take Coop into her hands.

Coop and Red Butler showed up at dusk. I cooked a tomato basil tart, red rice cakes, hoppin' John, cornbread sticks, and lemon raspberry basil sorbet, made by stirring chopped basil and lemon zest into store-bought raspberry ice.

Ava helped me set the table in the garden with Uncle Elmer's hunting dog china. Then I went to the kitchen and poured tea into brown crystal goblets. I wasn't sure who took sugar and who didn't. I was just pouring sugar syrup into a tiny pitcher when Coop walked up.

"How do you like your tea?" I asked him.

" 'In a glass, sweetheart,' " he said.

"Bogart said that in *The Big Sleep*."

"Yeah, I know."

"I didn't think you watched old movies."

"There's a lot you don't know, kid." He winked.

I put the glasses on a tray, added the pitcher of sugar syrup, and followed Coop into the garden. Ava sat next to him and told stories about a haunted dig site in the Carpathian Mountains, her wedding rings sparking in the candlelight as she waved her hand.

After the meal, I passed out Market Street pralines and the talk shifted from archeology to murder.

"Natalie is still alive," Coop said. "She's out of surgery. A bullet hit her lung. If she makes it through the night, she's got a fighting chance."

"Let's just hope she ain't brain-damaged." Red Butler crossed his fingers. "If she comes through, she can tell us who the shooter was. Prolly it's the same person shot Bing. And Teeny will be in the clear."

My future as a jailbird didn't seem to interest Ava in the least. She touched Coop's arm. "Any news on the skunk?"

"Not a word." He patted her hand. "We've got twelve more hours. Then we'll know."

"We got worse problems than rabid dogs," Red Butler said. "A serial killer is running loose in Charleston."

Serial killer? I dropped the praline bag and they spilled onto the pavement.

"Aw, Teeny," he said, "don't worry. You're gonna be safe. The police put an extra car outside. And I'll be here."

"Me, too," Coop said.

"And me." Ava smiled at me. Her eyes said, *He's still my husband.*

I know, mine said back. I turned away before she saw the rest of it: *but I've loved him longer.* I had no business being in a love triangle. Besides, I owed Ava, big time. She'd helped me steal my cookbooks and she'd found discrepancies in Natalie's documents. It was impossible not to respect her keen intelligence. She was interesting and courageous, but I still loved Coop.

I turned in early. The Spencer-Jackson House had six bedrooms, and I left my guests to puzzle out the sleeping arrangements. I went to the pink toile room and slipped into my prettiest dollar-store nightgown. If I was sleeping alone, I might as well do it in style.

Sir's tags clicked as he pawed the side of the bed, pleading for a lift. I set him on the covers, and he dug into the linen to make his spot just right. Outside my door I heard three voices. I put my hand over Sir's tags to stop the jingling. Coop told Red Butler and Ava goodnight. A door slammed. That was a promising sign, right? I heard the stairs squeak, and two sets of footsteps moved to the third floor.

I slipped beneath the quilt, and the weight of the day smothered me. I felt dozy-headed, as if I'd taken TYLENOL PM. I tried to take a satisfying breath, but it ended in a yawn—a sure sign that my nerves were in a jumble. Before paratroopers leap out of a plane, they'll yawn. It's nature's way of calming down. So, my breathing troubles weren't 100 percent physical. But how could I calm down when my boyfriend and his wife were having a sleepover? Sure, they were in separate bedrooms, but the weirdness of it had left me breathless.

I reached for my inhaler, breathed in the bitter fumes, and fell asleep.

thirty-nine

I awoke a little before dawn. My chest felt tight and I couldn't get my breath. Sir curled up next to me and licked my arm, as if trying to sooth me. I lay there a minute, trying to calm myself, but it didn't work. I groped on the nightstand for my inhaler and took a puff. The smell of Ventolin made Sir snort, and he rubbed his flat muzzle against the cover.

"Sorry, fella," I said.

Now I was wide awake, and hungry. Sir and I headed down to the kitchen. I turned on the light. A man stood beside the sink. Even though my brain registered that it was Coop, I jumped a little.

"Hey, Teens." He turned on the tap and water trickled into a glass. "I couldn't sleep."

"Me, either."

"I was just going out to the garden to sit awhile." Coop took a sip of water. "Keep me company?"

Would I ever. I shut off the alarm and we walked into the shadowy garden. Sir ran to the hydrangea bushes and lifted his leg. The sky was gray, edged with the grainy light that comes before dawn. A breeze rippled through the crepe myrtles, and fine white petals floated to the patio. I pulled out an iron chair and swiped my hand across the damp cushion.

Coop pulled off his t-shirt and laid it over the seat. "There you go," he said.

I wished he hadn't done that. Because it just made me love him even harder. He sat down beside me and traced his finger down my arm. I looked up at the house. Which window was Ava's? Was she a light sleeper? And why did I freaking care? I hadn't promised her doodly-squat. No, that wasn't true. I'd told her I'd think about her proposal. I'd been thinking, all right, just not the way she'd hoped.

I wanted to climb into Coop's lap and press my face against his neck and say, *I love you, O'Malley.* But I couldn't do that because Coop was in trouble with the DA over that photograph.

To keep from touching him, I wedged my hands between my knees, stretching the nightgown until the bodice dropped lower. Coop's eyes went to my breasts. I pulled my hands away and my bodice raised to a modest position. I didn't trust myself to be around him. I was keenly aware of his gestures, and each one evoked a physical reaction, like an oyster responding to a foreign body, building layers of pearl.

"I hope Natalie wakes up and tells the truth," I said.

"Even if she doesn't, it's clear you were set up," he said. "The police wouldn't have put extra men outside if they didn't have another suspect."

"But who?" My number one suspect, Natalie, was in the hospital. My number two suspect, the redhead, was dead. Just for a fleeting second, I saw my own death as clearly as I saw Sir nosing through the hydrangeas.

"The police traced those anonymous calls to a pay phone on Meeting Street."

"In other words, they don't know doodly-squat."

"Exactly," he said. Behind him, the sky had brightened to the color of a limpet shell with sharp, rippled clouds. A purple streak held over the rooftops. Sir growled and spun in a circle, chasing his stubby tail.

"He'll wake up the neighborhood," I said. "I better take him inside." I got up and started for the kitchen door.

"Wait, Teeny."

I turned and a gust of wind flattened my gown against my legs.

"Stay right there," he said. "I just want to look at you in the light."

Coop's gaze dropped to my legs, then back to my face.

He got up from the chair, walked over to me, and picked up my hand. The heat from his body pooled into the space between us. My pulse thrummed in my neck when he moved closer, his mouth inches from my mouth. He started to kiss me, and I stepped back, thinking of Ava and the DA.

"We shouldn't," I whispered.

"But it's almost over, Teeny." His lips brushed the back of my hand, then he glanced up. "You're worried about something else, more than the DA."

"No, I'm not."

"You sure? Did Ava say something?"

"No," I said a little breathlessly. "Not at all." Was this one lie or two? I decided it counted as one and raised my tally to seventeen. I'd promised to think about Ava's proposal, and I had. But my thinking ran in circles, like Sir chasing his nubby tail. It always came back to one thing: I was going to fight for my guy. It was every girl for herself.

He pulled me around the hydrangea bushes, past the oleanders, into a secluded corner of the garden. I looked up and saw the shadowy outline of a balcony where Red Butler had stood the other day. Now, a pinch of light squeezed through the oak branches. The night was ending and the sky was the color of a pewter goblet—gray, a quiet, neutral color, that no-man's-land between white and black, right and wrong.

Coop uncurled my fingers and kissed my palm.

"You know how to get to a girl." I drew my other hand along his chin, feeling the rough stubble, then I pressed my palm against the back of his neck. His skin felt so warm. He let go of my hand and gathered up my hair.

"I can't stop thinking about you," he whispered. "Do you think about me?"

"You don't know the half of it, O'Malley," I whispered back.

He released my hair and it fell between us. His mouth covered mine. Pleasure flickered up as I traced my tongue under the rim of his upper lip, alternately teasing and probing. The wind blew around us, smelling of roses and brackish water, and I was glad I hadn't promised Ava. My teeth caught the soft swell of his lip and I sucked the edge. My hands knotted in his boxers as if clutching an anchor to that long ago summer at Lake Bonaventure.

"I want you, Teeny," he said. "I've never wanted anyone this much."

He picked me up and I wrapped my legs around his waist. He pushed up my nightgown and bunched the fabric around my waist, then his hand moved lower and lower. When he entered me, I tried not to make a sound. His eyes wanted to know the truth and nothing but the truth. I answered with my body, my hands in his hair, my thighs tight around his waist, my tongue drawing unspoken words over his lips. No matter what happened, he was the guy I'd never forget, the one I'd always love, and that was the truth, so help me god.

The sky had lightened to bone when we finally slipped into the house. Coop carried Sir up the stairs, cupping the dog's tags so they wouldn't rattle. Outside my door, he handed me the dog and traced his finger over my lips. Then he went into his room and I went into mine.

The mattress squeaked as I crawled into the center of the bed with Sir. He began his routine of circling and digging. Then he froze. He lifted his right paw and cocked his head. His bottom teeth pressed into his upper lip, and he growled. A moment later, one of the upstairs doors closed—not an outright slam but a loud clap, a purposeful sound that didn't care who it woke, a sound that said, *You're busted*.

Through the windows, light was breaking over the rooftops, morphing into a scarlet glow. Had Coop meant what he'd said, that he'd never wanted anyone this much? If this was true, where did that leave Ava? He'd wanted her at one time, right? But how much? He'd wanted her enough to marry her. I liked to think he was more than ready to move on, preferably with me, but it was too soon to tell.

Love was complex and had more than one layer. It was like an onion. You could chop it, dice it, and pulverize it, but the flavor would still be there, even if it stung your eyes.

I pulled the sheet over my head and tried to think of a soothing imaginary recipe. What I really needed was Smother Your Love gravy, poured over Forget Him pork chops, with a heaping side dish of He's Better Off With Her pie. Whipped cream would be a nice touch. However, it's fragile. All those peaks and swirls can separate into curds and water. Then you've got a mess.

To prevent your whipped cream from separating—and it will, after a while—add a stabilizer. Some people swear by powdered milk, others add unflavored gelatin. These products are flavorless, more or less, and won't add unnecessary sweetness. Take care when adding new elements, such as fruit or liqueur. Despite the addition of a steadying agent, your cream is unsound and can dissolve without warning. Once it falls apart, you can't put it back together.

forty

From a long way away, I heard ringing bells. I sat up and pushed my hair out of my face. The noise was coming from downstairs. The doorbell rang, and a deep voice yelled, "Police! Search warrant, open up!"

Sir's head tipped back and he howled. I threw back the covers and ran to the window. Police cars blocked Adgers, blue lights swirling over the houses.

I pulled on a white blouse and black pants. Sir followed me into the hall. Coop was standing outside his door, stepping into his trousers. "Why are the police here?" I asked.

"I'll find out," he said.

Above us, doors slammed. Red Butler shot down the staircase in his underwear. "What the hell's going on, Boss?"

Ava leaned over the railing, her hair trailing down. "What's going on?" she asked in a sleepy voice.

The bell-ringing continued. "Police!" the deep voice called again. "Search warrant!"

"God," Ava said and pushed away from the rail. Red Butler darted back to his room. Coop zipped his pants and ran down the stairs. Sir and I were right behind him.

"Police! Open up!"

"Coming!" Coop yelled, then he glanced at me. "Is the alarm on?"

"No." I handed him the gate key.

He flipped the dead bolt and glanced over his shoulder. "Teeny, just let me do the talking."

He ran into the corridor. I gathered Sir into my arms, staggering beneath his weight, and walked out.

A man in a blue uniform banged a stick against the gate. "Police!"

Coop unlocked the gate. Across the street, blue lights whirled over the houses. A tall officer held out the warrant. Coop took it. "Come on in, boys," he said.

Six men shuffled inside. The tall one barked orders, and the men took off in different directions, pulling on plastic gloves.

Coop pulled out his cell phone. The keypad beeped as he punched in numbers. "I'm calling the DA," he said.

Two officers hurried down the corridor. They stopped as Ava walked out the gray door. She gave them a freezing stare.

"Why are they here?" she asked.

Coop shut his phone. "The DA got an anonymous tip to search your house, Teeny."

"That sounds dodgy," Ava said. "What are they looking for?"

"According to the warrant, a gun, marijuana, and photographs of the crime scene—not the official kind." He paused. "In cop-speak, that means they're pretty damn sure they'll find what they're looking for."

"They can search all they want," I said. "I don't have a thing to hide." Then I thought of Uncle Elmer's marijuana and the Templeton cookbook, with its fantastical recipes. I'd left it on the wing chair in the pink living room.

I put Sir in Coop's arms and ran into the room. The chair was empty. I yanked out the cushion. Nothing. Damn, damn, damn. I should've hidden that book. No, I shouldn't have written those fake recipes in the first place.

From the hall, I heard Ava say, "Do we stand here or what?"

I stepped out of the living room. Coop stood beside her, gripping Sir. "Teeny," he said, "take Sir for a walk."

Ava rolled her eyes and walked toward the back door.

"I don't think it's a good time," I said.

"It's a good time," he said. "Trust me."

I grabbed a leash from the hall tree and hooked it to Sir's collar. I could see through the dining room into the kitchen. The cops were pulling silverware from the drawers and piling it onto the counters. Another officer stood by the desk, looking behind cookbooks.

Coop tapped my hand and gestured for me to follow him to the back door. Sir made little gagging noises as I pulled him along, even though I'd loosened the leash. Ava sat at the dolphin table, talking on her cell phone.

"Stay here, Teeny." Coop walked into the garden. Ava looked up and smiled. He whispered something in her ear. She nodded and handed him the phone. He walked back into the hall, spoke to a policeman, and lifted my handbag from the bench. He tucked it under my arm and gave me the phone.

"Time for that walk," he said under his breath. His eyes bored through me.

"Okay," I said, a little uncertainly. "Come with me?"

"No."

I started toward the front door, trying to figure out what was going on. His hand closed on my arm. "Not that way. Better go into the backyard," he said and squeezed my elbow in short, rhythmic bursts.

A cop breezed by, his shoes slapping over the wood. Coop guided me toward the back door. I started to explain how I'd found the plastic bag, but he gave my elbow a sharp pinch. We stepped into the garden and he guided me past Ava, who gave me a pitying stare.

Coop stopped. "Keep walking," he said, his lips barely moving.

I curved around the sundial, and the phone rang. I'd forgotten that I was holding it. I clicked a button and said, "Coop?"

"Go toward the hydrangeas," he said.

Sir tugged at the leash, pulling me forward. I walked around the flower beds and glanced over my shoulder. I could barely see Coop.

"Don't look back," he said. "Keep walking."

I stepped past the hydrangeas. Bumblebees circled the heavy blossoms. "Coop, listen. I saw a bag of marijuana in Uncle Elmer's bathroom."

"Did you touch it?"

"No."

"Okay, good." He exhaled.

"Someone put it there," I said.

"Teen, listen very carefully. The cops just found a gun. It's blackened, like somebody tried to set fire to it."

"I don't have a gun. I didn't kill Bing."

"I know it. But they don't." He paused, and in the background I heard a man say, "Where is she?"

"Teeny, they're going to arrest you," Coop said.

"I figured that." I swallowed. "Why did you tell me to take Sir for a walk?"

"Because I know you're incapable of murder. My need to fix this is greater than my need to follow the law. They haven't arrested you yet. Leave the dog with Ava. Go someplace safe. I'm going to talk to the DA and see if he'll hold off the arrest until Natalie wakes up from surgery. When you're safe, call me. Just hit redial. I'll be waiting."

"For what?" Was he was telling me to run for it? If so, this was aiding and abetting—I knew that much from watching *Law & Order*. That carried a prison sentence and made his unprofessional conduct look pretty tame.

"We'll talk later," he said.

I stopped by an iron bird feeder and looked back at the patio. It was hidden by low branches of an oak tree. Farther up, hydrangeas spilled out like a petticoat around the trunk.

"Running will make me look guilty," I said. "They'll just catch me, and it'll be a thousand times worse."

"You're wasting time."

"I'm not afraid of jail. I'm afraid you're doing the wrong thing."

"It's the rightest thing I've ever done. Listen, I've got to talk to the policemen. I'm handing the phone to Ava."

"Wait!"

There was a scrabbling noise and Ava said, "Teeny?"

"Yeah."

"What's going on?" she asked.

"The police are searching the house."

"Yes. Other than that."

"Where's Coop?"

"Inside talking to the policemen."

I looked at the brick wall. It was a foot taller than me. I probably could grab the ivy and pull myself up. But I couldn't take Sir. I knelt beside him, dropped the phone into my lap, and ran my hand along his back. He was panting hard.

"I'm sorry, little buddy," I said. He pushed his muzzle against my leg. I kissed the top of his head. Then I glanced up at the house, trying to get one last look, but it was hidden by branches.

Ava's voice rose up from my lap. "Teeny?"

I picked up the phone and and dropped the leash. "Call Sir."

"What?"

"Just call him, please."

I heard her yell his name. Sir didn't move. "Scoot," I said, patting his rear end. He looked back at me, then he trotted toward the hydrangeas. A moment later, I heard panting.

Ava said, "There, there good puppy."

"Ava?" I stood. "Pick up his leash."

"Got it," she said. "What the bloody hell is going on?"

"Take good care of him."

"Sorry?"

"I'm sorry, too," I said.

"Teeny, what are you plotting?"

"Nothing."

"Whatever it is, don't do it," she said. "You'll make Cooper's job five times harder. I'm getting him right now."

I disconnected the call and dropped the phone into my pocket. I started to leave the purse on the lawn, but I'd need my inhaler and money. I tucked the strap firmly over my shoulder and grabbed a handful of ivy. I was over the wall in a flash.

forty-one

The morning sun pushed down on my head as I worked my way through the narrow gardens that abutted mine. I squeezed through a hedgerow and climbed over another brick wall. A man with a pipe yelled, "If you don't leave in two seconds, I'm calling the police!"

I cut down a walkway to Bedon's Alley and stopped next to a brick wall. I stepped into the cool shadows of a live oak, then I started up Elliott Street. The police had set up a barrier at the intersection of Elliott and East Bay. Two policemen blocked reporters. Another officer redirected a carriage. Beyond them, I saw Eileen's Winnebago.

I ran to Church Street and started down St. Michael's Alley. My plan was to hide in the church, but it was just too close to the Spencer-Jackson House. The minute the police realized I was gone—if they hadn't already—they'd shut down the historic district.

A gust of traffic fumes made me dizzy as I walked up Church. Perspiration slid down between my shoulder blades. I turned left onto Broad Street and paused to wipe my face on my blouse. If I kept going north, I'd end up at Queen Street. If Miss Dora wasn't out gallivanting, she'd hide me. A lot of ifs, but I was out of options.

I blended in with a group of tourists and waited for the light to change. The wind hit the back of my head, and strands of hair whipped in front of me like thin cracks in old china. I'd need to change my appearance. A box of L'Oreal's Chocolate Espresso would make me unrecognizable.

I reached inside the bag for my sunglasses and saw yellow Splenda packets, a red leather billfold, and keys hooked to a Big Ben chain. This was Ava's bag. Coop had gotten it mixed up with mine.

Tourists were bent over at a map, and I heard them talking about having lunch at Poogan's Porch. I tagged along, trying to act normal. If Miss Dora wasn't home, I'd need to buy a hat and keep mingling with tourists.

I left the Poogan's Porch people at the corner of Church and Queen and headed toward Johnson's Row. Miss Dora's house had been painted dark raspberry, which meant the historical society had vetoed the pink.

Her iron entrance gate stood open. I stepped into the long corridor, then I turned back. Maybe I shouldn't drag another innocent person into my troubles. But I hadn't been arrested, so technically she wouldn't be harboring a fugitive, right? Maybe she could take me to Bonaventure. I could gas up Aunt Bluette's old Pinto and drive far, far away.

I turned and hurried through the corridor, passing through a square courtyard where a brass pineapple spit water into an owl. I knocked on the French doors. From inside the house, I heard footsteps. Miss Dora opened the door and smiled.

"Come on in, girl," she said. "Get out of this sickening heat."

I felt another wrench of guilt as I stepped into the cool foyer. It smelled of potpourri. "Like the new paint?" she asked. "I don't. The hysterical society pitched the biggest fit you ever saw. I was so put out, I told the painters to paint the stucco Berry Bisque. And I left town."

"Where'd you go?" I plastered a cheery smile on my face and hoped I didn't sound as panicky as I felt.

"Sumter."

"The fort?" I asked.

"No, honey, Sumter's a little town off I-95. I'd heard about this little antique mall? It's supposed to have good prices. Ha! Even the junk was sky high. I was so disappointed. The podunk shops know the value of Roseville and McCoy."

The rise and fall of her voice was soothing. I caught the edge of it and coasted. She led me to her parlor on the second floor. The long windows gave a narrow view of St. Philip's Church. I guessed the historical society didn't have a say about what Miss Dora wanted in the privacy of her own home because her parlor was pink.

She saw me looking at the walls and waved her hand, her diamonds catching the light. "Don't you love the redo?"

"Oh, yes, ma'am." I sat on the edge of the pink piano bench. "It looks like something in a magazine."

"You are *too* kind." She smiled. "Pale pink and cream are nursery colors. The only thing that saves this room from being babyfied are the Tabriz rugs. They cost a fortune. But they ground the room so nicely. So do the black lamps and pillows. See how I judiciously sprinkled that color around the room? It's just like pepper. A touch of black adds pep and gravity."

"It sure is pretty," I said, trying to sound enthusiastic. I'd never given a flip for decorating. But it was Miss Dora's life, and I wouldn't hurt her feelings for the world.

"How is your cute lawyer?" she asked.

"Fine." Ava's purse emitted a low buzz. I reached inside and flattened my palm over the phone, trying to smother the noise.

"Isn't that your phone?" Miss Dora asked. "Shouldn't you answer?"

"It's a telemarketer."

"Don't you just *hate* them?" She rearranged two rose figurines on the coffee table, then she glanced up. "You look kind of disheveled. And you're pale as a haint. Are you feeling poorly?"

"I'm in a rush."

"Whatever for, darlin'?" She flashed a sharp, shrewd stare.

"Is there any way you can drive me to Bonaventure?" I asked just as casual as if I'd requested a cup of mint tea.

"I thought your lawyer gave you his car. Can't you drive yourself?"

"It's on Adgers. I walked here."

"You trying to lose weight or what?" She smiled.

"I need to go home."

"But what about your probation?"

"Can't worry about that."

She pursed her lips, as if mulling that over. "What's happened?"

"It's best if you don't know."

"Well, no matter. I'll be happy to drive you. Just let me fetch my keys. Did you leave your suitcase outside?"

"Didn't bring one."

"Then you're not staying long?" Her brow puckered. "Should I drive you back to the Spencer-Jackson?"

"No, ma'am."

"But you'll need some clothes, won't you?"

"I've got plenty at the farm."

"Teeny, what's really going on?"

"Please don't ask."

"Come on, darlin'. Level with me. You're violating probation, not to mention leaving your boyfriend, and you're going without a decent wardrobe?"

"That's about the size of it." I stood. "If you'd rather not drive me, I understand. I'll just make my way to Georgia. And I apologize for barging in like this."

"Are you telling me everything? Did that lawyer mistreat you? 'Cause if he did—"

"No, ma'am. It's just that I'm in a little trouble."

"What kind?"

I explained about Natalie and Faye and the search warrant. I omit-
ted the part about Cooper telling me to run.

Her face turned so red I thought for sure she'd call the police. Instead,
she leaned forward. "Tell me how I can help, darlin'."

"Do you have a wig?" I asked. "I won't make it out of Charleston
unless I disguise myself."

"No, but I've got hats galore. Run upstairs to the peppermint bedroom and pick you out a hat. I turned a walk-in closet into a hat-keeping
room." She walked over and appraised my figure. "I don't have clothes
your size, but check the bedroom across the hall. It's got a canopy bed.
I've got a slew of caftans in closets and drawers. One size fits all."

"Oh, Miss Dora, thank you." I hugged her so hard, she tipped backward.

"I'm pleased as punch to help." She pulled back and smiled. "You and
I have been crapped upon by Jackson men. We must stick together."

"Do you have scissors?"

"Why?"

"I'm cutting my hair."

"Don't you dare. It's too pretty to cut. Maybe if you pinned it up?
I've got bobby pins in the bathroom, so grab you some."

Praise the Lord for women with vast wardrobes. I ran up the stairs.
I'd only been on the second level once, at the engagement party. Where
was the peppermint room? I turned into one with white French furniture and fuchsia walls. The closet was jammed with winter coats.

The next room had pink walls and lime curtains. The closet was
jammed with dozens of hats, each one sitting in its own cubbyhole. I
lifted a straw boater with a floppy brim and hurried across the hall to
look for the caftans. I veered into a muddy rose room with pink clouds
on the ceiling. Four cannonball posts jutted up from a cherry bed—not
a canopy, but close enough. Little swatches of fabric were pinned over
the headboard, like she was testing a decorating idea.

I checked the closet, but it was filled with pocketbooks and shoes, arranged according to color. On my way out of the room, I stubbed my toe on a dresser with a marble top. I knocked over a perfume bottle, and when I straightened it, I saw two hairpins lying on the mirrored tray.

Just what I needed. I grabbed the pins and put them into my mouth. With my lips fanged shut, I opened the top drawer. Bobby pins were strewn along the wooden bottom. I coiled my hair into a bun and stabbed it with the pins. It still wobbled.

I swept my hand toward the back of the drawer, looking for more pins, and my fingers brushed against something plush. I inched open the drawer and saw a pink tassel. I lifted it. Heavy brass keys swung back and forth, tapping together.

forty-two

It was my missing key chain—minus Bing's house key. I reached deeper into the drawer and clawed out dozens of keys. I tugged on a long tassel. It wouldn't budge. A long thread was caught in the side of the drawer. I bent closer. The thread wasn't snagged on the wood, it was attached to something under the drawer.

I pulled out the drawer and looked underneath. A creamy white envelope was taped to the bottom. Whoever had put it there had accidentally caught a tassel thread. I started to shut the drawer. I wasn't a snoop. But I only hesitated a moment, then I grabbed the envelope, ripped open the seal, and pulled out a thick document with blue paper on each side. It crackled as I unfolded it. The letterhead belonged to a legal firm in Savannah, Georgia. Below this, I read *Declaration of Irrevocable Trust.*

My name was on the first line, *Christine Bleuet Templeton, Trustor.* But my middle name was spelled wrong. It wasn't Bleuet, the French way, it was Bluette, like the color. I remembered Bing's document—he'd been referred to as the trustor. And I'd been named trustee, along with a bank.

I skipped to the next line. Alice Eudora Wauford Jackson was named the trustee, bypassing the Bank of South Carolina as co-trustee.

I flipped through the pages. There were three copies, each one bearing my signature, only it wasn't exactly my signature. Each document was signed and notarized by Natalie Lockhart.

Ava's phone began to buzz violently. I picked it up and saw Coop's name on the display panel. "Thank god it's you," I whispered.

"I called a minute ago," he said. "Why didn't you answer?"

"Never mind that. I'm at Miss Dora's. Listen, I found my missing keys. And a fake trust. It's got my name on it."

"Where is she?"

"Downstairs."

"Teeny, listen carefully. Get out of the house."

"Didn't you hear? I found a bogus trust."

"Teeny, she killed Bing. Natalie woke up. She and Dora were in this together. But Natalie pulled a fast one, and Dora shot her. I'll explain later. Get the hell out of her house. *Now.*"

"Okay, I'm going. Don't hang up. Keep talking." I looked around the room for a place to hide the document. "Coop, if something happens to me, I'm sticking the trust under the mattress. It's in a bedroom on the second floor. All the rooms are pink, but this one has clouds on the ceiling."

"Teeny, for god's sake, go! If she tries to stop you, knock her in the head. She shot Natalie and poisoned Faye—she'll kill you, too."

"Wait." I glanced in the purse. Ava didn't have anything sharp. However, she had oodles of Splenda.

"No time to wait," Coop said. "Don't let her know you suspect her. Meet me at St. Philip's Church. I'm on my way." He clicked off.

I hurried down the back staircase and paused on the bottom step, then I dropped the phone into the bag. Miss Dora stood in the hall, primping in front of a gilt mirror. If she was planning to kill me, she'd gotten all spiffed up for it. She'd put on pink leather pumps, and a large straw bag dangled from her arm.

"There you are." She smiled at her reflection, then her gaze moved to me. "Love the hat. We have a slight problem. The Bentley's air conditioner isn't working. So I'm trying to reach Estaurado."

I gripped the banister. This was just the delay I needed. I looked past her at the door. Could I run for it?

She gave me the sweetest look, and I began to wonder if Coop was wrong. Hadn't the police been wrong about me? She'd been in Savannah when Bing was murdered. And she'd been in Sumter when Natalie and Faye were shot. Maybe she paid Estaurado to kill them? Maybe that's why she needed him now?

Her smile broadened without a hint of irritation, but she was giving off suspicious vibes. "Is anything wrong?" she asked.

"Miss Dora, I hate to ask, but could I please have something cool to drink? I'm just parched." I let go of the banister and stepped down. Everywhere I looked I saw weapons: heavy silver candlesticks, paperweights, clocks, bookends.

"Why, certainly." She turned toward the kitchen and caught my arm. "Come with me, darlin'. You can help."

I pulled away from her and ran to the door. I turned the knob. It wouldn't budge.

"Darlin', it's locked." She stepped closer.

"I just wanted to see if any police cars were out there," I said.

"Oh, for heaven's sake. Now isn't the time to get paranoid." She took my hand and pulled me to the kitchen.

"While I'm calling that damn Estaurado, why don't you fix us some mimosas?" She opened a massive refrigerator with a glass door and pulled out orange juice and a bottle of champagne. The champagne had been previously opened, and the plastic cork made a whoosh when she twisted it off. Standing on her tiptoes, she opened a cabinet and pulled out two oversized martini glasses.

"Make us big fat drinks, darlin'." She lifted the portable phone, punched in numbers, and stepped into the butler's pantry, blocking my exit.

I reached into Ava's purse and grabbed the Splenda packets. I ripped them open and shook the contents into a pitcher. White powder drifted up, sticking to the sides of the glass. My hands trembled as I stuffed the empty packets back into the purse. Then I tipped the orange juice carton over the pitcher. What if she tasted the artificial sweetener? Where did she keep her sugar?

Next to the coffeepot, I saw three pottery canisters labeled sugar, flour, coffee. The lids rattled as I peeked inside. Empty. All for show. I spotted a sugar bowl on the other side of the coffeepot. I dumped some into the pitcher and grabbed a wire whisk. I stirred the juice while slowly adding the champagne. Bubbles curved along the sides of the pitcher, moving like tiny waterspouts.

I filled the wide glasses, grateful she'd chosen them, so she'd get the maximum dose. I lifted a glass and took a sip. Sweet, tart, and effervescent. I didn't detect the Splenda. Wait, had I added enough?

"That damned Estaurado won't answer," Miss Dora said, stepping into the room. "He's probably watching *The View*. He's addicted to it. And after that, he watches *All My Children*."

I slipped my hand from the purse and handed her a glass. I glanced along the counter and saw a Splenda packet next to the sugar bowl. I cupped my hand over it and balled up the paper. She drained her glass, then twirled her finger, signaling for a refill.

"Aren't you going to join me, dear?" she asked.

"Totally." Keeping my hand closed, I refilled her glass.

A girlish, twittery laugh bubbled from her throat. She winked. "I don't want to be half-looped when we start our little adventure, do you?"

"No, ma'am." I lifted my glass, took a sip, then set the glass down.

Miss Dora's portable phone rang. She glanced at the caller ID display and said, "It's the Spanish bastard." She pressed the phone to her cheek. "Finally!" she cried. "Where have you been?"

Her eyes switched back and forth. I slid my hand behind the coffeepot and dropped the yellow fragment.

"Yes, yes, I know," she said. "Never mind. I need you to bring your car around. And I need you to do it now." She paused. "No, not after *All My Children*, now."

She clicked off and pointed to my glass. "May I?"

I nodded. Perfect.

She emptied the glass in four swallows. Then, as she poured a refill, she nodded at me. "Teeny, you need to lower that hat. Somebody could recognize you."

She started toward the butler's pantry. The kitchen had two sets of French doors. I ran to the first set and jiggled the knob. The door wouldn't budge. Then I saw the lock. It was the kind with a keyhole on both sides. I looked around for a key—most people kept them nearby in case of fire, but not Miss Dora. Apparently, she was fireproof.

I ran to the other door and jiggled the knob. Locked. I looked up. A key hung over the door, dangling from a hot pink tassel. I reached up, but Miss Dora's voice stopped me.

"Step away from the door, Teeny," she said. "And turn around slowly."

forty-three

I held my breath and did a half turn. I expected to see her with a stun gun. Instead, she held up a giant pink fly swatter. "Be very, very still," she whispered. "There's a wasp on your arm."

She stepped forward, the swatter raised like a wand, and flicked the insect away. It buzzed up and circled her head, then it floated to the counter. Miss Dora slammed the swatter again and again, like she was tenderizing meat.

"There!" She tossed the swatter onto the counter, then her warm fingers clamped down on my elbow. She escorted me into the foyer, opened a drawer, and pulled out a pink plaid blanket, the kind you'd see at a football game. Then she unlocked the door.

"What's that for?" I asked.

"If there's a road block, you can wrap up in the blanket."

"Won't that look suspicious?"

"Oh, you know me." She chuckled. "I'll charm the cops' pants off, and they'll forget all about you. Let's don't keep Estaurado waiting."

I walked behind her into the courtyard. Morning light hit the tiered fountain and the water pattered down in fine beads, spilling into the deep concrete bowl. Behind it, the stucco wall rose up, too high to climb.

My only exit was through the corridor. Then I had to get to St. Philip's and wait for Coop.

Miss Dora's spicy perfume burned my nose as I followed her through the corridor. Through the open gate, smoke drifted from the tailpipe of Estaurado's ancient Cadillac. The engine was running; he was getting the car nice and cool for Miss Dora.

I stepped onto the sidewalk, blinking in the glaring sunlight.

"Let me just lock up," she said, rushing back to the iron door. "Don't want to make it easy for Charleston's criminal element."

Estaurado stood beside the car, all hunched over. Behind him, a red truck drove down Queen Street, but I couldn't see the driver. Miss Dora bustled past me, her pink shoes clacketing on the pavement.

"For gosh sakes, Teeny, pull your hat down."

Estaurado helped her into the passenger seat, then he opened the back door for me. It gaped open, dark and cold, like the entrance to a cellar. No freaking way was I getting in. Estaurado cocked his head, his dark brows slanting together.

Miss Dora's hand twirled behind the window, motioning us to hurry. She pulled down the car's visor, peered into a mirror on the back of it, and applied fresh lipstick. A tourist bus drove by, followed by a police car.

"I forgot something," I said. I wouldn't make it to St. Philip's. Better to run after the police car and turn myself in. Estaurado tapped on Miss Dora's window. It slid down. He mumbled something in broken Spanish and gestured at me.

"What'd you forget, darlin'?" she called.

"Actually, I've changed my mind." I stepped backward. "I'm turning myself in."

The passenger door squeaked as she climbed out. I bolted in the opposite direction. Footsteps clapped behind me. A cloud of tobacco and hair tonic pushed up my nose. Estaurado lifted me off my feet and carried me toward the Cadillac.

"Put me down!" I balled up my fist and hit his shoulder. It was like striking concrete. His long legs switched back and forth as he hurried to the car. Miss Dora stood beside it, looking exasperated.

"Teeny, you're making a scene. What's the matter with you? Estaurado, put her in the car."

He dumped me into the backseat and slammed the door. I scooted across the ripped leather, toward the other door and reached for the handle. He ran around the car and slammed the door just as I opened it. Miss Dora flung open the other rear door and climbed in next to me. She gripped my hands and stared hard into my face.

"Did Estaurado hurt you, baby? 'Cause if he did, his ass is going straight back to the third-world toilet he came from."

I shook my head. She was very convincing. Could she possibly be innocent? Maybe Estaurado had killed Bing and Faye. But no, she was listed as the trustee on the fake document.

She was still holding my hands, mashing my bones. "Honey, tell me what's wrong."

"If you help me, you're breaking the law," I said. "I can't drag you into this."

"I'm not worried about myself, darlin'," she said.

I tried to squirm away, but her nails dug into my flesh. Estaurado got into the front seat and gripped the steering wheel. It was covered with brown fake fur, matching the hairs on the backs of his fingers. A set of trouble dolls dangled from the rearview mirror by a tiny noose.

Miss Dora let go of my hands and thumped the seat. "Let's get moving," she said. Estaurado pulled into the street. I planned to jump out at the first red light, but Estaurado sped through intersections, ignoring blasting horns. He cut down a side street and drove toward Calhoun.

"Where are we going?" I asked.

"It's your adventure. I'm just in it." She smiled. "Where do you want to go?"

She was playing with me. "I don't feel good," I said.

"Maybe the mimosa disagreed with you," she said.

"I think it did." I shifted my gaze, hoping the mimosa would do more than disagree with her. I hoped she would spontaneously combust.

She strapped me into my seat belt. "It's a state law," she said.

Estaurado hunched over the steering wheel, his fingers sinking into the fake fur. He turned on the radio, and the car pulsed with a Jimi Hendrix song—"Hey Joe," a great song for a murder.

I assumed we were headed to Old Santee Canal State Park where they'd probably stick me in a shallow grave, but Estaurado turned onto Meeting Street.

"I just want to turn myself in," I said. Between Estaurado's hair tonic and Miss Dora's perfume, I couldn't get my breath. Odors sometimes triggered my asthma attacks, and my inhaler was at the Spencer-Jackson House in my true pocketbook.

"Turn your pretty self in?" Miss Dora laughed. "Why on earth would you do that?"

"I want to do the right thing." I studied her face. She didn't show any sign of the Splenda allergy. Maybe I hadn't put enough into her mimosa.

"But you were all set to run," she said. "What caused this change of heart? You *are* innocent, aren't you?"

"What if I'm not?"

"Wouldn't that be hysterical?" She snorted. "You don't have a mean bone in your body."

"I do, too." I tried to twist away, but she grabbed my arm. "You're hurting me."

"Then stop fidgeting."

"I don't mean to. I can't breathe." I wasn't fooling. I couldn't get a full breath.

"Where's your inhaler?" She looked genuinely concerned.

"Home."

"Home?" she asked.

"The Spencer-Jackson House," I said.

"Estaurado, turn up the air conditioner." His hand moved to the dash, and the air hissed out, twirling the trouble dolls.

"Don't you have an inhaler at Bing's house?" she asked.

"He probably threw it away."

"Maybe not." She let go of me and raked her fingernails over her neck, leaving white lines on the pink flesh. The marks instantly turned dark red. "I'm just itching all over. Like I've got chigger bites. Estaurado, pull into KFC."

"*Qué?*" He looked flustered.

"Kentucky Fried Chicken, you nitwit," she cried. "I've got to put ice on these welts."

He swerved into the parking lot. "Ice or ice water?" he asked in heavily accented English.

"I'll just do it myself." She flung open her door and scrambled out. "But watch her."

The minute she started toward KFC, I unbuckled my seat belt. Estaurado leaned into the backseat, reaching past me, and wrenched off the door handle. Then his long arm shot out toward the other door, and he ripped off Miss Dora's handle. He flashed me a "take that" stare and folded himself into the front seat.

I looked around for another way to escape. The windows were electric. I pressed the button. Nothing. I pressed it again. Okay, homegirl, next idea. I reached into Ava's purse and got the phone. I didn't know how to scroll through her programmed numbers, but I had to try. Keeping the phone hidden in the bag, I glanced at the display and saw Coop's number. I hit send. The phone emitted a faint toot. I found the volume control and turned it up. A series of beeps cut through the music.

Estaurado picked up his cell phone and frowned.

"Please turn down the radio," I shouted, hoping Coop could hear. "Where are you and Miss Dora taking me?"

He ignored me and twirled the dial; the music faded.

"Estaurado, are you taking me to Bing's house?" I asked in a shrill voice.

"*Sí.*" He nodded emphatically.

"So, let me get this straight," I said, a bit louder. "We're going to Bing's house?"

"Woman, why you scream?" He flashed an irritated glance and turned up the radio.

Through the side window, I saw Miss Dora come out of KFC, clutching napkins and a tall cup. I poised myself at the door, ready to spring. Her face looked mottled. She was turning into her favorite color, head to toe. Balancing the cup and napkins in one hand, she reached for the back door, but it wouldn't open. Estaurado leaned across the front seat and flung open the passenger door. She stuck her head inside and peered into the backseat. Her eyes narrowed when she saw the missing handles.

"What happened?" she asked. "Teeny, did you try to leave us?"

I shrugged, as if missing handles weren't out of the ordinary. Coop, I thought, please be listening.

"Damn you, Estaurado. I told you to watch over her, and you do this!" She settled into the passenger seat, then poured ice into a napkin and dabbed it over her cheeks. "I just don't know what's the matter. It's like I've had Splenda."

"Your face is swelling," I said. "Maybe you should go to the emergency room."

"No, the ice is helping already. I'm just a highly allergic person. Estaurado, if you won't turn off that music, can you at least change it to something I like?"

He twirled the dial and Five for Fighting began singing "Dying."

"Much better!" She pointed to the road. "Go."

forty-four

Estaurado eased the Cadillac into traffic and headed toward the bridge. Miss Dora couldn't sit still. She flipped down the visor and peered into the mirror. "What the poop is going on with my poor skin?" she cried, scraping her fingernails over her cheeks. "I'm on fire!"

"Please go to a hospital," I said. "Estaurado can drive me to Georgia. Can't you, Estaurado?"

"I'll be fine. Just give me a minute." She pushed up the visor, reached for her ice, and ran it over her right ear. I pulled my collar away from my throat. My breathing hadn't worsened, but it wouldn't get any better without an inhaler. I'd kept one in Bing's medicine cabinet—unless he'd thrown it away. I tried to sit very still so I wouldn't be on Miss Dora's mind. She was preoccupied with her itching, and it was starting to interfere with her acting abilities.

Straight ahead, traffic flowed onto the bridge. The Cadillac's engine made a grinding noise as the car moved past the double triangles. I saw the USS *Yorktown*. The water was glossy, except for a broad ripple where the Cooper River touched Charleston Harbor.

"Please drive slower, Estaurado." Miss Dora glanced at me. "Let's just hope he understood me. The other day I told him to bring floral *sopa* and he showed up with chicken noodle soup, garnished with roses."

Estaurado followed Highway 17 past Mount Pleasant Towne Center, and turned onto Rifle Range Road. A peeling sign for Orchard Estates flashed by with Bing's name in bold letters. The Cadillac swerved into the subdivision and rushed by weedy lots, each one with a Jackson Realty sale sign. The Cadillac jumped the curb and stopped within inches of the yellow police tape and orange cones in front of the driveway.

"Move that blockade," Miss Dora said.

The Cadillac dipped as Estaurado got out. He shoved the cones to the side, climbed back into the car, then hit the gas.

"Stop!" Miss Dora flung out her arm. Estaurado hit the brake. "Quit thinking in Spanish," she told him. "You have to put it back together again, Humpty Dumpty."

"Who?" Estaurado's face knotted.

"Never mind. Just put those cones back like they were, and make it snappy."

He seemed to know what snappy meant. He climbed out and re-arranged the cones, stretching the tape across the driveway, then rushed back to the car.

"Finally!" Miss Dora said. "Drive toward the garage and park next to that big crepe myrtle—and drive slowly."

Three separate commands seemed to confuse Estaurado. The Cadillac inched through dappled sunlight into shade, then stopped next to the garage.

"Stop here." Miss Dora's hand disappeared into her purse and emerged with a Hello Kitty keychain. "I'm going ahead. Estaurado, bring Teeny."

"*Traiga a Teeny?*" he asked.

"Like I know what that means! Oh, for heaven's sake. Listen to me, Estaurado, and listen good. Take her into the damn *casa*."

She shot out of the car like a pink cannonball. The porch was blocked off with more yellow tape, and an official-looking sign hung on the door. She eased around the barrier and slid the key into the lock.

Estaurado opened my door and grabbed my arm.

"I can walk by myself," I said.

He yanked me out of the backseat. "No business of monkeys," he said.

My hat flew off as he pulled me to the porch. The front door stood open. He steered me into the foyer and called for Miss Dora.

"In here," she answered.

It could have been a scene from *I Love Lucy*, a sinister one where Lucille Ball had turned into Lizzie Borden. I tried to wrench free, but Estaurado dragged me into the hall. We found Miss Dora in the master bathroom briskly rubbing ointment over her swollen flesh. A tube of Lanacane lay on the counter. She glanced over at me.

"How's your breathing?" she asked.

"Not good."

"That's a shame." Miss Dora gestured at three monkey figurines on the countertop—See No Evil, Hear No Evil, Speak No Evil. "The infamous three wise monkeys—how tacky!"

She lifted the blue figurine, Speak No Evil. "Have either of you ever seen a blue monkey? No, I didn't think so. Bing's first wife was utterly tasteless. I chased her off but just look, the monkeys are still here. They had the last word."

I didn't care about monkeys. I couldn't get air. Each breath sounded like I was dragging a stick through gravel.

Miss Dora turned the figurine upside down. "Supposedly, if you don't speak, hear, or see evil, you will do no evil. But I don't believe it for one second." She dropped the figurine. It exploded on the tile floor. Blue china fragments skittered along the floorboards. She reached into the cabinet and pulled out my inhaler. I started toward her, but she jerked it out of my reach.

"Not so fast," she said. "You'll have to earn it. Where did Bing keep his documents?"

"I don't know." Did a lie under duress still count? I supposed it did and marked down number eighteen.

"You're a pathetic liar, Teeny. If I didn't have to kill you, I'd *buy* you a set of wise monkeys. Lord knows you need them." She pressed down on the inhaler and it whooshed. The smell of Ventolin drifted over. I took a greedy breath.

A buzzing sound came from Ava's purse. Miss Dora set the inhaler on the counter. "Answer her phone, Estaurado."

He reached for the purse. I jerked it away. He wrenched it from my grasp, and the bag went flying. Ava's keys, red wallet, and lipstick hit the floor. The Splenda packets fluttered to Miss Dora's feet like tiny yellow birds.

forty-five

M iss Dora walked over to me and shook a Splenda packet. "What's *this*?" she cried. "Did you poison my mimosa?"

"This isn't my purse," I said. "It's Ava's. Look at her wallet if you don't believe me."

"I won't even ask how you ended up with your rival's purse." Miss Dora threw down the packet and scratched her arm, leaving white marks on her scarlet flesh. "Get that damn phone, Estaurado."

I held my breath while he looked at the cell phone's display. "Is alarm clock," he said.

I tried to grab it but the phone slipped from his hand and hit the floor. A chunk of plastic broke off. The display continued to make a wounded buzzing sound.

Miss Dora reached for the inhaler. "One more time, Teeny. Where are Bing's documents?"

I didn't have the breath to make up a lie, so I shook my head.

She depressed the inhaler again. "You're running out of medicine and I'm running out of patience. Bing's documents belong to me, not you. I don't know why that little bastard left you everything. It's rightfully mine. I *worked* for it."

"Take it all," I said in a strangled voice. "I don't want it."

She set the inhaler on the counter, out of my reach, and pointed at Estaurado. "Get some *ropa* and tie up her hands and feet," she said.

He went into Bing's closet and emerged with two woolen scarves. "*Ropa*," he said.

"That's not what I wanted!" Miss Dora cried. "Oh, forget it. Just make sure she can't get loose."

She came toward me. My breath sawed in and out of my lungs. If I didn't grab my rescue inhaler, my throat would narrow to a pinpoint. I decided it was high time I dropped the Miss from Dora.

"Make her hold still," she told Estaurado. He grabbed my shoulders. I twisted away, slapping his arms. But he was too strong. I couldn't escape; I needed to make Dora see me as a person—as her former friend. I remembered our shared love for movies.

"Get your filthy hands off me, you damned, dirty ape," I cried.

"Charleston Heston." Dora clapped her hands. "*Planet of the Apes.*"

"Now you're dangerous," I whispered.

"Didn't Humphrey Bogart say that in *The Maltese Falcon*?" Dora laughed. "Oh, Teeny, I'm going to miss you like crazy. But don't you worry, I'll get over it in a heartbeat. The minute I move into the Spencer-Jackson, I'll be my wonderful, normal self."

She held me still while Estaurado looped a scarf around my ankles. "I'm sure you're wondering why I'm doing what I'm doing," she said. "Just think of it as a black-and-white movie called *They Done Dora Wrong*. Boy, did I get them back."

She helped Estaurado tie a better knot, one that lashed my feet together. Then she gripped my shoulders and guided me to the wall.

"Estaurado, run outside and look for a place to dig a hole," she said.

"Hole?"

"A grave." She waved her hands. "Cemetery. Day of the Dead."

"*Sí.*" He raised his hands and dug an imaginary hole.

After he left, Dora shut the bathroom door and turned back to me. "All I ever wanted in life was a pink house," she said. "When I first came to Charleston, I took a carriage ride down Rainbow Row and fell smack in love with the Spencer-Jackson. It was so *me*. I found out who owned it. I put the moves on Rodney, but he was such a disappointment. After the honeymoon, he gave me a mile-long 'honey-do' list. Like I was his administrative assistant. Can you believe the gall of those Jackson men?"

I started to shake my head, then decided I'd better nod.

"Rodney knew how much I wanted to live south of Broad," she said. "Queen Street is just too far north for my taste—and it's not pink. But he wouldn't give me what I wanted. One morning he was watching *Fox News*, all reared back in his leather chair. I thought to myself, 'Dora, get rid of his ass.' So I tased him. He didn't pass out, but he was paralyzed. He watched me put that ziplock bag over his head. I used the gallon size. Worked like a charm, too. He couldn't fight back."

A buzzing started in my head, like bees in an orchard. She was going to kill me just like she'd killed the others; but I wasn't ready to leave this world. I wanted my chance with Coop. I wanted to see him on the beach, backlit by sky and water. All my life, I'd been mindful of lies, maybe because I'd never told the truth about Coop: He was the one I'd always love. And now I wouldn't get to tell him.

"That left Uncle Elmer," Dora was saying. "By then, I'd hired Estaurado. He dumped Elmer's body in the harbor. I'd hoped Elmer's death would end it. I pleaded with Bing to trade houses with me—Queen Street for the Spencer-Jackson. I won't repeat the cruel things he said. So I hatched out a plot. But there was one little problem. I really liked you, Teeny. And believe me, I don't like most people. I didn't want to kill you. I just wanted you to catch Bing in flagrante delicto. So I brought in Natalie."

I realized I was holding my breath. I released a burst of air.

"She was my dead sister's daughter," she said. "Come to think of it, Natalie didn't favor Gloria one bit."

She was referring to Natalie in the past tense. I started to blurt the truth, that Natalie was alive and in the hospital, but I caught myself. If Dora knew a loose end existed, she would fix it.

"You want to know how stupid Estaurado is?" She twirled her hand airily. "He thought Bing and Natalie were cousins—just because I was married to Bing's father! Imagine anyone thinking I was a blood relation to that little asshole Bing."

The droning in my head got louder. I lifted my bound hands and pressed them against my right ear, trying to hold in the buzz and muffle Dora's words, but she kept on talking.

"I thought for sure you'd find out that Bing and Natalie were lovers." Dora peered into the mirror and fluffed her bangs. "Then you'd follow the peach trees home just like Dorothy followed the yellow brick road. But you didn't. So Natalie brought in that redheaded whore. My Lord— you caught him with two women and you still didn't run. You fought like a street urchin. So I had to switch plans. I put you at the Spencer-Jackson."

"But if you wanted the house, why did you put me there?" I cried.

"To keep an eye on you. And so you could look after the house. But then Natalie got ahead of herself and didn't follow my plan. When a plan goes awry, it opens the door for errors."

Dora lifted the inhaler. "I'll give you one little puff if you'll be good."

I nodded. She fit the mouthpiece between my lips. A second later, the Ventolin hissed out. I drew it in and held my breath. She set the inhaler on the counter and scratched her arms, leaving streaks in the white ointment.

"Better?" she asked.

I nodded.

"See? I'm not a bad person. But you'll need your breath to tell me where Bing put his deeds." She patted my arm. "I hope you know that I never meant for Natalie to put the Spencer-Jackson up for sale. Natalie did it behind my back. Bing went wild when he found out. He broke up with her and claimed he still loved you. But I didn't believe it for a second."

Tears burned my eyes.

"After that," she continued, "we had to kill Bing sooner than we'd intended. It was Natalie's idea to set you up for the murder—which was a pretty good solution, actually. You wouldn't have to die. And your housing problem would be permanently solved. But I didn't count on you finding a new boyfriend."

A tear dripped off my chin. "Did you take that photograph of me and Coop?" I asked.

"That was Estaurado's handiwork. I knew you were supposed to meet Bing at McTavish's—I had your phone tapped, darlin'. So I sent the Spanish bastard to take photographs."

"But why would you want pictures?"

"If you gave me trouble, I'd have proof you violated the restraining order. But I wouldn't have mailed the photos till after Bing was dead—they'd let the police know you were their girl." She paused. "Any more questions?"

"Were you calling me and hanging up?"

"How can you even think such a thing? Natalie called you once—well, that's what she claimed. She was trying to scare you out of the Spencer-Jackson." Dora bent closer to the mirror and ran her fingers over her swollen face. "But I *am* guilty of sending your kissing pictures to the DA. The last thing you needed was a boyfriend who knew the law."

Right. It was the last thing *she'd* needed. I cleared my throat. "You stole the pink tasseled key chain, didn't you?"

"Wrong again." She turned. "I distracted you in the garden so Natalie could steal it. She wanted your fingerprints on that key—odd that it never turned up. Natalie was the lady in the hat and sunglasses—the one the repairman saw. You thought it was Bing's sister, didn't you?"

I nodded, but I'd suspected Ava, too.

"Natalie returned my pretty tassel, and we continued with our plan. But first, we had to lure you to Bing's house."

"You sent the fake text message?" I asked.

"Darlin', I wouldn't know how to text if my life depended on it. Natalie did it."

"How'd she know I'd respond to it?"

"Because I know you, Teeny. It would have gone off without a hitch if I'd been there."

"You didn't kill him?"

"What do you take me for?" She rolled her eyes. "I sent Natalie and Estaurado to Bing's house. During the struggle with Bing, she broke a fingernail. She waited till you got there. Estaurado stun-gunned you, and Natalie texted herself from your phone. All that stupid bitch could think about was her manicure. She actually called the nail salon from Bing's house—how stupid is that?"

"Totally," I said.

"I'll say." Dora rolled her eyes. "Before Natalie left, she told Estaurado to take care of everything. He was supposed to put the revolver in your hand and fire it into a kitchen cabinet. The Spanish bastard misunderstood. He put the revolver in your hand, all right, but he didn't fire a bullet. He brought the damn gun back to my house. Flambéed it on my gas grill. I saw the smoke from my kitchen window."

Dora waved her hand. "He thought 'revolver' meant 'to turn something over.'" How was I supposed to know that? I looked it up later. Apparently some Spanish words sound like English. You'd swear they mean the same things, but they're different. They're called *falsos amigos*—false friends. Get it?"

More than false, I thought.

"Darlin', the bottom line is you didn't have gunpowder residue on your hands. And the darn murder weapon was blackened. I was so mad. I ordered Natalie to go back to Savannah. But she wouldn't leave. She wanted to sell the Spencer-Jackson and divide the money. Naturally I went along and worked behind the scenes."

"But Natalie sold the house to the Randolphs," I said.

"Poo, I wasn't worried about them. I had papers that would stop that sale in a heartbeat. I was more concerned about Natalie. When a partner gets greedy, you've got problems. If I hadn't tapped your phone, I wouldn't have known the half of it."

"Who hung that stuffed dog from my chandelier?" I asked.

"Natalie wanted you out of the house. She paid Estaurado to hang it. Isn't he the handiest thing?" Dora picked up a washcloth and wiped her fingerprints off the medicine cabinet. "By the way, it's not *your* chandelier."

"No, ma'am."

"I don't know what got into Natalie. She's always been so obedient. But she got spooked. She thought we needed to get the money and leave Charleston. She planted evidence at the Spencer-Jackson, then she decided to kill you. The evidence would be the icing on the cake if you'd committed suicide—or better yet, if you'd disappeared. So she called you, offering to exchange her sex tape for your cookbook."

"*She* stole my family cookbook?" That was the surprise? "Why didn't she mention it?"

"Oh, she just loved being mysterious. But she had no intention of returning your book. I think she meant to keep it." Dora dropped the washcloth into her handbag. "I was shocked at you, Teeny. Those recipes are pure evil. Toxins aren't playthings. Have you ever watched someone die of cyanide poisoning?"

I shook my head.

"Well, it's not pleasant." She picked up the Lanacane tube and rubbed more ointment on her arms. "Speaking of which, Natalie was going to serve you coffee and poisoned peach pie."

I remembered seeing a pie on Natalie's kitchen table and broken crockery on the floor.

"She'd planned to kill you and the redhead." Dora put the itch medicine into her handbag. "I knew you'd been delayed by the Randolphs and their designer, so I hurried over. When I arrived, Faye was on the floor, having convulsions."

Dora picked up the red Hear No Evil figurine and pitched it against the wall. The Sheetrock dented and china fragments skittered along the floor. "My stupid niece had ruined things again. I had no choice but to kill her."

But you didn't kill her, I thought.

"Of course, if Natalie had lived, I'm sure she'd say *I* brought that pie and forced the redhead to eat it." Dora opened a drawer, pulled out a hairbrush, and ran it through her hair. Because her face was so red, her eyes looked bluer than usual and craziness jumped out of them.

I pulled in a deep breath. Now that I could get air, I began to think about escape. I rubbed my wrists together, trying to loosen the scarves.

"Is there anything else you'd like to know?" Dora asked, teasing her hair.

"What if I hadn't come to your house?"

"But you did." She put the brush in her purse.

"Yes, but if I hadn't. What then?"

"Do you really have to ask?" Dora picked up the yellow monkey, See No Evil. "But the stars were aligned. You ran straight to me. I couldn't have planned it better myself."

A jolt of déjà vu swept through me, and I felt as if I'd been here many times, watching Dora and the three monkeys. Again and again, I saw her smash each one.

"Isn't this monkey hideous?" She swung it against the counter. The monkey's head broke off and hit the floor. "Just hideous," she said.

I was just like that monkey. Nothing more than an object, like a lamp, or pillow sham, to be used and discarded.

"Now, all I have to do is dispose of you and present a new trust to Quentin. And I'll be in the Spencer-Jackson before Christmas." Dora leaned forward. "Do you want to hear how I plan to decorate it?"

"No."

"Well, just *be* that way." She reached under her suit jacket and scratched her midsection. "I'm tired of this conversation. I'm going to let you decide how you want to die. Do you prefer cyanide or a bullet? I brought both. It's your choice. But if I were you, I'd pick the cyanide. It's over in three minutes, and it's less messy." Dora picked up a soap and smelled it. "Do you have any idea how hard it is to find a decent poison in this town? And not leave a trail?"

The door creaked open, and Estaurado stepped into the room. Dora reached for the inhaler. "One last time," she said. "Where are Bing's deeds?"

"Give me the Ventolin and I'll tell you."

She shook her head. "Talk. Then you breathe."

"Okay, they're in the garage. Hidden." A lie, but I refused to put it in the tally.

"Show me, darlin'."

"How? I'm hog-tied."

"Untie her ankles, Estaurado."

He squatted, and his cool fingers moved over the scarves.

"Please, my inhaler," I begged.

Dora set it on the floor, then stomped it. The cartridge shot out and the plastic casing shattered. She reached into her purse and pulled out a stubby gun. It was small like Ava's.

"Lead the way, sugar lump." She waved the gun toward the garage. "Just lead the way."

forty-six

Estaurado shoved me into the kitchen. I stopped beside the counter to catch my breath and glanced out the window. The driveway was empty. Coop wasn't coming; he didn't know I was here. Either the call hadn't gone through or he hadn't heard me over the booming music.

If I had one hope of surviving, I had to stay calm and try to outsmart Dora. She reached down and clawed her legs, her nails tearing her panty hose.

"My skin is absolutely raw, thanks to you," she said. "I'll end up in the hospital if we don't hurry."

Estaurado cut in front of me, and I fell back against the intercom. The stereo system clicked on, and the Beatles started singing "I'm Looking Through You."

"Hurry up," Dora said.

Estaurado opened the door to the hot garage. He gripped the back of my neck and steered me down the steps. I shuffled to a Peg-Board where tools hung from metal hooks. This fake treasure hunt wouldn't fool Dora for long. I inched my way toward the side door that led to the driveway. My hands were still bound, so I didn't know how far I'd get, but I was out of options.

"He's got a wall safe behind the Peg-Board," I said in a raspy voice. If this was lie nineteen, then it called into question every fib I'd ever told and I'd have to do a recount.

"You have to look careful because the safe is behind the Sheetrock," I added. "You've got to pull down the Peg-Board and look for the seams."

"Grab a tool, Estaurado," she said. "Pry off that loose edge."

He lifted a Phillips-head screwdriver, and Dora shrieked, "Use a flat-head, you nitwit."

As he studied the tools, I scooted next to the door. It didn't have a deadbolt, just a button on the knob.

"Oh, fudge." Dora pointed at the toolbox. "That one. No, not that one. Higher. What's the matter, Estaurado? Have you been smoking cilantro?"

I rubbed my wrists together until the scarf loosened. My right hand slid out and the scarf fell to the concrete floor. I grasped the knob, opened the door, and ran into the driveway.

From inside the garage, Dora screeched. I heard Estaurado's heavy footsteps slap against the concrete. I hurried down the driveway. I thought I heard traffic noises and a siren, but they were far away. They could be going anywhere.

I sprinted to the middle of the driveway. Something hot and sharp slammed into my shoulder, followed by a crack. I stumbled forward. My hands felt like they were still bound, but I'd dropped the scarf in the garage. Why couldn't I move my arm?

I got to my feet. Something warm and wet trickled under my shirt. Homegirl fails again. Homegirl's been shot.

Another loud clap whizzed by and the mimosa tree exploded. Bits of wood and blossoms flew into the air. I was pouring sweat. I lifted my good hand and wiped my face on my shirttail. The fabric was white on one side, red on the other. I drew in a breath. Climb that mountain, Teeny. The ground curled around me and I fell sideways.

Estaurado picked me up and slung me over his shoulder. My head and arms dangled upside down. Blood ran down my arm, curved across my elbow, and dripped off my fingers, leaving a trail as he moved up the pea gravel toward Dora.

I tried to reach lower and swipe my finger through the blood, spelling out *D* for Dora, but I was too far away. *Don't let her notice the spatters*, I prayed. *If they bury me, Coop will see the blood.*

Estaurado passed by Dora. I saw her tattered hose and red, swollen legs. Her thick ankles were stuffed into pink leather pumps. She grabbed my hair and yanked. I shut my eyes. But I could feel her gaze.

"Teeny?" she said. "Can you hear me?"

I held my breath. The bitch could draw her own conclusion. No need for me to keep track of my little white lies. It was open season on the ninth commandment.

"Did I kill her?" she asked.

"She breathes," Estaurado said.

"Well, not for long." She released my hair and my head lolled forward. "Just take her into the house for now. Wait, let me get that blanket. We don't want blood all over the place. And you better hose down the driveway, too."

"Hose?" he asked.

"Water. *Agua*. Just put *agua* on the goddamn driveway. *Limpio* the blood. Oh, forget it. I'll do it my damn self."

I cracked open my eyes and took a tiny breath. Dora was upside down. She ran to the Cadillac and returned with the pink stadium blanket. She threw it over me and everything went dark.

"Dump her in the house for now," she said. "If she moves, slap her. Then go and do what I said earlier."

"I dig hole?"

"Not yet. Get your Aztec ass back to the garage and pry off that board. *Then* go dig you a hole. A nice deep one. We don't want animals dragging up her body. She mustn't be found."

Estaurado carried me into the garage. Through a gap in the blanket, I watched blood hit the concrete floor, falling in a stream like pomegranate juice. Estaurado walked into the kitchen. Music still blared from the speakers. It sounded like the King was singing "He Touched Me," but I couldn't be sure. If I was too woozy to recognize Elvis, I was a goner.

Estaurado dumped me on the floor and returned to the garage. Over the pulsing stereo, I heard him rooting for a shovel. A high humming sound moved in the walls. It sounded like the hose was running. Dora was spraying the driveway. With all that blood, it would take a while.

I couldn't stay here. If I didn't hide, she'd finish me off while Estaurado dug that hole. I made myself sit up. Pain was everywhere, throbbing in my fingertips. Blood flowed over my chest. No spurting artery. That was good.

From the garage, Estaurado muttered something in Spanish. I heard him shuffle to the driveway, dragging the shovel behind him. The sound faded. He was going off to dig my grave. I wadded up the blanket and pressed it to the wound. As I grabbed the refrigerator's handle and pulled myself up, I felt all prickly behind my eyes. I didn't know how much longer I'd be alone. I had to hurry.

I took a step, and everything swirled. *You will not faint, Teeny Templeton.* Keeping tight pressure on the blanket with my good hand, I slogged toward the back staircase. I stopped and did a half turn, trying not to jostle my hurt shoulder. But I had to see if I'd left a bloody trail. Jagged drops led from the garage to the refrigerator then stopped.

I staggered up the stairs. It was a long way to the top, and I didn't want to leave any bloody smears. I wrapped a corner of the blanket around my hand, grasped the rail, and pulled myself to the second floor. All around me, water gurgled in the pipes.

I reached the upper hall and staggered toward the guest room. Spots twirled in the air like lint boiling in a patch of sun. If I couldn't get into Bing's closet, Dora would find me.

The pipes stopped rattling as I turned into the guest room. Light streamed through the windows. Beautiful, pear-colored daylight.

My knees buckled as I moved to the paneled wall. I shoved a panel. Nothing. I pressed harder. It still wouldn't budge.

From downstairs, Dora screeched. Footsteps pounded into the foyer, toward the front door. I heard the burglar alarm beep a harmless beep, which meant she'd opened a door. Dora yelled for Estaurado.

I studied the wood panels. Had I forgotten which one led to the closet?

"Teeny?" Dora called.

I held my breath and tracked the sound of her footsteps. She was hunting for a blood trail.

"If you don't show yourself, I'll kill Cooper." She paused. "I'll kill Sir. I'll make him suffer. I'll get Estaurado to hang him for real."

Her voice echoed, as if she was in the stairwell.

Keeping my fist tucked around the blanket, I moved to the next panel. I was too weak to push so I leaned against it. The door clicked open. Hot attic air drifted out, smelling of insulation and fresh lumber. I stepped inside the room and tugged the chain on the panel door, trying to close it, but it wouldn't move.

"Teeny?" Dora's voice sounded loud.

I looked down. The blanket was caught in the door. I held the chain with my good hand and kicked the blanket into the room. Through a crack in the panel door, I saw a shadow pass in the hall. I gritted my teeth and pulled the chain as hard as I could. The panel clicked shut; the light winked out.

"Teeny?" Dora's voice was loud. She was in the bedroom, I was sure of it. What if the paintings had tilted when the door had shut? For sure she'd straighten them. I wanted to curl up on the floor, but I gripped the chain and twisted it around my finger.

"Where are you, darlin'?" she called.

From downstairs, a door slammed. Estaurado shouted in Spanish.

"Oh, poo," Dora said. Footsteps shook the guest room, then faded. I let go of the chain and dropped to my knees. My good hand hit the floor. I slumped over. Warmth flowed under my shirt. It smelled like rust. My eyes adjusted to the dark, but I saw the edges of things. And I wasn't alone.

A woman stood over me. She wore a black, loose-fitting dress. Her face was in shadow, and her hair was long and bushy, like a horse's tail. Was I dreaming? It didn't feel like a dream. But the lady couldn't be from this world.

"Did I die?" I asked her.

She shook her head.

"This isn't heaven?" I was totally hoping it wasn't, because heaven would surely have a greeting party. I wanted to see Aunt Bluette, not some woman with too much hair. The woman's dress rustled, and she shook her head again.

"It's scary times," I said. "I can't breathe."

The hairy woman kept shaking her head. I had the impression she was an escort into the gauzy hereafter, or maybe she was like the cemetery guides in Charleston.

I slipped into a place where time was damaged. Yet I was acutely aware of my surroundings. I saw Jesus, clear as day. His hair was braided, and He had a unibrow. He wasn't listening to me. He was talking on a pure gold BlackBerry. It had little wings attached on each side, and every now and then it flew out of his hands, shedding green parakeet feathers.

"Jesus," I said, "if You let me live, I'll never tell another lie. It's the freaking truth. I'll even give up Coop. Just let me live."

Even to my own ears, I sounded desperate.

"I'll hold you to the first promise," He said. "But forget about the second one."

"Because the blood loss has confused me?" I asked.

"No, Teeny." He smiled. "Because giving up Coop won't solve anything."

"But Ava—"

"I know what she thinks. But it's not up to you or her—or Me, for that matter. The decision is up to Coop."

I lay there a while, then I heard shouting. I was too tired to raise up. I saw movement. The dark woman was back. She reached out to pat my shoulder, but her hand moved through me like a knife slicing through room-temperature butter.

The panel door swung open, and the woman's face became Ava's. It loomed over me, all gauzy at the edges. The secret room came into view, with its cubby holes and file drawers and the hard edges of Bing's safe. Ava pressed her fingers against my throat. My pulse wasn't beating there, it was behind my eyes, ticking like the gold dolphin clock on Uncle Elmer's desk.

Ava's lips parted with excruciating slowness. "Red?" she yelled. "I found her. Call 911."

My eyelids fluttered.

"Teeny?" she asked.

"I'm here," I said, or thought I said.

"Teeny, look at me. No, don't close your eyes. You're almost home and dry."

She pressed the heel of her hand against my shoulder. Then I saw Coop. He leaned over me, fit an inhaler into my mouth, and pinched my nostrils shut.

"Breathe in, Teeny," he said. I heard the hiss of Ventolin and drew in a raspy breath. He pulled off his shirt and balled it up. Ava moved to the side as he pushed the shirt against my shoulder.

"Stay with me, Teeny," he said. "Stay."

forty-seven

I awoke in a shallow grave. I took a little sip of air, trying not to breathe in dirt. I imagined the soil, black and grainy like cake crumbs. I reached up to dig my way through clumps of devil's food. A splinter of light pricked the dark. Within that light, I saw shapes.

"She's coming to," said a calm voice.

"It's about time," a gruffer voice answered.

I blinked. A clear tube ran from my arm up to a plastic bag like what you'd microwave rice in. Next to that was a purple bag. It resembled a pork tenderloin, the kind that's marinated in a preshrunk wrapper. Was I in Bing's kitchen or on a reality cooking show?

Then I remembered I was in Bing's closet, hiding from Dora. I tried to raise up, but those tubes held me down. A gray-eyed man gently pushed me back. "Don't move, sweetheart," he said. "You're in a hospital."

Yes, a hospital. Not a test kitchen. The tubes were IVs. Another machine tracked my heartbeat across a computer screen. I drew in a breath—a beautiful, dirt-free breath. Coop stood in front of the window. Behind him, through the glass, lights shone from tall buildings. It was night. How long had I been unconscious?

"Where's Dora?" I said. My voice sounded raw.

"She's in jail, homegirl." Red Butler stepped forward, his hands jammed under his armpits.

I looked up at Coop. "Where's Sir?"

"He's fine," said a voice with a cut-glass accent.

I turned in the direction of the voice. "Ava?"

She moved out of the shadows, to the side of my bed. I thought about the dark woman in the hidden room and what might have happened if Ava hadn't found me. I reached out with my good hand and pulled her into me.

"Thanks, Ava," I said.

"Not at all," she said into my hair, then she drew back and stood next to Coop. "How do you feel?"

"Like somebody dragged me over an oyster bed."

"Shall I ring the nurse?"

I shook my head.

"We thought you were a goner, Teeny," Coop said. "Dora insisted you weren't in the house. But there was so much blood. Ava ran upstairs and found you."

"You almost didn't make it." Ava said. "When the EMTs arrived, you barely had a pulse. The doctors didn't think you'd survive surgery."

"Natalie's on the floor above you," Coop said.

"She's one crazy bitch," Red Butler said. "The DA is with her ass now. When she and Dora weren't killing people, they were into mortgage fraud."

"Unbelievable," Ava said. "Why didn't someone catch them sooner?"

" 'Cause they was slick," Red Butler said. "It don't take a genius to steal a house. All you need is a blank deed, a signature, and a notary. Natalie was a notary. You can buy the blank deeds at office supply stores. Dora was a first-rate forger. But Natalie was an amateur. She made the mistake of forging the sale contract on the Spencer-Jackson. That's how you caught on to the signatures not matching, Ava."

"Praise the Lord for stupid forgers," I said under my breath.

"Amen," Red Butler said. "Dora's first husband was a used car dealer. He died in 1988. A heart attack, supposedly. Dora got the life insurance. $250,000. Not much, but enough for her to take a home decorating course and get some designer clothes. She dyed her hair, exchanged the Lee Press-on Nails for acrylics, and got her teeth capped. She attracted a guy who owned a garden center. He died in his sleep. No autopsy. Millions in insurance, plus the business, which Dora sold."

"I never suspected her," I said. Of course, I hadn't suspected a lot of things.

"You ain't the only one she fooled," Red Butler said. "The bitch is a pro. After she killed the garden man, she shanghaied a lawyer. Old Savannah money. They got married and Dora bought a place on Hilton Head. A year later, he fell off his boat and drowned. She inherited everything."

"I bet she stun-gunned him," I said, thinking of what she'd done to Rodney Jackson and Uncle Elmer.

"According to the coroner's report, the dude drowned. Whatever happened to him, he was alive when he hit the water. Maybe she bashed in his head, then pushed him overboard." Red Butler cracked his knuckles. "The bitch was prolly refining her modus operandi. Just like any serial murderer."

"I didn't think women did that," I said.

"Kill? Sure they do." Red Butler shrugged. "All the time."

"But a lady serial killer?" I asked.

"They're rare," he said. "Once some of them, they get a taste of it, they can't quit. They're like shoppers at Sam's Club. When these dames kill, they do it in bulk."

Ava and Coop laughed.

"Anyhoo, after Dora killed the lawyer, she got another makeover," Red Butler said. "She moved to Charleston and married Rodney Jackson. I got this from the lips of Nataloon herself. By the way, she's claiming Bing was in the shower when your cake school called. Nataloon took the message—so she knew your classes were rescheduled, Teeny.

She and Dora hired the redhead so's you'd be sure to break the engagement. Only it didn't go like they'd hoped."

"Then they got careless," Coop said.

"So, I'm in the clear?" I asked.

"You bet, homegirl."

"Except for one thing," Coop said as he moved to my bedside. "Dora's claiming you fixed her a poisoned mimosa. She says you knew she was allergic to sucralose."

My heart monitor began to squawk. I remembered my deathbed promise. Even if I went to the pokey, I was coming clean about the Splenda. "I was trying to stop her from killing me," I said.

Red Butler snorted. "Don't say that too loud, homegirl. Dicks are in the hall."

"Am I in trouble?" I glanced from him to Coop.

"No way, girlie." Red Butler's brassy hair fell into his face, hiding his eyes. "If Dora hadn't been itching, her aim might have been better."

"I wouldn't worry about Dora," Coop said. "But you need to explain something."

"What?" I asked.

"Red found a strange cookbook at Natalie's house."

"You ever heard of the *Templeton Family Receipts*?" Red Butler asked me.

Something fell inside my chest, but I managed to nod.

"Damn thing's full of handwritten recipes—poison ones." Red Butler leaned forward. "You didn't write them, did you."

It wasn't a question. I hesitated. How to explain I'd used these concoctions to soothe myself and my Baptist aunt had set me to doing it? "I wrote some recipes," I said, then turned back to Coop. "But not all. Aunt Bluette and her sisters wrote most of them."

I stared hard into Coop's face, looking for his eyelids to flicker or his jaw to tighten, but his face was smooth and blank. He'd had too much practice in front of judges and juries to show how he really felt.

"*You're kidding.*" Ava said, and I caught the tiniest look of surprise.

"It's an old family joke," I said and tried to explain. Even to my own self, I sounded crazier than Dora. But I'd promised Jesus, and I wasn't messing around with Him.

Coop shook his head. "The Templetons and the Borgias," he said.

I didn't know what that meant, but I was pretty sure it wasn't a compliment. My heart monitor shrieked, and the white dot galloped across the computer screen. "I never said I was a saint," I said.

"Who needs one?" Coop grinned.

"It's okay, homegirl," Red Butler said. "We can't have a vicarious poisoner going to jail. You might dream up bad stuff, but you'd never do it."

I lifted my good hand and grabbed the edge of Coop's shirt. "You *do* know I'm not dangerous, right?"

"Well, I believe you won't poison me, at least," he said.

My heart monitor began to whine. The white dot moved erratically. I felt sure it would fall off the screen and roll across the floor.

A nurse walked in, her white shoes squeaking against the floor. She fiddled with the machine, and the noise snapped off midsquawk. "How's the pain?" she asked me.

"Not terrific bad," I said—almost a lie, but not quite.

"If it gets worse, just press the red button." The nurse pointed to the IV machine. "Don't try to be brave. You've got to stay on top of the pain."

"If I push the button, will it knock me out?"

"Definitely."

Ava glanced at her watch. "I've got to run home and check on the dogs."

"Give Sir a hug for me," I said.

"Of course." She smiled, then looked at Coop. "Ready to go?"

He glanced at me, then her. "Sure," he said.

Oh, crap. I plucked the sheets with my fingertips the way Aunt Bluette had done before she'd died. Ava started for the door, but Coop lagged behind. He leaned over me. "When you're feeling better, we need to talk," he whispered.

I stiffened. "About what?"

"No more talking," the nurse said, pointed to the door. "Leave, all of you."

forty-eight

The next morning, when the hospital found out I didn't have health insurance, they couldn't get rid of me fast enough. The machine with the red button disappeared and was replaced by bitter, white capsules that made me woozy but cheerful.

The discharge nurse helped me into my clothes and put a sling on my arm. "Is somebody picking you up?" she asked, glancing at her watch. "Or should I call a cab?"

I eased over to the phone and lifted the receiver with my good hand. I started to dial SUE-THEM, but I kept seeing Ava's face. She'd saved my life. The least I could do was stop chasing her husband. So I called Red Butler and told him the hospital was turfing me.

"Be right there," he said.

The nurse gave me another pain pill and wheeled me down to the business office, which resembled an ultraexpensive hotel—tall windows, potted plants, and soothing background music. A darn good thing, too, because my bill came to $57,689.27. I all but signed a contract in my own blood, promising to pay monthly, then the nurse escorted me to the lobby.

Reporters from every Charleston news station waited outside, each one yelling my name.

"Miss Templeton!"

"Have the murder charges been cleared?"

"Who killed Bing Jackson?"

Red Butler's van pulled up under the port cochere, and the nurse steered me past the electronic doors. Humid, gasoline-smelling air blew into my face. A reporter with a ginger-colored crew cut rushed forward and pushed a microphone in my face.

"Will you sue the police department for harassment?" he asked.

Red Butler shoved the man aside. "Want me to pull a Russell Crowe and start throwing shit?"

The reporter shrank back as Red Butler and the nurse helped me into the van. Cool air blew out of the vents, giving off salt water fumes, and the radio was playing an oldie, "MacArthur Park." Mama would have paired that song with a recipe for key lime cake and Leviticus 7:12.

"Miss Templeton needs her prescriptions filled," the nurse said, pushing white papers into my hand. From the radio, Jimmy Webb was singing about cakes being left in the rain, and I wondered if my own cakes had been confiscated by the police or if they were still sitting on the kitchen counter.

Red Butler climbed into the driver's seat and, as usual, read my mind.

"Relax," he said. "Ava and me delivered them to the store."

Ava to the rescue. Again. Red Butler started the engine and drove off. I shut my eyes, and when I opened them again, we were parked outside the Rite Aid Pharmacy on Calhoun Street.

"Be back in a jiffy," he said.

"Wait." I did a one-handed reach for my purse. "Let me give you some money."

"Forget it." He climbed out of the van.

"I can pay for my own drugs!" I cried.

"It's the least I can do, girlie." He walked toward the pharmacy. The top of my head buzzed, a drunken dizziness that tasted like pinot noir. That damn pill. My eyelids dropped like heavy curtains. Then they changed into a silk prom dress that smelled of berries and vanilla. Vanilla, with its aphrodisiacal quirks. A pinot that pink cried out for grilled mesquite shrimp brushed with olive oil and bacon drippings, with a shot of chipotle and a hint of chives. Pile them on top of a deep bed of stone-ground grits and garnish with a wild onion and garlic salsa.

My mouth felt dry. If I had a bottle of anything, I'd drink every last drop, even though I wasn't much of a drinker. What I needed was sugar, maybe a praline cheesecake with a dark chocolate drizzle and a triple caramel brûlée chaser.

Red Butler got back into the van and set a white sack in my lap. "The doctor gave you a new inhaler, but you won't like it."

"Why not?"

"It's pink."

I peeked into the bag. Sure enough, the inhaler was pinkish purple. "Bing died because of that color," I said. "If only Dora had wanted a blue house, he'd still be alive."

"If-onlys are like wild canaries," he said. "Once they fly out of the cage, you might as well open the window and let them go."

"It's going to take me a while to let this go. I never once thought Dora was a killer."

"Maybe by herself she's not. But when you put a Dora with a Nata-loon, you get a third entity."

"A Doraloon?"

"Or a Natora." He drove out of the parking lot and turned toward the historic district. "Soon as the paperwork gets settled, you'll own the Spencer-Jackson and everything that goes with it. Maybe you can paint it yellow."

"Wait, are we going to Rainbow Row?" I leaned toward the wind-shield.

"Yeah."

"Drop me off at a hotel."

"Why, girlie?"

"The Spencer-Jackson isn't rightfully mine."

"The trust says otherwise."

"I'm splitting it with Eileen."

"You been freebasing Raid?"

"I won't take blood money."

"It's still cash. You got to eat, don't you? And you need a house."

"I've got one. Just as soon as Coop can fix things, I'm moving back to Bonaventure."

"You're talking crazy, homegirl."

"Whatever. Just stop at the next hotel."

"Okeydokey." He hung a right onto Market Street. "But if I was you, I'd go see the boss."

"I can't."

"Why not?"

"He and Ava need time alone."

"What the hell for?"

"To work things out."

"What things?" His forehead puckered.

"She saved my life. I owe her, big time."

"Come on, Teeny. If she hadn't been with us, we would've tore out every wall to find you."

"But she *was* there. And she loves Coop. She wants him back."

"Sure she does. But it ain't up to her—or you. The boss will pick who he loves."

"That's exactly what Jesus said."

"Who?" Red Butler looked away from the road.

"Never mind." I lifted my good hand and pointed to a hotel. "Here's the Marriot. Pull over. Hey, you passed it! Dammit, Red Butler, turn back."

"It's Red to you, girlie."

forty-nine

Red drove toward the Ravenel Bridge, but I couldn't keep my eyes open. The pain pill dragged me into a white, gauzy place, and I didn't wake until the van stopped in Coop's driveway. His red truck stood next to a palmetto. I didn't see Ava's motorcycle. That was a good sign, right? Only I couldn't trust signs. The last few weeks had taught me that life was quirky and unpredictable. Anything could happen in five minutes or five days—and it probably would.

Red opened my door and helped me out of the van. The briny air cleared my head as I walked crablike along the wooden stairs and crept up to the deck. Coop must have heard us drive up, because before we knocked, the front door opened and he stepped out.

"Teeny!" His smile morphed into a frown. "Shouldn't you be in the hospital?"

"They kicked her out." Red shrugged. "She didn't have no insurance."

"Why didn't you call?" Coop asked.

"'Cause she called me." Red gripped my good elbow and steered me into the sun-drenched living room. After I got settled on the black sofa, he set my purse and Rite Aid bag on the coffee table. Coop stood off to the side with his hands on his hips, but I couldn't see his face, thanks to the sharp beach light.

"I hope I'm not intruding," I said.

"Not at all," he said.

From the hall came a jingling noise, accompanied by heavy panting. T-Bone skidded around the corner, his tail whipping against the furniture.

"T-Bone!" Red cried.

"My Lord Hugeness got kicked out of quarantine," Coop said.

Before I could respond, a fainter set of toenails skittered in the hallway, and a second later Sir trotted into the room. When he saw me, he let out a yelp and ran to the sofa. He rubbed his stubby body against my legs, determined to scent-mark me. I lowered my good hand and scratched his ear.

"Poor little guy," Coop said. "He missed you like crazy. He wouldn't eat, so Ava fed him chicken and rice."

I was grateful, but I couldn't speak. My numbed brain was stuck between appreciation and angst, but I managed to look around for womanly touches. If Ava had been here, she would've left a mark. A hairbrush, lipstick, the latest *Vogue*. Everything was tidy except for law books, which were piled on the floor.

T-Bone pressed his nose gently against my hurt arm, as if sensing my mood. His mammoth chest vibrated as he smelled me.

"I just made egg salad for lunch," Coop said. "Anyone want a sandwich?"

I'd forgotten his love for egg salad. I imagined him spreading mayonnaise on white bread—and not just any mayo, it had to be Duke's—adding lettuce and a grind of pepper.

"I've got to run," he said, "but Teeny'll need something on her stomach. Give her a pain pill in three hours. If she gets winded, make her use the inhaler."

My cheeks burned. He could've been my mother, dumping me in a stranger's hotel room. I thought I'd gotten past all that. The pills had lowered my defenses, leaving me Teenified. Mama had been sick but she'd loved me. If she walked in the door, I'd put my arms around her, tell her I loved her, and cut her a huge piece of cake.

Red bent over to kiss my cheek. "You're on your own, homegirl," he whispered, then he looked at Coop. "Take care of her, Boss. She's a dandy."

The dogs followed the men into the foyer. I heard their low voices, then the door banged shut. Coop walked back to the living room, shooed the dogs onto the screened porch, then sat down beside me. His eyes were pure gray, not a speck of blue.

"Can you manage a sandwich?" he asked. "Or would soup be better? I've got tomato and chicken noodle."

"I'm okay." All of a sudden, I felt queasy. I remembered the uneaten birthday cake I'd made him in high school. I'd waited until the sunflower icing had gotten stiff before I'd finally cut a big slice and washed it down with milk. All these years later, I was still chewing on hard, unspoken words, but I couldn't hold them back another second. Last night he and Ava had left the hospital together. Now I was having déjà vu about him and Barb.

"Actually, I'm not okay," I said. "What's up with you and Ava?"

"She wanted to tell you herself."

"Tell me what?"

"She's going on another dig. In Peru, I think. One of her colleagues called while you were in the hospital."

I felt a surge of glee followed by doom. I didn't want to win the guy by default—if I'd won him.

"You didn't think she and I were together, did you?" he asked.

"I don't know what I thought." This was lie number what? I'd lost count.

He reached for my hand. "Can you walk to the kitchen?"

I wasn't in the mood for egg salad, but I got to my feet and leaned on his arm. As we passed through the dining room, I glanced at the yellow legal pads and beige law books that were strewn on the table. One book was spread open and a flat, brittle daisy lay on the page. Was that our daisy or just a weed?

I started to ask, but he turned into the kitchen and led me to the freezer. He opened the door and frosted air curled out of the glowing interior. He reached for a white box with The Picky Palate's logo, then pushed back the lid. I recognized the peaks and swirls of cream cheese icing.

"It's a red velvet cake," he said.

"I know. I baked it. You didn't have to buy one."

He opened the freezer door wider. Inside, metal shelves were crammed with white boxes, each one marked with raised blue letters. "Sweetheart," he said, "I bought them all."

He set the box on the counter and slipped his arm around my waist. "I'm in love with you, Teeny."

I slid my good arm around his neck and pulled his face close to mine. The moment our lips met, a bell rang. I'm not lying. It was an honest-to-god bell, only it wasn't a sign from the cosmos—someone was at the front door. We broke apart and looked out the kitchen window.

A little girl with blond pigtails stood on the deck. Something about the shape of her face and her upswept nose caught my attention. She reminded me of someone, but I couldn't think who.

"Probably a neighbor's child," Coop said. "I'll be right back."

"Wait, I'm coming." I grabbed his sleeve.

Coop opened the door. The child looked up with wide gray eyes.

"Are you Cooper O'Malley?" she asked, turning her heart-shaped face to one side.

"I sure am." He smiled. "Who are you?"

"I'm your daughter."

Recipes

Lavender Shortbread
Teeny's Vanilla Peach Pecan Coffee Cake
Espresso Steak Rub
Fried Green Tomato Salad with Cornbread Croutons

Lavender Shortbread

1½ sticks unsalted butter, room temperature

⅔ cup white granulated sugar

½ cup confectioners' sugar

½ cup cornstarch or rice flour

1 cup all-purpose white flour

⅛ teaspoon salt

3 tablespoons fresh lavender flowers, finely chopped

(or 2 tablespoons dried lavender)

Cream butter and sugars. Add flours a few tablespoons at a time and salt. Mix until crumbly. (You can mix by hand or put the ingredients into a food processor.) If dough is too thick, add 1 to 2 teaspoons cream. Add lavender. Chill mixture for an hour. Pat into a shortbread mold, or gently roll and cut dough with a cookie cutter. You can also shape the dough into a circle. If you aren't using a mold, place dough on an ungreased baking sheet. Prick the surface with a fork. Bake 25 minutes, or until lightly browned. Cool; cut into bars.

Yield: 2 dozen cookies
Preheat oven to 325 degrees.

Teeny's Vanilla Peach Pecan Coffee Cake

2 large eggs
1 cup whole milk
½ cup vegetable oil
1 teaspoon Madagascar vanilla
½ cup sour cream
3 cups all-purpose white flour
1 cup sugar (white, granulated)
1 teaspoon baking powder
½ teaspoon salt
½ teaspoon baking soda

Beat eggs. Add milk and oil. Whisk. Add vanilla and sour cream. Next, add dry ingredients. Mix. (It will be crumbly.) Pour into a greased 9 x 13 inch pan or well-seasoned cast iron skillet.

Prepare topping:
3 cups ripe peaches, peeled and sliced
2 tablespoons melted butter
1 cup brown sugar
2 teaspoons ground cinnamon
1 teaspoon ground nutmeg
½ cup chopped pecans
3 tablespoons all-purpose flour

Mix ingredients and spoon over batter. Bake 30 minutes.

Yield: 8 servings
Preheat oven to 350 degrees.

Espresso Steak Rub

3 tablespoons espresso beans, freshly ground

1½ teaspoons sea salt

3 tablespoons brown sugar

1 teaspoon ground pepper

2 teaspoons chili powder

1 teaspoon ginger

2 tablespoons Hungarian paprika

Mix. Brush steaks with extra virgin olive oil. Dredge in rub. Grill.

Yield: coating for 2 New York strips

Fried Green Tomato Salad with Cornbread Croutons

Step 1: Make cornbread.

Grease a 9 x 12 inch pan. Make your favorite cornbread recipe. Cool. Cut cornbread into cubes. Brush cubes with melted butter and place in a baking pan. Preheat oven to 375 degrees. Cook cubes 10 minutes or until crisp.

Step 2: Fry green tomatoes.

Vegetable oil

3 large eggs

5 large green tomatoes, sliced

1 cup cornmeal

Salt

Pepper

Heat oil in skillet. In a large bowl, add eggs and whisk. In another bowl, add cornmeal, with salt and pepper to taste. One at a time, dredge sliced tomatoes in eggs, then in cornmeal. Place in hot oil and fry till crisp, turning once. Cool. Cut tomatoes into wedges.

Step 3: Make the salad.
Mixed greens
Bacon, crumbled
Red onions, thinly sliced
Shredded cheddar
Sliced green onions

Mix. Add tomatoes and cornbread croutons. Serve with buttermilk dressing.

Yield: 4 servings

acknowledgments

The author would like to thank Ellen Levine, Jennifer Enderlin, Sara Goodman, Lisa Senz, Matthew Shear, Sally Richardson, Matthew Baldacci, Sarah Melnyk, Sarah Goldstein, Nancy Trypuc, Kevin Sweeney, William Brock, Darnell Arnoult, Laurie Ritchey, Nacnich, Nathaniel Whalen, Trey Arnett, Andy Martin, Jeanne-Marie Hudson, Jean Helton, Lori Wilde, and Egg Cream Man.